Con

P₂

The Weed Wife
    C. Allegra Hawksmoor   11
The Girls from Humaji
    Adrian Tchaikovsky   45
Dawn of Demons
    Eric Scott   53
The Sharks of Market Street
    Michael Ezell   80
Shirtless in Antarctica
    Justin Brooks   107
Under the Green Witch
    Colin Sinclair   143

Part 2

Girls Day Out
    Bruce Lee Bond   171
The Winter After
    Mikey Nayak   185
The Thirteenth Hour
    Michael Trimmer   214
Hope Street
    Dylan Fox   247
I Was Here
    Anne Michaud   277
Savage Times
    Paul Starkey   289

Part 3

Spring Semester at Halcyon High, 2123
    G.R Delamere   315
Bunker Buster
    Alec McQuay   331
The Unbroken Line
    K. Bannerman   354
Vanquish
    N.O.A. Rawle   361
The Eternal Quest Of The Girl With The Corkscrew Hair
    David Turnbull   376
Were Stars To Burn
    Kara Lee   404
The Dragon's Maw
    Cheryl Morgan   423
Sleep Sweet Children
    Nathan Lunt   426

Contributors

The
Girl
at the
End
of the
World

Also Collected by Adele Wearing:

Tales of the Nun & Dragon
Tales of the Fox & Fae

Fox Pockets Series:
Piracy
Shapeshifters
Guardians
Missing Monarchs

The Girl at the End of the World: Book 1

The
Girl
at the
End
of the
World
Book II

Collected
by
Adele Wearing

www.foxspirit.co.uk

Cover Art by Dave Johnson
conversion by handebooks.co.uk

ISBN:

978-1-909348-56-1 mobi
978-1-909348-57-8 epub
978-1-909348-58-5 paperback

A Fox Spirit Original
Fox Spirit Books
www.foxspirit.co.uk
adele@foxspirit.co.uk

For Jack C Young, K.A.Laity, Dana Fredsti, Chris Voss and the rest of the Wednesday evening crowd. Lock and Load.

Part 1

"Everyone, deep in their hearts, is waiting for the end of the world to come."

Haruki Murakami,
1Q84

The Weed Wife

C. Allegra Hawksmoor

Rest, seeker, and I shall tell you a tale from the very cusp of time, when all that we are stumbled on the verge of being. These were threshold days: when the last of the stone skyways still formed crumbling capillaries across the land, and their vaulted archways sheltered hundreds of the shivering, soot-covered refugees fleeing west towards the Coastlands in the ash fall and the embers. It was autumn, but the weed wife could see little of its mellow fruitfulness as she walked barefoot across the thin, cracked earth atop the ruined skyway. Suspended high above a countryside laid out like a colourless map between her and the horizon.

She called each living thing by name as she walked: her tongue feeling for their words against her teeth. *Couch grass. Birch. Ragwort. Teasel. Dandelion.* Life in struggling profusion all around her. Twisted thorn trees, bow-backed from elevation and high winds. Great knots of bramble and old man's beard spilling over the parapets and hanging down in the vast expanse of air. Like living icicles.

The ash fell slowly from a great, grey sky. Feathery flakes of almost-white that dissolved into dust the moment that they touched her. The embers fell more quickly and infrequent— barely visible in the daytime gloom as they followed erratic, meandering paths between the earth and sky. Two weeks now since the rain, and far, far below the waste ground and abandoned fields were blonde beneath their shroud of ash. Tinder dry. It would only take one fat, stray ember falling like a pellet of early autumn rain to set acres of these rich lowlands aflame.

Blackthorn. Foxglove. Fireweed.

A mother swallow whipped past the skyway, snatching a single, bitter-tasting cinnabar moth out of the falling sky and disappearing back beneath the arches where a clutch of her young squeaked weak with hunger. They were too late in the nest. When winter came, they would all starve.

The weed wife stopped beneath the partially-collapsed wall of an assay post and crouched down low to refill her waterskin from an ancient runoff. She scooped the ash and thistledown from its surface with open hands, and let the cool and clear water run between her fingers. It could have fallen yesterday, but left a bitter taste on her tongue when she raised her cupped hands to her lips. Her black and silver hair fell across her face, hanging down into the water like the tips of willow branches.

She lingered for a moment in what had once been a doorway. Within, all that was left of the last shipment of iron to pass through here was a thick heap of rust drifted in one corner, spotted here and there with bright flecks of broken glass. The flasks and alchemical equipment used to test its purity. The people who once lived within the pillar underneath had left no sign at all, as though they had simply scattered into the blowing wind like dandelion seeds.

The weed wife closed her eyes, and waited for the wind to blow, but all that came was a terrible stillness and the gentle snap of fire in the air. She retied the scarf over her nose and mouth, and began to walk. A small, dark shadow migrating against the low, grey sky. But the weed wife did not wander. She moved with gentle purpose: the faint echo of the sun blanching the smoke clouds at her back; bare feet caked in ash and making not a sound; eyes always on the distant horizon in the north. Her heart heavy with the weight of distant memories—of the time-before-time when this land had been swathed in forest from horizon to horizon. *Oak and ash. Elm and hazel.* The bluebells and the dappled light of late September, the colour of a beehive. Before the heartswood of the forest was cut and clamped for charcoal, and its cinders nourished the narrow patchwork of corn and oats and barley. Before those fields were blanketed in ash themselves, and their grains rotted down into the blackened earth.

These memories-beyond-remembering echoed through her like water dripping in the hollow deepness of a mineshaft, but she did not lose herself to them. She saw the dark elf at the roadside as she drew near. He was dressed in rags, with skin the colour of wet, blue slate. Half-starved amongst the fruiting brambles. Sleek, dark hair as tangled up as blackthorn. He watched her through the falling ash with eyes like freshly-minted bronze. Lips trembling, and long nails catching at his sleeves. There was an irreparable absence in those eyes. A distance that could never again be spanned. It left its yawning echoes underneath the weed wife's heart.

The plague.

It started in the fathoms of the hollow mountain, but now that the land was emptying it spread through the knotted clusters of survivors as quickly as despair.

The brambles almost swallowed the elf in a halo of dark fruit and twisted thorns.

'Please,' he whispered, his chest heaving against the smoke and ash. 'I'm so hungry.'

The weed wife crouched down, and picked the berries from amongst the matted leaves. They stained her brown fingers to ink black, and clustered in her palm like little jewels. He ate from her open palm, and she took out a vial of clear liquid from the leather satchel at her side as he struggled between food and breath.

'I must get to the city,' he said when her hand was empty and his lips were black as nightshade. 'Please, my lady, I am sick and I must reach the city. Do you know the way?'

It was an old memory. As old as the plague itself. Once, it would have led him to the Weaver King's salvation. Now, it would only lead him to the centre of a wound.

'There is no cure for you there, child,' she said softly. 'Not anymore.'

'I must get to the city,' he repeated blankly, squeezing her hand in his thin, slate-coloured fingers. 'You must show me the way. I am so cold. So thirsty. Please...'

His voice hitched in his throat. The weed wife's brow knitted together, and she offered him the vial.

'Drink,' she said.

And he did. And all through the long hours of the afternoon she sat with him as the hemlock slowly suffocated the life from him. It began in the muscles of his feet and fingers:

a slow and tingling paralysis that crept up through his body as she soothed and smoothed his blackthorn hair, until his diaphragm struggled to pull the poisoned air down into his body and he choked to death in her arms.

She stood then, and stretched the stillness from her legs and from her shoulders. She gave his body to the brambles and the blackthorn. At the very end of winter, they would dress his slate-blue skin with soft, white blossom, when much of what he was now had returned into the shallow earth atop the skyway, and only skin and tangled hair and bird-light bones remained.

It was in liminal time, when the earth twisted like metal towards dusk, before she saw her goal. Out where the ocean met the land. Between the valley and the high, white cliffs. Standing sentinel above the deathless sea. A grey sunset on grey water.

A cross-hatching of thin and strip-like fields radiated outwards from the old manor house. Matted patches of dull gold struggling amongst the weeds and soot. Poppies splattering the blonde like fresh-sprayed blood around the granite and half-timber hall. Its steep roof of purple slate bowed down in the middle like the back of an old horse.

This was an ancestral place. As old as the bedrock that it was rooted in, and as still as a freshly-opened crypt. It had stood there through the first age of ash and embers, back when the skyways were young. Now, it stood in its furrow before the chalk cliffs to see that time return again.

Nothing moved, and no smoke rose from the central spire of the chimney.

The slumped ruin of an assay office lent the weed wife its stairs down onto the valley floor, and she struck out for the house.

A salt wind blew inland from the booming sea, catching on the cliff tops and chasing up through the valley like a river flowing backwards. It brought clean air in from the ocean, and as the weed wife padded through the parched wheat and knotted weeds, she loosened the scarf from her nose and mouth and breathed it in full deep. The fields formed a cross-work over the low inclines of the valley floor, from the black and poison river mouth where fresh and salt water fought against one another through the rise and the fall of the tide. Thin strips of wheat, rye and oats interwoven with each other, divided here and there by scraggly lengths of hedgerow.

Hawthorn. Dog rose. Honeysuckle. Bedstraw. Great, antlered stag beetles and the tiny, tangled nests of dormice. The manor loomed black through the curls of smoke and ocean wind.

It was an old bastle house, built for defence and practicality. It stood parallel to the sea wind, its landside gable set with great, studded byre doors and a small hatch and lifting beam for winching hay into the loft. One of the great doors groaned back and forth on its hinges as the wind chased itself down the flanks of the manor. The weed wife caught the handle in her open hand, and the whole world tumbled back into silence and the rasp of air through grass.

It was warm and still inside the barn. Tawny brown. Thick with the smell of straw and dung. A pair of longhorn cows shifted anxiously in their stalls and flashed their great, white eyes. They were thin enough to count every rib and vertebrae, the sharp lines of their shoulder blades and pin bones rasping on the inside of their skin. The weed wife came in slowly, and fastened the door. As the latch came closed, two ewes and a young hogget bolted to their feet and backed against the far wall of their pen, bleating and whickering to each other.

She stopped at the foot of the ladder that led up into the hayloft. In the shadow where the wet stone of the barn wall met the rest of the manor, white sheets and matted cobwebs covered a mass of tangled metal. The long blade of a scythe curved out from underneath the canvas, blunted and dappled with rust. The weed wife peeled the covers back. *Scythe. Sickle. Pitching forks and ploughshares.* And amongst them, the polished metal of an arming sword and smooth face of a shield embossed with fronds of ivy. A breastplate bearing the same vines, beneath the hitch of an old plough. All going slow to ruin in the damp dark and sea air.

She left them there, opened the door that led into the rest of the manor and paused for a moment on the threshold, but there was only silence and darkness within. The kitchen garden around the weathered steps beside the house was tangled with masses of brown, dead leaves. *Mint. Sage. Soapwort. Feverfew.* All growing wild and raggedy. The door to the house banged closed in the wind as she came down the steps, and the small, dark windows stared down at her accusingly.

She ranged up towards the sea, and found the crypt on the very cusp of the world. It brought her to it with the smell of foreign flowers. A narrow passage cut into the chalky hillside in ages before remembering, clad in granite and planted with flowering wonders from lands so distant that few in the age of ruins could name them. Great waterfalls of purple wisteria trailed from the trellises like falling smoke, dusted with ash and blooming too late into the year amongst the muscular strands of green-black ivy. It overflowed with life, this long-house for the dead, while the gardens and fields all lay fallow and choking. The weed wife descended the foot-worn steps leading down into the earth.

In the purple dark, a woman sat amongst the stone urns and carved faces of her ancestors, her red-gold hair bound into an unruly braid that fell between her shoulder blades, her cheeks and bare arms freckled brown from years spent underneath the sun. The knight was lean with months of famine, and did not so much as glance the weed wife's way as she approached. There was a distance in her blue-green eyes. Unlike the blindness of the elf that the weed wife had left to the brambles, but almost as unbreachable. The knight's chest rose and fell heavily in the sweetness of the flowers and the smoke of the falling sky—the weeds all growing wild around her, as though she was no different from the statues of her kin.

'Ser Marchlyn,' the weed wife said. 'Your fields have gone to ruin and your cattle are starving. There are rats in your grain store, the rot is in your roof, and I have come a long way here to speak with you.'

The knight blinked her red-gold lashes only once, and slowly. She sighed into the cool sweetness of the tomb, and then fell still once more.

'Ser Marchlyn.'

'I do not own that title anymore,' the knight said in a voice like ash drifting into the open sea. 'It has forsaken me.'

The weed wife crouched down beside her, and watched the filaments of purple light play amongst the fresh bronze of her hair.

'It is not all you have forsaken,' she said. 'Where are your family, Marchlyn? Where are your thegns?'

'All gone.' Marchlyn bowed her head, and for a moment it sounded as though her voice would break. A look passed across her brow like the front of an incoming storm, and with the force of her will alone she sealed herself against it. 'Dead. Or else gone east to the city.'

The weed wife allowed a thin frond of silence to work between them, then dropped her voice to the gentlest of murmurs.

'Do you think that mourning them through all the passage of the seasons will aid them into death, child?'

Marchlyn's expression remained as impassive and featureless as stone.

'Nothing can aid them,' she said flatly. 'Nothing can aid any of us anymore.'

The weed wife frowned.

'I am certain you must feel that's true, girl.'

The vague sort of distance in Marchlyn's eyes slammed closed like a shutter in high wind and her eyes flashed hard and sharp.

'Let me be, woman!' She pulled away and straightened up to her full height. Once, she had been a thing formed of sculpted muscle and power, but now her clothes hung listlessly off her starving shoulders. The only echo of strength remained in the rip curl of her voice. 'Whatever it was you came here for, you shall not get it from me. Be gone with you!'

The weed wife stayed exactly where she was, crouched low in the purple shift of light and dark with the knight towering above her. She watched the heavy pull in Marchlyn's chest as her throat tightened and she struggled for breath against the air itself. It was only when the knight turned away and braced herself between the statues, choking and shaking, that the weed wife rose to her feet. She walked into the entrance of the crypt, where feather-light pendants of wisteria swayed in the salt wind. Marchlyn said nothing at all, and for the longest time the weed wife stood on the threshold between the living and the dead and watched the high clouds blow in over white cliffs. They wove a serpentine path of chalk between her and the horizon in the weak and gilded evening light. Great waves dashing against their feet—the colour of granite, dusted with the faintest breath of gold.

The smallest curl of ivy crawled at her feet, no bigger than the length of a hand and blanketed so thick with soot that it was barely there at all. She knelt down beside it, and brushed the ash away with her fingers and her breath. Its leaves were no larger than her thumbnail, curled over on themselves and as dry as brittle paper. The weed wife turned the frail vine over in her fingers, her free hand reaching for the black glass knife at her belt.

The blade was no longer than the ivy or the span of her hand, slick and notched and uneven from where it had been knapped out of the earth. She placed the edge of it against her lip, and let it cut until the blood dripped off the glass and splattered black and wet amongst the dry drifts of grey soot. Her mouth formed words and sounds beyond her knowing: forgotten languages that ran together on her tongue. She felt the power of it rise in her belly until it quivered like a harp string in the wind. Then, she spat out the final word with a thick clot of her own blood, and the tiny curl of ivy surged against her: thick, muscular vines seizing her about the wrists, grasping her arms and squeezing around her chest, its tiny aerial roots puncturing her travelling leathers and burying themselves into her skin.

The weed wife opened her eyes, and looked down at her arms where a thousand leaves the size of children's hands formed a patchwork over the leather and canvas of her clothes. The tiny, yellow-white flowers hanging heavy with their pollen. A terrible tenderness was upon her then. Tears shivered in her eyes, and she spoke to the ivy in a sotto voice as she unwound it from her body. The white, aerial roots only let go of her reluctantly, leaving rows of tiny puncture wounds behind as she laid the vines out in what sunshine that there was. She harvested a few of its great, dark leaves with a heart full of supplications. Only when she stood and wiped her tears away did she see Marchlyn standing at the back of the crypt, her blue-green eyes locked unmoving on the blade of her knife.

'Come inside with me,' the weed wife said.

Marchlyn did not move until she sheathed the blade back at her waist. Even then, she lingered for a long time in the evening. Beneath the tears of wisteria. Looking back into the host of statues, and the great urns of the dead.

The knight disappeared into the umber gloom and sat down beside the empty hearth. She had a sprig of the ivy between her fingers, twisting it slowly and studying its tiny cream-coloured flowers. The weed wife closed the door behind them, and allowed her eyes a few moments to adjust. The gruesome shadows of a dozen skinned hares hung from the crossbeams, swinging slowly in the breath of wind that had crept in through the open door.

Marchlyn looked up from the ivy, and watched her carefully.

'The smith's boy brings them,' she said gruffly, nodding to the hares. 'For all the good it does us both.'

The weed wife studied the lean lines of Marchlyn's shoulders through the coarse wool of her shirt. Not famine then. Rabbit starvation.

Too much lean meat and blood.

'When was the last time that you ate anything else?' the weed wife asked.

Marchlyn shrugged, and turned back to the sprig of ivy twisting in between her fingers.

'This does not look like any ivy that I have ever seen,' she said.

The weed wife crouched down beside the hearth, and began to sweep away the ashes. Her hands moved slowly and methodically. When she didn't answer, Marchlyn shifted irritably in her chair.

'What did you do to it?'

The weed wife collected the ashes into an empty scupper, and began to lay a fire.

'It is an old spell,' she said. 'Very old.' She took the large, dark leaves out of her satchel, and placed them reverently at the bottom of a small copper flask, topping it up with water from the runoff. 'She is much more like grandmother ivy now.'

Marchlyn frowned at the tiny flowers and their heavy, pollen-covered stamens.

'Why?'

'Because she was dying,' the weed wife told her. 'And the land here has already seen too much death.'

Marchlyn tried to swallow, but her mouth was too dry. When the weed wife stopped stacking kindling in the barren firebox and offered her water, she almost choked on it.

'The smoke that pours out of the city has done much more than darken the day,' she said as she worked. 'It has poisoned the rivers and killed almost every bee, hoverfly and moth from here to the Coastlands. It has been a little over five weeks since I last saw a butterfly.' She counted them as easily as someone might count their steps away from home. 'It was a dull, tired little thing. One of last year's tortoiseshells. Clinging to the parapet of the skyway.'

She felt for a piece of tinder fungus in her bag, and worried at it with the edge of her knife until the surface began to powder. Then she struck a fire steel against the blade until it caught. A thin curl of smoke melted slowly into the air, and when the weed wife brought the ember to her lips, it waxed against her breath. Marchlyn's own breathing came quickly and uneven, her eyes searching the distant shadows of the room, settling anywhere but on the glass blade of the knife.

'That ivy,' the weed wife explained, tucking the knife carefully away and wrapping the ember up in dry moss and bark. Feeding it air until the tinder caught. 'Has begun to remember things that have slept in her sap for many generations. She does not need the bees and butterflies any more. The wind will spread her pollen. If the smoke does not lift, she will endure.'

She placed the cracking, smouldering tinder into the fire-box, and bent down low to breathe upon it until tiny, bright flames jumped up out of the moss. Marchlyn twirled the ivy between her fingers.

'You made it older,' she said slowly.

'No,' the weed wife sat back on her feet, and arranged the kindling over the infant flames. 'I helped her to remember her past. What she did with those memories was her choice, not mine.'

Marchlyn tossed the sprig of ivy down onto the hearth and wrapped her arms around herself. The weed wife pinched off the leaves, one at a time, and dropped them into the copper beaker with the others. As soon as the fire was strong enough, she nestled the beaker amongst the flames and brushed the soot off of her hands.

'Where did you learn your spell?' the knight asked her. 'Who taught you?'

The weed wife shook her head.

'Not taught,' she said. 'These spells cannot be learned, taken, or stolen. They may only be given. Open hand to open hand. Mouth to mouth, and heart to heart. Between one world and the other.'

Marchlyn rubbed her skinny arms, and stared into the hearth. The warm light caught in the copper tones of her hair and drew deep lines of shadow underneath her cheekbones, until she looked as frail as the longhorn cattle in her barn.

The weed wife said: 'Is that not the answer you were expecting?'

'It is not how it was with Elidir,' she said too quickly, as though she was afraid that the words would burn her if she did not spit them out.

'I have heard stories of your friend,' the weed wife agreed. 'How he tore magic from books and scrolls. From his teachers. Rending memory as easily as paper. That the great rulers of people and elves brought all their best and brightest to him so that he could tear the knowledge from their bodies. Of how they dammed the rivers with stone and magic so that he could use their power as his own.'

Marchlyn's lips worked for a moment and her copper eyelashes glowed like liquid fire in the hearth light, but when she spoke, she only said, 'He was not my friend,' and looked away as though she could not bear the light. Her windpipe tightened, and the breath groaned through the narrow passage of her throat. Her eyes were almost colourless.

'Who gave it to you?' she asked. And then: 'The spell.'

'My ancestors,' the weed wife told her. 'Mine to call to hers. To parley with grandmother ivy through deep, deep time.'

'And who were your ancestors?' Marchlyn snapped, pulling her chair closer to the fire. 'Fair Landers?'

The weed wife looked down at her hands, the colour of red amber in the firelight. If there was any trace of her past in the deep lines of her palms, she could not see it.

'I don't know,' she admitted, sighing. 'I don't remember.'

'Don't remember what?' Marchlyn said. 'Your parents?'

The weed wife shrugged. 'My parents. My siblings. Anything beyond perhaps a year ago.'

The knight made a short, hard sound in her throat. It may once have been something like a laugh, but it had long since atrophied into something far colder and devoid of life. The weed wife eased herself onto the settle before the fire and held out her red amber hands to warm them.

'What is it that amuses you?' she asked.

Marchlyn shook her head, and drew her knees up to her chest.

'You cannot remember your past,' she said. 'And I have nothing but. We make quite the pair.'

'I suppose we do,' the weed wife said.

For a long while after that, neither of them spoke. Not until the water began to rumble in the copper beaker and the weed wife knelt down to retrieve it. She took her knife from her belt, and glanced at Marchlyn as she hooked the point of the blade through the handle and lifted it onto the hearth. The knight's eyes flashed white in the gloom, and the muscles of her narrow shoulders tightened. The weed wife nodded silently to herself, and retrieved a wooden cup and length of muslin to strain the ivy leaves out of the boiling water.

'You shall have to bring in the harvest soon,' she said

softly, looking sidelong at Marchlyn as she poured the water through the cloth. 'Or at least, what harvest there is. You must prepare your scythe, Marchlyn.'

'I have none,' Marchlyn said stiffly. 'And even if I did, what would it matter? The plague spreads further every day, and more and more of our people leave for the city. Soon the Weaver King will have an army larger than any force upon the earth. And we will all be dead if we are fortunate.'

'Perhaps,' the weed wife said, swirling the ivy tea in the bottom of the wooden cup and breathing in the smell of it. 'But hunger will kill you quicker than the Weaver King. You may be sure of that.'

'Why have you come here?'

Marchlyn stood, and knocked her chair onto the floor. The sound of the impact shot through her body like lightning, every muscle taut and ready to fight or run. When she could not hold her composure any longer, she turned away to hide her shame.

'Leave me alone.' Her ribs worked like bellows against the worn-thin wool of her shirt. 'Just... Let me die in peace.'

The weed wife came to stand behind her and placed a hand on Marchlyn's shoulder. She could feel every smooth bone and twist of tendon through her shirt, and when the knight twisted around, something hard and out of place shifted across the plane of her shoulder blade, embedded underneath the skin.

'Here,' the weed wife told her, offering her the cup. 'Let grandmother ivy help you to breathe.'

Marchlyn rubbed her dirty fingers over her closed eyelids and pressed her teeth together until her jaw ached and her eyes burned. She reached out to take the cup.

The weed wife woke between her first and second sleeps in the deep silence at the very heart of the night. Far off, she could hear the ocean against the white chalk cliffs, the sound of water resounding in the walls. Now and then, the wind pulled at a loose slat in the shutters, but the mournful whistling of it only seemed to make the silence deeper. The embers in the hearth burned low, the light blood-red on the bodies of the hares hanging high above her. It was one of the nights of early autumn when winter creeps through the hours of lengthening dark, and dull cold had worked its way into the walls.

The weed wife curled beneath the blankets of her bedroll by the fire, and breathed the darkness slow and even. Outside, Marchlyn's hunting dog howled for the high, black clouds passing before the waning moon from its kennel beneath the old stone stairs. The sound bled into the requiem the wind sang in the shutters, until the weed wife could not tell them apart. On the settle, the knight shifted fretfully in her sleep and murmured something that did not quite manage to form words. Her voice was a frail, tiny thing, and she rested like a woman used to sleeping on the wing. Always on the verge of waking.

Marchlyn struggled with the blankets as though they strangled her, and when the weed wife moved to cover her over again, she came awake with a startled gasp of air. Her hand flashed out for a sword that wasn't there, then shivered at the memory of the blade. She swept her palm through the cold sweat blistering on her forehead and drew away, sitting upright on the settle and sloughing the blankets off of her narrow shoulders. The weed wife stoked the fire, and sat down at her side.

'Focus on your breath,' she whispered, so as not to break the deep quiet of the night. 'Bring it in, deep and slow and steady, and think of nothing else.'

Sweat dripped from Marchlyn's chin onto the knotted blankets, and for a long time her whole body rose and fell like the pulsing of a heart. The air knotted in her throat and groaned deep within her chest, and every time it stammered, the weed wife squeezed her hand and breathed with her again. In the firelight, Marchlyn's expression was set. Hard and featureless.

Only when the sweat began to dry, when her hands and shoulders grew still and her breathing grew quiet, did the weed wife draw away to lay two small, grey segments of ash across the embers.

'Does this happen often?' she asked as she came to the settle.

Marchlyn sighed. 'Each night.' The lines of her face softened for a moment, and her voice grew terribly brittle. As skeletal as leaves. 'Goddess, what is wrong with me?'

The weed wife frowned and placed her hand upon the shrapnel buried deep in Marchlyn's shoulder.

'Nothing is wrong with you, child,' she murmured, watching the grey ash split and blacken in the flames. 'Nothing at all.'

Marchlyn rubbed her pale face with her cold hands. 'I'm dying,' she told the weed wife. 'I can feel it in my blood. I have been dying ever since the battle. Since Elidir...' She stumbled. 'Some nights, I wonder if the river was not the only thing he harnessed for his magic. Whether, now that he has gone to the Weaver King, he is sucking me down into death along with him.'

Something like a smile curled at the edges of the weed wife's mouth. She took Marchlyn's fingers between her warm and sun-browned hands, and brushed her thumb across her knuckles.

'You are not dying, Marchlyn,' she said. 'When you breeched the city, you fought for your life. Night and day, and hour on hour, for more than a month. You spent another fighting your way back out again when Elidir joined with the Weaver King.

'The things we see and hear and feel, they are like the food we eat and air we breathe,' she went on. Beneath the waning moon, the wind and Marchlyn's hunting hound sung to one another. 'When we bring them into our body, they must be broken down so that we can digest them. So that we can draw them into our blood.' She nodded to the dozen hares hanging like bloody pendants in the rafters. 'You find that you have trouble eating since you came back. That your body will not digest anything you give it.'

Marchlyn nodded mutely.

'It is the same with your mind,' the weed wife told her. 'The night that you entered the city, and in all the many long days and nights that followed, you focused only of the life of your charge. You kept yourself alive, kept Elidir alive with you, and allowed no other thoughts in to distract you. You knew that even the smallest of them could have left you both dead there in that place.

'All the things you saw and felt,' she said. 'All the things you heard and touched and smelled, they are all lying undigested in your mind, because your body was far too busy surviving that ordeal. They come back to you now so that you can begin to break them down and sculpt them into memories.'

'That isn't true,' Marchlyn snapped. Her hands stiffened, but the weed wife did not let her go. 'It has been a year since we came out of the city.'

'And every time that these thoughts have come back to you, Marchlyn, what have you done? You have pushed them away. You have shut them out in the cold and the dark of your mind. Because you are afraid.'

'I am not afraid!' Marchlyn's voice was a closed fist.

She pulled her hand away. When she tried to stand, the blankets knotted around her. She thrashed out against them, hot panic rising in her chest, and when finally she freed herself, she crouched down low before the fire with her head cradled in her hands.

'Why are you here?' she said miserably, her freckled fingers pressing back into her red-gold hair. 'How do you know all of this? How did you find me?'

The weed wife picked her water skin up from the floor, and drank deep of the bitter rain.

'I followed stories,' she said eventually. 'About you, and about the others who went with you into the city to slay the Weaver King. I listened to a stable boy on the road from Rock Savage and patched the sores and blisters on his hands as he told me about how men and elves had dug the heart out of the hollow mountain, looking for its metal, and found something waiting in the darkness there. Some fragment of a dark king, long dead to the age of ruins.

'I traded a salve to a leper girl on the outskirts of Stanlow for the tale of how our great kings and queens and chieftains came together when that fragment began to resonate with the song of its master and call him from his slumber. How they planned to turn the shard of the Weaver King's own soul against him, and how they took a young dark elf boy from the streets so that they had somewhere to bind it. How they forged a great and ancient mage from him, and from the shard inside the mountain. Someone capable of rescuing them from the horror that they had unleashed upon themselves.

'I treated scurvy in two sisters from the Coastlands who ran the ships along the Restless Sea. I fed them lemon juice and honey, and they told me how they had given passage to a great host of a dozen knights, archers, sages and savants, who were all accompanying an elf back east from the Library of Dinorwig towards the hollow mountain. They gave me the names of those they could remember, and descriptions of those who they could not.'

The weed wife sighed. 'With time, child, I traced each and every warrior, thief and scholar who went with Elidir into the city, and followed the stories of those who came back out of it. I have walked from the southern lands to these white cliffs, and from the Coastlands in the west all the way to the limits of the great city itself in search of each and every one of you. You are my last.'

The words fell heavy. Like the sealing of a tomb. Marchlyn shivered before the fire, and reached out a frail hand for the blankets knotted on the floor.

'You have seen Hoyle,' she said at last, pulling them about her shoulders like a shroud. 'Ser Maelogen and Grand Master Wylfa.'

There was hope in her voice: hot and fast as liquid metal. The weed wife turned the water skin between her hands. Her dark and silvered hair fell across her face like a rent veil.

'No, child,' she said, so softly that her voice almost melted into the gentle keening of the wind. 'They are all dead. You are the only one.'

'I...' Marchlyn stammered, choking on her words like clotted blood. 'No. That can't be true. Grand Master Wylfa...'

'Threw herself off of the skyway before she was halfway back to Rock Savage,' the weed wife sighed. 'Hoyle and

Gwynt y Môr have both gone into the city with the plague. Trawsfynydd died from it before I could reach her, shut up in her rooms until she forgot how to feed herself. Ser Maelogen led a vanguard back towards the city and was struck through the chest with an arrow. Maentwrog—'

'Enough!' Marchlyn spat, coughing against a sob that swelled in her throat like a tumour. 'I've heard enough.'

Her words were stretched out, thin and fractured. For a full minute after, she could only crouch there before the hearth and spit out angry tears.

'Why have you come?' she said at last in a strange, high voice, half-smothered in her throat.

The weed wife slid from the settle to kneel beside her, and stared into the fire.

'Because someone must sow crops in autumn for there to be a harvest in the spring,' she said, her brow knitted low over her dark eyes. 'And if hope is not planted somewhere now, then I fear the sky will fall forever and the Weaver King will rule in the smoke and embers through all the ages that remain.'

The silence sat between them like a great slab of unfinished stone.

After a long, long time, Marchlyn passed the back of her hand through the tears on her eyelashes, and swallowed hard.

'What must I do?' she said.

'Remember,' the weed wife said softly, studying her tear-stained face in the steady firelight.

Marchlyn flinched, the corners of her mouth grimacing like someone already dead.

'And then?'

'What you do with those memories is your choice, Marchlyn,' the weed wife said, running her hand down the sharp notches of her spine. 'Not mine.'

'Where do I begin?'

Marchlyn stood at the edge of the wheat field and stared into the blanching corn, splattered with the heartsblood of poppies and tangled with corn cleavers. The heads of the wheat were small and bent over from too little water and too much ash. Tiny grains at the centre of long awns that had grown into stiff needles. The weed wife followed her gaze out across the fields.

'I always find,' she said, kneeling to draw a long strand of corn cleavers out of the crop. 'That it is best to start at the beginning, and work in.'

Marchlyn passed her hand over a haze of red-gold hair that was working its way loose from her braid, and knelt beside her. 'As you say, my lady.'

The weed wife smiled, meticulously stripping the last few leaves off the cleaver and laying a blanket out between them to hold the parts that she could use. She worked in silence, and felt the wind roll in off the ocean. Marchlyn glanced across, and began to mimic her movements—her fingers numb and heavy. The weed wife showed her how to separate the tiny burs from the cleavers, and piled the long, barbed stems behind them.

'The plague had already begun to spread amongst the mine workers by the time I reached the hollow mountain,' Marchlyn said at last. 'Nobody really knew what was happening, just that the people who came into contact with the shard forgot how to care for themselves. They wouldn't even cover themselves with a blanket to stop themselves from freezing. Some of them left for the city. After that, there was an exodus.'

'Were you told stories of the plague, child?' The weed wife stripped another strand of corn cleavers from the wheat and began reducing it into what she could use for medicine, brewing and bedstraw. 'The old one. The one that brought the Weaver King to power in the first age of ash and embers.'

Marchlyn shrugged her bony shoulders.

'They told us that there was another plague, long ago. That the Weaver King found the cure, and people flocked to his stronghold to receive it.'

'The Weaver King was not always as he is now,' the weed wife agreed. 'When the plague came, he tried to heal the sick. But his cure was long and slow, so they built a city around his surgeons. Somewhere that the sick and their families would be safe until the healing work was done. They mined metal, because it was the only thing of worth on the blasted mountain where his stronghold had been built, and burned the woods for charcoal so that they could smelt iron for the forges. Then they built the skyways, so that they could sell their metal to other lands, and we all grew wealthy from the Weaver King's compassion.'

Marchlyn frowned, and picked at leaves.

'What happened?'

'Times changed,' the weed wife said. 'The forests were burned out. The metal emptied from the mountains. Years passed, and the Weaver King refused to die. He lived on far beyond his usefulness, and came into great power that festered at the centre of his city like a sore. The people turned against him. They left his empty body to slumber in his city, surrounded by the poor and the desperate that built their shelters in the ruins, and bound up the shards of his spirit so that he would stay there. That is what your people found at the bottom of that mine. A fragment. The smallest piece of him. But when it woke, it resonated with its master's song. The Weaver King began to stir, and the memory of the plague which had once drawn people to him shivered in the hearts of all who touched it. Not a real pestilence, but a reflex. No longer connected to anything at all.' Her fingers were turning raw with the barbs of the weeds. 'I suspect that it was around then that someone had the idea of turning the shard against its master.'

Marchlyn tried to swallow, pausing for a moment with her hands on the earth. Her fingers on the dry, green leaves of a cornflower. Blue blossoms nodding towards the earth.

'What shall I do with this?'

'Keep the flowers,' the weed wife said, not looking up. 'They can be used to clear the eyes. Here.' She held out her knife. 'Once you have taken them, dig the root out as best you can.'

Marchlyn grew pale, but reached out with an uneasy hand to take it. The weed wife held the flat of the blade between her thumb and fingers, and allowed her to grow used to holding it.

'Breathe deep, Ser Marchlyn,' she told her.

The knight closed her eyes, and breathed in long and slow. The cold wind stirred the wheat field, bringing the smell of salt in off of the ocean. Marchlyn took the knife, and went quickly about her work.

'I think that they found Elidir on the streets of the city,' the knight said, filling her head with words so that she did not have to think, cutting the flowers and digging out the roots. 'After all, who was going to miss one barefoot dark elf from the slum built atop its ruin?'

The muscles of her jaw flexed. She lay the blue blossoms on the sheet between them, and moved on to the next.

'They had already built the monstrance around the shard at the centre of the mountain by the time that I was called there. A great starburst of twisted brass. Like rays of sunlight around the glass where they had sealed Elidir...

'He was so still,' she said, studying the blue flower in her hand. 'Like he was sleeping. The colour of a clear summer sky quite long into the evening. I don't know what magics they worked to fuse him with the shard, or how long he had been in there. I think that it was very long. I think...' She licked her lips. 'I think that he had suffered terribly.'

The weed wife brushed her fingers down the stem of a forget-me-not and took hold of the base to work the root out of the earth. After a few moments, Marchlyn placed the cornflower down upon the cloth, and looked up into the sky.

'I have no idea what he was like before they put him in the monstrance, but when he came out, he was a damned pain in the ass.' She shook her head. 'I could never decide whether something deep within him had shattered, or whether he had always been a monster.' Her voice trembled for a moment, and she breathed in full deep to steady it. 'They gave him everything he asked for: spells, scrolls, magic-workers. Elidir sucked the life out of each one of them in turn to feed his own power. The more they gave him, the more that he wanted, and the more that he asked for, the more that they gave. I suppose... I suppose that they didn't have much choice. He was their last hope against the Weaver King. And so they dammed the rivers and worked the runes into the buttresses, and when he was in need, he would draw the runes upon the earth with his staff and the whole heart of the river would surge through him. It was...'

'Both beautiful and terrible,' the weed wife said under her breath.

Marchlyn sighed her agreement.

'I guarded him for months while he learned, working through night and day. He barely slept, barely ate, everything was given over to his work although... although I do not think that he hurried himself. Every week brought new stories of how the plague spread across the land. How the towns were emptied and the people all gone into the city. I don't think that Elidir cared. He simply drank in knowledge and power because it was in his nature to do so. Perhaps...' She stared down into the bloody heart of the first of the poppies. 'I always thought that if I had found some way to speak to him... Or if I had only listened I... I don't know.' She took the head of the poppy softly in her hand. 'What do you want with these?'

The weed wife studied her. Rain clouds blew in over the cliffs in flanks of dappled black and grey. The wheat waxed in the autumn wind.

'I think,' she said at last, reaching out to brush her fingers against Marchlyn's arm. 'That we do not have need of them anymore.'

Marchlyn swallowed, and nodded firmly.

'As you wish, my lady.'

When she broke the stem of the first poppy, the thunder rolled above them. A deep and lingering resonance that rippled clean and clear across the sky. Fat flecks of rain fell onto the baked, pale earth. Marchlyn stared into the poppy's heart, and placed it down behind her. The water softened the earth, ran through Marchlyn's red-gold hair, and soaked through the thin wool of her shirt until it clung to the starved lines of her body.

'It did not stop when we left the Library at Dinorwig,' she said over the sound of water drumming on the tight skin of the field. 'He seemed to grow stronger with every day that passed. The further that we travelled, the more we passed through lands already in the thrall of the Weaver King. In the beginning they were only suspicious of us, but as we grew closer they started to greet us with drawn steel.

'We cut across the open country,' she went on. 'And stayed off of the roads. There are ancient trackways leading up into the mountains that have not been walked for generations. We followed them as best we could—Elidir pushing us every step of the way. He pushed until the horses starved or collapsed from exhaustion, and then he drove us forwards on foot. I was grateful for the cold, and for the smoke that spewed across the sky. If the sun had been on my armour, I would have fallen by that road long before we came over the ridge and looked down upon the city. Lights burning in every window and smoke rising out of every forge.'

Her hands continued their steady work amongst the poppies: drawing them out of the earth and laying their fallen bodies down amongst the wheat. Lightning turned the sky to tempered steel. White hot, and clamorous as clashing swords. Marchlyn pushed her dirty fingers back through the wet tangles of her hair.

'How long must we go on?'

The weed wife rocked back on her knees until she was seated on her folded feet, and nodded towards the far side of the field. The rain crackled on her travelling leathers, and ran down the hollow of her spine.

'Until we are done,' she said.

For two days, the knight and the weed wife worked. Above them, the mood of the sky shifted between storm and smoke-shrouded sun. Their fingers grew sore, and within the manor house the hares were slowly joined by bunches of drying herbs, hanging high up in the rafters. They spoke as they worked, and Marchlyn grew used to the slow constricting in her throat when she talked about the journey. The electric flash of not-yet-memories against the inside of her skull. She worked until her whole body was on fire. So that she did not have to think.

On the third day, it rained fit for the end of the world.

Great, sinuous tendrils of blue-white lightning waxing against the sky, sprouting through the clouds like ivy growing through a hedgerow. In the empty stillness of the house, Marchlyn wrung the rain out of her hair, and dragged a wooden bath before the fire. Her shoulders ached, and pain shot like the lightning across her back as she placed an iron cauldron on the flames.

When the water was ready, she stripped out of her soaking, filthy clothes, and climbed into the bath. She closed her eyes, and for the longest time she felt as though she was suspended in pure and perfect dark. The rain crackled on the window-panes in waves, and the dark gathered its strength behind them. Marchlyn sighed, and sank deep into the water. Her great, fawn-coloured mastiff stretched out before the fire, and rested her heavy head upon her paws.

Time did not pass.

The world became a diffuse and insubstantial thing.

The weed wife crept in softly with bare feet, but the sound of the rain surged and swelled through the open door and a squall of tiny water droplets rattled on the floorboards. Marchlyn sat up in her pool of darkness, and allowed the light back in. She watched the weed wife hang her cloak beside the door, streaming with bright water, and set down a basket filled with struggling vegetables salvaged from the garden. *Turnip. Onion. Leeks and early carrots.* The weed wife climbed onto a chair to take down one of the skinned hares, and set about her work.

Marchlyn patted the mastiff's large, domed head absently as the animal nuzzled at her fingers.

'I think,' she said, her fingers creeping back over her shoulder to the jagged knot of muscle around the shrapnel embedded in them. 'That I am ready for you to take this out.'

The weed wife chopped the onions and smiled to herself, and Marchlyn waited while she fed the stew to the cauldron, topped it up with water, and wiped her hands against her soaking leathers. Waited as she drew her chair up by the fire, behind the curve of Marchlyn's neck, and began to lay her tools out on the settle: knives; forceps; a curved bone needle and length of linen thread. Marchlyn drew her legs up to her chest.

'Here,' the weed wife told her, placing a vial of dark glass on the edge of the wooden bath. 'For the pain.'

Marchlyn studied the vial, and wrapped her arms around her knees. The weed wife placed a hand upon shrapnel in her shoulder.

'Do not martyr yourself, Ser Marchlyn,' she told her. 'You shall need all your strength. Let the poppies ease your suffering.'

Marchlyn sighed, and drank. The liquid was thick and hot and bitter, and the warmth spread out from her stomach. She closed her eyes, rested her head upon her knees, and half-dreamed that she was suspended in a starless sky.

'Tell me about the city.'

The weed wife's voice cut through the perfect, wallowing dark. Marchlyn came back to herself slowly, as though she had been very far away. There was a strange pressure against her shoulder, and warmth radiating down her back. It took her some time to realise that the weed wife had begun her work.

She felt nothing at all.

Lazily, she opened her eyes and looked down to see the mastiff pressing her great, black nose against her hand. The corner of Marchlyn's mouth twitched with something like a smile.

'I don't know what we were meant to do when we reached that place,' she said slowly, her voice like slow treacle in her mouth. She turned her cheek against her knee so that she could stare into the fire. So that she could stop herself feeling as though she were being swept out into a great, black sea. 'Or how Elidir planned to defeat the Weaver King. We asked, but he would never speak to us. Perhaps... Perhaps he did not know himself.'

She raised her free hand to her brow, and rubbed her aching eyes. The weed wife's black glass blade worked between the muscles in her shoulder, and Marchlyn wondered if it would ever hurt.

'When I trained to be a knight,' she said, the fire wending around the blackened metal of the cauldron. 'The Grand Master used to tell us stories. To teach us how to live as knights. Only... in those stories... when they rode out to fight, it is always against some terrible monster. A mighty water dragon. A manticore or cockatrice. A great, black wolf...'

Her thoughts chased themselves out until they were extinguished. She thought that perhaps she drifted out of knowing then, but could not say for how long. When her mind came keen again, a low pain had begun to press out from her shoulder.

'Only...' she said, her voice hitching and knotting. 'It was not like that when we reached the city. We were not fighting monsters. We were fighting people who had been our kin. Sometimes, I even thought that I recognised a few of them. It was hard to tell. There was such a hollowness in their faces. Like the mountain where they sealed Elidir in that monstrance. As though their hearts had been cut out.'

She pressed her dry tongue against the roof of her mouth, and something nudged against her arm, but when she opened her eyes to push the dog away she found that the weed wife offering her water. She took the cup vaguely, and drank deep. The water cooled the insides of her body, but sweat trickled from her forehead and down between her breasts. Or perhaps it was her tears. It was difficult to tell.

'Breathe,' the weed wife said, her closeness stirring the tiny hairs on the back of Marchlyn's neck. Then she said: 'This will hurt.'

Marchlyn nodded, and pulled the air down into her belly. The pain started slowly, as though her body woke to it only when the weed wife placed the forceps in the wound to draw the shrapnel out. Marchlyn clenched her teeth.

'The sky was red and black...' she said, the cracks spidering through her voice. 'Like ink running into water. So much blood. So much of it on my hands that I could barely hold my sword. My armour was slick red. The others looked like golems formed out of butcher's scraps. They stank. Like rotten meat. I couldn't tell the difference between our people and the plague-carriers any more. I don't know what happened to Ffestiniog. I think...'

She choked. The weed wife's hand fell on her good shoulder. Slowly, the tears unwound themselves from her, and Marchlyn let them go.

'I think that perhaps it was my blade that killed her,' she said, her voice firmer. 'I think... I think that maybe she was not the only one.'

A sharp bolt of pain flashed through her body. The weed wife's hand tightened on her, and metal clicked down against wood.

'There,' she said softly. 'I have it.'

'Let me see?' Marchlyn pleaded, twisting around until the weed wife placed a shard of broken, bloodied metal into her open hand.

Marchlyn took it between her thumb and index finger, and turned it in the firelight. 'This comes from a blade,' she said. 'A shattered sword. I don't...' She frowned, and stared at the shard of blood and metal. 'By the end, most of the armour was broken from my body. Blood ran through the hollows in my breastplate. I didn't know if it was mine. And always... Always there was Elidir's magic. The flash of bright, white light like a storm of early summer. The high, reed-like song of his voice. All those words that I did not understand, and the runes of fire upon the bloodied earth. Goddess...'

The skin and muscle of her shoulder pinched and throbbed as the weed wife stitched it closed. Marchlyn looked down, and saw that the water had turned to blood around her.

'The main body of the host had gathered around the tower.'

The shard of sword slipped from between her fingers and fell into the bathwater. She watched it fall. End over end. Flashing silver-white through the blood. Her voice grew distant until she could barely even hear herself.

'When Elidir approached the host... They parted. Like the clouds separating for the sun. His red robes were black with blood. The hood drawn up over his face so that I could only see his eyes, shining like old gold. I wanted to call out. To break off from the fighting and ask what he was doing. But I didn't. I knew. I think perhaps that I had known for quite some time. Perhaps he had deceived me, but I think that maybe I had deceived myself. We all had. Somewhere within our bodies, we all knew that he was not going to the city to defeat the Weaver King. How could he?'

She drew a long, deep breath, and shook her head while the weed wife cut the thread and began to dress the wound with plantain and with bandages soaked in red wine. Marchlyn stared down at the faint glint of silver metal resting just between her feet, somewhere in the bloodied dark.

'How could he?' she murmured underneath her breath, the darkness reaching out to her and wending itself around her body. 'The Weaver King was formed out of the same matter as he was. Our enemy could not defeat itself.'

'Come.' The weed wife touched her side, and helped her slowly from the bath. Stumbling and blood-soaked like a newborn calf. She wrapped a sheet around her shaking body. 'We have done all we can,' she said. 'You need to rest.'

The crop was barely alive. The stalks too few, too stunted, and bowed-over from thirst. And yet, the messy hatch work of fields had all turned amber and in the flashes of late summer sun, reaching through the high haze of black smoke. The wheat shifted in the wind that broke over the cliffs, and it was the most beautiful thing that Marchlyn could imagine.

Life. Struggling against the dark.

She rubbed the top of her right shoulder, feeling the edges of the bandages and the deep ache that radiated far down into her muscles. It was a good pain. The kind that comes when the poison is out and the healing has begun. She had only been a week in the fields, but already her body was starting to feel stronger: the muscles across her arms and back coming back into themselves. Only the muscle she was gaining now was not in the places she was used to. It was not built to wear heavy armour. Hold a shield. Swing a blade. No. Her body was growing strong for the work that must be done kneeling. With hands in the earth, and fingers working through the roots and stones.

Marchlyn closed her eyes, and the weed wife came to stand beside her.

'It will not be a good harvest,' she said into the darkness. 'You were right. On the first day that you came here. I should not have let the fields go to ruin. Stupid. I was...'

'Suffering,' the weed wife finished softly, a twist of gentle warmth coming into her voice. 'You were a vassal to the past. There is no shame in it, Marchlyn.'

'Say that when midwinter comes and all my stores are empty,' the knight said with a sigh. 'Tell it to the smith's boy a month before Candlemas when all the hares are gone from here, and the only way I can repay his kindness is to starve to death with him.'

The weed wife touched her shield arm, pressing her thumb gently into the muscle and the sinew there.

'Marchlyn.' Her voice was deep and warm, like a full night of summer. 'Despair has ever been a greater enemy to you than famine. Do not allow it to take root.'

Marchlyn opened her eyes and stared out towards the cliffs.

At last, she said: 'You're right.'

The weed wife patted her forearm, and walked out into the crop. Her long, black hair was unbound down her back, streaked with filaments of silver. It billowed in the wind like a wave. No. Like the twisted tendrils of a thorn.

'Take heart,' the weed wife called back to her. 'We are not done here yet.'

'The harvest should have come in a week ago,' Marchlyn said, although she did not sound certain. Something fluttered underneath her heart. Something that had not moved for the passing of an age. 'It is too late. There is nothing more that we can do.'

'Is there not?'

The weed wife turned her head until Marchlyn could see the profile of her face. The deep lines around her eyes and mouth seemed to melt away in the flutter and the flash of autumn sun. There was a wicked glint in her eye, and the wheat seemed to wax and flood around her. As though it was little more than an extension of her body. Her bare toes twisting in the dark, wet earth.

Marchlyn tried to speak, but found that her voice was almost too weak to reach her.

'Who are you?'

The weed wife bowed her head, and her black-and-silver hair swept across her face. She was smiling. A young smile. One that penetrated all the way into the depths of her eyes.

'Do you think that I know?'

'I think that you would not tell me,' Marchlyn said. 'Even if you did.'

The weed wife laughed like falling rain, and turned back to face the fields.

'It's time,' she said.

And so it came to pass.

This is what the weed wife heard:

The voices of her ancestors in her mouth and in her ears. Singing the wind itself into being, in a language that only stone remembers. The living cloth of the earth against her feet, her knees, her hands. Oak brown. Stirred by wind and rain and sun. Stretching back from now into deep time. Deep as the far fathoms of the ocean, or the abyss of the night sky. Reaching on into the future like a hand, stretched out for the horizon.

And through it all: growth and death and birth and growth again. Life. Unfathomable in its tenacity. Incomprehensible to the arrogance of all these tiny, human minds. Seed and spore and shoot amongst the cracks between the rocks. In the folds of black stone on the flanks of the volcano even as it cooled, steaming in the bright, spring rain. The awns of wheat and grass expanding and contracting as day follows night follows day, boring down into the supple ground and sleeping through the long darkness of the winter. The seeds of fireweed and feverfew brought in through broken windows by the breeze. Rooting between floorboards. Breaking up the stones and rafters. Breaking the backs of the proud roofs.

Endless and indomitable.

It was fallacy to think that the Weaver King could destroy it. It would not bow to his demands. It would not bow to anyone. Life is, and was, and ever will be. Even when the sky grows black and silent, empty of birds and bats and moths and mayflies... Even when the leaves of ash and oak and hazel curl, brown and dead and black, and the skeleton trees rot down into the earth... Even when the grasslands burn from the city to the Coastlands, their embers dancing in the summer wind, and the rivers all run backwards and run black with soot and poison... Even then, the tiny parasols of dandelion seeds find their way into spaces wrought by water in the walls. Moss creeps over the flagstones. Clover follows it. Ground elder, well used to dark, cool places, finds its place beneath the falling sky. Much more than that. It thrives. Its leaves eaten in February and March before spring harvest. Bramble and ivy drape over the crumbling parapets of the skyways. Just as they have done since those skyways were young. Just as they will do until they topple down into the earth.

Life is. And was. And ever will be. She could feel it stretching out on every side of her into forever. Huge and messy and tenacious. Filled with tiny moments of triumph and despair. Burning out as fast as falling embers.

The voices of her ancestors in her ears and in her mouth, and the slow pulse of life in the wheat and oats and rye and barley all around. Their feet shallow in the earth and their seeds shivering in the cool sea wind. Remembering. Always remembering.

Spreading out from the short roots of her twisted toes, into eternity.

This is what Ser Marchlyn saw:

The weed wife drawing the blade of her black glass knife across her tongue. Lips moving, sounded and soundlessly, in a language that Marchlyn did not understand. Blood dripping off of each word into the golden wheat. The weed wife's voice like the boom of wind against her eardrums, or the peals of thunder in the sky.

Tiny tendrils of red mist and red-coloured magic. Blood atomised into the air. Growing like vines around the weed wife's body. Spreading through the air like branches. Feeling the currents of the wind. Her eyes open like polished jet, and skin like dirty amber as she sunk down to her knees.

The notched, black glass knife catching in the sun as the weed wife leant back her head and pressed it to her neck. Chanting and breathing. The blood running from the fullness of her mouth and snaking out into the air like living hair. Like roots. The blade held to her throat like one of the god-priests of old. Sacrificing themselves to the fields for fair harvest. Their hearts blood venting down into deep earth.

Gulls calling far above the sea, and a kind of waiting that built up in the air like the breath before a thunder crack. Clouds circling overhead in great, grey whorls. Waiting. All waiting. The words that called to something that Marchlyn could not name: something larger than a god, or fate, or time. Something terrible and beautiful that filled the air with a red haze and the snaking capillaries of blood.

The weed wife at the centre of it all. Like the beating of a heart.

The silent snap somewhere behind the air as everything came down at once: words tumbling end-over-end into silence and the wind; blood pattering down onto the wheat like falling rain; a great release that swelled up from the earth and settled in the bottom of her belly. The wheat and rye and oats all surging in towards the weed wife, kneeling at their centre point. Their seed heads swelling heavy. Their stalks growing different lengths and different colours. Awns lengthening like needles. A starburst of living gold all radiating in to her. The brambles and the cleavers at the edges of the field snaking out into the crop. Reaching out their splayed, green hands.

They are remembering, she thought, tears swelling up out of her chest. And, for a moment, the sound in her ears like the beating of an ancient drum that sunk back slowly. Into the beating of her heart.

Marchlyn stood before the field, shaking and breathless. The weed wife rose like a thing formed from wind and water vapour, picking her way back through the crop: the deep lines in her face scored with tears, and feet careful to avoid the stalks. Grandmother wheat shifting to enfold her like a cupped and open hand.

As she stepped out of the field she seemed to tread back upon the earth again. Marchlyn took her by the hand, and knelt.

'My lady,' she said in a voice too tremulous to break whatever power lingered in the air. 'I have not words enough for you.'

'Then you should save them for yourself, Ser Marchlyn,' she told her. Smiling. Eyes shining like obsidian. 'Because the year grows late, and words will not bring the harvest in.'

She touched her fingertips against the underside of Marchlyn's jaw, and tilted back her head so that she could look into her eyes.

'Fetch the smith's boy,' the weed wife told her. 'He must put an edge back onto your scythe.'

Ser Marchlyn pressed her lips together. She nodded slowly, and stood.

'And if it has already gone to ruin?' she managed.

The weed wife smiled.

'If it has already gone to ruin,' she said. 'Then he shall have to re-work your sword upon his forge.'

The Girls from Humaji

Adrian Tchaikovsky

Magda had been hurting for a long time before they brought her before Errek. She hurt from where they had beaten and kicked her, her skin a mottled patchwork of bruises, fresh red and older black overlaying the yellow marks of the first. She hurt from where they had burned her: arms, thighs, the soles of her feet. They had whipped her, too – that had been earlier, after they had first caught her amongst their slaves. Each weal had seared like fire when fresh, but now it was just part of the background murmur of her pain. Most of all she hurt where they had raped her. Errek wanted her for himself, to teach a very personal lesson, but these were the Yarokan, and so a good dozen of the guards and taskmasters had already held her down and thrust away at her, gripping hard enough that the marks of their hands were all over her body like cave paintings. There was a scream inside her. She had come very close to letting it out, each time they raped her, but she had held it down. It was important that she hold it down. For now.

For, now, she had been hauled into Errek's big tent and thrown down in its centre, curled in upon herself as though the arch of her naked back, her tucked in legs, would offer any protection. Errek had a good gathering of his cronies, his subordinates and favourites here. The tent reeked of them: sour sweat, old smoke, rotten breath and cruelty. Big men; hard men, wearing clothes made by their patient, abused women out of hides and furs and salvaged fabric from the Old World. Where Magda came from, in the Project, they grew flax and raised sheep, and wore linen and wool. The Yarokani slaves grew only what their masters could eat or ferment. The Yarokan were typical of the roving bands of marauders and enslavers – they were the strongest and the greatest of them, the warlords of misrule who had conquered most of the rest. When they overran another people they took what they wanted, kept what they could use and obliterated all else, especially anything that challenged their brutal philosophies.

'She have a name?' Errek grunted. 'Anyone got it from her?'

Nobody had even thought to ask. Her name to them had been Woman and it had been Witch and it had been Enemy. She had been the foreigner, the spy from the land they travelled to make war on, the intruder who had dared walk free to speak the unthinkable amongst their wives and daughters.

And they had caught her. Of course they had caught her. Most likely those same wives and daughters had run to tell their hard-fisted fathers, their drunken husbands. Such was the nature of growing up so shackled by fear that it etched itself onto the mind.

'Well? You've got a name?' Even speaking directly to a woman was something a Yarokani man should not need do. Women should not need to be asked to perform any task: it should already be performed by the time their men looked for it. Certainly they should not need to be asked twice.

Her voice, when she spoke, came out as little more than a croak. Only on repetition did she get out, 'Magda.'

'So this is what the Humaji have, is it?' Errek demanded, performing for the entertainment of his fellows. 'This is their soldier, their champion. This is what they send to stop the Yarokani!'

Their barbed amusement came to her more through the ground to her belly than through the air to her ears.

'Come sleep with me and cut my throat, yes,' Errek stated, 'if I was such a fool. Come poison our water. Come let our horses go. But you, you come whisper your lies to our women. Did you think you would make them like you? They know the will of God, and it is not for a land of women. That is blasphemy. That is the root of evil. So the Yarokani will grasp that root and tear it from the ground. We will show your woman nation how the world is, and what your place is in it. I think you have learned that place, now, eh?' and he kicked her, not hard, but hard enough.

Magda's wretched cry, loud even past the laughter and the jeering, was sufficient confirmation for Errek.

'Women were made in mens' shadow, all peoples know this, or else we teach them. Women are foolish and weak. They cannot live in virtue without men. Your Humaji, your kingdom of witches, it is the work of the evil. It is our duty to tear it down and bring the true way. It is our pleasure also, yes?'

Magda just clenched herself tighter, clutched about that scream that was building inside her, knowing that she would not be able to hold onto it for long.

'Some of you have spoken of the witches and their powers,' Errek addressed his audience. 'Not to me, but to each other, you have said they have magic from the Old World. You have said we should leave them alone, because you fear they will curse you and make your cocks wither between your legs. Any man who says that has lost his manhood already. Witches they might be, for the unnatural way they live, but that is all. They have no magic. Or do you, witch?' and he kicked out again, catching her hard in the shins. 'Turn me into a beast, witch. Baffle my mind. Fly out of here and save yourself. Come on, show me that there is more to you than just a woman.'

The scream was almost in her throat now, but she kept it down, just these few seconds more. To speak now would be to reap more pain, but she was so close to the end that she wanted him to hear her voice. She wanted to use her words because they were almost the only weapon left to her.

'You are a beast,' she spat out, and there was blood in her mouth. 'You are nothing but a beast, and what mind you have, you have baffled all by yourself.'

She thought he would lay into her with a vengeance then, but Errek was chief of all the Yarokan, and he was more than a brute berserker. Instead he laughed her words down, because nothing a woman said to him could matter at all. 'And yet you have not flown away, witch, so you are just woman after all. And I would not trust you to make food for me, or to stitch my clothes, but I will show you what a woman is for even so. Spread her.'

And coarse hands were taking hold of her, wrenching her out of her foetal crouch and forcing her onto her back, and although she kicked and struggled they pried her legs open, wrenching them hard, twisting every joint. And Errek had loosened his belt and let his britches drop, already kneeling in his eagerness to jam his swelling member into her flesh.

And when she felt his hands on her, prying at her body as though he was going to rip her apart, she let the scream out, and with it the fire.

The Yarokan camp was between five hills, a great sea of tents where the nomadic warriors, their women and slaves and children, had stopped for a time before continuing their advance towards the Project. They were neither herders nor hunters. Their progress was like a locust plague, and they left behind them enslaved and garrisoned villages, or else corpses.

The night was clouded, the moon only a pale suggestion within the dark sky, but the explosion lit it all up, sending hundreds of the Yarokan whooping and crying about the crooked, narrow streets of their transient city. The entire central tent, the greatest of their itinerant dwellings, was swallowed in the fierce fury of the fireball, and a score of nearby shelters were set alight from the blast. From this vantage on a hilltop, the cries of the injured, the yells for water or for aid, were distant and muted.

Errek must be dead, and with him a welcome bounty of many other leaders of the Yarokan, all close supporters of his way of life. This Magda knew.

And her other self, her more-than-sister, she was dead also, making the great sacrifice for the Project and for the future.

Beside her, Svethan grunted, impressed by the scale of the devastation but no more than that.

'Is that grief for a brother I hear?' Magda asked him.

Svethan was bigger than Errek had been, a great broad-shouldered man with arms that could have broken a bear. Beside him, Magda herself was tiny, a thing he could have crushed in a single hand.

'I spit on his ashes,' he told her conversationally. And it

was fair enough: Errek had killed two of his brothers already, and Svethan had lived this long by staying well out of his way and surrounding himself with men who had no reason to love his brother. 'You do not weep for your twin, witch?'

'She knew what must happen to her.' Magda would weep, later, but not in front of this barbarian. She would weep for what she knew her other self must have been put through, and because it could so easily have been her. 'What will you do now, last son of Aroc?'

Another grunt from Svethan, but she knew him by now: that sound meant he was considering. A pause for contemplation, rather than swift action, was not common amongst warriors of the Yarokan. He must have developed the grunt purely to show others that the wheels were still turning.

'I will gather my people,' he told her. 'We have heard who was with my brother. There are not many left of his favourites, but we will find and kill those who do not flee. This is the way of it.' He was eyeing her, waiting for her to object. She just shrugged, though. Although the Project would change the world for the better in the fullness of time, she herself could not remake the Yarokan in a night.

'You will make yourself chief.'

'I am Aroc's last son, as you say. I am a greater warrior than any. I do not think there will be a challenge.'

She took a deep breath. Now was the moment, if he was going to turn on her. A cut of his sword, a thrust of his knife, even a slamming blow from his hand could end her life instantly. 'And where will you take your people?'

'My people.' Plainly he liked the sound of that. For a long while he did not speak, thinking again, and at last he said, 'You think I will march still on Humaji.' He wrestled with the word, the best stab the Yarokan had made at the full name of the Project. 'I will not. You know why.'

'Because of your visions.'

He laughed softly. 'You do not believe in visions. You know where my visions come from,' and he brandished his talisman at her, but gently, for it was fragile. In truth, Magda did not know how a book had survived in the harsh world outside the Project for so long. But it had, amongst some now-conquered people or other, and it had found its way into the hands of this barbarous-seeming man.

When Svethan had been a child, she had been told, there had been a woman, a nurse, who had taught him some letters. He could not read much or well, but enough for the most basic sense of things. Later, one of his wives had found this out and, in the secret night hours between them, had encouraged him.

There were two dozen such wives and concubines amongst the Yarokan, women whose lives were now given over to the whims of these violent and proud men, but who had been born of the Projects' lineages. That was a secret that Svethan was not ready to know, that his own favourite wife was an agent of the Humaji.

'There are many who fear your witches. Many more after tonight.' His nod took in the fires still burning fiercely in the centre of the camp. 'Turning away from your people will be easy, for now. Others have wanted to trade, save that Errek would kill them for saying it. Now things are different. Now you and I, we have an understanding.'

'And what is your understanding, Lord Svethan?' she asked him.

'That you will make my people strong. You will show my people how to be strong as the Old People were strong,' and he brandished his book again.

'With our magic?'

'Do not test me.' The words were calm but firm, and she forced herself to remember that he was not the creature he appeared.

'You have no magic. You have...' His brow wrinkled, 'sceeyens. I know this. It is written.'

The religion of the Yarokan was a collection of self-serving oral histories devised to justify their place in the world, but Svethan had his own holy book, and he believed in it with a fervour that a prophet would envy.

'Our sceeyens, yes.' Correcting his pronunciation might anger him, and this was a delicate time.

'Sceeyens that makes you live without men, and breed only daughters in your wombs,' and, if there was some censure in his words, still it was a world away from Errek's hate-mongering.

'For now, yes.' She had seen the minutes of those early crisis meetings after the fall. How desperate had they been to preserve what they had; how much of themselves had they abandoned in order to save what was important from the wreck of history. There had been thirty-seven women working for the Human Genome Project back then. Now there were thousands, but only thirty-seven lineages, daughter after parthenogenetic daughter from the laboratories. It had been the only way to achieve enduring continuity in the face of a falling world. What cost, Magda wondered, to keep the last outpost of the Old World alive? Their progenitors had never intended the cloning to go on for so long. They had not known how far the world would fall.

'And can you do this to give a man sons?'

She had been expecting the question. 'It is a magic – forgive me, a sceeyens of women only. But we have other things to trade, when both our peoples are ready. We have food that you need, if you are not to spend all your lives taking from others until there is nothing left to take. We have medicines.' She stole a glance at him. 'Books also, we have.'

'I know there are other books.' He was trying to be casual but there was a yearning in his voice quite out of keeping with everything else about him. He was a man out of his time.

'Books of legends and stories, books of teaching.'

'Of Sceeyens.'

'Yes.'

'Books that can give all of it back,' and he was gingerly opening the pages of his treasure, leafing through the bright pictures: cars, aeroplanes, rockets, a bulky figure walking on the moon. On the battered cover she could still just read the words, *The Boys' Own Book of Science.*

'And you do not fear the unnatural?' she prompted. It had been a great argument of Errek and his like, when stirring up his people against the Humaji.

'What is natural?' Svethan asked her. 'To die young is natural. To go hungry. I welcome your unnatural.'

The women of the Project would go amongst the Yarokan. They would not come as invaders, but as teachers. They would be humble and gentle, but they would know much of curing the sick and aiding childbirth, of animal husbandry and efficient agriculture. And they would teach the sons and the daughters of this warrior people, generation after generation, and slowly the violent dark world of the Yarokan would turn towards a new dawn. Svethan would not see it. Magda would not see it – or this Magda would not, anyway. There would be other Magdas.

'It is a way of doing things,' Svethan said, almost nonchalantly, 'for two families who will be allies together, for there to be an exchange of wives.' He cast her a sidelong look, and it was the look of a man brave enough to take a witch to wife if it would secure him the future that he read on those brittle pages. And he was strong and intelligent, a remarkable man who might be the father of a new world just as Magda and all the women of the Project would be mother.

But: 'It is not our way,' she told him. Time enough for future generations to phase out the cloning and the lineages and return to nature. And when Svethan just grunted again, and nodded philosophically, she felt a spark of hope flicker and catch in her: hope for her future, hope for the human race.

Dawn of Demons

Eric Scott

'Thank you. I thought they were going to kill me.'

Dawn pulled the canteen from the boy's mouth, ignoring his gratitude. Cool water splashed her arm as he groped for more. He looked almost twenty, maybe a little younger. Black hair, thick on his chin, withered across his cheeks leaving splotches on his sallow skin. His hair, the colour of decaying bark, smelled of rotting flesh on an open spit. A bit of smoke seeped from his forehead and from behind his ears. Plum pouches beneath his dark eyes dragged the skin down. His eyes, greasy black dollops, darted from side to side, the puffy skin bulging underneath. All were clear signs of the change.

She pulled a small white towel from her leather duffle bag and dotted the sweat from his forehead. Steam crept from underneath the towel as his fever intensified.

'Can I have some more?' he asked, reaching for the canteen. Blood oozed around the edges of his fingers and the familiar green mould sprouted from his cuticles. His hands felt mushy and malleable when he touched her. 'I'm so thirsty,' he begged.

The boy's head dropped back and Dawn caught him before he slammed into the wall. She lifted the canteen to his mouth; his hands shook as he tried to hold it.

'Have a little more. But go slow, ok?'

The boy nodded, his mouth opening like a small bird in a nest. Dawn frowned as he guzzled the water, dumping more on his chin and chest then into his mouth. His sweat-covered forehead, almost too hot to touch, dampened her hand.

His time was short.

She eased his head down, letting go of the canteen. It wouldn't be of any use to her now. Her bag stuck to her side and she wiggled around to dislodge it from the piece of metal jutting from the stove that hung from the wall. The house looked to be in decent shape, at least the part that still stood. The chasm had sliced the house into two pieces. The one, like a prefabricated modular home not fully assembled, balanced on the edge while the other had disappeared down the red walls.

Dawn stared into the abyss. The fire licked the sides of the red walls, the rock branded black from it. Ash and dust rose from the depths manifesting cones of flames that swept across the chasm. The cones danced with one another, escaping in wisps that rocketed into the sky. Heat waves rolled over her and she wished she had saved some of the water for her dry and cracking lips. The blood that covered the red walls had turned dark. Dawn could still make out some of the long lines carved into the stone from the fingernails of all those who had plunged into the chasm. It had only been six months since the reckoning. An echo of a scream invaded her thoughts. She shook the memory away before it could take hold, and turned back to the house.

The part of the house that still stood reminded Dawn of her aunt's farmhouse in Pennsylvania. She had spent each summer with her Aunt Ginny, learning to cook, to crochet. She would spend hours on the porch reading or combing Aunt Ginny's collie, Bernardo. The summers were her favourite time growing up, just like most kids. But Dawn especially missed those times now.

Most of the gray vinyl siding had peeled away when the rift opened, leaving only charred plywood and gaping holes that, Dawn surmised, had once been windows. Black columns bowed under the stress of the collapsing weight. This house didn't have a fake fireplace like Aunt Ginny's, but it did have a decorative rock wall. A collage of stones: pink, azure and bottle green, covered the wall bordering the kitchen. Most of the stones had cracked around the edges, but remained intact. The house felt stable and would do for a few days, much better than the maintenance room in the subway. Dawn knew it wasn't the best idea to camp this close to a rift, but the area seemed dead.

The clang of the canteen on the stones surprised her. The

green lines running from wrist to neck climbed across the boy's chin looping into cross hatches of black. Time was shorter than she thought.

Rummaging through her bag, she found the silver tube of lip-gloss. It tasted like crushed aspirin as she caked her lips with the red liquid. She grabbed the boy by the chin, shaking him from his delirium.

'Hey, what's your name?'

His eyes rolled to white, the green invading and filling his retinas with the putrid filling. Dawn slapped his face. He leaned forward coughing, dark green bile pouring from his open mouth.

'Your name!' she screamed, knowing she might need to start running.

The boy lifted his head to face her, his eyes clear now, a deep brown and orange that made her think of sundown. The final glimpse of his humanity stared back at her. Grabbing his shoulders, she stared intently into his eyes, waiting.

'David.'

Dawn kissed him, the bitter taste of bile mixing with the acidic lip-gloss. His body stiffened and she pulled away, wiping the black ooze from her mouth on the arm of her grey sweatshirt. Ruined now, she would discard it after the ritual.

The boy's body convulsed, his arms and legs rigid as his body jerked from side to side. His wet hair straightened, caught fire and burned to ash. The remnants piled behind him, forming a halo that made Dawn think of her mother's picture of Jesus that hung over their fireplace. His fingernails, dark with green, black mildew, clawed at the rubble.

Dawn dumped the contents of her bag onto one of the large stones that had fallen from the wall. It was a smooth surface where she could spread out her ingredients. She placed the Coke bottle full of kerosene next to the salt. The boy had done her the courtesy of transforming on the granite kitchen countertop. It would make for an adequate pyre.

When she turned back, David was gone and only the demon remained. It turned its blue fluorescent eyes towards her. Black hash marks, like a million tic-tac toe games, covered its baldhead and flesh. It smiled, the teeth evaporating to reveal a twisting tongue that flicked in and out of its decomposing mouth. When it tried to move, the pain seized it, paralyzing the demon in place. Dawn tapped her lips.

'I give good kisses.'

'You will die,' it hissed.

'Yeah, yeah.'

Stretching her back, Dawn looked around at what was left of the kitchen. Some of the cupboards were still intact and might contain food she could eat. Running water would be a miracle to find. There were enough rooms still standing that could provide shelter and that was the most important thing, especially at night. She would grab Trista and come back, once she took care of old mildew-face.

The demon thrashed as if it read her thoughts. Its tongue wagged as she splashed the kerosene, forming a circle around the body. Salt was next. All she could find was sea salt at one of the yuppie grocery stores. She hoped it worked the same as regular table salt. She hadn't vanquished a demon with sea salt. If this didn't work, she wouldn't have much time to escape. The anaesthetic wouldn't last long.

After she completed the circle of salt, she dumped the rest of the kerosene on the demon for good measure. It couldn't hurt. The demon spat and howled. Dawn reached into her jean pocket and found the matchbook. Four matches looked back at her mockingly. Hopefully, there would be some matchbooks in one of the cupboards. She struck a match and stood over the body.

'David, I release you. We drive you from us, unclean spirit. I send this monstrosity back to the depths of hell.'

'You can't defeat us. For we are many.'

'You are charcoal.'

She dropped the match. Its guttural screams brought a smile to her face.

Trista sharpened the knife on the grindstone. Sinewy arms rested on her knees as she stroked the knife up and down. Her white tank top, spotted with soot and dirt, blended with her dark brown khakis that hugged her thin frame. Blonde hair chopped short and tight, so different from the frizzy mess of four months ago. Her feet, boots untied again, slid back and forth across the gritty cement floor. It amazed Dawn how different Trista was from the frightened waif she had pulled from under a pile of cereal boxes.

The cackles were the first sound Dawn heard when she entered the grocery store in search of supplies. She didn't know how long the demons had tossed Trista between one another, the way an orca plays with a baby seal, before she had come along. What she did remember was the way her heartbeat had slowed and the calmness that washed over her. She saw the entire scenario in her mind. The same way her father had taught her to use board vision to see a chessboard, all the moves leading to checkmate.

Demons weren't bright creatures, which helped. These three still had on their nametags, which made it easier to give them a proper deliverance. She kicked a can of peeled tomatoes across the aisle. All three turned in unison, their eyes glowing in the dim light. Dawn blew them a kiss. They ran after her, tripping over the scattered boxes and cans.

She led them away to an aisle lined with salt. When she reached the far end, she hurdled over the line, giggling as she heard the three bodies' crash into each other. Doubling back to the other side, she emptied a box of salt, trapping them in the aisle. When they tried to blow the salt away, Dawn laughed and held up a bottle of honey.

'The floor's really sticky in here,' she said, plopping one of them on the head with the empty bottle.

They hissed and clawed at the air as Dawn inched the lines closer together. Once she pushed them to the other end, she doused them with lighter fluid and watched them burn, satisfied with their screams.

After the flames died, she found Trista laying amongst the cereal boxes with pieces of cereal stuck in her hair. When Trista got up and tried to run, Dawn grabbed her and saw the fear in her eyes, tapping primal senses. Dawn pulled her close and rocked her in her arms, picking the cereal from her tangled hair.

When Trista's breathing slowed and Dawn was confident

she had calmed down, Dawn stood and took Trista by the hand. She led her to the ashes of her tormentors.

'Wanna help,' Dawn said, holding out a broom.

Trista took the broom, confusion in her eyes. Dawn picked up another broom and started sweeping the bits of bone into a pile. Trista watched, her eyes studying Dawn.

'You do know how these work, right? You just push the bits together like this,' Dawn said deliberately sweeping a larger piece of bone into the center of ash. Dawn held out the broom, beckoning Trista to help. Trista began brushing the remaining ash and bones. They swept the remains into two neat piles.

'Now comes the fun part', Dawn said, handing a hammer to Trista. They sat silently in the grocery store, smashing the bones into dust. They burned the remains in a Weber grill. Good times.

For the first couple of days, Trista was guarded, her speech pattern low and sparse. When she finally started to talk more, Dawn noticed she had trouble maintaining a train of thought and she made wild connections about what had happened. She blamed God, the government and even aliens. Trista was looking for an explanation. Dawn had gone through the same thing, so she understood. But she didn't need the world explained anymore. She knew that until the demons were gone, nothing could change.

Dawn shifted her bag to the other shoulder. Trista stopped sharpening her knife, cocking her head in Dawn's direction. Dawn smiled. All of her teachings were finally starting to pay off and it gave Dawn a sense of pride, but more a sense of relief. Maybe she didn't need to worry about leaving Trista unattended. Demons weren't the stealthiest of creatures, but they could sneak up on you from time to time. In only a few months, Trista had transformed into a cunning fighter. No different from herself she supposed. She was very different from the college girl who majored in sociology and wanted to change the world. The world had gone and changed all by itself.

It was as if time didn't exist before the apocalypse. It had only been six months ago, but it seemed longer. The shift had been sudden and complete. There weren't news reports or predictions. It just happened on a Wednesday morning in September.

Dawn made sure to spend every Wednesday with her parents. They ate carryout and watched Everybody Loves Raymond reruns. Dawn's college roommate, Cindy, always tried to get her to come to happy hour with the rest of the girls. But Dawn had always been a homebody and she loved her parents, especially her father.

Her father was picking off pieces of pepperoni when the rumble shook the house. Dawn thought it was a bomb or maybe an earthquake. A booming voice thundered from all sides. Dawn didn't recognize the language, but her father did. He rushed into the kitchen, frantically rifling through the shelves of the pantry.

'What's going on?' Dawn yelled. 'Mom?' Her mother collapsed from her chair and shoved the small oak coffee table aside, sending drinks and pizza sprawling across the room. Dawn started for the window.

'Get together,' commanded her father.

He shoved Dawn down onto the living room floor. The itch of the shag carpet felt rough on her bare legs. He recited prayers in Latin and Dawn held her sobbing mother. Her mother shuddered as demons, like vermin scurrying in the walls, tore the siding from the house and ripped the shingles from the roof. Her father pleaded for her to run to the church and Father Lucas. Dawn didn't want to leave them, but he slapped her across the face and screamed at her to run before it was too late.

Dawn stumbled to the back door. Vertigo took hold of her as she grasped the doorknob. She looked back. Her mother rocked on her knees, praying to an ineffectual God. Salt splayed across the room as her father tried to create a shield. But the waves of heat lifted and destroyed the protective circle. The beasts engulfed them as Dawn stumbled out the back door. She didn't turn back when her father screamed, his voice carrying above the roar of the earth splitting.

Screams filled the streets as the earth transformed into a fiery abomination. Huge rifts opened and swallowed the lucky ones. Demons poured out, having transformed from the dead, infesting the ground like locusts. Tears cascaded down her burning cheeks as Dawn raced toward the church, the cries of her parents still echoing inside her head. When she reached the church, demons danced around the collapsed steeple. Father Lucas stood at the front doors yelling words of faith, his round face lathered in sweat. Strands of thin hair wavered in the blistering air. The black cassock shredded as faithful parishioners clawed at him and exposed his flushed skin.

Even in her panicked state, Dawn knew they had to run. They weren't safe on the front steps of the church. Dawn pleaded for them to come with her, to escape before the hordes fell on them. A large woman wearing a brightly coloured floral dress shoved Dawn down the steps.

'Leave us alone ,' she shrieked.

Wincing and grabbing her side, Dawn retreated behind a parked minivan. She watched the demons seize the parishioners one by one. The flesh burned and peeled away from their screaming bodies as they transformed. They kept Father Lucas alive the longest, not allowing the transformation to occur. Stuck like a pig on a spit, they urinated and defecated on him, raped women in front of him, all the while performing mocking praises to God.

The demons would have found her if she hadn't spotted a small child's boat, cobalt with white stripes across the sleek frame, plummeting into the storm drain. The opening was dark and smelled of damp leaves, but it was her chance to escape. She slipped through the narrow opening, scraping her back as she landed in the wet muck. Facing darkness on either side, Dawn stayed close to the opening. Bugs and vermin scurried through the pipe.

Sleep only came from exhaustion and when she woke, it was always with a start. Dawn cowered in that dark musty pipe for two days, unable to block out the cries above her. She shed all her tears in those two days - tears for her family, for humanity, for herself. When the screams faded, replaced by eerie quiet, Dawn climbed up to the deserted street. This dank subway room reminded her of those first two days. It was time for a change.

Now, Trista whipped knives at a makeshift wooden dummy. Each throw, expertly placed, struck the wood with a thunk. When the final knife hit the target between where the eyes would be, Trista let out a satisfied laugh.

Dawn eased around the corner, the stale smell of old water and garbage filled the air. They had come across this small alcove by accident while running from a group of demons. It was an abandoned segment of the Baltimore subway. The room overlooked a cavernous space at least six stories high, decorated with graffiti. Just above the tracks between the names professing love, someone had scrawled: '*GOOD MORNING LEMMINGS*'. With the subway vacant, the words always gave Dawn a chill.

Metal barrels smouldered around the walls. Dawn noticed that some would need replenishing before they turned in for the night. A platform with dusty wooden benches and rusty turnstiles curved around the corner. A lone ladder led to the street and gave them an escape route in case a demon wandered into the subway. So far, none had.

The scraping of her shoes on the grate caused Trista to spin around, knife cocked.

'Just me.'

'How long you been here?' Trista dropped her arm; the white top clung tightly to her chest, damp from sweat. Dawn stared at her, noticing for the first time that she would need to start looking at bras for Trista.

'A few minutes.'

'Shit. I knew I heard something.'

'Don't sweat it. You're getting better. Just trust those feelings when you get them. Even if you're wrong. When you need to be right, you will be.'

'What'd you get?' Trista asked pointing to the overstuffed bag that hung from Dawn's shoulder.

'Bunch of stuff. Crackers. Sardines. And...' Dawn raised a box of matches in the air and shook them.

'Sweet. Some of the fires are getting low.'

'I noticed.'

'Of course you did,' Trista said as she walked over to the wooden dummy. She started pulling the knives out. 'Maybe we can have something hot to eat now, Ms. Survival?'

'Maybe. But the best news is I found us a new place.'

Trista sighed. 'We've only been here a couple of days. You said it was safe here.'

'You know we have to keep moving.'

'Why? Where do we have to go?'

'Move or die. You know the drill.'

'You read that off a bumper sticker.'

'No discussion. Let's pack things up. We can leave in the morning before...'

Dawn heard a high pitch whistle that started from above, but quickly surrounded them. She felt a rumble and then everything went black.

'Are you awake?'

The crackling voice jostled Dawn. She wiped the spit from her mouth, realizing she was drooling. When she rolled over, a sharp pain shot through her spine and the vertebrae in her back creaked in tune with the metal cot. Her eyes fluttered open, adjusting to the bright fluorescent lights. The room was small, all white brick except for the glass wall in front of her. The tile floor felt cold on her bare feet as she swung her legs around and sat up. Her white gown itched and splotches of red covered her arms. She hugged herself, trying to shield her body from the cool air that blew from the air duct above.

A man in a white lab coat stood on the other side of the glass. He jotted notes in a small black leather book. Beneath the lab coat, Dawn could see the olive drab cargo pants of the military.

Great, another one of these.

The man pushed a button on the speaker built into the glass. It hissed before he spoke. When their eyes met, he smiled, wide and expressive.

'You are awake. Excellent. Can you tell me your name?'

'Where am I?' Dawn asked as she stood. She stretched her arms over her head and began doing toe touches.

'You're safe. This is a government facility. One of the last ones, actually. You're lucky we found you in that rubble.'

'I feel lucky,' said Dawn, hoping her sarcastic tone was heavy enough for a government employee to recognize. 'Where's the girl that was with me?'

'You mean Trista?'

Just great. They already know too much. They won't want to let us leave now. They'll want to help.

'Trista is doing great,' he continued. 'She's in the main dining hall having some dinner. She checked out.'

Dawn's eyes narrowed. 'Checked out for what?'

'The disease. She's clean. We're still waiting for your results to come back from the lab. Everything takes much longer than it used to. Sorry about that. It shouldn't be too much longer and then we can get you something to eat.'

'You think I'm a demon?' Dawn said, raising an eyebrow. 'You do sound like the government.'

'I understand. It does seem like the apocalypse.'

'Yeah, all the demons killing everyone tipped me off.'

The man laughed, but his eyes stayed focused on Dawn. 'It's a disease. We're looking into antibodies to combat it as we speak.'

Dawn walked over and started examining the glass for imperfections, even just a crack. 'You guys know the Deltas?' she asked.

'From Virginia? Yes, we haven't heard from them in some-time. Do you have any information about...'

'They're dead,' answered Dawn, tapping the glass with her knuckles.

The man's smile disappeared and he shut his eyes tightly, his face flushed with anger. When he looked at her again, he blinked quickly, his voice a whisper.

'All of them?'

Dawn nodded and her fingers squeaked as she slid her hand across the filmy glass.

'How do you know that?' He stared at her, moving closer. Dawn rested her nose lightly on the glass. He'd restored control of himself. But within his stare, she saw pain mixed with anger. She needed to be careful.

'They picked us up about three months ago. We ran into them at a Radio Shack. The one in charge was a Chris something.'

'Davidson,' the man finished.

'Right. He gave us the speech about being safe and finding a cure. I tried to tell him, like I'm trying to tell you now. We aren't safe. Demons sense large groups of us. We can't mobilize to fight them. We have to attack them in small groups, no more than five. Anything else, draws them.'

The man grinned sardonically. 'We've been here for about two months. Fifty of us. We think we're making some progress on a cure.'

When he spoke, his gaze kept shifting to the right. Dawn leaned against the glass so she could squint around the corner that faded into darkness. The glass was cool on her cheek. She spotted another man right before he shifted around the corner and out of view.

'It's not a disease,' she said, throwing her hands in the air.

The man raised his hand and took a step back. 'Ok, you need to calm down.'

Dawn moved away and held up her arms. 'I am calm. We don't need your help. Just let us go and we'll be on our way.'

'We saved your life,' he said in disbelief. 'The explosion destroyed your little underground safe house. It could have killed you. We pulled you out and nursed you back to health.'

Dawn pounded her fist on the glass. It shimmied, but didn't give.

'That's enough,' a voice announced from the shadows.

A large man appeared. Army fatigues bulged around his midsection. Bits of gray peaked from under a dark green cap. His right cheek had a fresh scar, deep and jagged from a poor stitch job. A permanent frown and wide nose made him look like a man who never smiled or even understood the definition of laughter. His eyes, bright white with globes of black, like the center of a bullseye, stared through her.

He walked over and examined Dawn feet to head, cataloguing and taking stock. His stare made her uncomfortable, his eyes moving deliberately across her body. He motioned to the man with the notebook. Closing the book, the man nodded, backed away, and disappeared around the darkened corner.

'You in charge?' Dawn asked.

A suppressed chuckle escaped his clenched lips. 'How old are you?'

'Didn't your mother ever teach you not to ask a lady her age?'

'I'm guessing you're twenty-two or twenty-three. I'm fifty-eight. So I've a few years on you. Listen up. You need to cooperate. We're here to help. I understand that things have gone to hell.'

'No pun intended,' interrupted Dawn.

'I'm Colonel Daniels,' he continued, ignoring her. 'I'm going to be straight with you. You seem like the kind of person who would appreciate that.'

Dawn snickered. 'That's the first honest thing I've heard in a while.'

Daniels smiled, more a tight-lipped frown, but Dawn guessed that was as good as it got. Daniels turned and grabbed a rusty metal chair. He dragged it over and Dawn noticed he favoured his left side. She couldn't tell if the injury was old or new, but the information was worth filing for later. The metal groaned as he eased into the chair. He stretched out his right leg and released a deep breath.

'Ok, here it is straight. There are only fourteen of us in this facility. We've been here for about two weeks. Before that, we were all from separate units. Well, most of us anyway. A few of my men survived and came with me. This facility was designated as a rally point. As far as we know, we're all that's left of the east coast division.'

Dawn watched his face for any indication he was lying. All that stared back at her was a stone slab that had spent years squelching tears. She wondered how many times a mother stared into this flat affect while Daniels read an incident report of her son's death. 'I'm very sorry to hear that. But Trista and I will be fine on our own.'

Daniels shifted and stretched his leg further out. A grimace flashed across his mouth. He moved his leg back and forth until his knee popped, like the cracking of a knuckle.

'I'm sure you would be, but I have other considerations.'

Dawn folded her arms and met his stare. 'What considerations?'

'You think this is the apocalypse, right?' he asked. Dawn continued to stare at Daniels and he went on, not waiting for her to answer. 'We haven't made that determination. We still think this might be... something else.'

'Like a disease?'

'That's one theory that like you, I do not share. However, I'm a man that believes it is good to look down every avenue. But apocalypse doesn't fit either. If it truly were the biblical version of Judgment Day, why are we still here? Shouldn't we've ascended or descended, depending on our souls?'

Daniels didn't drop his eyes from her stare and when he talked, he gestured often. Her father had told her liars were like stiff boards and lies rolled off their lips. But Daniels could just be a skilled liar.

Dawn felt the cool air sweeping across her skin again. Her eyes traced the path to an air duct in the right corner of the room. It was about twelve feet from the floor, but if she stood on the cot, she was sure she could reach it.

'A valid point, but I know a little bit about demons and I can tell you, that's what these things are.'

Daniels stood, wincing as he slapped his right leg. He ambled over and leaned on the glass with his hand above his head. 'Tell me what the salt is for.'

They had her bag. Part of her wanted to trust Daniels, but his intense stare cautioned her to go slow. 'Look, Colonel. I'm sure we can figure out a way we can help each other. How about you let me out of this cage?'

'I'd like to,' Daniels said nodding as if he was agreeing with her. 'There's a faction in our group that believes the disease scenario is plausible. So let's just talk for now.'

'Salt binds them. It holds them in place temporarily. Just long enough so I can burn them.'

'You burn demons?'

'That's right. And then I take the leftover bones and I grind them up until they're dust and then I burn the dust.'

Daniels let his arm fall to his side. His thin eyebrows rose, adding youth to his gruff face as a grin widened on his narrow lips. 'Who taught you that?'

'My father. He was a professor of religious studies and he liked to tell me stories.'

'And he's dead?'

Dawn flinched, covering her mouth as she faked a cough. She hoped Daniels had missed the flinch. But when their eyes met, she knew he hadn't missed anything.

'Look, I'd love to chat about our families and where we spent our summers, but let's cut to the chase. I can show your men how to trap and destroy demons. There's plenty of them to be killed and I could definitely use the help. After that, Trista and I will be on our way. We can set up a weekly rendezvous point if you want, to make you feel all warm and fuzzy inside. I don't care. We just can't stay together.'

'Your dad tell you that too?'

'Yes, he did,' said Dawn. He was really starting to irritate her. 'So, what do you say?'

'I'm sorry. I told you there are other considerations.'

She remembered Daniels had avoided answering her question about what considerations. Panic rolled over her, but she maintained her stoic stare. What were they doing with Trista?

'What's your name, dear?' Daniels asked. His voice was quiet and his eyes softened.

'My name's Dawn.'

'That's a pretty name. Dawn, I need us to have an understanding.'

'Of course. I'm all for that. We can help each other, like I said.'

'We're all men here.'

Dawn took a step back from the glass. Daniels rubbed his chin and let out a deep breath.

'I have to think about the future. You're the first women we've seen since... Jesus, I don't know how long.'

'Where's Trista?' Dawn clenched her fists, her head pounding. Urgency bubbled inside. She spoke deliberately as she tried to mask the anger that filled her. 'You want us to be friends? Let me see she's okay.'

'You need to understand. We have to make sure the human race survives after, whatever this is. We can protect you.'

'I understand. Where's Trista?'

An alarm blared. Daniels eyes widened as two men bolted passed him. The man with the leather notebook followed, his hands shaking and his forehead creased in concern.

'There's been a breach.'

Then the screaming started.

The air duct smelled of rat droppings and puffs of dust rolled past Dawn as she manoeuvered through the tight corridor, scraping her elbows and feeling the breeze across her bare ass. A hint of heat mixed with cool air flowed across Dawn's naked body. She had lost her gown while climbing through the vent opening. It had caught on a sharp edge, tearing down the side and Dawn had ripped it off in her frustration. With her arms bloodied and the heat intensifying, Dawn regretted leaving the gown behind. Red lights every few feet illuminated the metal in a crimson glow. Screams echoed through the vents and for the first time since that night in the sewer, Dawn was scared.

She needed to find Trista. The air duct would make a safe hideaway for the two of them. Once the soldiers were turned, the demons would leave and search for the next batch of survivors. Demons never lingered. She and Trista could hole up for however long it took and then take their time checking for supplies, especially some clothes. Maybe even camp for a few days in the base.

A beam of white light disrupted the bloody glow of the aluminium tube. Dawn inched closer to the vent, feeling the heat swarm her face. Six demons huddled over one of the remaining men, like hyenas around a kill. The smell of singed hair touched Dawn's nostrils and she had to put her hand over her mouth to stave off a cough. The man's clothes were torn and his chest smouldered under their outstretched hands. Each demon slashed and clawed at the boy, leaving his scored chest a bloody jigsaw puzzle.

He's so young, thought Dawn. *He's more a boy than a man.*

A figure, dressed in army fatigues, sauntered into the room. Even with the skin transformed to green and black, Dawn recognized Colonel Daniels. His firm jaw had drooped, as if the skin melted from his face and then hardened into a grotesque mask that made Dawn think of the gargoyles of Notre Dame. His skull, caved in on the right side, oozed dark liquid from black and white gashes. The skin creased like the bellows of an accordion.

Daniels walked over, his limp a distant memory. The boy recognized him and he struggled to break free, but the others held him down. Daniels crouched and licked the side of the boy's face. His acidic tongue left a long gash and blood dripped from Daniels' lips. His eyes, black pools of oil, ignited and flames lashed out, engulfing the boy's head.

Dawn turned away and continued forward. Daniels wasn't a good man by any means, but another human was lost. A wave of futility consumed Dawn and she rested her forehead on her crossed arms. Daniels and his men had been trained in combat and survival. They hadn't lasted an hour. What hope did she have against such odds? Wouldn't it be easier to give up and let the demons take her?

'They were not trained in the ways of demons', her father's voice whispered.

And there was Trista. She had to find Trista.

She heard the sound of metal scraping from around the next corner. Pushing forward, she spotted another vent. A voice, struggling from exertion, resonated from below. Dawn eased to the vent and stared down into a small room with dim lighting. A hand flashed in front of the vent.

'Shit.'

'Trista?'

'Dawn? That you?'

'Who else?' Dawn pounded her fist into the metal grate and it rattled. 'Get back.'

Dawn slammed her fist into the grate again; the reverberation shuddered through her arm. Turning on her side, Dawn clasped her hands together and struck with one forceful blow. The grate exploded from the air duct and clanged on the hard linoleum floor. She shoved her head through the opening.

Trista stood by a large metal door, worry lines wrinkling her forehead as she ran her hands through her hair. Perspiration glazed her face and arms. She wore a white gown, the same kind Dawn had worn. A red streak, light around the edges but darker in the center, lined her side just below her ribcage.

'Are you hurt?' Dawn asked, pushing her arms completely through the opening.

Trista glanced down and frowned. 'I fell trying to jump up there. It's not bad.'

'It looks bad. Let me see.'

Trista rolled her eyes and raised her gown, exposing a makeshift bandage. It was about eight inches long and leaked blood around the edges. Trista had torn the bottom of her gown and stuck it to her side. It reminded Dawn of the way her father stuck toilet paper to his neck when he cut himself shaving.

'Is it still bleeding?'

'Can we discuss this later?' Trista looked over her shoulder at a large door. Sounds of claws scraping metal grew louder.

'Good idea. Give me your hand.'

Trista stood on a folding chair. Balancing on the tip of her toes, she reached for Dawn. Their hands were about a foot apart.

'I can't reach,' Trista said through clenched teeth.

'You're going to have to jump up and grab hold. I can lift you.'

Fists pounded on the metal door and Trista whipped her head around. Puffs of plaster clouded around the buckling hinges.

'Come on. Jump up,' urged Dawn.

Trista jumped. Her hand slapped Dawn's hand, but slipped off. Screws rocketed from the door as pressure bloated the struggling hinges. Panic swept across Trista and she started to shake, tears rolling down her bright red cheeks.

'Hey,' whispered Dawn. 'Calm down. Wipe your hands off and breathe. Focus on my hand. Your hand to my hand. Bend your knees and give me one good jump. You can do this.'

Trista gnawed at her bottom lip and she shook her head

violently. The fear was overtaking her. The pounding intensified as the door began to separate from the frame. They were running out of time.

Trista isn't going to make it.

The thought seeped into Dawn's conscious mind. She'd been thinking it for weeks. This new world wasn't a place for a young girl like Trista. If anything, Dawn knew she would be better off without Trista slowing her down. Dawn looked into Trista's terrified eyes and knew she had only one choice.

'I'm coming down.'

Trista shook her head as Dawn started to squeeze through the opening. 'No, don't. Just... you'll be stuck down here. I can do it.'

Dawn spread her arms out. 'Well, come on then.'

Trista hopped back onto the chair and wiped her hands on her gown. Bending her knees, she leapt and caught Dawn's hand. Tendons screamed in Dawn's shoulder and her forehead furrowed as she lifted Trista. Trista's legs kicked as if she were swimming through the air.

'Grab the edge,' Dawn instructed. 'Pull yourself in.'

Trista's head popped through the opening and Dawn moved back to give her room.

'Turn right. Not towards me. We need to go that way,' Dawn said pointing.

Trista crawled to the right, her gown riding up her back.

'Now go,' Dawn said pushing Trista's feet. 'Go!'

After labouring through the air duct, they reached a vent that overlooked a large open area. Dawn grabbed Trista's foot and motioned for her to stop. Dawn had a clear view of the room from where she lay, but Trista was far enough ahead that she couldn't see anything, which was what Dawn wanted. She didn't want Trista to see any conversions.

Rows of long tables filled most of the room. Doors from adjacent rooms hung from jagged frames. The floor, littered with cans of food and loose paper, looked far away. They needed to be patient. Once the rest of the men were converted, the demons would leave and they could find a way down.

Dawn watched them, some in army fatigues and others completely bare, as they moved through the rooms, searching for more victims. A monstrous being, wide as he was tall, rumbled into view, clumsily knocking over tables and chairs. His mouth was larger than most demons. It was as if his jaw, loosely dangling from his head, had been unhinged. Bending over, dark black sludge gushed from his gaping mouth. He absently wiped the muck away and tilted his head, sniffing the air. He looked into Dawn's eyes. She dropped her head, hoping she only imagined the look of recognition on his gruesome face. She waited for her pounding heart to slow before she raised her head. The behemoth disappeared around the corner and Dawn exhaled a breath she didn't realize she was holding.

When Dawn was positive the last demon had left, they dropped out of the air duct and onto the floor. Blood, sticky on her bare feet, covered the linoleum. The sharp smell of ammonia mixed with excrement filled the room. Trista dry heaved and when Dawn put an arm around her, she pushed her away and rushed into one of the other rooms. Outlines of bodies sketched the floor, the blood dark red on the white tiles.

One of the rooms housed uniforms, t-shirts, underwear and boots. Dawn grabbed two sets of fatigues and boots. The stiff cloth felt hard on her skin, but it was better than being naked. She spotted a knapsack with blood spattered on one side in front of an open door. It was partially full of cans and bags of food. Dawn picked it up and walked into the small room.

Bags of sugar, oats, flour and rice filled the shelves. Dawn dumped out the contents of the knapsack. Whoever had packed it had done so haphazardly and Dawn wanted to fill it with items that were more essential. She found plastic containers of honey, which would be useful for its antibiotic properties and wound healing, not to mention sweet taste. There were rows of canned vegetables and fruit. Dawn shoved pinto and kidney beans into her bag. She grabbed tuna, sardines and canned ham.

Trista walked into the room, the white gown barely hanging from her frail shoulders. Dirt smudged her cheeks and forehead. She looked exhausted.

'Find another bag,' said Dawn. 'There's some clothes and boots on the table out there. Put them on and then help me.'

Trista leaned against the doorway, a blank stare on her face as she rested her head against the wall.

'Look what they have,' said Dawn waving a bottle of peroxide in the air. 'They have matches, bandages, vitamins and bottled water too. Come on. Hurry up and help me.'

Trista twisted around and shuffled out the door. As Dawn watched her slink away, she considered giving Trista time to regroup. Even though the smell was horrendous, this place was good shelter and the chances of any demons coming back was slim. As Dawn contemplated where they would sleep, she realized she was scratching a spot on her arm. A deep red mark just above her wrist swelled and she rubbed it. The area, hot to her touch, was about an inch wide and rose a bit on her skin. They needed to leave.

As they walked out of the building and into the parking lot, Dawn spotted an old trailer just outside the fencing that surrounded the army facility. Silver siding, faded from decades of winters, covered the hunk of metal. Rotted tires sat flatly on the brown grass. The door squealed from rusty hinges and the interior reeked of dead animals. Dawn didn't like being in such an open area, but they were both exhausted, mentally and physically. They could spend the night outside the trailer and at least have some semblance of shelter.

Staring up at the night sky sheathed in the orange hue from the rifts, Dawn scooped some pinto beans into her mouth, the mushy texture warm and soft against her teeth. She hadn't wanted to start a fire, especially out in the open, but she could see from Trista's body language - shoulders slumped forward, head down, eyes glazed over - that she needed a treat.

Looking into the fire brought back memories of the camping trips Dawn had taken with her family each fall. Her father had inherited an old singlewide trailer from an aunt he barely remembered. The first trip to upper Pennsylvania felt more like an adventure than a vacation to Dawn. A long gravel path curved off the main road and plummeted down the hillside that led to the trailer. It rested in the center of an oasis of trees, like an old shoebox in the back of a closet. Leaves and twigs littered the roof. A large tree towered over the area with an old tire hanging from a frayed rope. It swayed gently in the cool October breeze.

When her father opened the front door, the odour of mothballs greeted them. Even though Dawn was only nine, she could jump and touch the ceiling. Between the kitchen and bathroom, bunk beds lined one of the walls; the other wall had built in cabinets and drawers. Dawn loved the top bunk because there was a small window that overlooked the woods. Deer would wander through the back and Dawn would slide the white lace curtains aside to watch them, especially the fawns.

Her mother hated coming to the old trailer, but Dawn and her father loved it. They spent most of their time on the front porch. Enclosed in mesh, the tiny porch built onto the side of the trailer only had enough room for a card table, two chairs and an old wood stove. Her father used a small metal shovel to stoke the fire, sending orange sparks into the air, like fireflies spinning in circles. They played gin rummy and listened to the ambient sounds of the forest. Crickets, cicadas and the occasional howl of wolves serenaded them each night. Her father told stories about ancient religions and their beliefs. Mostly, he talked about demons. They were his fascination and they became Dawn's as well. Dawn never thought the stories were survival lessons. Life was funny sometimes.

Sitting on a log they had rolled over from a nearby woodpile, Dawn pulled out a bag of marshmallows and shoved one onto a stick. She handed it to Trista. While the army fatigues were loose on Dawn, Trista looked like a child dressed in her daddy's clothes. She had rolled up the sleeves, but the cloth bunched up around her shoulders.

Trista stared through the fire, eyes unblinking. She hadn't

said much since they'd left the army facility. Dawn was afraid she was regressing back to the scared little girl from the grocery store. Dawn never had to deal with an upset little sister and her maternal instincts were lacking. She needed to try something to get Trista talking again.

'My dad and I use to roast marshmallows when I was a kid. Just let it hover right above the flames.'

Trista let her marshmallow inch closer to the fire. A lick of flame caught it and it blackened on her stick.

'When we wake up, we can head to that house I was telling you about before,' said Dawn, the enthusiasm sounding to optimistic even to her ears. Trista didn't answer. She dropped her stick and folded her arms across her chest.

'You ok?' asked Dawn sliding closer. 'It's over. We had a scare, but we're ok now.'

Trista turned to face Dawn, her eyes squinting through the smoke. 'No, it isn't and no we're not. We're going to die and we're going to turn into one of those things.'

'I won't let that happen.' Dawn rested her hand on Trista's arm. Her skin was warm from the fire.

'You can't promise that.'

'I know it seems hopeless, but we have to keep fighting.'

'I liked one of the boys,' Trista blurted, her cheeks reddening.

Dawn frowned, not knowing what to make of the comment. 'Ok, but we can't dwell in the past.'

'It was only yesterday.'

'I know but...'

'No you don't,' Trista wailed. Raising her hands, she rubbed her temples, as if trying to force the memory back inside. 'His name was Sam and he had dimples and he liked me.'

'Trista, those men were not good men.' Trista's eyes widened and Dawn realized she'd said the wrong thing.

'Sam was,' Trista insisted. 'He put me in that room when the alarm went off. He said I'd be safe in there. Before he closed the door, he told me everything would be all right and I believed him. Just like I believed you.'

Trista turned backed to the fire, her eyes swollen with

tears. 'I believed him.' Her tears flowed, carving wet roads across her dirty cheeks.

'We don't need them. We're doing just fine,' Dawn said making circles with her fingers across Trista's arm.

'You don't believe that.' Trista stood and started to pace. Dawn hated when she paced.

'I know what I'm doing. Trust me. Haven't I been right about, oh I don't know, everything.'

'We can't just keep running,' Trista said, her arms flailing.

'We don't just run,' Dawn corrected. 'We kill demons along the way.'

'Yeah, like one a day. Big whup.'

'Look, I know you're freaked out.'

'I'm not.'

Dawn smirked.

Trista rolled her eyes. 'Ok, maybe a little,' Trista continued. 'But I'm pissed too.'

'Good. Funnel that anger. Use it to kill these bastards.'

'No, I'm pissed at you.'

Dawn stood, grabbing Trista by the shoulder. 'Stop pacing. You know I hate that.'

They stared at one another, waiting for the other to look away. Trista finally conceded.

'You can be pissed off at me all you want. I know what I'm doing.'

'No you don't,' countered Trista. 'You just know how to kill them. You don't have a clue about what to do.'

'Killing them not working for you?'

'There's like a billion of those things. You going to kill all of them?'

It was Dawn's turn to look away.

'We need to find more people,' Trista pleaded.

'People are just as dangerous, sometimes worse.'

Trista grabbed Dawn by the arm and twisted her around. Her blue eyes shimmered in the flames as she looked into Dawn's eyes. 'No, never worse.'

Dawn nodded. 'Ok, you're right. But what do you want me to do?'

Trista reached around her back and pulled out a booklet with a red cover. She held it out to Dawn.

'I found this when we were looking for stuff.'

Dawn took it and read the cover. 'Project Humanity?'

'Yeah, I read through it while you were colleting wood. There's a place in New York...'

'Not New York. You wanna guess how many demons are running around New York. We're better off staying off the main highways and away from any big city, especially New York.'

Trista started pacing again. 'I know. But we have to try.'

'Stop pacing. Sit down and let me look at this.'

Trista sat back down, but her feet bounced with nervous energy. Dawn sat next to her and started flipping through the pages. She felt Trista's anticipation boiling over as she read over the bulleted aims of the report. The heading, 'Continue the Species', was a section she hoped Trista hadn't read.

'See that,' Trista said pointing to the heading, 'Who can save the world?'

'Yeah, so. Did they really write that down?'

'I think it might be you.'

When Dawn saw Trista's even stare, she started laughing.

'It's not funny. I'm serious,' Trista said flatly.

'What makes you think it's me?'

'Uh, duh. You got us out of there with your super powers.'

'My super powers?' Dawn was laughing again. She closed the booklet. 'These are the ramblings of a bunch of nerds trying to make sense out of something that is unreal to them. It's bullshit. I don't have super powers. No one does.'

'You sensed those demons. You know how to bind them.'

'So? My dad taught me. You know that.'

Trista grabbed the report from Dawn's lap and opened it to an earmarked section. 'There may be one or more agents on Earth that possess an innate sense of pre-Adamite activity.'

'Oh, Jesus,' Dawn said, the corners of her mouth rising as her eyebrows dropped into a dubious gaze.

'Reports of survivors locating and leading others through dens of pre-Adamites have been reported,' Trista continued reading, unfazed. 'These senses may continue to manifest over time. Harnessing the power within these individuals may be the key to humanity's survival. Testing has begun at the Queens facility. Transfer of all potential pre-Adamite sensorial individuals is mandatory.'

'Just like the government to try to control an uncontrollable situation.'

'You want me to have hope and all you do is crap on everything,' Trista said slamming the booklet shut.

'Come on. This is ridiculous.'

'Why? Because you don't believe it?' Trista asked, shoving Dawn.

'Because it's silly,' Dawn answered, shoving her back. 'It isn't a super power to have common sense.'

'Ok, what about Towson?'

Dawn ignored her and picked up a loose stick. She shoved a marshmallow on the tip and angled it just over the fire.

'It wasn't your fault they didn't listen,' said Trista. She placed her hand on Dawn's arm, the consoling roles reversed. 'You told them to stay away from the mall, remember?'

'Everyone thinks they know what's going on but none of us know. Not really.' Dawn pulled her arm away.

'You knew not to go that way.'

Dawn shook her head. 'I just thought it wasn't the way to go.'

'That's not true. You told them you had a feeling it was infested.'

'A gut feeling is not a super power.' Dawn pulled the stick back and took a bite of the marshmallow. It burned her tongue and she threw the stick down.

Trista set the booklet down. 'Dawny, I care about you and I know you think you're looking out for me.'

'I want you to be safe,' said Dawn kicking the stick away.

'Maybe you don't have super powers. It's crazy, I know. But you're smart about these things. You saved me. Maybe you can save other people. Maybe what you know is kind of a super power. But we can't just keep running.'

Dawn looked at Trista and shook her head. She blew out a long breath. Trista was right about one thing. They couldn't keep going like they were. Eventually, they would get cornered and killed or worse, turned into one of those disgusting creatures. Dawn stared into the sky, hoping to find some wisdom hidden behind the orange glow. She wished she could see the stars again.

'This is crazy.'

Trista jumped up and started clapping her hands. 'I knew you would go. Yes!' Trista danced around the fire, wiggling her thin hips and pushing her hands up in the air as if to keep an imaginary ceiling from falling down. She tugged on Dawn's arm and pulled her up.

'I hate New York,' Dawn said, unable to hide her smile.

The next morning Dawn watched the sunrise. A yellow hue broached the eastern horizon, mixing with the constant orange glow. The fire had died. Only a few orange embers glowed in the retreating darkness. Trista slept soundly next to her under a wool blanket, a smile creeping at the corners of her mouth. Dawn stroked Trista's hair, gently brushing the stray pieces from her forehead.

As she stared into the morning sky, a sparkle of light, dim, but unmistakable, caught Dawn's eye. A star. It flashed in and out of her vision, as if a hand cupped over a flashlight and then released the light again. It was the first star Dawn had seen since the reckoning and it was the first time she felt hope.

The star hovered in the sky and Dawn knew New York rested under it, beckoning her. Her father would have told her the ancients would see this phenomenon as a sign from a higher power. Dawn's logical side told her it was just a star. But a part of her hoped it was meant for her.

She watched the star until the morning light blotted it out. Even though she couldn't see it, she knew it was there, waiting. She knew she would follow it.

The Sharks of Market Street

Michael Ezell

The twin hulls of Rita's skimmer parted the dark water with hardly a ripple. Having little body fat to keep her warm, Rita shivered and pulled her sweater tight against the predawn chill. Three months shy of sixteen, she still hadn't put on the extra weight that was expected of a bride. (As Pops often reminded her.) She hugged her own skinny chest and looked ahead into the fog. Nothing but grey. She'd left the last of High Ground long before light. She wanted to make sure she reached the 'scrapers just as the sun came up. That's when the sharks seemed most active. The big ones, anyway. The ones that could eat boats.

In the time between people walking on the flooded streets below Rita and now, the once endangered Whites had come back with a vengeance. Bigger than any oldster had ever even *heard* of, and territorial to the point that anything giving off a steady vibration in the water was torn to shreds.

With this in the back of her mind, Rita added to her skimmer's momentum by gently tugging the guide-rope that ran from High Ground to the first 'scraper in the rope line. The earliest Salvies had been all about helping each other, kind of like the Hippies who once lived in this submerged city. In that spirit, the first Salvies set up the rope system Rita now used to reach the closest of the buildings folks once called 'skyscrapers.'

Nowadays, no professional Salvie would ever run ropes to his or her favourite buildings. If you wanted to dive the big 'scrapers, you had to have the kind of guts that got your name on the wall at Tunny's.

In other words, you had to be willing to skim open water without an anchor rope to guarantee your return.

And since generations of Salvies had picked the closest buildings clean, if Rita wanted a chance at the best swaggity goodness, she had to skim serious open water. Way out Market Street, closer and closer to the 'scrapers of old Downtown Frisco.

For most folks, the tops of those old 'scrapers sticking out of the water were just bitter reminders of a time when the world was normal, when a body could just buy food and goods as they needed. Looted ages ago, the topmost floors were useless to anyone who survived the bio-weapon and the following floods.

But then along came a guy who called himself 'Sly Eric.' He was the first official Salvie, the first guy to get his name scratched into the wall of the tumbledown shithole bar called Tunny's. Sly Eric figured out that the sharks left drifting objects alone, so he made the very first twin hull skimmer, shoved offshore and floated over to the nearest 'scraper. Once there, he broke out a window on a floor half under water and took his entire skimmer inside. With no air tanks and set of balls the size of Kansas— *as Tunny liked to say*— Sly Eric dove down an elevator shaft to the flooded floor beneath him. When he came back up carrying a framed collection of gold coins from some VIP's office wall, a legend was born.

A legend that many brave divers, including a skinny girl named Rita, would follow onto the water.

Just as the top two floors of the first 'scraper in the rope line loomed out of the fog, something big rippled the water fifty feet to Rita's left. She held her breath and locked her eyes on the window her skimmer was aimed at. The glass had been scraped from all the frames long ago, allowing Salvies to glide right into the relative safety of shallow waters inside the buildings.

Closer, closer...

A dark back five times longer than Rita's skimmer broke the surface to her right— A lazy roll, not an attacking rush, but Rita's heart still hammered in her chest. Hard to tell in the fog, probably just a young whale being curious. But if he bumped the skimmer and spilled Rita into the water, she was as good as dead. Maybe this close to the building she'd get lucky and a current would carry her in. But if she so much as started to tread water, she'd meet the same fate as the legendary Sly Eric. This thought made Rita reflexively check her ankle chucks.

In a bit of gallows humour, the pioneers of 'scraper salvaging had named their ankle weights after an ancient type of ankle-high shoe. All true Salvies wore these decorated strings of lead weights around their ankles. If you flipped your skimmer and couldn't get back on, at least your fate was in your own hands. Better to drown quickly than to feel those teeth crushing your ribs, or ripping off a leg to let you bleed out before they finished the meal.

Rita released a breath she'd held to a painful point, as her skimmer cleared the window of the first building and she glided into darkness. Safety. The big predators didn't like to swim into the buildings. Rita had a theory that it somehow disoriented them and the shallower waters inside the office floors made them nervous.

The grey rectangles of light on the other side led Rita across what used to be a place where people worked. When the sun came up, Rita would be able to see the submerged skeletons of rusted desks and the floors of the offices, now carpeted with seaweed, coral and anemones. She reached up and let her fingers scrape the stained ceiling as she drifted through a huge hole cut into a partitioning wall. Squiggly faded letters told the story of past generations of Salvies who'd made their mark on the ceilings of the closest buildings. The farther out from High Ground, the fewer names on the ceiling. No one's name was anywhere on the big pyramid. But Rita meant to change that soon.

At the windows on the far side, Rita stopped her skimmer for a moment. She checked the two tiny plastic skimmer models behind her for what had to be the hundredth time. Still there. All the mechanics intact, nothing out of place. Natch. Rita had painted their little hulls herself. Black and white, like the Killers. When the Whites had come back in force, so had the Killers. And the Whites didn't seem to like them too much. Which had given Rita this insane idea to begin with.

The grey sky got lighter by the moment and Rita wanted to be at least over Market Street by the time the fog burned off.

This is where the rope system stopped and it became every Salvie for herself. From there, you had to rely on your Sling to get your skimmer from building to building. No problem going out. The killer was coming back. You could only load so much stuff on a skimmer and still have the power to sling yourself back to the roped buildings. Get greedy, try to bring back too much swaggity goodness at once and come up short on a sling… Well, you just had to pray that tides and currents would carry you to a building instead of out to sea. You could always take a chance and try to row a few strokes without attracting the Whites. But the walls of Tunny's were lined with scratched-in names of Salvies who'd tried it and hadn't made it back.

Rita took a deep breath and pulled on the rope. Her beautiful skimmer skated across the water toward the next building. Rita designed the skimmer herself, and crafted it out of sheet metal and rubber she found in the scrap yard behind the shack where Tunny served homemade potato liquor and fried fish. No way she had the upfront scratch for all that stuff, but old Frank Tunny laughed off her payment plan.

'Girlie,' the grizzled bartender had growled from the side of his mouth that wasn't paralyzed, 'You only got till sixteen anyways, so live it up. I'll just take the boat back when ya get married. We got a deal?' (The mouth thing came courtesy of a wicked knife scar that made Rita think of Tunny as a gnarly pirate captain.)

Like a real old-time Salvie, Rita had spit in her hand and slapped palms with Tunny. Pretty disgusting, actually, but Rita managed to walk outside before she wiped the stray splashes of her own spit off her face. Tough like that.

Passing the halfway point between buildings, Rita glanced up at the sky and saw blue replacing the black of night. Like a physical weight on her shoulders, the sky reminded Rita that soon she'd be wearing bridal blue and Tunny would be the owner of a brand new Salvie skimmer.

As her skimmer drifted into the next building, Rita thought about her upcoming wedding and frowned. The Salvie dudes respected her because she braved the waters, but she knew she'd never get to be a legend like Sly Eric or Wiz, the Wizard of Twin Peaks. Wiz was the only guy so far who'd made it out. Found a hoard of gold in a locker down there and bought a pass across the Arizona border and a piece of High Ground far enough inland that his children's children wouldn't have to worry about the encroaching waters. Nope, she'd never make it out like Wiz, because it took him twenty years of diving to hit it big. Rita started at thirteen, which had given her just three short years to make her mark. Not fair in any sense of the word.

And she was lucky to get those years. Pops thought it was beneath a lady of her upbringing to risk her life doing Salvie work. Only 'urchins' did this kinda thing. But Pops couldn't very well ban her from salvaging. The same *Words of the Prophet* that said she had to marry at sixteen also said that young girls should be allowed to sow their oats before sixteen so they get it out of their system. (Blasphemous rumours suggested the Prophet came to this opinion after being accused of plying a fourteen year-old girl with wine.)

Being a devout follower of the Words of the Prophet, Pops just gritted his teeth and put up with Rita's wild side. Rita had once joked that Pops should look at her salvage work in a positive way; if the Whites got her, he wouldn't have to pay a dowry to Fat Calvin's family. Pops hadn't talked to her for a week, and to this day Rita still felt guilt about the wounded look on his face.

As the fog began to burn off, Rita skimmed her way into the last building that had a rope line. She could see the gleaming top of the pyramid building sticking out of the fog miles away, reflecting the rising sun off its white and silver skin. The tallest building in the old city, over half of it still stuck out of the water. The Salvie Bible said there was a great treasure in the lower floors of that place. The kind of treasure that would buy you a house smack in the middle of Oklahoma. *No sharks there, Dear Rita, none at all.*

Rita stopped her skimmer on the western side of the building and anchored a line to a spike in the wall. The Salvie Bible also said that Sly Eric drove all these spikes himself. Rita didn't really buy that one. There had to be hundreds of anchor spikes in the walls of the leftover 'scrapers. She doubted Sly Eric had enough time to make his legend as a Salvie diver and still drive all these spikes.

Rita set about preparing her scale model skimmers for what would most likely be the only journey they'd ever take. She pulled the first one to the front of her skimmer's platform deck and sets its little black and white hulls in the water. About three feet long, from a distance it kinda looked like a baby Killer. Kinda.

Rita twisted a wooden dowel and wound a length of salvaged elastic until it was bunched up in a tight coil, full of stored energy. Plastic ties attached the elastic to Rita's rowing contraption. A simple cam that drove two paddles that spun around as long as the elastic still had power.

The lonely bark of a seal out there in the fog reminded Rita that the Whites would be expecting food to hit the water soon. Depending on the building, the water sometimes came to just the bottom of a floor, or made an island out of an exposed rooftop. Pods of seals gathered there to both rest in safety between hunts, and let their pups get big enough to evade the sharks.

The swirling fog thinned and Rita could see them now. A large pod, over two dozen on the roof of a shorter building to the north. Rita had spent countless hours sitting on the edge of an upper floor, watching the Whites feed on the seals. Sometimes Rita even brought chicken blood and used a seine net to catch shiner surfperch on her way out. She'd chop up the little fish and add the chicken blood for a nice chum. The other Salvies thought she was crazy, but Rita was doing research. She'd seen pods of Killers cruise the deep waters near old Downtown and she would purposely try to draw the Whites close to them.

Once the Whites realized there were Killers in the area, they invariably left. As big as the Whites had become, the Killers had been huge beasts to begin with and they had grown in equal proportion over the last century. Rita couldn't say for sure scientific-like, but she figured maybe the world had gotten sick of what people did before. Nature made sure the ocean's critters were big enough to kick 'em out if they tried to rule the water again.

Whatever the reason, the Killers kept their spot at the top of the chain and that made this design spring full grown into Rita's quick little brain.

Rita let the scale model skimmer go and the elastic band began to unwind. This spun the little wood paddles and the miniature skimmer splashed its way toward the next 'scraper about a hundred yards away. Rita snatched up a piece of slate and her special rubbing sticks. She'd spent weeks experimenting, checking subtle differences in materials rubbed against her slate. She'd found a bit of something the oldsters called nylon that gave her the same frequency as the calls of the Killers.

Rita held the slate just under the water and started rubbing the nylon rod against it, mimicking the underwater call of a Killer. Or near about, anyway.

Her brave little black and white skimmer paddled and paddled, splashing its way closer to the other 'scraper. Rita kept her call going and the skimmer made it to the shadow of the 'scraper. Nearly there!

Rita had just enough time to see the telltale swell of water below the skimmer—

A grey and white behemoth *exploded* out of the water, crushing the toy skimmer in a ring of razor teeth that still had room for Rita and her real skimmer. It seemed to hang in the air, all white teeth, pink jutting gums and a flat black eye that Rita swore looked straight at her.

The White twisted to one side, finishing the breech with a massive splash that sent a wave all the way back to Rita's building. Rita shivered even though the sun had risen high enough to warm the air. *That fucking beast dwarfed the horse old man Thierry used to pull his plough.* Rita would hardly be an afterthought, a skinny little bag of bones bouncing around in that giant mouth.

Pulse hammering in her neck, Rita hurried to prepare her next toy skimmer. This twisted elastic engine drove a willow rod attached to a flexible paddle that stayed underwater. The flexible rod and paddle configuration undulated beneath the water in the same motion as a Killer's tale.

'Go, baby.' She whispered, and let go of the second toy skimmer.

Same as before, Rita used her slate call to create something close to Killer-speak. The little skimmer moved with a peculiar up and down motion, but it arrowed toward the far building just like the first skimmer. Rita made long, drawn out calls as she watched the black and white skimmer go. A pain in her chest told her she'd been holding her breath again. She exhaled as the new skimmer made it to within fifty yards of the next 'scraper. Then the elastic band crapped out and the skimmer slowed. The morning current started to carry it wide of the building and Rita watched it until a swirling eddy took it around a corner and out of sight. Not one bump, not one swell of water anywhere near it.

Success.

Now if she could just do it full size without getting ripped to pieces.

Rita pulled her skimmer out of the water and nudged it into line on the broken asphalt alongside the dozen or so others. She'd waited two hours to give the Whites time to chase the seals out to sea before she pulled her way back along the ropes. She had no time for diving today. In fact, if she changed right now and ran like mad, she could just make it back to the Compound in time for her dress fitting. Pops had paid special to have Rita's dress made by the spinster Agatha. Agatha had never taken a husband and had devoted her life to her craft. She made the finest wedding dresses in the Compound. Maybe in the world, for all Rita knew.

Rita grabbed a macramé bag made from coarse hemp twine and headed for some bushes to change out of the sweater and trousers she'd worn against the morning chill. Even though Rita hated wearing her *shari*, the traditional dress of a single girl, she knew Pops would only tolerate so much rebellion.

A shrill whistle came from down where the road widened into an ancient turnout, near Tunny's bar and scrap yard.

'Hey Rita girl! You need some help puttin' on your church clothes?'

Rita didn't even slow down. She flipped a middle finger in Flounder's direction and hustled into the bushes. She didn't need to look to know it was Flounder. His flattened nose made the words so nasally they were almost a foreign language. Flounder found salvaging after learning the hard way that he wasn't meant to be a bare-knuckle boxer.

Ducking behind the thickest cover she could find, Rita quickly stripped off her clothes and hauled the white cotton *shari* dress out of her bag. Through the screen of green leaves, she could see Flounder's moon face teasingly moving around as if to get a view. 'Fuck off, Flounder! Else, I'll tell my old man you tried to show me your dingus.'

Flounder let out a mock howl of pain and covered his crotch as he ran into Tunney's. The men who lived inside the Compound of the Prophet's People had a nasty habit of castrating men they thought had defiled their daughters. And they considered showing a girl your man business to be defilement.

Rita slipped the tight dress over her head and pulled it down until it hit the middle of her thighs. Most girls her age had to wriggle their way into their *shari*, but Rita basically had the build of a twelve year-old boy. Gangly, with no hips to speak of, the scoop neck of the *shari* wasted on the modest bumps peeking through the white cotton on her chest. Pops didn't really care if she ate the Diet of Anne or not, since Fat Calvin had made it quite clear that he'd marry Rita if she was a knobby skeleton or the curviest woman in the Compound. He didn't have a lot of options.

And it wasn't even a matter of rebellion for Rita. She didn't object to the high fat diet that made the girls so curvy. The food was great. But as her sixteenth grew closer, Rita wanted more and more to be out on the water, diving her buildings, communing with death every day. To her that was life. But it also meant she was not present for communal meals, and she wasn't allowed to take food from the compound just because she wanted to be 'self-centred' and eat by herself on the water.

That meant Rita subsisted mainly on a diet of fish she

caught herself and rice she bartered from a group of Koreans who lived on a tiny spit of land to the north. Rita once gave them a fading sign with pictures of food and Korean writing on it that she salvaged from something called a Food Court. From that moment on, the old Korean women made sure Rita got only the best rice they had, not that crap the men normally reserved for the religious nuts in that compound.

Rita jammed her sweater and trousers into the macramé bag and hustled for the main gate of the compound. The sun had climbed much higher in the sky than she thought, so she was lucky the main gate was so close to the water.

She waved at Muncie Williams up in the guard tower and he waved down at someone inside the compound. The walk-in gate cut into the giant timber main gates swung outward. Rita smiled at Gordon Plum and he waved her in with his shotgun.

Quick-walking, as a lady doesn't run, Rita made her way to the longhouses in the residential block of the Compound. Since Pops sat on the Council of Five, their family had an entire timber and stone longhouse to themselves. Rita, Pops, three of his original five wives, and Rita's two unmarried brothers. All of her sisters had long ago married and moved to other families' longhouses. Rita was the last daughter in the house.

Rita's mom was one of the two wives Pops lost. Elvira, the Original Wife, died from the 'flu long before Rita was born. Pops lost Rita's mom Margaret, and very nearly lost Rita, during Rita's birth. This carved a permanent soft place in his heart for Rita. Though she felt guilty, she still sometimes took advantage of this, pulling out the weepy peepers when she really wanted something.

Rita hurried into the front of the longhouse, dropped her bag on a chair and stopped short. Jersey, her eldest sister, stood there with a smirk on her face. Since she was inside her own family's home, Jerz didn't have to wear the blue modesty veil that told the world she was married and off limits.

Jersey stood next to the spinster Agatha, a thin woman of sixty with a sharp face. The black plait of hair down her back was shot through with grey, but braided in the style of a single girl who still lived with her family—

Shit! Rita had forgotten to braid her hair. She didn't need a mirror to see the wind-whipped mess. She could see it in their eyes. Agatha shared Jersey's smirk and said, 'I see you hurried here to keep your appointment.'

'Of course she did. She knows how important this is.' The sound of Pops' voice made Rita's stomach clinch. He stood at the side entrance of the house, his overalls covered in dust from the soy fields.

'Pops?'

He took off his wide-brimmed hat and wiped away sweat with the sleeve of his old hemp fibre shirt. Rita recognized the patch on the shoulder. It was an old shirt, his favourite, and Rita had sewn that patch herself. Countless passes over the washboard had beaten the shirt into the soft, warm thing Rita remembered burying her face in as a young girl.

Pops gave Rita a tired grin, his age showing on his face today. 'You look so surprised to see me. Don't a father always come to see his girl try on her weddin' dress?'

'Well… I know you're in charge of harvest this year, so that means you're crazed biz, and you've done this so many times already.'

'I am 'crazed biz,' if that means what I suspect.' Careful to knock the dust from his boots, Pops stepped in and put an arm around Rita and whispered in her ear. 'But that don't mean I'd miss my last girl for nuthin'.'

He straightened and put on his gruff voice before anyone could see the moisture in his eyes. 'You've made Miss Agatha wait long enough, I'd say. You get on with puttin' on your finery and I'll fetch a nice bottle of cider for her to take home to make up for your lateness.'

As Pops walked out of the room, Jersey gave Rita the second of roughly six hundred and seventy-three smirks she'd suffer that afternoon. But for his sake, Rita took it. Twirling about in a giant puff of sky blue taffeta that was strapped to her body with a rib-crushing corset, enduring the pokes and prods of Agatha and Jersey, and finally all five of the other sisters for the final fitting.

Hannah, Clarita, Tania, Beula, and Gennie all showed for their turn to tease Rita about looking like someone put a dress on a skinny fisher boy who lived on the tide-line.

Jealous bitches as far as Rita was concerned, with their giant gross lumps squeezed together in the necklines of their dresses, and big asses that would sink a skimmer to the gunwales in a second. All of them were over thirty; hell, Jerz was *forty-two*. Pops was sixty years old when he had Rita, the last of his children. The family watched Pops sit vigil at Rita's crib-side, waiting to see if she would make it through that first long night, his big rough hand sneaking in to touch her fragile cheek now and again. From the start it had been clear that he loved her above all else. And that had led to a hard road for Rita among the 'girls' of the family. But the rebellious streak that led her to fight them had a breaking point when it came to Pops. Because in reality, Rita loved him above all else, too. But she still wished he'd let her talk to him about some of the Prophet's Words without blowing a head vein.

They all shut right the hell up when he came back in. He'd taken off his dusty field clothes and put on the purple cotton of a Council member, as if this were a formal ceremony and not just a skinny girl who stank of saltwater trying on a dress.

Pops absentmindedly handed the bottle of hard cider to Agatha, his eyes on Rita in her blue bridal gown. Rita's sisters all smiled, but their eyes glared as Pops touched her face with a shaking hand. Rita looked up at the rough beams of the ceiling to try and hold in the tears. She felt him take hold of the blue veil attached to her bridal headpiece. He practiced putting it across her face and tying it in place as he would after Rita and Fat Calvin spoke their vows. 'One night, the fourth night after you was born, I thought you stopped breathin' on me. I held a fine piece'a blue jay feather over your lips to check... For a long tic, nothin' happened. Then you blew that little feather outta my hand with a cry and you haven't stopped yellin' at me since.'

Rita laughed to keep the tears away, but neither of them fared well with that. 'You're a special girl, Rita. You'll be a beautiful bride.'

Rita wanted to shout— *I don't wanna be a beautiful bride! I wanna dive, I wanna find a treasure, I wanna see the world!*

But she didn't.

She just blubbered like a newb who forgot to tie down her skimmer and lost it on the tide.

Jersey stepped in and blotted Rita's eyes roughly with a kerchief. 'There, there, girlie, don't go getting' your veil all stained with tears. Leastways, not before the weddin' night.'

'Ew, Jerz!' Rita pushed away from Jersey and went to let Agatha unhook the back of this torture device. As she watched Pops leave, Rita smiled and put up with this last bit of pinching and pulling.

But she had visions of Jersey paddling across Market Street, a pack of grey shadows swimming beneath her…

The sun burned off the fog as Rita watched from her perch on the top floor of a small 'scraper she'd staked out to dive. She looked out at the strange forest of building tops between her and the open ocean. Feeling more alone out here than usual, Rita's mind turned to the fight with Pops last night.

They took a walk in the soy field under the stars, basically the only way to find privacy in a place where everyone was jammed into communal homes. He was excited to talk about the wedding. Instead, she rambled about her experiment with the small skimmers.

Pops begged her to apply that genius to farming techniques to help her husband, but she flamed out and told him that Fat Calvin was getting more than enough food; he didn't need her help. This had made him crazed mad, of course. Pops didn't like that disrespectful name for her future husband, no matter if she'd been calling him that since they were both five.

'As much as I love you, girl, you got to control that tongue. Not even your mother had such a mouth on her,' Pops had growled. 'You need to remember how important this is to your family. Joining with Calvin means our family is tied to more acreage.'

'Which means everything to my brothers and scrappi-ty-doo to me and the other girls.'

'The Prophet has given your brothers the task of caring for their wives, as Calvin is to care for you. We have also been given the task of repopulating the world. That, my baby girl, be more important than your personal desires.'

'Says who? Can you look me in the eye and tell me you know for certain that it's God's will for me to stop my life at sixteen and start honkin' out kids and sweepin' up after my man?'

'In the End Days, when all of humanity was a-chokin' on snot and hawkin' up their lungs because Man had finally made his greatest evil, the Prophet give us a chance through his healin' hands. All he asked in return was that we follow his Words—'

'And give him a few teenage brides.' That earned Rita a warning scowl that she unwisely ignored.

'Careful, girl. I am an Elder in this community. I am a direct descendant of Eduardo, the first follower of the Prophet, who saw the Prophet healin' folks with his own eyes.'

'Pops, the Prophet was just some dude who had medicine. He didn't know God's will any better than anyone else.'

She practically leaned into it when he slapped her. Both of them looked a little stunned in the seconds afterward, but the tide had already made its mark, as Salvies say.

Rita stomped out the front gate and spent the night on her skimmer down by the water. She had less than three months before she turned sixteen. Less than three months to find enough treasure to buy her own spot in Oklahoma, and she'd dive every waking hour to make it happen.

Her rebellion had been a magnificent gesture, but not really thought through. Her sweater didn't cut it against the night air that brought the thick fog with it. But she stub-bornly shivered herself to sleep on the deck of her skimmer. Some of the O.G. Salvies hanging at Tunny's had seen her and told the old bartender. He'd come in the night with his scarred face and clumsy hands and laid a blanket over her. Rita had no idea, but her heart had become legendary among these men who had no choice but to ply the waters for survival. That she had a warm place to call home but chose the cold water made the skinny kid a kind of mascot they all came to love.

Rita shook herself as the last tendril of fog burned away. No time to waste, so she climbed down to her skimmer and set about prepping her tank for the dive. Visibility looked great, with sunlight filtering down four floors below the surface.

Rita rested her tank on her skimmer and pushed over to the elevator shaft she'd scouted. There were very few initials scrawled on the ceilings of this building. Rita had done scouting dives and believed she'd found a room no one had entered. She zipped her stitched-together wetsuit to her chin and tugged the hood over her head. She tied off her skimmer and made sure her tool bag, goodie bag, and knife were secure on her belt before she hauled her tank into the belly sling.

A quick test breath and Rita put on her mask, slid into the clear water and swam down the cold elevator shaft. In the dim light, her own breath rattling in her ears, Rita passed elevator doors she'd already pried open on her scouting dive. That dive had been in pitch darkness, her heart hammering, feeling the sharks under her dangling legs even though she knew they didn't live in elevator shafts. Now the opened doors let in enough light from the glass walls for Rita to see her goal. Three floors below her skimmer, Rita swam through the elevator doors and entered what was once a well-appointed outer office.

The flood had not been sudden for floors this high. The thick safety glass survived on a lot of buildings and this floor had just one slight break in the glass. Only small creatures, shrimp, crab, a few clownfish, lived among the chrome skeletons of what must have been very modern furniture. Rita kicked past a built-in desk that curved out from a wall.

She swam to a set of double doors that looked like wood, but were in fact metal. When she first discovered this, Rita's heart had leapt. Maybe someone had made this place secure for a reason. Could be crazed amounts of treasure just the other side.

Rita took a hand pick from her tool bag and laid into the wall to one side of the locked doors. It didn't take long to hack through the waterlogged panels and expose the building's skeleton. When the cloud of debris settled, Rita got her first look inside the locked room. One giant rectangle of safety glass dominated the far wall. The greenish quality of the light filtering through a layer of algae gave the office an eerie feel. And it was definitely an office. Rita had seen hundreds of desks in these buildings, but this behemoth of smoked glass and chrome spoke of an owner who wanted people to know his importance. Picture frames on the walls contained paintings in various states of ruin and a second door inside the office looked like it led to a private toilet.

Closest to her new entry point, Rita saw something that almost made her laugh in her respirator. A full bar, pretty as you please. Glasses still upside down in racks, rows of bottles intact on mirrored shelves.

She retrieved an old hacksaw blade from her tool bag and set about hacking through the metal wall studs to create a Salvie Glory Hole, as the boys called it. She didn't really get why they all laughed any time she said it. It took a helluva lot of work with the dull blade, but she managed to cut through one sheet metal crossbeam and that was all the room Rita needed. Anxious to get to her new find, she eased inside the office and swam to the bar.

As she took in the stone counter top, the chrome sink fixtures, Rita's thoughts turned to Tunny. If she had to bring this out piece by swaggity piece, she intended to give the old man a new bar. But for now, she perused the bottles on the top shelf. Rita knew scrappity-doo about liquor, but she figured this must be good stuff given the size of the guy's office. She glanced over and saw a wooden box peeking out of a shelf on the side. She eased it out of hiding.

The little brass clasp was still closed and the box felt heavy. Rita laid it on the fancy stone bar top and flicked open the clasp. Gold letters gleamed at her as she opened the box and saw the bottle inside. Seal untouched, cradled in what looked like white silk, the label still a flawless deep blue with bright gold letters. Given that the label was blue, Rita thought it a little redundant to name the whiskey inside 'Blue Label.' This Johnnie Walker guy may have made high end liquor, but he clearly needed someone to help him come up with names for his stuff. Tunny's potato 'whiskey' was called Star-Spangled Salvie Blinder. Now that was a name.

Rita could already see the slanted smile on Tunny's face. The label and box wouldn't survive contact with the air, but the bottle and whiskey would. This bottle alone would probably make him part with all the material she needed for her special skimmer. And once she had that, she'd be well on her way to travelling the known world, to buying a place smack in the middle of Oklahoma.

For a brief second, the weight of the real world fell on Rita. It would take at least three months to build her new boat. After that, she'd be a married woman and wouldn't be allowed to leave the Compound.

The golden letters gleamed in her peripheral vision and Rita shoved all those thoughts aside. She put the bottle into her goodie bag, the wonderful label already sloughing off just from moving it. Then Rita stopped breathing. In the mirror of the bar, the greenish light revealed two things behind her.

A safe on the far wall, opened and empty.

And a shoe, seemingly still on a foot poking from behind the giant desk across the room.

A cold that had nothing to do with the water settled into Rita's stomach. She swam over slowly, not sure she wanted to confirm this find. A block of something clear rested atop the desk. The words 'Barry Crane – CEO' were etched in the block. Rita stopped at the edge of the desk to steel her nerves. She peeked over the top...

A skeleton dressed in a suit sat against the wall beneath the open safe, one leg tucked under and one sticking straight out. A metal briefcase sat in the dead man's lap, opened so that only he could see inside it. Rita didn't think she wanted to know what was in there, given that the skeleton's skull had a small hole on one side and a large hole on other side. A rusted pistol still lay in a bony hand. Creepers. Rita had come across skeletons before, but nothing like this. What was in that case that someone wanted it to be the last thing they ever saw?

Rita swam closer, her own passage disturbing the water enough to make the dead man's suit billow around his bones. Torn, she didn't want to take the briefcase off his lap, but she didn't want to lean in close to look inside, either. She called herself a dirty coward in her head until she worked up the nerve to peek around the top of the briefcase.

A dead electronic device caught her eye first. One of the larger flat ones with a picture of an apple on the frame. Tunny liked to collect these, but Rita figured to leave this one right where it was. Resting atop stacks of puffed up old world money. Fat stacks banded with rubber, the top bills marked with '100.' They hadn't floated away because the dead electric device held them down. Beneath the stacks of money were crumbling papers edged with gold. Some type of 'bond' from what little Rita could make out. Rita backed away and stared at the dead man for a moment.

Whoever he was, she felt for him. He had obviously died alone since no one had removed his body. The world was dying and even if he was one of the immune few, his life as he had known it was over, so he came here of all places to die. He took out all that hoarded money, put a gun to his head and waited for Rita to find him. All those bucks were nothing but a weight to hold him down when the ocean took over his glass-walled crypt.

Rita knew it was time to leave without checking her air regulator. Experience gave her a superb internal clock and though she hated to leave, she knew none of this meant anything if she didn't come back alive. Later, she'd return and go through Barry Crane, CEO's desk and bring down a bigger bag to pick up all that liquor. She patted Tunny's whisky in her goodie bag and kicked back to the hole in the wall. Rita tucked her arms in and wriggled through the hole she made— but suddenly jerked to a stop.

Not stuck, not at all, she thought as she inched a hand down her body to find out what had caught.

Relief washed through Rita like a cool wave when she found the problem. Her goodie bag was hung up on the metal stud she'd cut to get in. Rita gave it a tug. Stuck good. With a burst of strength, Rita yanked the bag free— and the sharp metal stud slashed her palm to the bone.

Rita floated into the reception area in shock, her hand feeling as if someone had set it on fire. She put pressure on the wound, but the blood came out in a thick cloud. Nothing she could do but swim.

Up the shaft in the dim light, her hand throbbing, treasure forgotten for the moment. When she broke the surface, Rita forced herself not to look at the wound. She shoved her tank onto the skimmer deck and hauled herself up after it.

Like a pro, Rita went straight to her Ouchie Kit. She unfolded the plastic bag that held her idea of medical supplies and grabbed a strip of thick cotton cloth. Rita shoved the wadded cloth onto the wound and watched the deep red slowly advance into the white fibres. She'd seen just enough of the cut to know she didn't want to see it again. She put the back of her hand flat on the deck and knelt on the pressure bandage as she used her free hand to rummage for another strip. Using her teeth to hold one end, Rita managed to get a fairly tight wrap on the bandage and she finally stopped to assess the level of shit she'd stepped in.

Hand throbbing, but likely to stay on her arm. Dizzy, nauseous, but the weight of her goodie bag did a lot to dampen that so she must not be too bad off.

She tied her dive gear down to the deck and got ready for the hard part. She had come out two 'scrapers past the last pull-rope setup, so she'd have to Sling twice to get back.

Every Salvie had a hand-crank winch on their skimmer. To get to a building without a pull rope, you set a bungee line hook on the outside of the window you want to leave, skim back to a wall opposite the exit window and hang onto an anchor spike. Then loop the bungee line through the winch and crank it until the cord is tight enough to play a banjo tune on. Let go of the anchor spike and *whoosh*, out the exit window, the hook falls loose when the line goes slack, and you reel it in as you skim to the other building. Repeat as necessary, chil'ren.

Rita's first Sling back gave her a panic attack. Her throbbing hand had convinced her that she had enough tension in the line, *so stop cranking already and let's go.*

Her speed bled off surprisingly fast and Rita figured out how stupid she'd been about fifty feet shy of her target building. She lost almost all headway and the current began to pull her wide of the window she wanted to hit. Prayer suddenly became a priority as the front of the building slipped by. If she didn't get into this one, the current would take her wide of the area called Downtown and shoot her all the way out to sea. As the last window threatened to pass her by, Rita reached out with a gaff hook and a Hail Everybody—

The clang of metal never sounded sweeter.

Rita pulled her skimmer into the building and negotiated the torn out interior to realign herself with her exit route. She noticed how saturated her bandage had become and stopped to change it. She had plenty of daylight to get back to shore by, but she could already hear the barks of seals coming back for the evening. Soon, they'd be jammed together on rooftops and floors not covered by the tide, safe from the Whites for another night.

Dressing a wound without looking at it came difficult, natch. But Rita struggled through, ignoring the fresh well of blood that spattered onto the skimmer's deck. Once she had a new bandage in place, she set up for her final Sling. She just knew the nausea would pass once she got into the relative safety of the guide ropes.

This time she ignored her yammering hand, cranking until the line sang with tension, and the Sling went flawlessly. She arrowed straight through the window she aimed for with speed to spare. The only hitch came about halfway across when a sudden breeze threatened to push her off course. Thankfully it was only a puff of cool air and she stayed true. She didn't notice her old bloody bandage blow off the deck and slowly spread a little red cloud in the water.

Once inside the building, Rita didn't even slow down. Getting to the ropes didn't make her feel as good as she thought it would and the panicky feeling had risen into her throat now. She just wanted to be home, with Pops chastising her as he cleaned her hand and sewed the wound up good as new.

She got straight onto the ropes, giving a mighty pull at the first exit window and skimming easily toward the next 'scraper. She couldn't say for sure which came first, her realization that a rivulet of her blood had run off the edge of the deck, or the inquisitive bump from below. They came so close together and in the end, it really didn't matter.

Rita had just enough time to kneel in the middle of her deck when the strike came. The White erupted from the water, slamming into one hull of Rita's skimmer, raw power flipping the whole thing in one insane fraction of a second. The burn of the rope on Rita's forearms and the backs of her calves registered long before the desire to actually go for the rope. Her body simply reacted.

The skimmer flipped into the air, striking the rope on the way down and the shark flopped the other way, a fourteen-footer easy. The splash washed over Rita and she clung to the pull-rope like some high wire artist who was seconds away from slamming into the ground. Only there was no ground under Rita. She bobbed up and down over swirling water, grey and white death thrashing her skimmer to pieces just three feet from her.

The line bounced so much, Rita's hair and her goodie bag hit the surface on every downward bob, dipping her into the water like a jiggy bait you used to catch sea bass off the high rocks. She tried not to scream, concentrated on holding onto that freakin' rope for all she ever had.

Rita couldn't see below her; she could only see blue sky and 'scrapers. The one closest to her looked to be about thirty yards away in Rita's upside down view. While the shark thrashed her skimmer to pieces looking for more of that tasty blood, Rita started to shimmy. The rough rope quickly burned into calves and ankles left bare by her diving shorts and Rita couldn't have given less of a shite. She pulled and shimmied, her injured hand screaming at her to stop, her panicked brain driving her hand to grab that rope and *pull, damn it!*

Close, so close now. If she could get inside the building, she knew there were reinforced shelves along the walls. Leftovers made stronger by Salvies who used the buildings in the rope system as staging points. They liked to be able to spread their tools out on something besides their skimmer deck if they needed to make any repairs going out or coming back.

With just twenty feet left to go, she felt the slickness on her calf. She knew the rope burn had turned into an open wound that was bleeding into the water now. Rita choked down the fear and pulled like hell to make those last twenty feet—

The refraction of the water gave her the only fighting chance she'd ever get. That close to the water, of course the White could see her. That moving thing up there above the tasty blood must have something to do with it.

With a bull rush that started ten feet down, it tried for her. An explosion of white foam and rough unyielding flesh struck Rita, knocking her senseless. The slight refraction from the water caused the shark to misjudge Rita's position by mere millimetres and the serrated white razors snapped shut just behind Rita's legs. But the impact caused the rope to jump and Rita could only hang on blindly until she felt the cold water envelop her— Water??

Rita let out an involuntary scream underwater as she woke to a real nightmare. She still held the rope; how could she be underwater? She realized with fatal certainty that the beast had cut the rope. She felt the tug of her ankle Chucks, the lead weights offering to let her race the shark to the bottom.

Something burst in her brain, bright and clear, and letting the Chucks take her down suddenly seemed like the dumbest thing she'd ever heard. Rita pulled on the rope, willing herself to clear the edge of the building. Cold silent water surrounded her as she pulled, her ears registering the *whoosh-whoosh* of her progress through the water. And something else, on the edge of her hearing, a rushing sound...

Rita pulled hard on the rope, made the edge of the window it ran through— and something *yanked* her out of the water, smashed her against the side of the building. In the blessed air for a brief moment, then back into the cold water. But this time her arm hooked on the ancient windowsill and she levered herself through with the manic energy of full panic.

Rita grabbed the slack pull-rope and yanked herself farther into the room just as a mighty commotion erupted behind her. A wave rushed into the room as the White followed her, thrashing against rusting desk skeletons and crumbling office partitions.

Rita screamed and screamed as she used the rope, her arms, her legs, anything to get space between her and the shark. She reached the anchor point of the rope and hauled herself out of the water. She clambered onto a Salvie shelf, knocking off a pile of anchor spikes and a bong someone had made from salvaged PVC pipe. Still the shark pushed toward her, crushing every obstacle in its path.

'Leave me the fuck alone!' Rita screamed.

The White ignored her and slammed through the metal beams that once held dry wall in place. The front half of the massive body rose over a pile of rubble and steel rebar, bloody teeth gnashing a foot away from Rita—

And then she realized that the thrashing had become something different. The top half of the shark's body wasn't sliding back into the water. It had impaled itself on a length of rebar grounded in the cement floor below. The White thrashed and thrashed, but couldn't free itself, couldn't get its gills back below the water. Foam and blood spattered Rita and she screamed again, the sound lost in the roar of water being pulverized by two thousand pounds of pissed off animal. After what seemed like an eternity to Rita, it finally stopped moving. The black eye stared at her and Rita felt her own vision dim.

As she wondered why she felt so weak, the insistent pounding from her foot registered on her. When she looked down, she couldn't understand what was hiding the front half of her left foot from her view. Then she saw the ragged edge of meat and bone, and realized what had thrown her out of the water. The shark hadn't missed as badly on that last pass as it had the first. Rita knew it would rather have taken off her leg, but at this point, her foot would do just as well to kill her.

But as Pops often reminded her, she'd inherited a stubborn

streak from a mother she'd never met. Rita untied the bandage from her hand and knotted it hard just behind the wound on her foot. Her trusty tool bag had stayed on her belt and she used a screwdriver to tighten the tourniquet until Rita and her foot both screamed in pain.

Rita laid back on the shelf to catch her breath. If she survived this, they'd carve her name into Tunny's wall for sure. Maybe even if she didn't. With that thought, she turned to the side and vomited her breakfast into the water. It only made things worse when a school of pipefish swam into the puke like it was a free feast.

Wanting to look at anything but that, Rita looked back the way she had come. Out the windows on the far side of the building, she saw the sun sinking behind the orange and white behemoth Tunny said they used to call Sutro Tower. She couldn't tell if the sun was going down faster, or if her vision was just going dim. *Probably a little of both,* she thought, as her eyes fluttered shut.

Some time later, Rita heard the voices calling her from the other side. Pops had told her those who loved us would be waiting when we passed over. She wondered if she'd recognize her mother's voice. At the moment, only male voices seemed to be calling for her. She opened her eyes to blackness and knew she was dead.

A bright light suddenly flared from the center of the room. 'Rita?' A man's voice called out.

'Is that you, God?' Being dead hadn't seemed to make her any quicker on the uptake.

'Dear Lordie.' She heard the voice whisper. A swirl of water around twin hulls and the light drifted toward her, growing into a hissing gas lamp. When she saw the pilot of the skimmer, Rita thought she'd gone bonky instead of dying. Tunny didn't go out on the water anymore. But it was him, all fatherly concern with wet eyes and a gentle nature Rita had never seen from him. 'You still with us, girl?'

'Appears so. But I think they'll have to let out my weddin' dress on one side to hide the fact I'm lopsided.' She gave him a weak grin as he lowered her onto the deck of his skimmer and looked at her in the light. When he saw her foot, his face went slack and that made Rita worry more than anything so far. He turned and swung his gas lamp near the window. When he shouted, his voice cracked with emotion. 'I got her, I got her! Start back now. And tell the Compound they need to bring their doctor!'

Lights winked on momentarily in other buildings, then winked out again. Running lights over open water at night was crazier than, well, than coming out on open water at night to begin with. Rita couldn't believe they'd all come looking for her. Tunny covered her with his jacket and put out his gas lamp. He gave a mighty pull on the guide rope and they glided across the water with more power than Rita could generate in three pulls. 'Am I gonna be okay, Tunny?'

'Course you are. Now hush, girl. We're gonna get you right as a summer rain, just you wait and see.'

Even in the dark, Rita thought he looked like a liar. As the blackness crept in again, she thought of Pops. She wanted more than anything to see him before she went, to hug him and feel the soft hemp fibre of his shirt against her cheek. To tell him she was sorry.

But she could still do without Fat Calvin.

Rita climbed out of the depths, the beast behind her, her hands raw on the rope, pulling, pulling, screaming as she felt the rush of water under her feet—

'Hush now, child. You're in my arms again.'

Pops' deep voice put her right at ease, right as a summer rain. In her bed again, safe here with him sitting beside her. 'Pops, I'm so sorry. So, so sorry.' She wept into his shirt as he pulled her against him.

'I'll hear none of it. You're a young girl yet and you speak your mind as such. I'm the elder here, so's I should be takin' them things into stride.'

'Oh, Pops.' Hot tears coursed down her cheeks as memories flashed at her. Scrambling feet carrying her on a makeshift stretcher, rushing past the gate of the Compound, faces drifting in and out of her vision like runaway moons. Tunny's crooked mouth, Flounder's flat nose, Hezra, the ancient doctor of the Compound, her brothers and sisters blurring into each other, except for Jersey's ruddy face. It struck Rita that she had never seen tears run down Jerz's face before this. You find out who loves you at the strangest damn times.

Of course Pops was there all along. Rita had rubbed her face in his shirt like a blind pup finding its mother, and he clung to her with a desperate strength that made Rita feel small for the things she'd said to him last.

Pops let Tunny stay the first night to see whether she made it through. In the morning, Rita had woken up feeling strong enough to bitch until Jersey brought her goodie bag and presented Tunny with the bottle of fancy whiskey. The big brawler of a bartender with the nasty knife scar had blubbered like a babe and hugged her so tight Rita heard her back crackle.

Someone cleared his throat and Rita realized she and Pops weren't alone in the room. She looked down to see Hezra putting the last touches on a new bandage around her foot. Pops had already stitched her hand up himself, in the old way as his folks had done.

Pops and Hezra exchanged a look that got Rita's dander up. Pity. She'd be damned if anyone was gonna—

She saw Fat Calvin standing in the corner, his wide-brimmed hat in his hand. He headed up the canning of food for the Compound, so his overalls weren't covered in field dust. His greasy hair lay flat against his skull and his sweaty cheeks shined as he smiled and nodded at Rita. 'Rita, my love.'

'Hello, F— uh, Calvin.'

Pops patted her hand and said, 'He's just here to see how you are. We don't have to talk about other things just now.'

Rita looked into his eyes. 'It's okay, Pops. I'll do whatever you want. I know what this means to you.'

Hezra closed up his bag and made ready to leave. 'Well, she'll take a while to heal, but I believe she'll recover true enough. 'Course she'll never be able to walk normal.'

Pops closed his eyes and put a hand on Rita's head.

From the corner, Fat Calvin smiled at Rita. 'That's okay, I'll still take her. Though my father might want to talk about the level of the dowry a bit.'

One second, Pops was sitting in his chair stroking Rita's hair. The next, he had the back of Fat Calvin's collar bunched in his fist, his other hand on the seat of Calvin's pants. The stammering young man landed in the foreyard of the longhouse amid the gasps of onlookers. 'She's too good for the likes of you, you soft-handed ninny!'

With that, Pops stalked back inside and plopped down beside Rita's bed. Shocked, she could only stare at him.

With a wry grin, he asked, 'Well, what shall you do now?'

Rita laughed like she hadn't since she was a little girl. 'I'm gonna travel the world, Pops.'

'Of course you are, my darlin' girl, of course you are.'

He kissed her forehead and Rita drifted off to sleep again, dreaming of plying the open waters on her black and white skimmer, old Tunny manning the sounding board to keep the Whites of Market Street at bay.

Shirtless in Antarctica

Justin Brooks

Sometimes I dream of a meadow. A small, peaceful meadow. Lying down in the grassy folds of its heart, I watch the sky peel off like irradiated skin. Its baby-blue hue bleeds down to Earth in weighty rain drops that resemble thick paint. Once there is nothing left of the sky to shed, the grass is drenched in aerial blue blood, and up above remains only the raw red flesh that lay beating underneath.

I never got good sleep. Since my teens, I'd wake up from dreams like that at least three times a night; the digital red numerals of my alarm clock burning bright through the surrounding darkness. Each unwilling reprisal greeted me with a new expression: 2:00, 5:00, 7:00 AM... I always made faces back.

Hunger willed me reluctantly out of the heavenly embrace of my bed. Escaping the floor's obstacle course of domestic debris in the dark was a challenge, but I emerged victoriously into the narrow kitchen hallway (only tripped on two things this time.) I don't believe in windows—a lot of bad things can come through windows, like cats and bullets and bombs and cars—so my humble abode becomes a vast stretch of shadow in a day's nether hours.

On the way through the kitchen's tight passage I picked a knife up from one of the counters flanking me. The dim wall-perched lamp barely illuminated it, so my fingers did the work, lightly tracing its fine edge in silent satisfaction: millimetres thin and at least two inches wide. The perfect tool for trimming animal brawn into the elegant pieces of bite-sized meal.

Out the kitchen and around a corner waited the door to my workshop, which opened with the creaks and shrieks of age. I flipped the light switch by the entrance to get a good view of the morning's ingredients. A fresh few pounds of meat squirmed feebly against the restraints of its chair; placed strategically in the centre of a spotless, white bathtub the night before. It was ripe and ready for me.

I made sure the knife was visible as I approached the tub's side. The meat's struggle became more relentless with each step, fuelled more by fear than any hope of escape. A tear glided down the smooth surface of its fair flesh before tangling into a patch of gruff, grey beard. I watched this happen a few more times as the tears kept coming. It was trying to provoke mercy and it almost worked, but I wasn't going to play its little game like the others had.

Instead, I brushed my hand up its side, slowly exploring the ridges of its ribcage with the forgiving fingertips of my left hand. The right hand had a different attitude, however. After the left hand withdrew from its merciful expedition, the right viciously thrust the knife in and out of the trenches separating each rib. The gaps were tight, it took a degree of wedging to go hilt deep, but soon he was a leaking cork of holes.

The squirming gradually eased along with the flow of blood as his heart sputtered through the final moments of its suffocation. His muffled screams shrunk to a low moan, barely audible through his mouth's duct tape penitentiary. I backed up to appreciate the whole scene: his eyes soon tilted up for an intimate view of inner-skull while the rest of his head tried to follow suit, bending back against his neck. Meanwhile, red rivulets flowed steadily down his torso—he looked like the sculpted centre of some satanic fountain. It wasn't long before the man died knee-deep in a tub of his own blood. The gashes still dripped out the thinning remains of his crimson sustenance.

There was no remorse in draining him dry of life. He wasn't fit for it, only manipulating its opportunities to satisfy selfish needs. The man had cannibalised five people before I could catch him vulnerable (never take a dump in the bushes, I might be waiting.)

As I played these thoughts in my head, I absent-mindedly retrieved a mug from one of the neglected tables in an equally lonely corner of the workshop. This room was to be avoided except for occasions like this. With the mug firm in my right hand's palm, I knelt by the side of the tub and took a gracious scoop of its pooling liquid. Some of it spilled over the cup's mouth and onto the back of my hand; still warm. Fresh blood always borrows the lingering warmth of its host.

It was hard to enjoy. The bad world outside had once again been rid of another toxic soul, but I felt like his sins were stored in the liquid discharge of his departure. There was no backing out now, though. The thirst won over and I shut my eyes to any second thoughts, narrowing my conscious to the thick slither of salty copper down my throat. Not exactly delicious. I retreated back to the privacy of the kitchen; it seemed kind of inappropriate to drink a dead man's blood in front of him. He wasn't good company, anyway.

So I drink blood. Please don't judge, it's kind of like recycling. These bad guys waste their life aiding themselves, so I give them the opportunity to actually help someone. While some people need their morning coffee, I need my monthly cup of Joe. Assuming all of my victims were named Joe, of course. See what I did there? I've been holding that pun for a while now, I hope you like it.

Also, sorry about all that elaborate 'the meat was ready to be carved.' That's just what I tell myself to get psyched for each meal. Never works, but I hope repetition will finally just set its message as an unconscious fact.

Anyway, back to the story, on the wall next to the kitchen table are etched the scars of my wanna-be calendar—a notch for every passing day. The notches were pretty abundant, becoming a sort of wicked wallpaper. I used a knife (other than the one Joe felt, by the way) to create the markings, and that knife now added another to the collection. June 15... I forgot what year it is. That doesn't matter, it's the day that counts. Time to enjoy it.

Guzzling down the rest of my gore, I rushed back into the workshop and began packaging as much of Joe's blood as I could. Cold blood lacks that key warmth, but it'll have to do for the next few weeks. I can't sit here hitting the drink all day like Dad would at his bars.

It took a while to wrap things up. First, that piece of trash

Joe didn't want to get into the garbage bag. You know what he gets for that, right? I was going to slip him into a bonfire tonight (How did the dead man get in there? Must've been one of those gangs again, darn.) The maggots can have him now for all I care. At least that's giving back to the environment, maybe I should dump bodies that way more often. Never thought I'd worry about being green while killing people. Second, the generator outside had another heart attack, so I had to feed it some more gasoline and pat it alright before storing the rest of the blood. The thing is as demanding as a baby so I treat it as such. At least it doesn't poop.

The tub would have to be scrubbed clean later, the patience the task required wasn't present, and I really didn't want to stain my PJs again. That stuff never comes out. Even if you can bleach the stain, the smell is still there. Trying to go to bed with that scent is like if you were to lie down next to a nice fire-grill armed with your severed limbs. Hideous. The odour jams itself up your nose, squeezing through that slim conduit to your brain and roasting the night's dreams into a restless clown-house. I really hate clowns.

So after filling a fair amount of plastic with slushy red, I avoided the tub and exited the garage. Back to the bedroom and up to the closet door, I opened it to greet Mother. I met her gaze through some spare slits in the hanging wall of jeans, shirts, and coats. Just two green eyes floating in the dark; their owner fully clothed in shadow. They watched as I selected a pair of holed jeans to complement a brown and red t-shirt (red in swirls not through design, by the way, but I like pattern anyway.) It was summer; all I needed was a little bit of clothing to cover up the itching scars.

'Elaine, you shouldn't wear rags like that. You're too pretty for them, way prettier than the other girls,' she was no more than two feet from me, but her voice was faded as if spoken from a few yards away.

I stuck my tongue out at her, 'All the other girls are dead, Ma.'

The eyes disappeared. I closed the closet door.

I wonder if Tom's Mom still talks to him? He's a strange

case, but I'm pretty sure we're best friends. I'm really not sure what I think of him, everything we do is so lax that a serious discussion of emotion would be indecent. Not that a deep, tearful purge of feelings is something I look forward to. I don't think I've ever given a hug, and the last time I received one was years and years ago.

Still, Tom is part of my life. I always find an excuse to see him should a day go by void of his companionship. That almost never happens, though; he needs me to help him hunt food. I have a knack for sniffing out the smell of blood as you may have guessed. He doesn't know why though, and he should never learn about my occasional cups of Joe. Don't tell him, alright?

This makes me recall one of the hunting trips I spent with him a couple of months back. We were silently scoping out the wasteland in the prime of a spring day. The stealth was broken after I tripped over some stray rubble. The collision was loud, but my string of barbed curses bullied it away (along with any chance of game.)

'Shit, lady, where the hell's your mouth been?' that was Tom's response.

He wouldn't like the answer to that question. My little basement blood-drive has remained a secret to everyone but me and my victims. I'm sure Tom has his own little guilty pleasures, and there's no way I could judge him for it. I would never want to hurt him, but that lack of leverage feels vulnerable.

Out of the kitchen and up a wooden staircase that shouted its age under each step waited my front door. Its hatch was parallel with the ground above, and opening it flushed my ill-prepared eyes with a fury of white sunlight. The glare was harsh on the optics but gentle on the skin; dulled by a cool, caressing breeze. I focused on the dirt ground to prolong blindness, closing the hatch behind me and resetting the layer of dirt that had previously been its camouflage. The bad guys only get to see my place when I want them to. I'd seen too many stray people become prey out here.

It took about a minute for my eyes to tolerate the morning sky, but when they did adjust I saw the city outskirts decorate the horizon. Even next to this lonely highway three miles away you could see concrete slowly crumble off the steel framework of sky-scrapers; every new day dedicated a chunk to time's decay.

People lived in those buildings. Not because they were safe, but because they're familiar. Sure, the ceiling may fall on them in the middle of the night, but if it doesn't they get to wake up with a face-full of sun. I haven't awoken to the sun in years.

Tom's house was within the urban edge, and I had to cross a few streets to reach it. Some of the sad people peered out at me from behind the (relative) safety of their shattered shelters. Their faces were covered in dirt, the blackness broken in streams by the tell-tale riverbeds of dry tears. Everyone cried these days. Except Tom. The guy seemed almost too happy. He should share a little of that.

I stepped up to his sheet metal shack, debating whether I should ask him to donate, but instead just ended up making a harmony of knocks upon his rusted door. The rhythm was my password; something I knew that the bad guys didn't. That's one reason I liked Tom, he was just as paranoid as I was. We never wanted some Joe sneaking up on us.

The door had a wide slit reserved for peeks of the porch (which I so humbly stood upon), and its cover slid open; the void it left framed Tom's turquoise eyes.

'Hey, Elaine, what brings you to this corner of the Earth?' he spoke through the door, 'My beautiful lawn, huh?'

'What lawn?' I asked it innocently enough. A glance around made visible only a sole patch of barren dirt.

'Yeah, I'm working on that. Don't rush me. So why are you here?'

'It's my birthday, Tom.'

'Ah shit,' that part came out low; a swift whisper. He desperately reinforced the rest of his words to radiate false confidence, 'How could I forget? Because I didn't.'

'Sure, Tom.'

'Wait here a second.'

The door's view-slit closed with the raspy cough of metal on metal, and Tom's eyes vanished behind rust the colour of cauterised blood. His return saw the door turn on its ancient hinges (like my staircase, this age was painfully audible) as he stepped out by my side on the porch.

'Where are you off to?' I asked. He was in a full hunting outfit: a faded grey duster tattered down the muscle-wired length of his body from the wide support of his shoulders. The coat was a scroll of survival: tears, rips, cuts, and even the neat bites of bullet holes were all frequent in the fabric. Despite all the damage, it was thin enough to encourage agility while still maintaining protection from nature's basic elements. And misfortune, too, apparently. Whenever asked, Tom would proudly boast that good luck was sewn into every single thread. Sucker.

I also noticed his belt holstered an array of blades and that his bolt-action rifle was slung over a shoulder.

'It's your birthday. Let's get you a cake,' he smiled at me.

And thus we were whisked away by the winds of adventure: today's episode a raid of the local supermarket.

'I snuck in there a couple of days ago and saw a few of their refrigerators were still working,' Tom explained.

'The power still works in there? Sounds like a trap.'

'Hey, I'm not that stupid, I checked it out. A generator outside had been rigged to the thing, but I think it belonged to one of those nomads. Must've moved on a few days ago because the generator had just a sliver of juice and everything was cleared out. Inside the fridges was... well... there was a dead guy in there. I guess he locked himself in. But I'm sure none of his blood or anything got on the cake that was next to him.'

I've never tried it as a topping. Maybe that'd make it easier to get down.

'Dead dude cake? That's nasty,' I gave him one of my exaggerated expressions, this one leaking disgust.

'Hey, if there is any blood, I'll lick it off for you,' he surprised me.

'....Really?' there was such hope in my voice.

'Just kidding! But I will cut off any piece of the cake that looks a little soggy. A carved cake is better than no cake, huh?'

'Yeah... sure,' my tone was deflated.

The conversion sort of withered away after that—I was too depressed to carry it to a comfortable end. I was always getting depressed though, so Tom just shut up accordingly. Speech would only distract from the beauty of the ruins around us anyway.

Walking through the remains of the city, we were currently in a district dubbed the 'Rib Works.' My uncle came up with that one back when he was still alive. He always had good names for everything.

This name fit particularly well because this was an area of the city stripped bare of any resemblance to its urban past. The cement that once reinforced the thin strands of metal in each building's framework had been completely swept away. Here and there, a chunk could still be found hanging on for dear life, but its eventual rot was inevitable. Maybe some realised this and just decided to give into death without all the struggle. Maybe that's why some people commit suicide.

The framework itself was a bit more durable, warped by wind but still rooted to the ground. The steel skeletons took on several new manifestations now. Some were just a scrap-yard mess: grimed girders twisted together in bows to produce sloppy yarn balls of rust. Others were more elaborate in their decay; mangled into shapes that faintly resembled other objects. Your imagination could make a whole art gallery out of this place. Like the way people used to look at clouds and project different shapes upon them. To the right was a make-shift centipede frozen in mid-wriggle, to the left was the shadowing exoskeleton of a great scorpion, and to the right again, what vaguely resembled an enlarged specimen of severed tongue paralysed in a final writhe of pain.

Right now Tom and I were passing under a sculpture my uncle dubbed 'Hell's Hand.' To make this monstrosity, the metal had twisted upward into the sky to resemble what might be an arm from the elbow up. At its skyward end the metal strands twisted off in five different directions, making up the palm and fingers of the Hand. They reached up into the virgin expanse of sky in a spiteful attempt to strip it of purity. Or maybe the Devil was just trying to dig his way up to the real world, which was now a more appropriate hell than anything he'd ever watched over.

Soon we were past the dismal art gallery, now on our way down a more intact street in a more preserved part of the city. This urban corridor was lined on each side by cratered structures, their decomposition a little more repressed than that of its neighbouring zone. On the fringes of this ghost town's heart waited the supermarket. A short but stocky building, it dominated a great plot of land, half of which was consumed by a parking lot. We crossed that mote of concrete, full in its emptiness, to get to the store's front door. Tom seemed slightly unsettled; he stopped with a grimly straight face.

'What's the matter?' I asked.

His lips parted slowly as he un-slung his rifle, 'I closed the doors on my way out.'

The automatic doors, paralysed for a great passage of time, had been yanked apart to allow a chill air to yawn out of the darkness beyond. The sunlight to our backs illuminated a few patches of the store's lobby: an empty shelf there, the ravaged bones of a check-out station here, the brown shreds of plastic shopping bags strewn across the dry-tile floor.

I turned back to Tom, 'Didn't leave it like this, huh?'

His eyes wouldn't stop scanning the darkness, as if he could actually see through it, 'No… you know what kind of a neat freak I am.'

He never let me inside his shack, but I still never doubted the hygienic paradise that must be within. I once dropped a candy wrapper on his boot, which he promptly picked up and threw back at me without the slightest flicker of guilt.

I could tell he was nervous, 'I don't need a cake, Tom. Here, let's go back to the Rib Works and I'll teach you how to climb the scorpion's tail.'

'No, we'll be fine. I'm sure they've left by now.'

'Then why don't you put away the gun?'

'Just in case.'

I whipped out my switchblade as I followed him over the threshold of the doorway. Tom turned around to address me with a raised right eyebrow. As far as he knew that thing was only used to scare away some of his rabid neighbour kids. I'm not sure he's ever seen me gut someone before, but I'd been assured of the knife's lethality in the past.

'Just in case,' I repeated his words with a smile of reassurance.

He shrugged. We both moved swiftly through the shadows of Aisle 1 ('Cereal and Breakfast!' as the sign above stated.) That sign had claimed we would find several items, but now there were only bare shelves. The dark's optical oppression gradually lifted as my eyes became accustomed to its illusory mask. What was once just a tease of silhouettes became absorbed with the promise of detail.

The absence of light wasn't complimented by a lack of sound; down the aisle echoed the light tones of casual conversation, which became louder the closer we approached. Tom, hearing this and hoping to hinder the soundtrack of his footsteps, slowed into a catlike creep.

I followed suit and soon we were at the aisle's open end, with Tom peering around its right corner. Stray orange light flickered faintly on the far wall, cast by what could only have been a candle or oil lamp.

The conversation was clarified by our approach: two men going back and forth:

'So, what did you do to him afterwards?' said a gruff voice.

'He cried. Begged me not to hurt his family. 'Take me instead! Wah! Wah!' I cut out his tongue, I just couldn't take the noise anymore. The funny thing was that he still tried to talk me away from his family, tongue-less and all. Tried so hard,' this came proudly from a huskier source.

'But you didn't stop there, right? That's going too easy.' Gruffy was interested.

'It was years ago, man, only a few months after the bombs went off. You'd really have to ask his family. I can't remember what I did, but whatever it was must've been bad; they all cried harder than Tongue-less.'

And such was another fine specimen of the post-war human race. I think that's another reason I enjoyed Tom's company; he wasn't constantly gunning for my throat. Just now he turned and put his face in front of mine.

'Four of them. Two asleep, two on watch,' the words

arrived soft as clouds to the point I struggled to make them out, 'We're leaving.'

I wasn't about to argue, the odds were against us. Still, disappointment wallowed in the cavity of my chest: those were the kind of people I'd invite over for a drink.

We backed away just as Husky was trying to remember if that was the family he forced to bury his victim alive, or the one he had forced to burn his victim alive.

'Audience participation makes everything better,' he said with a chuckle weighed down by his deep voice.

'You're a sick fuck, mate.' Gruffy commented.

'Hey, if I hadn't of done it to them, someone else would've. Suffering is everywhere, my friend. If you can learn to enjoy it you'll lead a happy life,' Husky was a philosopher.

He was right, though. As disgusted as I was by what he did, I understood. Because at that very moment I wanted nothing more than to make him suffer, draining slowly into my tub, watching helplessly as I continued to cut his life away. And I didn't completely want it for the justice of his victims. It made me feel good to want to hurt him. The horror these people show when they realise how powerless they are is delicious. They're so used to being the ones that deal out the pain that when the situation is reversed, they can barely utter words. And when they do they're usually very mean. I guess that's where I get my potty mouth from.

While my mind was mesmerised with this inner-revelation, my muscles responded automatically to Tom's fleeing movements, matching them subconsciously. Sunlight reached out to us from the store's open entrance, a scared mother about to reclaim her lost child. The warmth filled me inside-out, and when it was interrupted by two silhouettes in the doors' threshold, I was dumped abruptly back into the cold's frigid grasp.

Tom stopped and had to halt my torpid approach with an outstretched left hand. The two new visitors pulled the automatic doors shut behind them, and it became clear that the store's new residents had painted over the previously transparent windows at some point. We were wrenched from Mother

Sun's grasp with the shriek of the closing doors, dragging reluctantly against the floor.

We waited there in the darkness for a moment or two, eavesdropping on the new conversation that tumbled down the length of the aisle. The two hadn't noticed us in those brief seconds of sunlight.

'So what do I tell them?'

'They'll be pissed no matter what.'

'You gotta tell 'em for me, man.'

'What? I wasn't the one that stomped the living shit out of those rabbits.'

'I had to, man... they started talking to me... telling me to cut off my skin and feed it to them. They wouldn't stop,' the speech was frantic and distorted, much like their owner's mind.

'You are one crazy motherfucker, you know that? I think it's about time the rest learned that, too. I've been keeping your secret for too long; I'm tired of hearing about your little flirts with the walls and rabbits and whatever else 'talks to you,' said the one I now dubbed Dickhead.

'Wait, man, what are you saying?' Crazy was on the verge of crying.

'Hey, you just pissed away the day's meat. I'm not going back there empty handed. Maybe if you're easy about it I'll convince them to knock you out first. Like we did with Jeff.'

One set of footsteps began to echo down the aisle. In pursuit was a desperate cousin, undoubtedly that of Crazy. I could vaguely see their frames, detail-less in the dark but growing with proximity.

'Please, man,' he was definitely sobbing now, 'You saw what they did to him.'

'Yeah, well so did you. I didn't see you flinch a bit as we handed you his shin. Now get the fuck off me-,' he cut himself off.

A spectrum of blinding light encompassed my vision, Dickhead had just turned on a flashlight that now spotlighted our presence.

'Who the-,' the crack of Tom's rifle cut Dickhead off this time. His speech drowned in the pool of blood filling his now open throat, producing a struggled gurgling. The flashlight hit the floor with a solid clang, painting our feet in its ghostly gleam.

In the same instant I heard Tom realign the bolt on his rifle, punching a new bullet into its barrel with a metallic snap. More noise flurried from behind us; the store's sleepy encampment rustling to action in response to the gunshot. Crazy audibly scrambled back down the aisle to the relative safety of the lobby's aphotic vista. Right now that didn't seem like such a bad idea.

I nudged Tom with an elbow, 'Hey, let's get out of here!'

He began to move toward the lobby in agreement when a fountain of lush red light ballooned out of our periphery. Turning revealed a flare, hot red embers sparking from its enkindled tip, held high above a man's bald head. Below this virtually hairless scalp squinted a pair of dark eyes, complimented by the stupor of an agape mouth, plied apart by surprise.

'Who is that?' the jaws un-slackened to churn the question out. It was Husky, and he wasn't alone. Behind him skulked three others, the emanation of the flare painting their faces in eccentric shades of red. Their expressions were hollow save for anger, the ragged clothes adorning them were dotted in a crust that was probably blood (it was impossible to distinguish for sure under the flare's cardinal dance), and their weapons were gripped tight. They didn't have guns, instead relying on the intimate brutality of melee tools: in one hand hung a baseball bat spiked with bent, black nails; another hand gripped the hilt of a machete, its blade rough with dirt and disease.

Husky smiled at us, his black gums struggling to grip the remains of his rotting teeth. Licking his lips hungrily, he stuck two fingers in his mouth and whistled an abominable tune that screeched to piercing octaves. Those waiting restless behind him leapt out, weapons swinging.

They only rushed to their doom as Tom lit his own flame beside me. He had stuffed a drunk rag into the mouth of some old liquor bottle; the rag's exposed end flickered to life with the persuasion of a match. He tossed the Molotov

Cocktail at the assaulting herd, and the explosion swallowed them in a scraggly patch of flame. The roar of the fire added a sort of distorted harmony to the tortured screams rising out of its belly.

'Time to go!' Tom yelled at me.

'Well yeah, man, shoot the glass!'

The recent bonfire sprinkled illumination across the front doors' opaquely black windows. There was the crack of a rifle. One of the windows shattered apart, buckling under the force of Tom's bullet. A second crack. Now both windows lay fragmented on the floor, and our grateful Mother Sun frantically flowed through the new gaps with her rays, that like caressing fingertips cooed away the cold, stale supermarket air lined with the stench of cooked flesh.

I reached back to it, the light was so inviting. Tom was right behind me. And then he wasn't. As soon as we made it out of the aisle his hazy form slipped from my periphery.

Spinning around, I took in the scene rather well for what it was: Crazy had Tom pinned to the floor and was raking abnormally long fingernails up and down his sides. Great trenches in his flesh cascaded over with blood, contributing to a gathering puddle under the two. Meanwhile, Tom had his hands full around Crazy's jaws, keeping the biting teeth away from his face. Crazy's breath was so tainted that it visibly resembled a green cloud of algae. That gas poured out onto Tom, and he looked like he was going to pass out any second—either from the smell or the pain.

In a second—less than that—I was standing over Crazy's scalp (which was the sick colour of shed snake-skin) with my switch-blade in hand. My arm was pulling back, ready to deliver the blade into the back of his head, when a burning pain erupted from my own. My hair was getting pulled cruelly backwards, resulting in the loss of my balance and consequent fall to the floor. The ruthless tugging didn't stop there as the perpetrator dragged me back across the cold, tile floor. Tom and Crazy faded away fast with distance. I finally turned a corner into the lonely intimacy of one of the aisles, and was spun around on my back; whoever the attacker was wanted me to see them.

Husky smiled down at me with that grin of his—that grin that was likely to rot off any day now. I still had the switch-blade, and I thrust it up at him. It was a pretty powerful strike, but futile nonetheless, as he anticipated it and grabbed my wrist, pinning me down with his foot so he could work with both hands. With his right hand he twisted my wrist with a crunch of shattered bone; with the left he caught the recently released knife. To free his hands, he thrust it into my stomach, and its slender, deep tooth bit through my nerves.

'Just calm down, sweetie. The more you move, the more it'll hurt,' there was that smile again. A smile of satisfaction— domination pleased him.

That smile was delightfully wiped clean from the bumpy slate of his face as I gripped the front of his stained shirt and pulled his throat close.

'What are you-,' he was silenced by the sickening crunch of my chomp on his jugular.

Warm blood poured thickly onto my tongue and spurted down the tunnel of my throat. Husky struggled away in horror—the horror of helplessness I enjoy seeing in his kind—but I dominated his movement, holding him close, holding him still as more blood overwhelmed my taste buds. My skin prickled with goose-bumps, and I wanted to cough it all up really bad. I kept to the task, though; it was the only way out of this alive. At least I was used to the taste.

It took only a few minutes for his muscles to slacken, lethargic without their crimson coal. I removed my jaws from the ragged cavity pitting the side of his throat to take advantage of this; snapping his neck, removing him from this world with the flick of my (unbroken) wrist.

There wasn't much time to savour the rush. Footsteps were coming. I shoved Husky's heavy corpse to the side before ripping the switchblade from my belly. Any pain was glazed over by the hum of adrenaline, allowing me to shoot up onto my feet and face the coming adversary.

Tom rounded the corner and any threat he represented was purely emotional: an assault of fear and relief. Relief: Tom was alive. Crazy hadn't made a meal of him. Fear: What if he sees Husky's body?

'Oh god is that all your blood?' he was holding a cracked flashlight, presumably Dickhead's, that lit me up. I squinted in its glare, but was more worried about the red liquid drenching my clothes. Some of it was mine, but most of it was Husky's.

'Yeah, it's all mine… I got shanked pretty good,' I hoped the lie sounded genuine. Husky's body was just out of the flashlight's range, but if Tom moved it slightly, his drained corpse would be naked of darkness. He instead lowered its gaze to face his feet, finally noticing the pain its light shot into my eyes.

'Let's get out of here,' he tried to limp towards me but collapsed during the delivery of his body. His weight was becoming too much for his bloodless legs. I couldn't see the damage, but Crazy had done a number on Tom before I was pulled away, and that had only been a few minutes ago. That's definitely time to lose a lot blood, the heart pumps as fast as it can until death.

I went down on both knees next to him, brushing a comforting hand up his chest. It was completely soaked.

'What are we gonna do?' he asked me, the words slurred slightly through the blood that began to soak his tongue.

'We're way up shit creek,' I put my arms under his back and began to lift, 'Time to get to shore.'

He probably thought he was screwed. I had different plans though, and supported his journey to his feet. When it was complete, I pushed his arm over my shoulder; my neck in the notch of his armpit which was damp with either sweat or blood. Maybe both.

We made the clumsy jumble to the front door, through its cracked windows and into the vast plain of parking lot beyond. This lot became the sun baked canvas of our desperate charade. We'd take a few steps. Tom would fall. I'd help him back up, we'd lean into a few more steps, and then find ourselves leaning into the ground. It was like that all the way back to the Rib Works before we finally collapsed for good under the scorpion's steel skeleton. The children of the sad people, using some of the twisted frameworks as jungle-gyms, swiftly descended from their perches high above and scattered back to the wreckages of their homes. Our collapse wasn't Tom's fault this time, it was mine.

Husky had made a fair incision of my belly, and it had drained a trail of blood all the way to where we lay. My head was heavy with a lack of blood. Tom had taken advantage of this reprieve to finally pass out, and I knew I wasn't far behind. Looking up, I saw the scorpion stare down at me, its rusty tail bent high above, tipped with a tetanus venom. The disorientation attacking my conscious made it more life-like than ever; as my vision swirled around it, its joints skittered and danced over my head. The pinchers of its mouth snapped back and forth with excitement—some fresh meat had just delivered itself right onto its plate.

I descended into darkness; entering another session of captivity in the penitentiary of dreams.

The mushroom cloud on the horizon bloomed with the promise of death, its atomic touch ready to reach down any helpless throat for a finger-food feast of organs. The insides of the general population would be melted to a pink soup by the end of the week.

That was years ago, but the theatre of my dreams preserved it with the clarity of a present moment. The radioactive wind fiercely whisked away strands of my air, nipping at the flesh on my face until there was nothing left to hide my skeletal smile. At least that's what I wish had happened. No, I was one of the 'lucky' survivors.

Before my apartment building became part of the blast radius, my uncle burst from the door behind me, carrying me off the roof as the nuke's impact swept local civilization away in a dusty wave. We made it to the underground parking structure right as the wave arrived: a sick metallic twist screamed down to us from above. The building was in such excruciating pain, yelling out for help as the bomb crunched its steel bones into some insidious manifestation. Mixed in with this and the rumble of crumbling concrete were the screams of my neighbours. They couldn't escape fast enough.

We had to dig our way out of there a few days later: scraping the remains of apartments and their residents off our path to salvation. If salvation could even describe our lives after that.

Outside was a wide trench of road dividing the abundant rubble of surrounding city, as if God had desperately used a scalpel in hopeless surgery on His dying Earth. We followed this geological incision out of the city. I remember the afternoon sky was covered in swirls of caramel clouds; I wanted to fly up there and help myself to a thickly sweet scoop. There hadn't been much food in that parking structure—only one poorly stocked vending machine.

The road led us out of that city and through several more like it. Everywhere we went, death had arrived first. We found some nice people; they begged us to let them die in our arms. My uncle did this part for me, but those people were so sad. They were bleeding out all over the floor, skin peeled by the jagged blade of radiation poisoning, but their main fear was dying alone. We made sure they didn't. My uncle held them, but I grasped their bloody hands tightly. That was back when blood still disturbed me; I wanted to pull away so bad but forced myself not to. If I was ever dying like that, I'd want someone to hold my hand.

We met bad people, too. Desperate people, or just those that wanted to take advantage of civilization's weakened state to advance the pursuit of their own desires. They were sad too, but my uncle carved a smile on their face with his switch-blade—the same one I would later inherit and have stuck through my own body. Mom had said that he had lived in jail for a little while, but he didn't seem like such a bad guy. He took me away from Mom and Dad, for example. I remember that day too well:

'Hey, schizo, am I real or just in your head?' my father's breath reeked deeply of booze.

'Stay away from her, Dan,' Mom solemnly threatened.

He ignored her, 'Say your name, schizo. Say it!'

'Scizzo, shizzo…' my four year old tongue couldn't exactly mold the word.

'Look she can't even say it!' the scent of alcohol spewed intensely from his laughter.

'God damn it, Dan, I'm going to call Jonah! He's home down the hall.' Mom threatened again.

'Call that crazy bastard, he'll be her friend. You know, a real friend. You're all too crazy for me,'

In less than a minute Uncle Jonah was through the front door and dragging Dad into the kitchen. Mom tried to stop him, but he was too strong and merely pushed her out of the way, locking himself into that wide room with Dad. All I could see through the glass door were Dad's feet sticking out from behind the wall. They fluttered violently as he screamed and screamed and screamed.

Uncle Jonah came back out of the kitchen with a lot of blood on his hands, and Dad wasn't moving anymore. Mom was standing over him and crying.

'He'll live, but he may not like it. I made it so he'll never drink again—that's my gift to you,' Jonah had told her. He then lifted me up and told me that he was taking me somewhere safe.

The next few years of my childhood were spent hidden in another state, under his care. He made sure I went to school and got an education. Would be really pissed if I didn't read one book a month. He also taught me some things of his own.

'The Slam is kind of like school, Elaine. You're trapped in a little room for hours against your will, but you do walk out a little smarter than before,' he had told me one day.

He passed his prison lessons on to me: how to bleed someone out quickly, how to snap a neck, fifty bad places to hit a man that aren't his balls, etc. He told me that the world can be a scary place, and that I would have to be scarier. These tips were taught in the hope that I'd never need them, but then the bombs came down.

In the aftermath we roamed from place to place, searching for a part of the world that might've remained magically unscarred. That dream dried out after a couple months worth of searching.

'What are we going to do now, Jonah?' I asked him as we set up camp in one of the decaying buildings that decorated the day.

'Well, kiddo, I really don't know... we're shirtless in Antarctica,' he replied. *Shirtless in Antarctica*: that was his term for being the utmost screwed. Stuck in a freezing place naked of hope, protection, food, and soon life. And it was true, we had just run out of meat and water. Jonah wasn't about to resort to cannibalism like so many of the sad people already had.

He surprised me a few days later with a cup of cherry-hued juice.

'It'll taste kind of weird; it's way past expiration, and it was some bad flavour anyway. But drink up, your life depends on it,' his smile kind of sunk into his now gaunt cheeks, but I accepted its comfort nonetheless.

The juice did taste awful. As if someone had made it out of melted copper pennies and stirred in a couple of salt capsules. It kept coming, though, and I was too thirsty to refuse. All the while, my uncle began to look worse and worse; soon too weak to even stand.

'Elaine, I'm running out of juice. You're gonna have to find your own soon,' his hand was slowed by a lack of energy, but he still managed to press the hilt of his switchblade into my palm, 'Use that.'

'What? Why do I need a knife for juice?'

His wrist was wrapped in bandages, which he unwound to reveal the truth underneath. He had been cutting himself; the juice had been his own blood. I had been leeching life off Jonah for the past few days.

'You can't live off blood forever, it's toxic, but it'll keep you going until you can find some real food,' he continued. I could only watch, held from any action by either hunger or horror, 'You gotta leave me, kid, I'm dead weight now.'

But I didn't. Shock wouldn't allow speech for the following hours that made up the rest of his life span, and I held his hand tight the whole time. I didn't let him die alone. The next morning under a storm swallowed sky, I left our camp by myself. Rain that fell from the charcoal clouds above tided over my thirst for the next few days as I scavenged food and, occasionally, people.

I used to blame myself for his death. He'd be alive if I had died earlier. That's how I would've preferred it: Jonah living and me dying. If anyone had the optimism to rebuild civilization it would be him. He fed me his own blood if that's any symbol of his dedication. I've adopted the task of killing off as many sickos as I can. Their blood comes in handy when I can't find any more water (that's not as rare an occasion as you may guess.) I have no real plan for curing the world's craziness, though. I never really liked psychiatrists and couldn't imagine being one myself

A few years after Jonah's death I built my underground bunker from the remains of an old house: tearing down the first two floors until only the basement remained. Those underground passages are what I transformed into my happy home hidden from the rest of the world. The next year I would meet Tom, and my blood-drinking would be substituted by actual meat. His dad had been in the army before the bombs went down, and he put the inherited skills to good use.

My eyes beat vision through my battered brain in the first few seconds of awakening. My head, now a husk of pain, was comforted by a relatively fluffy pillow in a relatively comfortable bed. Above, the smooth planks of a wooden ceiling stared back at me instead of the metallic scorpion I had passed out under.

I had been moved. I jolted up in bed and was surprised when it didn't require a fight with restraints. In fact, this room looked more like a child's bedroom than a prison cell. The walls were painted several oceanic shades to radiate an aquatic atmosphere. Layered within the waves were a variety of sea-life, all captured by the artist in some fluttered swim.

Covering some of the ocean were pictures, elegantly framed in beige edges. Within the borders smiled a woman and a little boy, both content with the genuine pleasure of their camaraderie. Except it was obviously something more than that: the love between a mother and her child.

I got up out of the bed with stoic ignorance to the wound that tugged at my torso's nerves. The room's door was locked, but that wouldn't stop me. I yanked its doorknob off (Jonah taught me a specific technique for the task) and pressed lightly on its surface to get a crack of vision at the space beyond: A hallway lit dimly by a candle holstered to one of the warmly orange walls.

Faded voices were coming from down the hallway, and I pursued them to another door at its end. This door had been cracked, as well, and Tom's deep voice became unmistakable as I listened further. I opened the door and walked silently into the room.

Inside, Tom lay on a bed I presumed was covered in his own blood. He looked a lot better, though. I noticed that my own wound was bandaged up and stuffed with enough Neosporin to kill even HIV. He was talking to an older women whose back was turned to me. Her hair was abundantly grey although a few black threads could be picked out here and there.

'Hey…' Tom saw me.

The lady turned to me and I recognised her instantly as the woman in the photo with the child. Maybe a decade older—couldn't have been more than fifty. Scars decorated her face but didn't obstruct the expression of relaxed facial muscles within.

'You feeling better?' she asked me.

'…Sure.'

'Good to hear. You must both be hungry, I'll bring in some dinner.'

After she left I turned back to Tom, 'You've got some explaining to do.'

'What? I just woke up a few minutes ago. She said she found us out in the Rib Works and brought us back here. I don't think she's going to hurt us. She spent enough work bandaging us up, after all,' he said.

It was true, but I still didn't like it.

'You think something's wrong here, I can tell,' he spoke again.

'Have you ever read Hansel and Gretel? The story where the witch takes care of a few kids just so she can eat them later?'

'That's not why I want you,' the old lady returned to the room with her blank slate of a face and a plate of steak.

'Why do you want us?'

'You're a very grateful bunch,' she sneered, 'But you're right; I do need you for something,' she paused, laying the bait for out curiosity.

'I don't think I taste that good, lady, I haven't bathed in a few weeks and I smell it righteously. I haven't even licked any part of my skin in fear of AIDS or something like that,' Tom told her.

'What?' then what he was implying hit her, 'I have enough cat food to last me a couple of months. Tastes like trash but I'd rather eat trash than you two,' I looked at the steak and noticed how it smelled. I was going to pass on dinner.

'I'm glad to hear it. So why do you want us?'

'Bait. I left those gang-bangers a nice little note with my address on it at the store you raided. Told them they'd find you both here,'

'No fucking way!' Tom said, struggling through his wounds to get up.

'I wouldn't do that, your bed is wired with a few pounds of C-4. It'll blow if you do more than sit-up, and even then I wouldn't risk that. I wasn't the military marvel my husband was, and I'm not sure I hooked it up right. Could blow at the slightest vibration.'

Tom stiffened up at that last sentence.

She turned to me, 'Don't take it personally, I'd really prefer to do this another way. But there is no other way. I've been tracking that gang you just hit for a while. You think that bunch was the whole package? 'No fucking way' as your friend likes to say. That was just a pocket. There's a lot more, and they're all on their way here for your heads.'

'So tell me why I shouldn't just lift Tom out of bed so we can all blow up in this room right now? Since we're all going to die anyway.' A really worried expression twisted up Tom's face at the sound of my words.

'If all goes well, we'll all make it out of here alive. We just have to go through at least fifty gang-bangers first.'

'And you're just going to single-handedly wipe them out?'

'No… you're going to help out. Your friend is too messed up to move, but you're doing ok. I saw that you were pretty nifty with that knife. Are you just as good with guns?'

The lady and I went to work out and around her little family house. It was reinforced solely by thin, wooden walls that'd buckle before any bullet, so my job was to make sure most of the gang didn't make it close enough to shoot. I had told her I never really used guns, but that I did enjoy setting traps.

The house was part of the city suburbs, but the buildings around it had completely collapsed and left a ring of a dirt clearing. When I asked the lady how her house had survived, she explained that she had blown the buildings up with C-4 explosives earlier in the week in preparation of today; she didn't want to give the enemy any cover on their approach. So I guess those weren't earthquakes a few days ago.

Sunlight was retreating below the horizon by the time my nasty surprises were rigged and ready to go. The lady owned quite an arsenal. She was busy laying it out on her dining room table when I stepped back into the house. Her husband used to be in some branch of the military (the lady didn't specify which) and had rushed home from his post when it had become obvious the bombs were going to drop. Brought as many weapons as he could: claymore mines, assault rifles, shotguns, sniper rifles, combat knives, grenades, and ammo boxes were neatly organised on top of the table. The lady was busy loading all of the guns.

'What happened to him? Your husband, I mean,' I glanced around and noticed another picture of the lady and the child, 'And that kid? Where are they?'

If looks could kill, her eyes would've shot nails through my head, 'There's a reason I'm going after this gang.'

I sympathised with a nod. Maybe the lady wasn't the psychopath she appeared to be.

'What do I call you, anyway?' addressing her as 'the lady' was getting mentally tedious.

She looked up from her task once again, 'I guess it doesn't matter if you know or not… just call me Mia. It's not my real name, but it's short enough that if you need me it'll only take a second to call it out. We can't waste much time when shit hits the fan,'

She's a real planner. 'In that case, my name is Eli.'

I stuck out my hand and after a little hesitation Mia gripped it tight. That was probably the firmest handshake I've ever received, and I had a feeling the strength might've spawned from guilt.

Her vital, blue eyes leaked a sort of regret, 'I'm sorry I had to drag you and your friend into this. I have to do this… why do they get to live if my little Elijah gets to die? I promised him there were no monsters in this world. I promised I would protect him.'

I couldn't say anything. A little taste of her pain had reached me upon Jonah's death, but he wasn't my son. And from what Husky had said back in the supermarket, this gang wasn't the kindest when it came to executions. So I just stood there and nodded. I felt bad for saying nothing, but there was nothing to say.

It was nightfall by the time the first of the gang arrived. The first of the gang to die. They trod over one of my trip-wires and unleashed Trap #1. Floodlights ringing the perimeter of the house ignited to exhilarating life. The gang bangers were now blinded and lit up for easy pickings (Mia and I were behind the lights' range, inside the house.) From one of the house's windows, Mia manned a heavy turret (I had asked her for its name; she replied with a flurry of numbers so I just referred to it as Jackhammer. Sounded like one, anyway.) Its bullets ate large chunks of the poor guys—within seconds the dirt outside was muddy with their blood.

Around eight or nine of them went down before Jackhammer was silenced by a shattering *CRACK!* Mia fell back from the window as gun fire tore it apart. The turret flew off the window pane and landed near enough that I could see a bullet had snapped it in half. A sniper was doing his job somewhere in the distance. Luckily he wasn't too good at it.

'Keep away from the windows, I think they've got sniper rifles.' I told Mia. She nodded and crawled into the dining room to acquire another weapon. Her belt was already heavy with pistols and knifes, but the good stuff was waiting in there.

Thunder erupted from outside as the gangsters hit Trap #2. When I had suggested we rig the place, Mia had introduced me to a couple of dozen anti-tank mines. With a shovel I had gone to work planting them in a ring yards away from the house. Soon we had a moat of explosives, ready to blow should someone be unlucky enough to step over one. Guess today just wasn't their lucky day.

Mia came out of the dining room with some brand of grenade launcher gripped in both hands. Definitely not their lucky day. She went to work blowing the battlefield to shreds; body-parts now flew among chunks of dirt. When her clip had emptied, silence only rang in from outside. Mia knelt down next to me, safely away from the window.

'How many of them do you think I got with that one?' For the first time I saw her smile. Good for her, she deserved this.

The silence was then cut by a shriek. It sounded like a she-beast banshee was coming for our souls, but as the walls around us enveloped in flame, I realised it was something much worse. The gang had a rocket launcher.

The blast threw us out of that room and into the next, but the affected walls ceased to exist now and left a gaping hole in our defences. It wasn't long before gunfire poured into the room. Mia and I rolled in opposite directions, away from the cavity between us. Once I had some cover behind an over-turned chair, I brought out a little remote I had stored in my pocket: Trap X.

It was supposed to be the last resort should everything go to hell. Seemed fit for the current situation. I mashed the remote's sole red button and listened as several warning sirens screamed out from around us. Mia had collected a bunch of the old wartime bomb sirens to scatter around various pockets of the field. It would only slightly annoy the gang, but it wasn't meant for them.

The gunfire stopped as screams rang towards us from the

gaping night. Looking out from behind my cover, I saw one of the gangsters get quickly dragged out of the floodlight's range. Gangs were one problem, but then there were the sad people burrowed under the world's concrete skin. Living underground in the drained veins of sewers and subways, these people rode life's harsh tide with a castaway loneliness. They couldn't look at themselves, the radiation had warped them beyond any past self-familiarity. This misrecognition wasn't skin-deep either, as all the pain seeped deep through their pores and eddied into the comfort of their mental faculties. They looked like monsters, felt like monsters, and became monsters.

Always reminded me of the vicious predators that had previously stalked African plains. I had once watched one hide in the darkness of a street's manhole, waiting like a trapdoor spider for some unsuspecting prey. It wasn't long before a guy, drunk on the alcoholic fruit of a good night's loot, stumbled past the manhole's mouth. The monster became the manhole's tongue as it shot out to cling on with pale, rotting limbs and drag the poor drunk into the swallowing darkness to be undoubtedly swallowed himself.

The sirens had been meant to summon them from their underground dwellings: loud sounds usually meant people, and people were food. The creatures were already taking away the gang members. A swarm of pale, tattered flesh overran them—the creatures would've scratched at their prey had their nails not rotted away, so instead they just bashed them out of consciousness with bony fists. Once a gangster was down, he was dragged away into the darkness outside the floodlights, back into the sewers to be subjected to whatever hell lay below (no one who'd ever gone down there had returned sane, if they returned at all.)

'Time to go!' I shouted to Mia. Once the gangsters had been picked clean from the field, we'd be next.

'Go get your friend.'

'What about the C4?'

'What C4?' she smiled again.

Damn. I made my way to the bedroom and picked Tom up from bed.

'No, don't!' he shouted as I helped him to his feet. He relaxed as I pushed him up without triggering an explosion.

'We're all good, but only if we get as far from here as possible. Hey, Mia!'

She stepped into the hall with an assault rifle in hand, 'Follow me.'

Mia led us back to the dining room and threw aside its one rug. Underneath was a flat, wooden hatch that blended in with the surrounding oak floor. She raised it up and handed me a flashlight.

'There was always an old service tunnel running below the house. Got abandoned long before the bombs, but no one decided to recycle it. I'm not sure if it's completely clear, but you'll have a better chance down there than up here,'

'You say that like you're not coming,' I told her.

'I'm not. I've got to make sure every single one of those bastards was wiped out,'

'Trust me, nothing in the area's going to be left alive—including you if you don't follow.'

'...Maybe it's better that way. I've made my choice,' she watched me reluctantly lead Tom down the hatch's staircase and into the dark tunnel below. I turned to look up at her one last time.

'It's been a pleasure, Mia.'

Her eyes communicated melancholy expressions, but I knew it wasn't because she had denied escape. In that moment, I deeply hoped God and Heaven existed just so she could see her family again. She closed the hatch after giving me another sad smile.

The service tunnel only spanned two directions: north and south. While I was out setting traps around Mia's house I had managed to recognize what district of the city we were in just in case the opportunity of escape ever showed its face. The place was just a few miles south of Tom's shack, so we were heading north right now.

The tunnel lacked any lights, but Mia's flashlight illuminated the cracked, cement walls closely flanking us on either side. They were bare save for the occasional pipes travelling along its length before heading into the ceiling or floor. Some spider-webs decorated the pipes in a few places, and I made a point of avoiding them. Radiation didn't just give people its twisted facelifts. It didn't seem to manipulate their size, but have you ever seen a four-fanged spider? I have. The venom gets altered for better or worse as well.

The journey looked like it was going to be pretty smooth until I noticed candle-light flickering up ahead from behind an open door in the tunnel's right side. I turned off the flash-light and set Tom down on the dusty floor.

'I'll be right back. I've just got to check this out,' I told him. Mia had patched him up pretty good. He was still going to die without any food, but at least he wasn't bleeding out anymore.

'Ok, just make sure you bring back dinner,'

'Whatever,' I replied as I started a cautious gait towards the light ahead. A little mouth-made tune hummed out softly from the doorway. I put my back against the wall next to it and peeked through the threshold.

Inside was a small room lit by an array of candles. It looked like a household kitchen: there was a stove at one wall, an oven next to it, several cabinets decorated another wall. A bathroom sink had been bolted to the final wall, and in front of it was a small table with enough room for four chairs to be placed around it. In three of the chairs were... things.

I know that's not very specific, but that's the only word I had thought of at the first sight of them. The room looked empty, so I stepped in for a closer look. The humming stopped, but I didn't notice it then. I was focused on the dolls—that was the word that did them the most justice. A bunch of brown, burlap sacks had been sewed together into the form of life-sized humanoids. They each had burlap arms, legs, a head, and stitched joints to bring them all together. One was masculine in form, another feminine, and the last was small enough to resemble a child.

They were all sitting around that table, motionless as if waiting for supper. That's when I realised the humming had stopped. I turned to investigate and found myself starring

at a robed figure, covered head to toe in black rags. A hood
draped over its head but failed to hide the weak strands of
grimy, grey hair that hung out.

'I'm sorry…' I backed away. I was trespassing after all.

'*Please stay,*' the words were fought out. It sounded like
a women's light voice, but it was hard to tell through all its
rasp.

The figure gestured me toward the table with the dolls. It
pointed at the masculine one, '*Daddy.*' Then at the feminine
form, '*Mommy.*' Then at the child form, '*Tommy.*'

I noticed there was a picture on one of the walls. It was of
a girl who couldn't have been out of college, smiling pleas-
antly through bangs of blonde hair.

Following her gestures, I pointed to it, 'Is that you?'

The figure didn't reply as it took the last free seat at the
kitchen table. It looked at 'Mommy' before speaking again,
'*Dinner?*'

She got up and went to the stove on the far side of the
room. She had a whole sack of skinless, raw meat from god-
knows-where. It was then that I noticed the cartridges of rat
poison spread around the room. Guess I was skipping dinner
again.

'I'm sorry I dropped in, I'm just going to go now if you
don't…'

'*Please don't!*' the desperate tone of her voice could've suggested I was her executioner.

'I won't, I won't…but why?' the question seemed fair
enough.

'*I haven't had visitors for years. The last ones weren't too nice.
Are you nice?*'

'I like to think so.'

'*Don't joke! The last visitors joked around and now Daddy's
dead!*' she almost fell back after shouting this. She kind of
cringed forward and began sobbing before running over to
the Dad doll, '*I'm sorry, I didn't mean that! You're not dead, I
didn't mean it!*'

She stood there nodding for a few seconds as if the doll
were talking to her, then calmed down, '*Thanks, I'm sorry.*'

She turned back to me, '*Daddy was kind and let a few men*

*in a long time ago. I knew something was wrong with them—
they had a lot of knives—but Daddy said that was wise in a
world like this. He said we were lucky to have this shelter, and
that it would be wrong not to share.*

'*So we shared. I woke up the next day and Daddy and
Mommy and Tommy were bloody. The men were laughing. I
ran out yelling but wasn't strong enough. They began to carve
and carve and carve. But Daddy was still strong. I thought he
might've been dead but he got up and hit them. I finished them
off for him. And then I found Mommy and Daddy and Tommy
some new skin,*' she patted the nearest doll's burlap covering.

'I'm... sorry,' It was another one of those moments where
you wanted to say something but just couldn't.

'*It's ok, we're all happy now. Do you want some supper?*'

'No, I got some stuff waiting at home. Speaking of which,
my friend outside is really having a bad day, and I'm not sure
how long he's going to last so I have to really go. Do you
know a quick way to the city outskirts from her?'

I still couldn't see her face but her body language communicated sadness. She helped anyway, '*Daddy says I shouldn't
keep you. You do seem like a good friend, though. Please visit
again.*'

'Of course,' I'm not sure how sincere I was. All I knew was
that I really didn't want to piss her off.

'*There's an old service elevator in the back of the house. It'll
take you to the surface. You don't want to keep going down the
tunnel... scary things live farther down there.*'

I really didn't want to meet whatever scared her, 'Thanks...
I'll be right back,'

I backed out and found Tom again, 'Brace yourself,
alright?'

'Huh?' he said as I dragged him up and supported his walk
into the room, 'What...?'

'What a comfortable place,' I cut in smiling like a chap,
'Where's that elevator, again?'

'*Follow...*'

She led us out of the kitchen and through several other
rooms furnished to resemble those of a family's home.
Pictures, dressers, TVs—the works. Soon we found the big

service elevator and climbed on. The robed girl stood outside by the lever and got ready to pull.

'Please visit.'

I only nodded. As we began our ascent I caught a shift of movement by the door to the elevator room. It was only a glimpse, but it looked like the three dolls were standing by the doorway, waving.

It wasn't far to Tom's shack. We arrived just as the horizon hefted dawn above its head; the first morning after my 22nd birthday. I made sure to always keep updating my home-made calendar; the days would just blend together without it.

The sun was shining through the hollow buildings' broken windows, casting mystically twisted shadows across our path. The street used to be scattered with rusted, old cars but those had been scavenged away over the years. A car's hull makes a decent home, I know that for a fact. There was of course always chunks of building debris you'd have to worry about tripping over, but even those were being scooped up to complete rudimentary cudgels.

Tom told me that was the reason he built his shack with sheet metal. It was battered and wouldn't take a bullet or three. Pretty useless compared to all the concrete littered across the city. That, and it was small enough to be an outhouse.

We walked up to the shack's door, its grey sheen was dulled by dirt smeared on by some past storm's savage fit. He gave me the three keys that would finally open its insides to my eyes. It took me a while to unlock all the chains (wrong key here, wrong key there), but finally three satisfying clicks rewarded all the effort. I opened the door to reveal... a toilet.

'It really is an outhouse?' I dropped Tom right on the floor. When I finally realised this, 'Oh shit, I'm sorry!'

'It's all good, I was about to ask you to set me down anyway,' he crawled over to the toilet and took a seat.

'What are you doing?' I asked,

He stretched his arms out in each one's respective direction and pointed back to his sitting figure, 'What does it look like?'

'I can't believe this...'

He pressed down on the toilet's grimy flush lever, and all of a sudden the shack's floor rumbled out of a slumber. The sound of cranks and machinery echoed up from below. I watched as the floor began to sluggishly descend—toilet, Tom, and all—into the depths. It was an elevator. Tom's smug smile only confirmed it.

'You're a sneaky, little...' I left the insult hanging as I jumped in after him.

'Please close the door behind you. I need my privacy,' damn that smirk. I closed the door anyway.

After about two minutes we arrived at the secret floor a few yards below. A gas generator much like my own (but without all the noise) was connected to the elevator and overhead lights through several black tendrils—wires. The place was beyond spotless, almost sparkling, and comfortably furnished by an array of couches, chairs and other must haves of the nuclear family.

'Hope you like it, I try to keep it organised.' he said as he limped past me.

'It's nothing special,' it was probably the most beautiful thing I had seen in ages.

Tom only managed a few limps before collapsing to the floor. I rushed over to kneel down beside his panting form.

'Think you should give the exercise a break for a while, champion,' I mimicked his sly, little smirk.

'Too many lunges... my bedroom's in there,' he pointed to an open door a couple of feet away.

I lifted him back up and hauled him onto his queen-sized bed. The place was as spotless as the previous chamber. Various paintings decorated the walls with their sad swirls of blue or eccentric flurries of orange.

'I don't know what's the better question: How you got all this stuff, or how you got it all down here?'

'It was a challenge, but I don't regret a thing,' he smiled a little, 'This'll be a comfortable place to die.'

'…funny joke there, my man,' my expression showed anything but humour.

'Oh come on. Look at me, I've lost enough blood to drown a small child, and there's no way I'll be able to hunt. There's no food around here anyway,'

'I can hunt fine,' I was kind of pissed.

'I know you can, but that's not what's important. There's no water; the little pond a few miles away finally dried up. I was going to tell you yesterday but seeing as it was your birthday and all…'

'I'll search for another,'

'Don't kid yourself. That spirited old lady in the house was a good doctor but not good enough. Have you checked your cut recently?'

I looked down at my shirt. Its side was drenched in blood. I pulled up the soaked cloth just enough to see the wound; open and unprotected. The bandage could've been pulled off at anytime in the past few hours; I took a bazooka hit after all. Pulling Tom across town didn't do anything to relax the injury either. I guess adrenaline must've made me stoic to its presence, but now that I noticed it my head did feel dizzy. Really dizzy. And when was the last time I had a sip of water?

'Have you felt your lips?' upon his words I licked my lips only to greet rugged, cracked flesh that burned against the slightest moisture. Good thing my mouth was almost dry.

Tom continued, 'I've searched around here for other water sources knowing the pond wouldn't last. Found nothing. And I've searched the whole city and a few miles around it. I was going to suggest we both move, but I don't think that's going to happen anytime soon.'

'I thought you were the optimist.'

'Hey, this is good for me. I could've died a couple of times yesterday, but I didn't because of you. So I've chosen YOU,' he laughed a little at the exaggeration of the word, 'You stay around here for a while until you feel better. And if I'm still better you can save me one last time. But if I happen to close my eyes for a while, don't sweat it. I'm real tired anyway.'

I wasn't too sure how to respond. He just laid there smiling at me with his foolish grin. He knew his fate was sealed but was trying to soothe it all over for me. So I did the only thing that seemed right: I smacked one of his boots and promptly strode out of the room with a face redder than all the blood caking his chest.

I sat against the wall on the other side of his room weighing out the options. I wanted to go out to find water but Tom was right. I could tell I'd only last about a mile outside before collapsing for good. It was getting hard to focus, but I went at the task ruthlessly. Finally I realised a solution. I smiled sadly at its irony and pulled out my switchblade.

'Here's a cup of juice. It might not taste right, it's old and salty, but it's all you got. Drink up,' I handed him a mug a few moments later, its red contents sloshing over its mouth during the transfer. The whole time I kept my left arm behind my back, hiding the recent cuts draining its wrist.

'Where'd you find this?'

'Cook's secret recipe,'

'Well, I won't argue. You're a genius after all. Make sure you get some yourself, you're starting to look a little more weak.'

I left his room again and prepared another cup. I made sure to mix in the ash that had gathered on my clothes earlier in the day to mask the taste and scent of the stuff. Tom, being a hunter and all, would recognize it pretty easily otherwise.

I'm not sure how long I'll last. Everything is slipping away from me: vision, hearing, happiness, sadness... care. It's like I've slipped into apathy's hot tub; I have no desire and it's the best feeling I've ever had. Restful. I'd always been so tense in the past. Not now.

The only chore I forced upon myself was the continual cutting. The blood had to keep coming, Tom would need it. He was already looking stronger; sooner than later he'd be able to hunt at least a rabbit. Then he wouldn't need me, and I'd probably be gone by then anyway. Malnutrition is his worst enemy at the moment; the blood won't take him far, but far enough to fix things for himself.

My uncle saved me the same way. I told you I couldn't think of anyone else prepared to save society. That still hasn't changed, but I might as well donate to the one person that keeps me rooted to this world. Tom would be depressed for a long time, but he'd trudge on with his walking stick of natural optimism (he did just smile as he told me he was dying.) If I lost him I'd probably stay in my room forever feeling bad for not doing anything about it. So here I am doing something about it, and it feels pretty damn good.

Thanks for reading my little autobiography. Kind of funny that this would be considered some sick horror story in the past, but I'm afraid this is my life. At least it'll be over soon. I'm going to hide these pages somewhere Tom won't find them. I know it seems silly, but I still don't want him to know about my secret. If you ever run into him, just don't tell him alright. Take care, whoever you are. I'm just going to close my eyes now. Lifeis exhausting.

Under the Green Witch

Colin Sinclair

A good crowd, this night.

Frost loiters off one side of the makeshift stage, watches while Kale runs through his Typical Guru Business.

Sixty, seventy citizens at least are bunched up in front of a waist high pile of flattened earth, all of them quiet and listening careful. Not all of them are scavver kids from the island neither, so whatever Kale's doing out here, it's building something. No question there. They gather for the moving pictures, stay for the deep chat after.

Skies are smooth and dark above and everything beyond the glow of chem-sticks and barrel fires is shading purple into nothing. Frost can't see much of the ruined towers out beyond the deadground.

Shit, she can hardly see the island from here.

'What's my motivation?' says Kale—edge of the stage now, looking to every eye—and the crowd leans forward hushed and waiting.

Kale points behind him. Nadine and Tone flanking the stretched taut white sheeting that served as a show-screen early on.

'You've seen the vidclips. All those scattered images of the Before. When people—some people—found time to do more than worry about food in the belly and a roof overhead.'

Nods and mutters in the gloom. No argument from Frost.

'Actors on a stage,' Kale continues, moving back and forth, hands clenched, using the space. 'Strutting their stuff on screens like ours. Telling their fantastic tales of wonder and woe.'

He's getting to the point now. Frost has seen it all before.

'Because they didn't live it they needed to ask: what is my motivation? Why am I doing this instead of that? What are my needs and wants?'

Kale stops marching up and down.

'Vital questions. More than that: an important lesson for us all.'

He's holding the focus of the audience. They're quiet except for breathing. Solid and still.

'Do this one thing for me…'

Scarcely a sound from any of them and it's all good. Except-

'…just one thing…'

Too much crowd for the shotgun, Frost has her pistol in hand and one-step-two-

'…ask yourself…'

Night and darkness and the crowd narrow to this, here, now-

'…what have I done, what am I doing…'

Stiff neck, tan coloured coat, crowd's edge on her left-

Frost steps in as the man pulls up a weapon: glimpse of gleaming black, short barrel, long magazine-

Tancoat's deadeye gaze directed right at Kale-

Frost raises her pistol as that stubby gun swings round-

'…what's my motivation?'

Frost puts a bullet in Tancoat's chest, puts him down before he has a chance. Thunder blast brightness of the gunshot shakes her vision. Roar of the crowd and shouts and squeals and clamour as they run. Good-good. Long as they're running away, it's not her problem to solve.

'What are you doing!'

Kale, at her shoulder, still on the stage and shouting over the furore as his following scatters for home.

Frost doesn't look. She keeps her eyes fixed front and scanning all the approaches. Reaches up to grab a handful of Kale's jacket and hauls him off the stage. He's still shouting when he hits the ground.

'Quiet time,' Frost says, crouching in.

More protest. Squirming. Frost holds him tighter.

'You keep this up, Kale,' she says.

Was that movement over to the right?

'You keep this up and I'll let these fuckers kill you.'

Kale twists a little more then stops.

There's a definite solid shape, out there, sliding past the darkening horizon.

Far as it goes, this position has its good and bad, defensively speaking.

At Frost's back, the stage, Nadine and Tone will do what they can, and behind them the solid reassurance of the Green Witch. No-one's approaching that direction.

It's all up front. Wide almost-circle of flickering light; worn out oil-barrels packed with burning rags and wood scraps. Couple on the left are fading down to cinders and dust at this hour, a few on the right still blazing strong.

Left for shadows, or right for the cover of the smoke and flame?

Could go either way, couldn't it.

That's what makes the challenge.

That's what brings the buzz.

Of course, maybe they'll take a hint and skidaddy backways to the hole in the ground they crawled from. Easy to find better things to do than catch a bullet in the face, isn't it?

'How many are there?' Kale's voice is kinda muffled, result of being pressed face down in the dirt.

'Stay low,' Frost tells him. 'Hard target.'

Moment of silence whilst she scans the approaches-

'You didn't answer the question.'

Some people clearly don't want saving, right?

'I'll let you know,' Frost says. 'Whenever they're all dead, I'll be sure and take a moment to update you with a final count.'

Sort of a sigh from Kale. 'Soz, Frost. It's just. I mean. No-one's ever tried to kill me before.'

Welcome to the real world.

'I mean, not in particular,' Kale goes on. 'In the past there's plenty of goons and bulls have tried to chop me, but that's just average day-to-day. Don't need to tell you this, now do I?'

Welcome to life in the After.

Frost shrugs, but keeps her gun steady and pointed out there.

'You grow accustomed to it,' Frost explains. 'Also, figures

you got to be doing something useful, right, if people want to take you down and out?'

Kale mutters something Frost doesn't catch.

'It's either that or you're being an asshole,' Frost says, takes another look at the man she took out of the game.

From a quick glance, deadguy doesn't look familiar. He's sprawled out cooling and oozing a few feet away. The weapon near his hand is clean and neat. A temp-hire gun thug from any one of dozens of scattered holds and hideaways in the region? Best guess, that is, and no less true because it happens to be obvious. Now he's just another average joe with a ragged hole punched through his heart.

'Know that man?' Frost asks.

Kale twists his head around and snatches a look.

'No. Should I?'

'Don't matter. Private contractor. Nothing personal,' she tells him.

'I'm not feeling reassured.'

Frost shrugs. 'It is what is.'

A couple of things are clear.

They don't have overwhelming force or they'd be in her face already.

They could have cleankilled Kale from three maybe four hundred yards out if they'd had the required equipment and-or the relevant skill set.

So:

It's a support crew of two or three, armed with short stuff and hanging back waiting for an opening.

Fair enough. Makes things easier.

'Tone,' Frost says. 'You on my six?'

Gruff answer from somewhere behind her. 'You know it, doll.'

Tone's the driver, a somedays tech-guy, an old-timer with old-world attitudes. Thinks women should be soft and warm or some shit like that? Still, he can shoot straight—at range—and tends to carry an AKM rifle that don't take prisoners.

'Cover fire, silvy-play. In ten. At my eleven o'clock. You set?'

Some shuffling and a heavy click of safety-off. 'Set.'

Frost nudges Kale. 'That shell-scrape ditch over there. When we get in I want you to lay flat and hug dirt till I get back.'

'Wait. What?'

'If I don't come back. Good luck and-'

'I don't understand what you're saying.'

'I'm saying. Run.'

Frost is already moving, dragging Kale along with her, when Tone opens fire.

Distinctive crack-crack, crack-crack rips open the silence of the night.

No looking back. Just hop-skip-jump and slip-sliding dive into a dust dry trench about two foot deep and thirty long. Concealed behind a spoil of dug earth and caught at the flickering edge of oil-barrel light.

Final rumble of reflected thunder as the shooting stops.

No return fire.

'Good-good,' Frost says.

Kale is on the ground, breathing hard.

Frost leaves Kale where he is: strict instructions not to stand up, or wave his arms, or generally make a nuisance of himself.

Probably doesn't need to be so specific, but you never can tell.

Frost is skirting the tumbled greyed out edge of the Witch's land, this whole place kind of jutting up from the once-was-a-seabed plains of the deadground.

There's torn and broken earth, shale and gravel cascades, long drops to nothing.

Not the safest route, but that's kind of the point, isn't it?

You don't win by doing the always expected.

Final hands-and-knees crawl up a low mound covered in struggling crabby grass. Directly ahead, Frost spots a shooter crouching down behind some weather worn concrete blocks. His head is jinking left and right, sneaking looks ahead towards the stage, both hands death-grip clutching a fat automatic, all soft edges and satin sheen.

Frost draws her own pistol. A bulky revolver, dull metal

giving back nothing, black tube of a scope running down the top of the barrel. At this range the glass isn't good for much more than seeing the sweat on this guy's brow. She can't really miss.

He stops moving long enough to read some graffiti scrawled on the scuffed cement surface of one of the blocks. Whatever it says, it makes him smile.

He doesn't see Frost.

Doesn't hear the shot that splatters his brains across the concrete.

Frost throws herself over the crest and stumble-runs down the other side. Keeping low, moving quick. Heading for the new deadguy.

A roar in the darkness.

Anger, pain?

Frost skids to a halt, thumps against the body. Presses close to the shelter of the blocks and-

Chatter of gunfire.

Blast of dust and fragments as bullets slam into the concrete.

Someone serious.

Frost risks a glance and sees:

A woman.

Long coat, white hair, face of howling outrage. Gun in every hand as she charges headlong towards Frost. Muzzle bloom and boom.

Frost snaps off a round. It goes wide and Longcoat keeps running. Rounds still rippling out and chewing into Frost's protection.

Choking billows of dirt, grit and grime.

Longcoat is almost on her.

Frost coughs. Breathes. Takes aim. Steady.

A puff of red at the side of Longcoat's head and she falters, stumbles, falls.

The hollow crack sound of an AKM arrives as the woman rag-dolls to the ground.

Big piece of her skull is missing.

Frost left hands a thumbs-up in the direction of Tone.

Quality or luck don't matter at that point.

Frost scoots over to check-out Longcoat. Very much dead, as expected.

Clothes are worn, but not cheap. Weapons are well tended and likewise expensive. Old school. Family heirloom stuff. Someone wants Kale really-real dead, prepared to pay top rate for the-

Hammer blow punch rips into Frost's back.

Gunshot.

Armour vest takes most of the heat, but she's down on one knee, hot pain grinding into her side.

Frost shoots wild at a shadow lurching up from her right. Watches it drop.

Keeps watching. No movement. No shooting.

Clear.

Frost risks a breath.

Takes time to reload her pistol.

Damp and sticky stench of death is all around her.

'Just a kid,' Tone says. Pointing at the last body. Blond hair, fresh faced, neat hole in the back of his jacket. Apparently he'd been running away when Frost shot him.

They dragged all the bodies up near the stage. Well, Kale and Tone did most of the heavy lifting.

Frost walked slow and policed the firearms and ammunition. Pretty good haul for short work.

'You want this?' Tone prises a little silvered revolver out of deadkid's hand. It's a baby-sized .38 or something. Anything more substantial would have burned right into Frost and out the other side. Whole different end to the evening. Thanks for that, kid.

Frost shakes her head. 'Not really my style.'

Tone nods. 'True enough. That hog-leg you carry's the kind of thing you can for beating sumbitch to death if you run out of bullets.'

His laugh is loud.

'Cheeses, you people,' Nadine says, turns her back on them, walks away.

Nadine handles what's left of computers in the After; runs

Kale's guru show with lights and sounds and vidclips. Wears a neat little auto-pistol in a shoulder holster, sure she does, but Frost's never seen her pull it. Ain't cut out for fireworks and blood.

That's Frost's business.

Bodies lined up on the ground.

There it is.

Tancoat, Longcoat, Reader and the Kid.

Show's a lot of coin laid down for a man like Kale. Plenty easier ways to take him out, but this is what happened. Maybe whoever wanted this action needed to stand well off and no-one connecting the dots later?

Now they're out costs and the world's still rolling on same as it ever was.

This might not be an end of it, then.

'Can we head back now?' Kale asks.

'About that,' Frost says.

How it is: you don't want to be scrabbling around in the deadground in darkness. No telling what might be waiting out beyond the lights. Frost explains all of this to Kale.

'I'm not afraid of threshers, or wrigglers, or whatever,' Kale insists. He tries a smile. 'I've got you to protect me, right?'

'It's not just the local badnews monsters, Kale,' Frost tells him. 'There are other forces at play, this particular evening. You get me?'

Kale tries again. 'The gathering all ran out into the dark about a half-hour ago. How come they're allowed to travel the deadground at night time, eh?'

He's got his stern look aimed at Frost.

'No one is trying to kill them,' she says.

It's all agreed.

The night passes quiet.

Frost sits on the edge of the stage—pump action shotgun laid across her lap—watches the sky turn.

Sure, there's the odd bout of howling from out there and far away. Distant rumble and crackle of heavy gunfire—prolly a thresher raid against a relig, or a merc company staking a claim—shimmers of red and white flares lighting up the march of broken, blank windowed towers out to the west.

The kind of stuff that passes for normal in the After.

Radio waves that'll boil up your mind; monsters that could-have-been, might-have-been, maybe-once-were people.

What happened to the world?

Frost gives it some thought, time to time.

No-one knows much. All the wise heads can say is that it was sudden and catastrophic. All anyone knows is that it fucked everything upside down to hell and back.

Not many people left who even remember the Before. There's pictures. Artefacts. Some other-time technology even – although half of it doesn't work so well in the After. They've got vidclips, and songfiles stored on shiny metal chips or lumps of black plastic. They also have books; piles of dusty and decaying words in neat stacks, abandoned in these old-style warehouses of knowledge.

You can learn a lot from books, Frost's mother always told her. So Frost has done just that.

There used to be vast masses of people living in things called cities.

All the cities are gone away. They've been replaced by burning pools of light that send you mad-hat if you look at them too much. Rip your brains out through your eyes if you stray close or linger long.

Majority of the people are gone too.

The step between the Before and the After was short and sharp, days not weeks of brutal, violent nightmare.

The kind of thing science liked to call an Extinction Level Event. Except, there's still something left, at least. The world ain't kicked its last just yet, has it?

Folks are still here. Carrying on with the same old shit. Fighting over scraps, warring over this, or that, or nothing.

What was it worth in the end, if that was-

'Shouldn't you be sleeping?'

Looks up at Kale, standing closer than she'd like.

'Just thinking about the past,' Frost gets to her feet.

Kale backs off. He clambers up on the low stage. 'There's too much of it, you know.'

'Thinking?'

'The past,' Kale says. 'Too much dwelling on whatever used to be and not enough coping with the now.'

'It's like you read my mind,' Frost says.

'Well.' Kale grins at her. 'I am the guru, aren't I?'

'You mean what you said,' Frost wants to know. 'What we do, how we live, motivations?'

Kale nods. 'No word of a lie. This scrabbling and scratching in the ruins of the old ain't cutting it no more. We have to change up and move on.'

Kale raises a hand. Points out there, to the unknown.

'Gotta look out for tomorrow, and tomorrow and the day after that.'

Morning's late this time of year, beginning slow and cold.

Frost is wide awake and feeling a core-deep thud of pain from where the bullet slammed her. Nothing to it. Bad bruising at most. Anything worse she'd be dead already, yeah? Time enough to sort it out when she gets home.

Frost stands and looks at white sky, grey land, and the Green Witch towering above it all. Battered and war-weary, sure she is. A slight lean in her stance, maybe. Spell book in hand, though, and the other hand – the ruined one that used to hold her wand - raised up to… well, who knows?

'What dread battles witnessed by these eyes,' Kale says.

'Just a statue,' Frost replies.

Kale shakes his head. 'No. It's way more than that. She's a symbol. You don't create something this big unless you're making a statement. Sending a message.'

Frost stares up at the weatherworn vastness of stone and metal. Always looming on the horizon of Frost's life, isn't she?

'So what's the word?'

'Who knows,' Kale says. 'Meanings drift over time anyway. Might start as one thing. Be a completely other thing now. Different things to different people even.'

Frost nods. Stares up again. 'What it's saying, to me. Even with the broken hand, I mean, it all says…'

A moment or two of silence.

'Yes?' Kale asks her.

Frost looks at him.

'Don't fuck with the Green Witch.'

Tone runs a piece-of-crap four-wheel-drive vehicle that never saw a good day. Some Brit thing, he says, but time and tide have scratched off all the labels and distinguishing marks. Lot like me, Tone always says.

Big soft tires, wire mesh or plastic sheet instead of glass for most of the windows, flat metal bed in back with plenty of space for this and that and—just in case—a thick post topped with a belt-fed .30 calibre machinegun.

'Old school,' Tone says. 'Take you to hell and back.'

No one argues with this.

They load up the bodies and the gear; stack them along with the offerings Kale accepted from the gathered the night before. His people like to bring him things these days: tins of who-knows-what, random coins and trinkets. It all helps, Kale says, if not me then someone else.

Nadine and Kale perch in back.

Either the dead are getting to Nadine or she's pissed off at Kale for something. Doesn't say a word the whole while they're getting set.

Frost's in the cab with Tone.

Takes him a few tries to turn it over but soon the engines rumble-chugging away. Belching bio-diesel smoke and vibrating fit to tear itself loose.

'That's my baby girl,' Tone shouts. Big smile for everyone. 'Never lets me down.'

He sticks it in gear and they power down slope. Leaving the Witch behind. Soon they're weaving through high berms of fractured rock, skirting poisoned pools and hollows filled with damp and sticky ashes.

Crossing over the deadground.

Heading for home.

Home is the island.

Like most things it had another name in the Before—lots of names most likely—and now it's just the island. Crumbling plateau of blocky buildings, crammed together housing plots, squares of open ground for planting and growing. One corner is boss territory. High walled compound set up as a hold-out for the Bon and his guards and all the island royalty. Frost's a part of that scene—by default, mostly—gets a little respect and recognition. Sometimes.

The After is all about family, about connections and linkages. You ain't got that you don't run long.

Frost's mother, Sear, she worked hard decades as merc command for the Bon's father; veteran top-boss known as Coombs. This is how Frost and the Bon grew up practically together whilst the already growed-ups played out all that politics and war stuff.

Leading to the here and now where Coombs is dead and the Bon is ruling the show.

Sear is gone too—some kind of retirement she calls it, at a relig this is, ten days along the coast—leaving Frost as…

Well, who knows, really?

Frost's a personal friend of the Bon, there's that for a start. She's a stand-up plays-for-keeps shooter with the island militia besides, and a roving protector of scavvers and visiting notables alike.

What's to think about? Frost just does her thing and no-one gets in the way. Nothing gets close.

Not often, anyways.

Now and then, Frost gets a special case. Like this thing where she trails around with guru Kale and his motley.

'Just a piece of look-and-learn,' the Bon tells her, couple of weeks back. 'I just want to know what's going on in that head of his. You with me, Frost?'

Frost nods.

'With you, Bonhomie,' she tells him.

Because life is about connections.

The mass of the island is ahead of them now; this last piece of deadground not-exactly-a-road is an arrow-true, steep incline upwards between thick concrete barriers. A route that funnels them towards a red brick defence station topped with a sandbagged metal hide and-

Tone hits the brakes and they shudder-stop.

Rattles and thumps from the back.

Frost unhooks the plastic sheet of a side-window on her door and leans out. Holding up a playing card. Ace of Diamonds.

'It's not like she don't know our faces,' Tone says.

Up on the top of the defence station, Frost can see a waving hand. She slides back into the cab. 'You savvy Rook,' she tells Tone. 'Always best to play things by the written rules. That girl, she does not fuck around.'

Tone gets them moving again.

'Look who's talking,' he says.

They roll through a thick portcullis gate that shudders up and down on chains and metal tracks. It thuds to a final close behind them.

A cracked tarmac courtyard is surrounded on all sides by high walls. Militia shooters are visible everywhere Frost looks. Not relaxing yet.

They stop again and Tone steps out slow. No need for an itchy situation. Best to take things easy.

Clang-clang-thud of boots on metal steps and-

Rook comes barrelling down the rickety rusted fire escape steps off the station roof. She's sliding down the last five feet of ladder when shouts and squeals erupt from beyond the inner walls. Doors burst open and a mob of raggedy children swarm out, swamping Kale as he climbs down from the back.

'We'll talk later,' Kale shouts as the gathering sweep him out of view, deeper into the island.

Nadine walks away without a word or backward glance.

Frost gets to work packing what she needs to bring along.

Rook arrives at Frost's side, dusty camo cape fluttering in the light breeze, goggles pushed high up on her grimy hair. She's holding a scoped rifle that's longer than she is tall. Carrying it like it's No Thing.

'What did you find outside, Frosty. What ya bring me this time?'

'You leave the approach unguarded, Rook.'

Rook shakes her head.

'Who's up?' Frost asks.

'Cupid's on it. No worries.'

That's fair enough. Cupid's got a good eye. Still learning the ropes though, isn't he?

Frost thinks it over, nods. 'Okay then. You keep a tight rein on him. No wasting bullets shooting shadows. No capping anyone that matters.'

Rook throws out a rough salute. 'Sure-sure, Frosty. Loudclear.'

Frost hands over the deadkid's .38 pistol, a few rounds she collected.

'It's not much,' she says. 'Just a back-up if you can't keep your distance.'

'If the sitch gets all uppity-close and personal?'

'That's it,' Frost tells her. 'You can end up right in the middle of things.'

'Do I have to?' Rook says. 'Sitch like that? Sounds like major suckage.'

Frost crosses the main open ground of the island, turns up a broad avenue between worn down houses from the Before. Beyond that are new-built shanties of brick and block and wood, pressed up against old shipping containers more rust than steel by this point. People go about their day; chattering and barter, kids working homelife chores, younger kids chasing through the early crowd.

There's cook fire smoke and the smell of roasting meat.

Frost nods and smiles her way along the street; handing over a couple of spare cans of food to Drea the blacksmith near Redtree, leaving a few not-too-mushy apples with Miggy Dalton at the brewhouse on the corner.

'Not sure you can use them,' Frost says.

'Use anything,' Miggy tells her, rolling forward in her

wheelchair. 'Anything at all. Get blood from a stone, I'll throw that in too.'

Miggy's laughter follows Frost out of the door and up to the edge of market square.

Bad summer is long gone, and a hard winter is heading in. Not a lot to show on the stalls and spread-blankets of the market. A fair few off-island traders aren't making the trip these days. Mercs, bandits, monsters. There's a lot out there to stop you leaving home or ranging too far.

Thin faces turning Frost's way as she passes through.

Not much hope to offer them.

Ordinary folk aren't high on the Bon's list, are they?

More militia guard the gates to the Bon's compound. He doesn't like the outside getting that close.

Frost gives the nod to Haslett, hands over a scruffy duffle bag containing the rest of the weapons and ammunition she picked up the previous night.

Low whistle from Haslett as he feels the weight, looks into the bag.

'Do you ever have a quiet evening, Frost?'

Frost shakes her head. 'Not lately.'

Inside the compound are storage areas, guard barracks and housing for the Bon, his brother Harm, the rest of their chosen few. All of it tangled up and threaded out between a few scraggy trees, abundant ivy and some vegetable patches that barely feed the goats and pigs they keep out back of the main building.

There are solar panels on every rooftop, wind turbine blades swoosh-whooshing overhead, and somewhere close by is the chug-chug-chug of the generator that pumps up water from the deep wells below the island.

They sell energy. What's kept them going this far along. Recharge batteries for barter or trade. Let people plug-in and power-up whatever breed of old tech they care to bring. That's the island, then, that's how things have worked out, up to now.

There's a lot of wasted space in the compound. Open ground given over to rusted out shells of cars, piled high broken televisions, scattered with all shape and manner of other relics that no-one's ever going to need.

Over by the Whiteline—long low building for the better class of compound dweller—Frost can see some folk in ones and twos. Dressed in finer clothes, primped up and promenading like the world never ended.

Frost heads around the side of main building.

Chalice is waiting at the door.

The big cat is sitting quiet at her side.

Chalice came in with a dried out, worn down circus a few months back.

Saddest, weakest circus of all time, no question, and Chalice had no place being with them, but there it was.

They brought creepy clowns, bad magicians, and inept jugglers. A whole drag of a show performed under ratty canvas sewn together from the sails of dead ships.

The crowd watched—the wrong kind of awestruck—as a magic man got trapped in a box, spent time wishing the jugglers would hurt themselves with an ill-timed knife toss, got to wondering why anyone so obviously mean would ever even want to be a clown...

Chalice wore a full face mask and a flowing red dress, didn't seem to do much more than introduce the acts—apologetic for the most part—and pad around the performance area accompanied by an almost pure white cheetah she introduced as Cassius.

'Like most of us,' she said to the crowd, 'he has a lean and hungry look.'

When the circus left, under a cloud, under cover of darkness, Chalice stayed behind. Cassius stayed with her.

Her mask is a thin metal, burnished to catch the light, crafted as the most perfect replica of a face. Maybe Chalice's face, maybe not.

At first, Frost thought it was just for the circus act, all part of the show, but Chalice never removes her mask in company.

Frost doesn't need to know why, but Chalice told her anyway, one long night in quiet darkness:

'It's not to cover damage or disease,' Chalice said. 'It's just... this world. Laid open, stripped bare. It's good to keep some mystery, no?'

Now, at the side door of the main building, Chalice gives Frost a welcome hug, holds her close whilst Cassius sits nearby and fusses at his claws.

'Staying out all night,' Chalice says, her voice light. 'You're as bad as Cass.'

Frost winces slightly as Chalice's arms slide down around her waist.

'You're hurt?'

Frost shakes her head. 'Nothing. Bee-sting. Worrynots.'

Chalice stands back, arms across her chest. Looking for more signs of injury.

'I'll tell you all about it, once I see the Bon.'

'I trust you not to be foolish,' Chalice says.

'You know me best,' Frost tells her. 'I brought some tinned goods. Might find something there that's worth it. Also... we left some fresh bodies back by the main gate. That's if Cassius would-'

'He's not a scavver,' Chalice declares.

'I'd say we're all scavengers, these days,' booming voice from inside the building, and Grantham steps out—shielding her eyes from the weak sun—letting ash drift from a half-smoked cigarette.

'Hey, doc,' Frost says.

Grantham waves a hand. 'Stop calling me that. I'm a graduate in veterinary science at best, I don't presume to higher things.'

'You do wear a white coat,' Chalice argues. 'Well. Off-white would be most accurate.'

'We all have our disguises,' Grantham tells her.

Chalice gives a slight bow of the head. 'Touché.'

'Look at Frost. Supple leather. Solemn weapons. Some slightly damaged armour—emblazoned with faded letters spelling out the single word POLIZEI—what are we to take from all of this?'

Frost digs a battered pack of cigarettes from her trouser pocket. Hands them over to Grantham.

'Presents for everyone,' Grantham says, busy unwrapping the cellophane with thin yellowed fingers.

'The deadground provides,' Frost says.

'There are quicker ways to let it kill you,' Chalice tells Grantham.

She's already lighting up, taking a puff, smiling at them through the smoke.

'We've been over this before, dear. I'm already dead. Already holding back a bone deep cancer with the sheer force of my will. Would you deny me the little pleasures Frost brings?'

'I just...'

Chalice stops. Shakes her head.

An awkward moment of silence.

A messenger arrives—the Bon does love his little theatricals—with word for Frost.

'The boss would like to request to see you.'

'Is it urgent,' Chalice asks.

The messenger tugs at the collar of his starched shirt and shrugs.

Looks at Frost. 'You know him better than me?'

The messenger leaves.

Frost leans in close to Chalice. A momentary embrace. 'Duty calls, as ever.'

She kisses Chalice on the neck, near where the edge of the mask meets the smooth warm skin below. Chalice smells like cinnamon and soap.

But duty calls.

'A quick word with the Bon,' Frost tells her. 'Then I'm all yours.'

Chalice nods, squeezes Frost's hand, lets it fall.

'Later, doc,' Frost says to Grantham.

Grantham grunts and waves her away.

Like walking underwater, this is. A curved corridor sided with damp and pitted plaster work, windows made of endless cloudy squares of glass. There are broken panes here and there – leaves and snarling ivy forcing their way inside – and all the light and every surface glowing pale and green.

Even Frost – sleek and brisk as ever – finds that moving slow feels somehow natural here. Every limb and thought gets itself a-tangled up in dull and languid push and slide. It's easy to hate this long-long walk to the Bon's court, with its walls too near and limited sight lines. Frost is open air, long range and see-for-miles. That kind of thing is what people call her natural medium. Anything but indoors and locked up tight. Anything but this.

Frost keeps walking.

One hundred steps more and the path ends up at battered wooden double-doors that are set back into a tiny cracked-floor alcove. The way forward is guarded by one of these lean and leery bladecrew sorts that Harm has taken to calling his Scorpions. If you can believe that? He's been doling out little metal insignia and everything.

'No troubles here, ammy,' Frost says. 'I'm up to see the Bon.'

Clatter of boots and ruffle-thump of glossy pages hitting floor as the guard straightens up. Blinks and stands as Frost just loiters back aways and makes no sudden moves.

Barely out of his teens, this guy. Raggy denim, tough leather jacket, with a crumpled blue-white tag on his chest:
HELLO MY NAME IS DANTY
Above the name badge—new, out of place—shiny bright scorpion of twisted silver wire.

'No guns in the throne room,' Danty announces. Like this rule applies to Frost.

He's checking out the artillery now, his eyes sliding past the holstered pistol at Frost's hip and taking in the tape-wrapped stock of the shotgun where it sticks up over her shoulder.

Harm doesn't let the Scorpions carry firearms near the Bon; knives and clubs only, for reasons of safety. Danty looks jealous.

'Worrynots,' Frost tells him. 'I got special dispensation from boss-man-Bon.'

Frost watches Danty's line of thought go stumble-sprawling over that Big Word she dropped into the sentence.

Finally, he abandons further effort with: 'What's that about then?'

'It says I'm gold-star,' Frost quicksteps past, pushes on through before he thinks of something else. 'It means: don't trouble yourself.'

The room is nothing much.

Broad space, warped wooden floor and peeling wallpaper, ceiling hanging low in places. A couple people standing around, not many weapons on show, lot of stern looks. A typical day at the court of Bonhomie.

Near the doors, the windows are covered with flat boards nailed in place. Lines and spots of light squeeze through to play with motes of dust in the chill air of the room.

The Bon is on his throne, up at the far end of the room where the windows are free of cover, natural light shining on his open welcome face.

Harm is standing by his side, holding a short heavy-looking club.

The only other person in the room—Frost takes a second look—Nadine.

Frost is two steps in when Harm speaks first:

'Leave the heavy by the door,' he says.

Harm's pointing at the low table to her left, one hand on the pistol at his waist, other hand up and using the club for emphasis.

Frost nods, wheels about, unhooks the shotgun from her back and sets it down gently. Starts moving again.

The Bon leans forward. Hands tight holding the arms of his chair. Some kind of dentist or barber thing, this throne of his; bolted to a stepped dais in the centre of the floor, olive coloured leather worn thin, scars and slits where the stitching splits or the foam padding peeks out. The Bon's dainty shoes squeak against the metal footrest.

'What time you calling this, ammy, coming home?' the Bon asks her.

'Had some troubles, this and that,' Frost says. 'You know what is. Some nogoods tried to clip Kale. I put them off.'

The Bon looks to be thinking that over. Casts a glance at Harm, then one for Nadine too.

'Ain't Nadine told the tale already,' Frost asks. 'It was flash-bang a hectic show. I figure you'd be wanting all the gory?'

The Bon ignores that. Shakes his head.

'He's got opinions. This Kale of yours.'

Frost shrugs. 'Don't see anyhow he's mine. You being the one and all who said he need some looking after.'

'He wanted watching, is what,' Harm says. 'Before he gets too big for boots.'

'Ha,' Frost says. Grins at them. 'Harmony is running scaredy of some scavver kids and a crowd of lowlys out of Tenville?'

Two quick strides and Harm is at her side, fronting fierce.

Frost smiles and looks back to the Bon.

'He's has his notions, is what we're saying,' the Bon continues like nothing's going on. 'The question is...'

'He making a move?' Harm finishes. 'That the deal? Kale gonna try and take us?'

'Like I was telling,' Frost says. 'Childrens mostly. He can just about fair organise a sing-song.'

The Bon leans back in the chair. 'Some people like to hear what is he saying. All that jabber–jib about the growing crops and change our way of thinking. Getting out the box.'

Frost takes a step forward. 'It ain't so wicked wrong, you know. We've had a good run here and all, but I figure it might be time at least to listen what the man is saying. I mean, it's not like we can...'

A blink of a look between the Bon and Harm.

That's all it takes.

'You weren't supposed to save him.'

The Bon's voice is flat.

All those years. Family, history, connections. Gone.

'You left me in the line,' Frost says. 'Standing out front when the shooting starts. Bonhomie, I can't believe you'd-'

'Big enough to take care of yourself, you says. Always a winner,' the Bon's voice is high, words coming fast. 'Harm had concerns. You know. Doubts. Your loyalty. Harm needed to...'

Before that sentence ends, Frost watches the Bon as he looks at Harm and gives a single, slow nod.

Frost's already reaching for her pistol, wrapping her hand around the grip, swinging the weapon free and-

Fierce pain explodes along her arm as Harm steps in and slashes downward with that heavy metal club. Frost's pistol falls away, slamming into the floor as she holds back a scream.

Her leather jacket soaked some of the blow, but the shock of it is still enough to drive her to her knees.

Bone could be broken. Fingers barely moving on that side. Sparks of sharp agony dance up and down from her wrist to her shoulder. Way more than a bee-sting, this one. Foolish mistakes and look what happens. Chalice is gonna be pissed...

The Bon is talking at her now. Leaning out and looking down from his throne.

'This is the way things are,' the Bon tells her. He's regained his calm, brought things under control. 'We don't need this Kale, don't need him upsetting the apple core. Been giving people unsettling notions about what could happen and who should have control.'

'We are in charge,' Harm spits at her. Adds a boot to make his point. Frost manages to turn enough that it hits her back and not her already-fucked-up arm. Barely feels the impact.

'Do we kill her now?' the Bon asks. 'Maybe wait and do them both when Kale gets here?'

Frost's pistol is lying not so far away.

She'd be dead before she got a hand to it.

Frost glances over at Nadine. Frozen in a corner.

No help there.

A little distraction and she can make her next move. That's all she needs. Maybe if Kale-

Some commotion going on back by the entrance, with raised voices and shouts and then:

Opening of doors, footsteps coming closer and Frost risks a look.

Chalice strides across the room.

She does not stop or falter in her path.

Harm moves up to intercept, waving that club around.

'You can't be here,' Harm's saying. 'Anyone wants your company, we'll come get you, right? So you just back the fuck off, before I put you down.'

On the last word he reaches out and places a hand on Chalice's shoulder.

'Do not touch me,' Chalice tells him. 'No-one touches me unless I wish it.'

Harm raises his arm to swing the club and Chalice seems to merely flick her hand across his neck. Spray of red as Harm stumbles backwards. Dropping the club and clutching at his throat, fingers doing nothing to stop the steady spurt of blood.

Chalice steps back, holding a thin ceramic dagger.

Harm's eyes are wide confusion as Chalice swings around and jabs the dagger deep into his ear. He makes no sound as he falls forward on his face.

A choking grunt from the Bon. Frost turns as he leaps from his chair, hand inside his jacket as he searches for a weapon.

Frost bites down on pain and reaches for her pistol with her left hand, manages to grasp it just as the Bon comes up with a fat barrelled derringer of a thing in one fist. He points the gun at Chalice, changes his mind and aims instead at Frost.

The Bon fires—the little gun barks loud—and misses as Frost shifts position.

Frost puts a bullet in his knee-cap, sends him squealing-sprawling on the floor.

Frost stands up. Steps over to the Bon. Notices the derringer now lying out of reach as the Bon clutches at the ruins of his knee.

Frost points her pistol directly at his head.

This is how it ends. How the past falls away.

'I never betrayed you,' Frost says, and pulls the trigger.

It's very quiet when the echo fades. Outside the world moves on.

'This one?' Chalice asks, holding another ceramic knife, indicating Nadine; still standing motionless to one side.

Frost shrugs, winces, shakes her head slow. 'She made some bad choices. We all do that from time to time.'

Nadine looks up, surprised.

'Maybe she can do something useful and go get the doc,' Chalice suggests.

'Yes,' Nadine answers; almost runs from the room.

Cassius slopes in silently and sits down alongside Chalice, stares at the blood where it pools around Harm's body. Chalice wipes her mask with a delicate silk handkerchief, removes any scattered traces of red.

'What now,' Chalice asks Frost.

That's the question, isn't it?

'Just a start…'

Frost steps up and collapses into the barber's chair that once was the throne of Bonhomie.

It feels comfortable enough, for now.

A knock at the door and a low cough.

Danty looks in, takes in the view, says:

'Someone here to see you…' barely a pause '…boss.'

A quick learner.

Chalice nods assent and Danty disappears.

A moment later, Kale arrives. Looks around.

'Not quite what I expected,' Kale says.

'Including these two,' Frost tells him. 'I count six people wanting you killed.'

'I'm not sure what to say…'

'Worrynots,' she tells him. 'It's the dead past.'

Frost leans back, with her left hand—still holding her pistol—resting easy on the arm of her chair.

Out the grimy cracked windows to her left, Frost sees the Green Witch standing tall and strong. Always moving forward.

She looks back at Kale.

'Here we are,' Frost says. 'Let's talk about the future.'

Part 2

*Infected are normal, law-abiding citizens who,
through no fault of their own, have been infected
with a horrible virus. This makes it okay to kill
them.*

— *Infected* game manual

Girls Day Out

Bruce Lee Bond

The young man howled as Fauna tightened the chains on his wrists. She smiled and cinched them further before she grabbed a rag and wiped spit bubbles from the corners of his mouth. 'Didn't expect this, huh? His pain reddened eyes rolled to her face and she studied the tiny capillaries zig-zagging around hazel orbs. He made a croaking sound, and licked cracked lips.

'Here,' She brushed a palm over his damp shaved scalp and lifted a cup of water to his mouth. She tipped it slowly as he drained it, and set it on the little table beside the sweat stained mattress. 'All better, ready to talk?'

'Fucking cunt!' The young man lunged in his bindings and yelped in pain. He moaned, and sunk against the wall with the back of his tattooed head red from rubbing the bricks.

'That's so articulate dude.' She stood in her faded leather shorts and calf length moccasins, and adjusted her gun belt with its worn .45 on her left thigh. His eyes ran over her blonde braids and bare skin before landing on the belt buckle beneath her navel. For a moment he seemed to have forgotten his situation before hatred replaced lust.'Your friend stinks out there,' She blew a strand of hair away from her face and glanced out a crack in the boards over the basement window, 'Gotta move him, he's covered with bugs.'

'Good luck, bitch!'

She dropped to one knee and shoved the barrel of her pistol under his chin. His skin didn't show any of the growths typical to his kind and he actually looked normal. Her eyes lingered on the dragon tattoo across his muscular chest before she pressed the muzzle harder into his throat. Davy's head ground against the bricks and he gagged. 'How many of your friends are out there?'

'That's for me to know and for you to—'

She brought the barrel down hard across his forehead. Blood spattered the bricks as she opened a gash across his right eyebrow, split the crude tattoo of a skull and Davy went limp in his bindings. Fauna stood up, grabbed his shirt from the chair and wiped off the slide of her pistol. 'You're *not* fucking unconscious, asshole! I can tell!'

Davy sprawled to one side as a rope of drool unwound to the floor. Fauna placed the sole of a foot on the wound where the slug from her pistol had exposed a rib that morning, and pushed. He made a low moan, but that was all.

'You fuckin' punk! I know your friends are out there. They sent you first because you look okay and then that warty ass-hole came behind you. You're gonna tell me how many, and *where*, or I'm gonna remove your fuckin' dick in about one minute flat!'

Davy didn't move.

She sighed loudly. 'Okay, dude'

Fauna unsheathed a worn Ka Bar knife and ran the index finger of her right hand across the blade. She'd sharpened it this morning, just like every morning. It was part of her ritual, like hauling water from the arroyo, cleaning her guns or scanning the empty two lane highway for traffic in the first light from a hill to the south. It was a month since she'd heard an engine. The last battered truck coming from the east, the direction of the Yellowstone Event, had passed with a half dozen heavily armed Mexicans with the growths, no doubt seeking women and richer pastures. If they'd known there was a leggy blonde just fifty yards to their right there was no doubt what would have happened. She'd have used up most if not all of her precious ammunition for both the M-4 and the shotgun, and of course she could have died. It would have been nice to have caught one to find out where they'd got the gasoline though.

A truckload of warty scum had caught Shauna last fall when they'd been hunting antelope. Fauna had found what was left of her staked out in the desert with the bodies of the three she'd killed around her. *Why the fuck did they have to eat her heart?*

She lay awake at night thinking about it and hating herself

for not getting them all. She'd cut across the hills to where the road doubled back and got one who'd wandered from their camp, but they were too many and too heavily armed. His dried penis and scrotum hung from a thong over the kitchen sink. Fauna had more hanging in the windows of the house; talismans against the mutants whose only purpose was to hunt down any remaining women like a pack of feral pigs. The male trophies, *god's eyes* she'd made of twigs and twine and a colourful mobile made of old cell phones decorated the place, along with the cans and chimes strung inside the high brick walls surrounding it.

She blinked back to the present. She'd awoken with a headache at the end of a sleepless night, a regular thing since Shauna's death, but now there were these other fuckers to take care of, starting with Davy. She glanced at the shallow cut she'd made on his thigh while taking his pants off, and Fauna gave his closed eyes her best pre-apocalyptic smile as she cut off his underwear with her knife.

His eyes flew open, and she grinned. 'Nice dangle there. You look clean I gotta admit. Too bad you're never gonna get a chance to use it again.' Fauna squeezed his balls hard, and he let out a strangled gasp.'Hum. first the balls, then the dick,' she lilted,'these will make a nice window hanger. or maybe I'll hang 'em in the garden for the crows. Guess that's why they call it a pecker.'

'Du...*don't!*'

'Wanta keep 'em?'

'Goddamn it, I had to join up to *survive!* You know that, you gotta! There's so few women left and men are a dime a dozen! I would have been killed! It's reality out there. It's all gangs. I don't have any tumours and I never wanted to hurt you. We were just looking for food and fuel, I swear. Indian looks shitty, but he's a good guy honest. He lost his wife and daughter to the gas. 'Davy tried to smile through swollen lips. 'Listen, you and me could—'

'I *said*, dude - do you want to *keep* it?'

'Yes! Please!'

Fauna sneered as she lifted his cock with two fingers like touching a dead animal and placed the edge of her knife

173

under the head, turning to hide the scar on the side of her throat where somebody had cut it. Davy's eyes were as big as golf balls. 'Last chance pal, who are you with?'

'All right, just two, honest! Pepe's got a pump shotgun and Don's got an Uzi, a semi-auto. They're down at the old BP station waiting for me and Indian to come back.'

'How long will they wait?'

Davy shook his head. 'I don't know, Pepe's got some whiskey we found at a house in Pahrump and Don's got a shitty ankle and he's lazy as fuck so they'll wait a while. They're trying to find fuel.'

'They got tumours?'

Davy nodded and glanced around. 'What time is it?'

'Time for a nap' She yanked the knife away, drove a fist into his face and his head bounced off the wall leaving a red smear as it came away. Davy slid down with the chains holding his arms. He was out this time.

She had a ridiculous urge to kiss him and growled at her weakness. He looked perfect, so he had to have come from somewhere beyond the gas. The asshole wouldn't say anything about where though, and with no internet or satellite and the only radio some loon in Pahrump spouting Book of Revelations shit and telling women to come his way she didn't know what was going on anywhere. She wiped her hands on his shirt and stared at his penis. It was the first time she'd touched a live one in a very long time. She tried to not think about it.

She grabbed her black M-4 carbine and loaded all six magazines. She had five mags for the pistol, and stuffed all of them and a small pair of binoculars into the pouches of a camouflage vest stained with the blood of a guy who'd surprised her last year when she and Shauna were going through a store. Shauna had shot him while he was on top of Fauna with his big rough fingers around her throat and the other hand parting her legs, and pieces of brain had splattered across Fauna and got in her eyes as she stared up at the frozen look of surprise on Mr. Tumour Face. She couldn't get the goddamn stains out, no matter what she tried. *Fucker.*

She filled a canteen, put her first aid kit in the pouch by her right shoulder and drank her fill of the water carried from the arroyo. She'd have to leave the canteen when she got close due to the noise it made sloshing but it was a hot walk. Hopefully she could take them at a distance. Fauna adjusted the least scratched pair of sunglasses she owned, and walked out the door.

The body of the guy called Indian sprawled in a blackened halo of blood in the driveway between cactus and dead foliage inside the gate. Yellow jackets circled amongst a horde of flies in his matted beard and remnants of a face surrounded by a collar of tumour growth like a lumpy yoke, and a coagulated black hole swarmed with insects between his legs. Something scampered into the bushes as she approached, and turkey vultures circled overhead that somebody could see for miles.

He had a nice carbine that she'd slid under a tangle of dead morning glory vines. It was a Ruger .44, and she probably wasn't going to find much ammo, but it could be good for trade if she ever found someone who needed it that she trusted, and was normal, and didn't have to kill first.

'Stash it!' Shauna commanded in her mind. Fauna adjusted the gun belt, and rubbed her stomach. She retrieved the gun, went back to the house and locked it in the basement, checked on Davy who hadn't moved and got a piece of rope. It would be great to have some downers to shoot him up with to make sure he didn't get loose but she and Shauna had used up the last when they'd partied with the contents of some gangbangers' SUV in June. At least she thought it was June. She hadn't seen a calendar for three years and counted out days on a notepad, but it had been near the end of the month so it could have been July. They'd really wanted the Escalade, but the fucking thing began to burn and exploded before they could do anything except grab what they could and run. They'd pretty much trashed it with all those bullets anyway.

She should kill him and get it over with, but if she were

gone all day he'd be pretty foul before she got home. Fauna sighed. He looked so *normal,* a lot like a guy she'd gone with in high school except for the tattoos. She checked his bindings while trying not to stare at his cock and went back outside.

She scanned beyond the gate with the scope on the assault rifle before setting to work on Indian. After several tries she lassoed his foot without getting stung by yellow jackets, and dragged him down the driveway with the rifle in one hand. She locked the gate and stuffed the key in her shorts. Not that it would keep anybody out who really wanted over the wall. The road to the once lovely abode had a steep edge to the right that dropped into a canyon, and after dragging the body a good hundred and fifty yards with the rifle in one hand and the rope chafing her shoulders, swearing, stopping to rest and switching sides she got him to the spot.

Fauna swatted at a wasp contesting her possession of the ripe meat. She untied the rope, checked his pockets now that she was away from most of the bugs and found his stash of ammo, a knife, some bloodstained money and a condom. She put the ammo, knife and money under a boulder, slid the condom in her vest and rocked the body with a foot into the arroyo. It disturbed a yellow jacket nest as it came to rest in a tangle of sagebrush and they rose in a cloud. She smiled. There wouldn't be anything but bones in a few days.

She stepped into the shade of a Palo Verde, wiped her brow and took a drink from her canteen. The cream-coloured Moorish style house with its red tile roof and solar panels surrounded by walls on the hill was easy to spot from the air, and she and Shauna used to wave at the rare airplane until they'd watched a helicopter destroy a semi truck with a missile a year ago. They had no idea why, but had quit waving.

If Davy had lied about his friends, or how many there were, she could be walking into a trap followed by the inevitable gang rape. At least nobody had been waiting to shoot her. The Yellowstone Gas Event, as they'd called it before everything went to shit, had killed seven times as many women as men. Soon, packs of surplus males with those cancerous growths had come from the east acting like crazed sharks at a feeding frenzy when they caught a girl. Something rumbled in her chest. You'd think they'd protect and cherish women, instead of going berserk. Davy had been truly scared though, and he didn't look like one of them except for the tattoos. She blew a strand of hair from her face and kicked a pebble with the toe of her moccasin as the feel of his cock returned. 'Goddamn it.'

It would be fun to ride him once, enjoy his mixture of arousal and terror while having a much-deserved orgasm at the same time. Hell, a *bunch*. Tomorrow she'd be twenty-one, or maybe it was today. She couldn't keep track. It was her birthday and she deserved it. She couldn't scare him too much though, and had to let him think he'd go free. Otherwise, he probably wouldn't get it up unless she fed him Viagra or something.

Fine. Shauna had found a bag of that on a guy she'd shot and the blue pills were gathering dust above the sink. Fauna rubbed her eyes. It had been way too long since she'd had a man of her own volition. She barely remembered the mating dance she'd considered herself an expert at as a freshman in college. A vision of herself in a little black dress erupted, but swiftly blurred when she tried to focus on it.

She put a hand in her vest, fingered the ring in its foil sheath, and glanced at the turkey vultures that had followed Indian's funeral drag to the arroyo like black gashes against a hard blue sky as they rode the hot updrafts in silence. Fauna adjusted her sunglasses, checked her weapons and headed down the road.

The old BP station sat beside a rest stop that had reverted to desert where the highway emerged west of the mountains. Fauna stuck to the ridgeline where she could glass with binoculars while keeping just to the far side, occasionally edging out between boulders and brush at the top for a look and keeping her silhouette hidden. In the distance stood the cone of a volcano that had sprouted in the last two years with its black peak bleeding smoke across the teeth of the Sierras.

Shauna called it *Satan's Crank,* and had sworn she could see it growing bigger.

Fauna knew the rusted vehicles at the station by heart, and sure enough there was a new one; an old Chevy pickup with bullet holes in the bed. They couldn't have found any fuel. The place had been gone over for a couple of years, and even the sludge in the diesel tanks had been siphoned out by the last big rig that had come through; a Peterbuilt with the cab sheathed in boilerplate and some kind of crap on the back for cooking down hydrocarbons. That was pretty cool.

She crouched in the shade of a twisted pinion pine and scanned with the binoculars. After ten minutes, a tattooed bald guy emerged shirtless with a bottle in his hand and a shotgun slung over his shoulder to piss an arc in the dust. Fauna watched him through the optical sight on the M-4 with the red dot dancing on his chest. The tumours on his back and neck made him look like some kind of part-dinosaur, part-man. A whoop carried across the desert and echoed off the cliffs around her, as he yanked a pistol out and took aim at a lizard on an oil drum.

'No way, he's not gonna waste—'

The shot cracked the dry air.

'What a dumb shit'.'The man laughed and stuck the gun in its holster. He had the shotgun, so if Davy was telling the truth it had to be Pepe and Don with the Uzi must be inside. A shotgun and a 9mm were virtually useless at this range. If Don would appear, she'd gladly shoot both of them and go down to investigate.

Pepe stretched, turned, and disappeared in the station.

Fauna rubbed her eyes, slid down in the shade of the pinion pine and took a drink from her canteen.'Fuck.' She had to climb down the long way so as not to expose herself and flank them. She took off the vest and stood up to dry the sweat on her bare skin, absently scratching the scar over her left kidney where some guy had cut her the day everything fell apart and the cops couldn't stop the hordes from the east anymore. Fauna hadn't realized how loud gun battles could be. She remembered how freaked-out she'd been when she had time to tend to the cut and the adrenaline had subsided, and how she'd panted like a scared puppy as she'd tried to staunch the blood.

It wasn't even that bad. She'd had lots worse since. He'd been her very first kill and she remembered crying, but it was as if she were at a distance watching someone she couldn't understand. She hadn't cried for a long time since, at least not from getting hurt. She'd sewed up her own wounds with a needle and dental floss a few times, and swore a shit-load, but never *cried*. Dental floss made great stitching material, and if you found a package that had never been opened it was sterile too.

She'd cried when she found Shauna, a lot. Shauna had been a nurse, which was really cool when you're wounded, and could sew up cuts way better than Fauna ever could and with much less scarring. Fauna thought of the time Shauna had dug a slug out of her back while talking to her in the most soothing tones as her fingers probed so gently, and Fauna had begun to laugh through the pain. Fauna had been a freshman in college with plans to get a job with a financial firm and a part-time model when the shit came down, but Shauna had lived enough to save her ass a few times.

She chuckled and drank from the canteen, savouring the warm water as she recalled their attempt to dig a well at the bottom of the arroyo. She remembered Shauna's fair face turning red, crying as she threw down her shovel at dusk that first day with her freckled skin flushed and long red hair plastered to her neck. Shauna looked at her broken nails, and wiped the sweat from her face before she gave Fauna a blue-eyed stare and laughed. They'd laughed until tears came, hugged, kissed, and went back to work with parched throats and blistered hands as darkness fell and coyotes howled in the hills.

It took three days to hit water and after it had risen from the forgiving earth they'd become lovers. Fauna wasn't sure how. She wished Shauna was there to tell her. Not that she knew either. It just happened. She'd always expected to survive an apocalypse with some guy, but the only ones left roamed in packs like wild dogs and needed killing. There had to be another kind somewhere, but she had no idea *where*.

She should use Davy. He looked like George in high school except for no hair and the tattoos. That was the kid's name, *George*. Davy had great skin and a hell of a dangle and probably hadn't used it for as long as she'd gone without herself, except some guy's butt maybe.

The thought of changing Davy into somebody she could trust appeared from some long lost place, and of awaking enfolded in his arms. Safe from the monsters so many men had become.

A vision of him beating some girl and raping her with his gang replaced the fantasy, and her nose wrinkled. 'Fuck that.'

It took an hour and her head ached from lack of sleep. She took one last pull on her canteen, placed it in the hollow of a juniper's roots and began crawling the last fifty yards wishing they'd show themselves while she had the advantage of range. A rattlesnake buzzed from the shade of a tree, and she scooted across an open patch to the next cover.

Abandoned gas stations always brought out violent reactions from people, and the place was riddled with holes. Fauna made it to the rear wall and pressed her sweating back in the cargo vest into the roof's sliver of shade. She lifted the receiver of the assault rifle to her lips, blew dust off the bolt and slipped off the safety. It would be nice if it were full automatic, or capable of bursts, but it was a commercial job she'd had since that first day in Reno and she was lucky for that. It would be great if those guys had ammunition for it. She bit her tongue to take her attention off the fluttering in her stomach. Fauna tasted blood, and let out her breath. 'Two sets a' balls comin' up.'

'Ha!'

The voice sounded right beside her and she jerked to the right, then spun to the left.

'Motherfucker I'm bored! Let's go lookin''

'And leave her alone? What if somebody comes by?'

'Yeah you're right. Hand me that bottle.'

There was the sound of something metallic tipping over and a crash. 'Fuck!'

A girl made a high-pitched yelp, and something rippled up Fauna's spine.

'Whatsamatter honey, you wanta little drinkee too?'

Fauna sprinted around the building, kicked a tumbleweed out of the way and leapt through the side door of the station. The dimness nearly blinded her and she tore off the sunglasses. A man stood silhouetted against the open garage bay with an Uzi in hand and she squeezed off three quick shots. There was a gargling howl, and he hit the floor. She swung to the right.

A naked adolescent girl kicked at the air, lifted off the ground by the dirty forearm of a shaven-headed man who sneered over her shoulder. *Pepe.* His shotgun leaned against the garage door, but he held a knife to the bruised breast of the girl and raised it to her throat with a grin.

The man on the floor made gargling sounds as his feet scraped the concrete and Pepe's knife glinted in the light coming through the shattered windows. The collar of tumours around his shoulders rippled like the pebbly skin of a gila monster. 'So, bitch, you want her for yourself?'

'Fuck you!'

'You gonna have to decide. Let me have my gun and go, and you can have her.'

'What do you think I am?'

Pepe scowled, lowering the girl until her feet just touched the floor. 'Hey cunt, you--'

The girl drove a heel backwards into Pepe's groin and he slashed at her as she burst free. That was all Fauna needed. She put two bullets in his face and he was dead where he stood. He toppled like a timber, and bounced once as blood splattered the bay.

The girl wrapped damp arms around Fauna and sobbed. Her tears soaked Fauna's vest, and Fauna pushed her away and tore it open. It was wringing wet with sweat. 'Any more?'

'Yes! Two guys who left this morning!'

'Davy and Indian?'

The girl's blue eyes widened. She nodded.

'That's all?'

'Yes,'

'Good.' Fauna walked over to Don, nudged him with a toe and his mouth fell open in a death rattle. She picked up his Uzi, checked the action and put it on a crate. 'Davy didn't tell me about you of course. How long have they had you?'

The girl ran her hands through tangled hair, and burst back into tears. 'I don't know, a week.'

'Did they leave you any clothes?'

She nodded. 'Somewhere.'

'Get 'em.' Fauna pointed at their truck. 'Any fuel in that?'

'Not much, maybe ten miles.'

'That'll do. Want a bath?'

'Yes!'

'Okay, get dressed and go to the truck.'

'Can I have a gun?'

'Sure, and pick up all the magazines and ammunition you can carry while you're at it.'

The girl swept up Don's Uzi and checked the action. She ran her hands over the gun like stroking a beloved pet, wiped her face, and grinned. 'I'm Denise.'

'Fauna. Nice to meet you.'

'Thanks so *much!*'

Fauna took a pull from the half-full whiskey bottle, corked it, and unsheathed her knife. 'Wait in the truck.

The truck had canned food looted from Denise's home where she said the men had killed her family. Denise leaned back in the shredded seat, opened a pack of beef jerky and talked nonstop on the way up the mountain about how she'd been living in a town in Oregon with a functioning police force, how the eruptions and earthquakes in California had sent hordes of people north and how after the tsunamis on the coast her family had sought refuge in a remote corner near the Nevada border. She shook her head. 'That was a fucking mistake.'

'How old are you?'

'Twelve'

'Shit,'

Denise's fingers traced the scar on Fauna's neck. 'How did you get that?'

'Somebody tried to cut my head off.'

'That's fucked up.'

Fauna nodded.

'Are we safe here?'

'Safe as anywhere I guess.' Fauna got out at the gate with the motor running and the Uzi in hand. 'Take off the safety on the black carbine and keep an eye on the hills. If you see somebody put the red dot on them and shoot, quick.'

'Okay,'

They pulled into the yard, locked the gate and parked the truck in the garage next to two rigs devoid of gas. Fauna stepped out with a bloody canvas bag in hand. She put it down, and opened the door of the house with her .45 in the other.

Denise followed her in and glanced around. 'Cool.'

A moan came from the basement.

Fauna rubbed her eyes. 'Here, put this in the sink.' She handed Denise the bag and slid her knife out of its sheath. 'There's water in the bathroom. You can take a bath but you're going to have to help me carry that stuff in and haul more water before nightfall. You'll get used to it. Make yourself something to eat. Wait here, I won't be a minute.'

Denise tore a bite of jerky and nodded. Fauna kissed her cheek and headed downstairs.

The Winter After

Mikey Nayak

1

He sat on top of the train, and howled at the grey sky.

The snow fell around him, collecting on the furry lapel of his coat, the dull wool of the thick beanie that covered his ears and most of his sloping forehead, and his lips as he thrust them up to the sky and let another piercing howl rent from his throat. On the street below him, the cracked cement was quickly colouring in with white. The top of the train had collected almost three inches already. It had been stranded in the middle of LoDo, since the first attack, like his life in many ways—suspended, waiting to start again. He let his mind drift away for several minutes, till the piercing cold brought him back. It would be time to seek shelter inside the train soon. Soon, but not yet.

The snow fell faster now, a thick curtain, catching in his beard, brushing against his cracked lips. The wind picked it up and blew it against his weathered face, bringing the sound of boots crunching against the new snow to his ears.

He reached into the deep pockets of the dingy green coat he had worn since the first fall wind had swept into Denver. It was ugly but forgivingly warm, with pockets that could hide a week's worth of food… or two days' worth of Chablis. Even when the world had been a sane place, and it had been dirty cheap, he had enjoyed the sharp, pungent burn of Chablis wine. Now it was all for the taking if you knew where to find it. Three men came into his peripheral view - all young, huddled close together, guns slung over their backs on worn leather straps. His muscles tensed, but he stayed where he was, Chablis bottle held loosely between his fingers, face pointed up at the sky. More of Hoatam's minions, he thought contemptuously. He uncapped the bottle, fingers trembling, and thrust the bottle aggressively to his lips. Beautiful bitterness tumbled into his mouth, and he howled fiercely at the sky.

The gangsters looked around, jerkily, scrambling to their guns, then they caught sight of him—a dark, crouching shadow on top of the train, behind a curtain of dirty grey snow, a bottle dangling from his hand, neck craned as if to catch sight of the moon through the snowy clouds. He looked over at them and guffawed drunkenly, the bottle swaying perilously. 'Hola!' he screamed. 'Welcome to the end of the world!'

The man in the centre let his gun drop to his chest, a disgusted look coming over his face. He was a little Vietnamese guy, just over five feet tall. He turned his collar up to the wind and shouted against it. 'You crazy hobo,' the Viet said. 'There's a storm coming!'

In response, he raised the bottle of Chablis to them in a mock-toast, then jerked it against his lips so hard that the cold glass knocked against his front teeth. The Viet shook his head and spoke to his two companions. 'One day this fucking bum is going to die, and I hope I'm there to see it.'

'I don't know,' the second, taller, darker minion replied. 'He keeps managing to find food, and he's always drunk. Wish I knew how.'

The Viet approached the train, lips baring to reveal his rotted, yellowed teeth. 'You got a stash, don't you, hobo? Hoatam thinks you do. You better hope he doesn't decide to come looking for it.'

On top of the train, the bum laughed; the wind picked up his laugh and slung it around the LoDo plaza. 'The poppy is in the corner hat!' he shrieked down at them. 'It's a raccoon!'

'Let's get out of here, Po,' Tall and dark said. 'It's getting nasty out.'

The Viet stared at the bum for another few seconds, fingering his gun thoughtfully, then shrugged. They backed away from the train and headed across the plaza, the Viet throwing one last look at the lonely man huddled on top of the train, as he let out another howl toward the frozen sky.

The bum watched them go from under narrowed eyelids.

They weren't interested in him if he didn't give them anything to climb the food chain with. Sometimes they were more aggressive, when they were bored or wanted some sport, and he would jump up onto the dead electric wires above the train, run away with an agility born from a previous life, cackling all the way. But the outcome was always the same.

Even at the end of the world, a bum was just a bum.

2

The migration from the East had begun. As the cold set in across a ruined America, survivors of the nuclear winter began to get desperate. The cities became war zones, gangs coalescing to stake out food, guns and warm places to spend the night. But without supplies coming in, the metropolis ultimately became an overgrown palace for an impoverished baron, and city men and city women began taking their pugnacious tenacity into the wheat bowl states, trying to commandeer safe havens in small towns with un-radiated food and water. Jupiter had seen it coming. She knew that with the right stockpile of supplies, they could avoid the inevitable rural hostilities and build a fortress like no other in the city. She had bought the family west, out of the small town in which they had spent most of their lives, two hundred miles into the big city to take over the Windsor Heights Apartments in downtown Denver.

Now she looked out of the frosted window on the penthouse floor, scowling as she watched the snow tumble out of the grey sky that hovered above the city. It was like the world had been swallowed whole by the sky, and they were the last bubble rising up into that hungry mouth. The clouds were impenetrable, but knowing Denver, Jupiter guessed that the flurries would turn into a white-out, filling the streets below with powder and hiding the other downtown skyscrapers from sight. She was counting on it.

She sensed his presence behind her and turned irritably. Joshua was watching her with a half-sullen look on his square face and she tried to wipe her expression to neutral.

'Looks like a storm.'

'We should hurry before it gets too bad. Is Donald ready?'

'Should be here any second.'

They stood in uncomfortable silence, Joshua fingering the shotgun shells hanging from the sling around his neck, the sullen look on his face expanding the longer she said nothing. *I don't owe you anything,* she thought stubbornly. *If you're pissed that I'm not jumping on your cock any more, that's your problem.*

The door opened and Donald strode in, his confident-man walk pasted on. His white whiskers were growing long, threading down the sides of his face, hiding his leathery cheeks and the deep dimples that were his saving grace when he smiled and showed his rotting teeth. He wore too many guns - four pistols, two in quick-draw holsters on his hips, two Air Force issue M-16s over each shoulder and a double-barrelled shotgun in his arms. Jupiter wanted to tell him that all that firepower would only slow him - and therefore her - down, but she didn't want to deal with that fallout. Especially in front of his sulking son.

She leaned down and picked up the only gun she carried—a modified 5.56 mm M4 sniper rifle with a telescope sight installed over the top rail. A mag light was strapped onto the bottom of the barrel in place of the bulky M203 grenade launcher it was equipped to carry. It was not her only weapon - she had a long hunting knife with a curved blade tucked into a leather sheath under her thick white coat, and it was a weapon she hated intensely.

'Windy out,' Donald said loudly, putting on his authoritarian tone. 'You should change that rifle out for a shotty.'

'I'm good with my gun, thanks,' she said shortly, already striding across the empty room to the door, trying not to get herself angry and upset. She needed her wits about her, more than ever since they hadn't stepped out of the skyscraper onto the deserted streets of the city for almost a month. Joshua and Donald followed her down the hallway, Donald talking stridently about 'idiot women that didn't listen to anybody'. Joshua didn't respond, but he didn't interject on her behalf either, as he had when they had been together. He knew she was listening, much as she didn't want to.

The door to 2408 was open, and as they passed, Meg's strident voice screeched out at her. 'Are you going outside? Get Blake some new toys, for fuck's sake!'

Jupiter kept walking, keeping her eyes on Willy's proud deadlocks at the end of the hallway, and Megan thrust her head out of the door at her retreating back. 'Don't you forget!' she yelled, and poked at Donald as he walked by. 'Dad, don't let her forget Blake needs new toys!'

Blake was three; he would be happy with a goddamn piece of gum on the end of a stick, Jupiter thought bitingly. But Megan just had to nag the hell out of everyone. *One day someone will throw you off the roof, and I hope I'm there to see you splatter twenty-five stories below.* She shook her head. *I'm turning into a real bitch,* she thought. *I wasn't like this once.*

At the end of the hallway stood the door to the stairs, hidden behind a roll-up metal shutter. Back in the summer Jupiter had spent sleepless, unimaginably hot weeks bolting the shutters together and welding cross-braces into them to increase their strength. Donald and the others had thought her nuts, of course, and offered nothing but criticism. 'There's no one in this complex. No one's gonna even know we're here!'

She ignored him, as she had grown used to doing after five years of dating his son, and installed locks and shutters on both sides of the stairwell door. One day, panting her way up fifty flights of stairs to the penthouse, she had paused for breath on the seventeenth floor, and heard a door slam behind her. Jupiter's hunting knife came jumping into her hands and she had almost skewered Megan in two as the girl had come into the stairwell. Megan screeched her head off, and raised a ruckus with the whole family, but the incident stuck in Jupiter's head, and that week she went back to work. By the end of the month there were locked shutters on stairwell access doors on every floor. The only way up to the penthouse was the stairs from the lobby, with no refuge to duck into, then through two sets of shutters.

Megan had thrown another tantrum, bitching that with

no access to floors 1-23 she had no space, nowhere to go to be by herself. Post-apocalyptic troubles be damned, the family swung her way, as always. Take the shutters down, Donald said imperiously, as if they were a royal court and he was the King.

Jupiter firmly refused to hand over the keys to the shutters. 'If you think you have no space, I don't care,' she told Megan flatly. 'There was a time you did just fine in a trailer with ten other people. Without those shutters, one day someone will be prowling around one of the lower floors, and you'll be bleeding your guts out before you know it.'

The shutters stayed. She was the brain trust, whether Donald wanted to acknowledge it or not. She was the brain, they were the unwilling, cancer-ridden organs, and they were all part of the same, miraculously functional body. And as the first days of below freezing weather began to appear on the almanac, the gang-bangers in the city suddenly woke up to the fact that the cruel winter of the high plains was here.

Some played Darwin, and eliminated their own, cleaning house till their supplies could last a chosen few through the winter. Others turned to preying on lone survivors and California refugees, hunting for victims to keep themselves alive. There were eleven people living on the top floor of the Windsor, and it wasn't long into fall before they were found.

Tommy, Megan's first cousin and former lover, was shot and killed as he walked into the lobby, shotgun still securely around his shoulder. That was the night their building was stormed by a local gang. It was jungle rules now - defend your water-hole. We've peed on this building, boys, it's ours now, and if you come in here and slurp our water, we're going to tear you limb from limb.

Jupiter's fortifications saved the family. With only one way up to the penthouse - up the stairs, around blind corners – it was a massacre. Donald, Joshua, Willy and Rip lost count of how many they killed. It seemed like the entire city of Denver wanted a piece of them that week. The body count was too high for sustained invasions, but it put their backs against the wall. Venturing beyond the building was now exponentially more dangerous, because their enemies knew where they were. But Jupiter had planned for a season-long stay, and as long as they stayed up in their penthouse, they were safe. *Now we're headed back out*, Jupiter thought with a touch of fear. Out from the water-hole into the wild jungle. Back into a world that was once sane.

And that dumb bitch is worried about toys for a three-year old.

3

They sprinted from bullet-ridden cubby hole to cubby hole, guns out, but the stairway was silent as they progressed down the floors toward the lobby. The stench of frozen death grew more cloying. Over the banister, Jupiter saw the edge of the pile of bodies that had been tossed down almost two months ago. Their homeboys hadn't bothered coming back for them, so now they just lay at the foot of the stairs, faces frozen to the cold marble, limbs untidily heaped together, denied the simple dignity of burial. Jupiter felt a shudder of revulsion start and grow till it racked her body visibly, causing her gun to stutter against her gloved palms. Donald looked back sharply and she grinned uneasily at him, her breath clouding around her face. 'Fucking cold,' she said.

Jupiter unlocked the shutters on the ground floor, and Joshua and Willy put their backs into heaving the heavy metal upward. The shutters screeched unpleasantly before they had enough room to shove the stairway door behind it open. They slipped under and let the shutter crash to the floor behind them.

Jupiter looked behind her, worried about leaving it unlocked. They would have to be back before anyone noticed... tried their fortifications and found them wanting. Jupiter knew the law of the jungle was in effect; had anticipated it better than most. Her weakness, though she refused to see it as such, was her core values.

Deep in her heart, Jupiter believed that the taking of human life was wrong. She believed in a life after this one; believed that the same ten laws that had applied when man was wandering around the Sinai desert with little food applied two millennia later, when man was wandering around a once bustling city with little food. Thou shalt not kill.

She had tried to share this with Joshua once, an experience that still frustrated her. 'But you carry a gun,' he had argued. 'If you don't believe in killing, why would you carry a gun?'

Ultimately she let him win; smiled and nodded along. But she knew why she carried the gun. She would rather kill than be raped; would rather blow her own brains out than starve to death like an animal. But that didn't mean she had to be like Donald and Joshua, who had competed to see who could scalp more gangbangers in the bloody stairway. 'Like sitting ducks,' Donald had laughed over the sound of ricocheting gunfire, and Jupiter had been sick to her stomach, because this brave new world was meant for men like these. Men with no remorse; men who didn't just kill, but enjoyed killing.

They stood in the darkness of the shallow loading dock, breaths coalescing around them in frigid clouds. Jupiter felt cold, and not just because of the storm driving in. She didn't want to live like this. Perversely, she wished she were like Megan, fed and well-kept in the Windsor, no closer to the snow blowing through the streets than the picture windows. But she also knew she couldn't trust anyone else with her own survival. While Donald and Joshua and Willy were good killers, they were not survivors. She kept them alive, and they killed for her.

Donald looked at her in the shadowy light filtering in from the grimy skylights embedded in the concrete. 'Grab your map, Jupe, where are we headed to?'

Jupiter had spent the last two weeks memorizing Denver street maps, but she knew if she just pointed a direction, Donald would frown at her until she pulled out the map. She felt her teeth clenching and took a deep breath, the cold air burning in the back of her throat, then unzipped her pocket and pulled out a map.

They were headed to the industrial district, past the Rockies stadium and the once-popular Lower Downtown or LoDo. There was no food left in the stores, but maybe, just maybe, some supply warehouses hadn't been cleaned out yet.

She had a list of possible factories to check out. Under cover of the storm, with a little luck, they could find a stash and bring it back to the Windsor before anyone was the wiser.

'East till we hit Landsown Street,' she said into the darkness.

4

Dane shivered, and it racked his body for what seemed like forever. In the back of his chilled brain, he wondered if he could actually shiver himself to death. What if the spasms never stopped? He blew hard on his hands, but the cloud of frost from his mouth just iced up the windshield. Outside the derelict bulk of the Cadillac, the wind was gusting to forty miles an hour. Slowly and steadily, the temperature inside was dropping, sucking the warmth and life out of his body.

Dane huddled into the cloth seat, drawing his jacket even tighter around him, and wished for the strength to kill himself and end his misery. Snow piled against the windshield, blocking its view, but through a tiny patch in the frosted passenger window he could see the doors he was supposed to be watching. If they were even still in there, they would be stupid to come out now. Now was the time to be indoors; watch the sky spit cold flakes all over the city from the relative warmth of the tower.

Dane wanted to quit, bust open a window somewhere and crawl indoors, but he didn't dare. He had drawn this duty because he had screwed up, and if he screwed up again, he might as well strike east out of the city, because there would be no more Hoatam protection for him. So he would lay here, watch the loading dock doors, freeze until his heart almost stopped, and then he would take his chances in the basement of the apartment block across the way.

Once upon a time, Dane had been what you would call a ladies' man. Booze, dope and pussy, master of the club scene, dancing and partying like there was no tomorrow. Then America woke up to the aftermath of a nuclear apocalypse, and here he was, feeling the cold silently take hold of him, gaunt from exhaustion, nerves showing across his face and pathetically stripped hands, as far from his old life as was imaginable.

As he always did when high on cocaine or barely clinging to life, he felt his brother's voice in his head, thick with the Southie accent Dane had tried so hard to lose in college. *Don't you dare go to sleep on me, little prick, or I'll skin ya alive, ya hear me?*

Images of warm summers spent climbing trees and rolling in tall grass came to his mind, so vivid he could almost taste the pollen in the air. Dane groaned, and the sound filled the frozen car, hovered in the air between the crucifix dangling from the rear-view and his stained blue jacket.

Your moment's coming, brotha. Better be ready, ya hear me?

The small door in the alley beside the loading dock opened, and Jupiter poked her head out into the storm.

5

The four of them walked briskly, guns cradled in their arms. The storm had moved in rapidly, faster than Jupiter had anticipated, blanketing the city. There was comfort in the pounding snow. No one could see them coming. She led the way down silent sidewalks, keeping out of the streets, clinging to the shadowy buildings and back alleys. Beside her, Willy kept pace, eyes scanning vigilantly.

Past shells of cars and meaningless traffic signs, building heights dwindled as they crossed the 20th Street Bridge, then began to grow in the distance as they headed west of the city, towards the southern industrial side and Jupiter's first prospective target. They heard voices at one point, directionless, carried to them from blocks away. Donald cracked the safety on his shotgun back loudly. She threw an annoyed hiss over her shoulder, and Joshua glared back from under his hood.

An hour after leaving the Windsor, she stopped outside what had once been a Van Heusen suit store. Donald and Joshua bumped into them and she said, 'Let's stop here for a while. I want to let the snow cover our tracks.'

Willy went around the back, disappeared into the alley, and they waited silently in the blowing snow till the door snicked open and his dreadlocks poked their way out into the wind. 'Place is empty,' he said in a low voice. 'Come in.'

Willy locked the door behind them, and they walked quickly into the back, away from the display windows. They collapsed behind a service desk, the guns around Donald setting up a messy clanking. 'Where are we?' Joshua asked.

I could tell you we're at 101st and Hades, and you wouldn't know the difference, she thought with contempt, but she replied civilly. 'We're just past Seventeenth Street. We want Eleventh Street, then we head North till we find the Traffire plant. Traffire made flash-frozen foods. Beef jerky, canned sausage, the kinds of things you packed when you were going camping up in the Rockies for a week. That's our first prospect, about half an hour away.'

'We should press on,' Donald said. 'The storm is getting worse.'

'Which means we should conserve our strength,' Jupiter said. She was tired, and she knew the old man was too, underneath his macho act. Despite his faults, he was a strong old shit, and she admired his toughness. 'Let's eat, what do you say?'

Around them, the warmer jackets had been stripped off the mannequins, but most of the store was intact. Silk ties and flimsy cardigans lined the walls, below crystallized pictures of fakely smiling models staring off into the distance. It all seemed so vacuous now, Jupiter thought, as she looked up at a picture of a woman captured in a large, toothy smile, jumping into the arms of a shirtless, muscled man. You fucked for comfort now; whomever was convenient.

Willy sat on his haunches, eyes cast down but alertly listening as he ate. Jupiter watched him as she wolfed down her food, not tasting the salty bitterness of it anymore. He was a good companion, she thought. Another survivor, alert and silent, he did what needed to be done.

He looked up, meeting her eyes squarely in the small, dark enclosure behind the counter, and she felt something like desire stir in her nethers. She stood slowly, feeling her knees pop and the muscles in her thighs protest. 'I'm going in the back to pee,' she said to everyone, but to Willy in particular. 'Might be a while.'

Jupiter walked out of their sight, her muscles clenched. She could feel warm wetness spreading through her old, worn panties. It was mostly the danger of venturing out past the safety of the Windsor. But it had been a while since Joshua. It would be criminally stupid with her ex in the next room... but if Willy followed her back here, she would let him have her, furiously and silently, while the mannequins in fashionably pointless designer clothing watched them dispassionately.

She waited, heart beating, in the semi-darkness of the sweater vest section. Gradually the arousal wore off and the cold began to seep in. She backed into a corner, pulled her pants and underwear down, half-crouched against a wall for balance and let her bladder go into a still-folded pile of hideously effeminate cardigans. When she was done, the silence of the store came back to her. Willy wasn't coming, and that was probably for the best.

She stood up, panties collecting around her ankles, and caught sight of herself in a low mirror. Once she had been a somewhat desirable woman. Joshua still wanted her. Once she had looked into a mirror and cared about what looked back. Now, her sad, overgrown bush looked back at her, below painfully bony ribs and patchy, whitened skin, and all she could think of was how fucking hungry she always was. *Fuck this body. There's nothing I want to give it except food.*

She pulled up her pants, buckled her belt, and headed back into the next room. Joshua's large eyes watched her silently; Donald lay against a dead computer processing unit, exhaustion showing on his lined face. She almost hated to do it, but they had to get moving. 'Time to go,' she said. 'Another half hour and we'll be at Traffire.'

6

Dane huddled against the dumpster, clutching himself, but

the cold had penetrated deeper than his bones. Snow piled up at his ankles, blowing his jacket up into his stubbly face. The shivers were back, and they lasted longer now, racking his full body till it stuttered against the metal of the dumpster. He was freezing and half-dead from the cold, but he couldn't give up now.

This is our chance, brotha! Luck is breaking our way. Hoatam's been desperate for payback on these assholes. We won't be bottom of the chain if we grab them… or even kill them.

Dane felt under his jacket, and the hard butt of the Glock 23 pressed back. He had fancied himself something of a crack shot with it, until he had fired a misplaced bullet into Lenny Small's face two months ago. He hadn't fired it since, but if his back was against the wall, he'd open fire without hesitation. He was almost at the bottom of the food chain.

The food chain was Joe Hoatam's response to the Darwinian situation unfolding in Denver as the fall chill set in. There simply wasn't enough to go around. Hoatam had his core group, of course, and they couldn't be touched, which was why shooting Lenny had landed him in so much trouble. The only reason that he hadn't been taken outside the Traffire plant and shot in the head was that Lenny had been on the outs with Joel Hoatam, Joe's brother. But if you weren't in the Hoatam inner circle, and were one of those who had begged to be taken in after the fall gang wars that had pillaged the streets of downtown, you had to earn your keep.

Whether that was scavenging apartments for food to be stockpiled in the Traffire factory vault, gathering intel on other gangs or food stashes, or providing sexual favours on demand, you had to earn your daily ration. And if you were at the bottom of the food chain, you weren't pulling your weight. The collective could do without you being fed once a day, bathed twice a month and allowed to sleep in the warmth of the cellar. If you had been at the bottom for a while, you knew to run into the cold, run east, or one day Joel would be waiting to put a bullet in your brain.

Dane knew that being assigned to Windsor watch was the gang's way of telling him that he was almost at the end of his rope. But here was his lucky break. Everyone knew about

Hoatam's losses in the stairwells of the Windsor. He had been on a high after coming out on top of the gang wars, but the failed assault on the skyscraper had lost him half his best men. Hoatam was still furious, and if Dane could bring one of the Windsor gang's heads back to the plant on a platter, he would be secure for months. The very thought warmed him, though not for very long.

And if he could bring Hoatam the Windsor itself?

We might even find ourselves in the inner circle, right, brotha? Not going to tell a damn other soul. We'll take care of this ourselves.

From his perch in the alley, he could see both the back and front entrances of the Van Huesen store. Every so often he felt the Glock under his jacket, steadily drawing more and more comfort from it. He watched.

And from his perch on top of the electric lines of the LoDo train, the bum watched Dane.

7

Jupiter stepped out into the cold of the alley.

The wind assaulted her right away, bringing tears to her eyes. She coughed, took a deep breath of chilly air and stood there for a long moment, one foot in the door.

Dane watched her, muscles tensed, hand under his jacket on the butt of the gun. She was half a block away, but he could see her clearly, see her brown hair blowing across her face, the snow swirling around her ankles, head cocked into the wind to discern any movement. A block north, the bum moved, his shoes dancing lightly over the electric wires. The wires moved under his feet and he swayed with them effortlessly, as he always had, eyes focused ahead. He stopped as he caught sight of her and gently dropped between the wires onto the top of the hulking train.

The bum saw the situation in one quick second. He had seen many such situations unfold from his perch atop the train, and his escape route over the wires, especially as the crisp air of fall had descended from the mountains. The gang wars raging in the streets had shown him the worst of post-apocalyptic America, mocking the effigies to civilization that had been the once-prosperous LoDo plaza.

The wind was in the girl's eyes, but he could see her perfectly clearly. In another life, he might have classified her as ordinary, but she shone out to him now against the dull landscape. Another survivor. One gun, travelling light, looking around alertly. She couldn't see the guy behind the dumpster, but the bum recognised him. Had seen him walking through the 16th Street LoDo plaza many times, on his way back and forth from the Windsor. Had classified him as one of the degenerates soon to be naturally selected out of the equation.

Jupiter and Willy made their way around the building, onto 17th Street and the LoDo plaza. Donald and Joshua trailed behind, watching their backs, their footsteps swallowed up quickly by the falling snow. Half a block behind, Dane trailed them on the opposite side of the street.

And between them, the bum walked on the electric wires, watching it all. Mostly, he watched Jupiter.

She was clearly the leader, the others following her, watching her back. He hardly saw women on the streets anymore. They were either dead, or property. Such was the way of the new order. And if Hoatam and his thugs had it out for her and her clique, she wouldn't last long. Especially if she was headed right into his territory.

The bum had no one, and answered to no one. He watched silently, without interfering. It interested him to see how quickly the fabric of civilization unravelled in the absence of a need to maintain that fabric. He considered himself a silent chronicler of humanity's fall from glory, in full sight of its mightiest accomplishments. In the plaza around them stood electric trains, once-bright neon, towering buildings and the latest ways to buy meaning to one's existence, now all reduced to the bare minimum. A man lurking in an alley with a gun. Four people clinging together in the cold trying to survive.

And him above it all, a silent watcher, invisible and unseen on the wires.

The bum didn't feel anything anymore. Not pity, not sadness, not desire, just reflection. There was certainly enough time for it. There were no jobs to go to. No artificial deadlines to meet. He went back to his stash once a week, a trip not without peril because he had to make sure Hoatam's men weren't following him. But the rest of the time he merely sat, watched and thought. And as he left the train behind, and continued walking on the telephone wires in the storm, he thought about this mysterious girl, and her odds. He began to think that maybe she deserved a fighting chance. Perhaps to stick it to Hoatam and his psychopath brother Joel. Perhaps it was a sense of fair play. Perhaps it was neither, and he just wanted to see what would happen.

He reached into his pocket and with a silent grimace, the bum hurled the half-full bottle of Chablis into the snowy air.

8

The bottle smashed against the windshield of a dead truck.

Dane froze, ducking down behind a car, eyes trying to peer through the snow and locate the source of the alien sound.

Jupiter's gun snapped up into her hand as the little group pressed itself behind her into the doorway of what had once been the Hard Rock Cafe. 'What the hell was that?' Donald hissed.

'Probably just the wind,' Joshua offered.

'Or something heavy enough to smash,' Willy muttered ominously.

Jupiter stayed riveted, her eye up against the sniper scope. 'What do you see?' Donald whispered urgently.

Now you wish you had my gun, don't you, you brainless shit. 'Quiet,' Jupiter grunted. 'I'm looking through a fucking soda straw here.'

She started back at the edge of the 17th Street block and scanned slowly north, across the plaza and the snow-strewn road. The wind made it hard to discern movement but she stayed as still as she could, breathing through her nose, rotating the scope up to clear the upper floors. And then every muscle in her body went stiff, because a block back the way they had come, there was someone suspended in the air looking at her.

The bum and Jupiter stared at each other for what seemed like an eternity. His bearded face was clear in her lens, hanging lightly from nothing, his image gently shaking with her breathing, eyes sharp and staring right at her. Then his hand moved slowly - she stiffened, finger creeping inside the trigger guard - and she realized he was pointing down at his feet.

Jupiter's shoulder began to hurt with the effort of holding the rifle snug, but she followed his hand with her scope, down his ragged snow pants, and discerned the suspended wires on which he stood, effortlessly balanced. She scanned back up, ignoring Donald's continued whispers, and he was looking right at her. His hand moved again, and he pointed down across the street, toward a green VW Beetle.

She followed his direction, the Beetle jumping into sharp focus. There was no one inside. She scanned back up to the wire, but whoever had been balancing on it was gone.

She swept across the wire, her heart beginning to hammer, but it was quickly swallowed up by the gloom of the falling evening. Panic struggled up in her chest but she fought it back, and returned her scope to the Beetle. The whole world narrowed, centred on that scope and the green car window within it. Nothing moved –

Then Dane's head poked up on the other side of the window, squinting through it in her general direction.

Jupiter's finger touched the trigger. Almost automatically her body began to relax around the gun, her breath collecting in her throat and exhaling slowly, taking up the slack in the trigger. His forehead, and the blue hood of his jacket, was square in her sights. She could end his life right now.

She tensed, ready to take the shot, but her finger didn't move.

She couldn't do it. She couldn't kill him in cold blood.

Then he ducked back down, out of sight behind the Beetle. Jupiter let out a strained groan and snapped the gun down, pressing back into the alcove.

'What the fuck, Jupe?' Joshua said, urgently.

'We're being followed,' she responded. 'About half a block

back, someone was hiding behind a green car on the other side of the plaza.' She thought about mentioning the guy balancing on the wires, and decided against it. Not just yet.

'Shit,' Donald hefted his shotgun. 'Joshua, see if you can get a shot from that blue SUV. Willy and I will–'

'No,' Jupiter said brusquely.

Donald stopped mid-sentence, and she could almost see his moustache bristling. Behind her, she felt Willy tensing. Ordinarily she would have found a better way to broach it, but there was no time for niceties now. Their stalker was probably relocating himself to another hiding spot as they hesitated.

'I barely saw him,' Jupiter continued. 'More out of luck than anything. There are probably more of them somewhere back there.'

'You got a better idea, honeybuns?' Joshua sneered.

Jupiter felt her jaw tighten with annoyance. Even now, two months after their break-up, he couldn't let go of the need to constantly one-up her. And suddenly, so abruptly it hit her with the force of a two-by-four, she realized she'd had enough. She had carried this family this far, ensured their survival, and had fought them every step of the way to do it. She had done it because they had been her family, too. But not anymore.

'Yes, I do,' she said evenly. 'He doesn't know I saw him. At Fourteenth Street, we'll split up.' She turned around to face them, breath filling the alcove, fierce strands of fear and excitement mixing in her mouth. 'We'll force them to divide their numbers. Willy and I will keep heading east. Donald, you and Joshua head north, down Fourteenth. There's a park two blocks down at the intersection of Fourteenth and Livermore. Should be a wide open area. Get past the park and find good position; anyone following you will have to come across the park to get you. We'll do the same, and meet at Ninth and Livermore, in an hour.'

She looked at Donald, who was already growing a frown, and felt savage satisfaction at ramming this down his throat. 'Ninth and Livermore, one hour,' she repeated. 'Willy, you with me?'

Joshua opened his mouth, words already spilling out about

how this was a terrible idea, what the hell was she smoking, but Willy's quiet nod cut him short. 'Let's do it.'

Without a backward glance, Jupiter pushed out of the alcove and into the street. Willy hurried to drop into step beside her. Her neck, her whole body tingled, heart pounding furiously. There was someone out there following her—maybe more than one someone - but she didn't care. She had done it. She had finally drawn the line in the sand.

Behind her, Donald and Joshua kept tossing looks over their shoulders, trying to penetrate the gloom of the winter twilight. Fucking idiots, Jupiter wanted to scream. Why don't you wave a flag to tell them you know they're there? She picked up the pace. For months, she had worried that they would get her killed, and now that she had made up her mind to split ways with them, it couldn't happen soon enough.

15ᵗʰ Street and she increased her pace even more. 'What's the plan to lose *our* tails?' Willy muttered to her, as they leaped over a crater in the concrete sidewalk, caused by some unknown explosion.

'Just stick with me,' she replied. 'I know the layout.'

'I know you do,' he replied.

Willy and his family had been their neighbours, back when life had been simple in Eastern Colorado. He had lost his family in the early days, and they had banded together. Never given to loquaciousness, after his diabetic wife hadn't pulled through he had grown even more silent. But he was a sure gun hand, and a reliable partner. With him, Jupiter had a chance.

They crossed 14th, and Jupiter kept walking without a backward glance. For a fleeting second she wondered what would happen if Donald and Joshua kept following her, and her breath came up in her chest, but a block later, there were no footsteps behind them.

She cast a quick look over her shoulder, up in the air, and thought she saw a shadow behind the snow, hovering somewhere above the first floor level, but when she blinked it was gone.

Jupiter walked faster.

9

There are all kinds of survivors, the bum mused.

There are those who will do whatever it takes. Some try to think of all the angles, and manoeuvre themselves into the upper hand. Fewer still know when to cut their losses.

The bum watched Dane and almost felt sorry for him. Felt his confusion and fear as he watched Donald and Joshua go one way, Jupiter and Willy go the other. Saw him follow them both with his eyes, hesitating, unsure, until both were almost swallowed up by the grimy snow. Followed him on the wire as he picked, predictably, the less threatening pair. Donald looked like a walking armoury, while Jupiter carried just the one gun. Less threatening they may seem, he mused, but they were more likely to bring him to his end than the other pair.

Then Dane surprised him, by veering sharply to the right, abandoning their trail, breaking into a shambling jog away from them. The twilight swallowed him up quickly, the wind erasing his tracks in the falling snow. All kinds of survivors, the bum mused. The odds had changed, and he was cutting his losses. Perhaps he wasn't doomed for Darwinian elimination, after all.

The bum watched Willy's dreadlocks till he couldn't distinguish them from the gray of the sky anymore, and then turned back toward the 16th Street LoDo plaza.

Every now and then... it was interesting to induce a little change in the way the dice fell.

10

Dane ran faster, east down Livermore, then north onto Brown Street. He took the 12th Street Bridge and sped around the curve of the once busy interstate ramp, jumping over fences and cutting through alleys and back roads he knew well.

His brother was talking to him again.

They saw you, brotha. Don't doubt it; they didn't break them-selves in half to make it easy on you.

Are you sure, Mikey? You're positive they saw me?

There's a trap here no matter whether you take door A or door B. Take door C and cash in while you still can. Let the guys know what you know—there are people from the Windsor wandering around the city. They'll have to head back at some point... and you know Hoatam will want to be waiting to welcome them back home.

Dane's chest began to hurt sharply and he slowed down to a fast walk, but his brother kept talking to him. *You're still ahead of the game, brotha. Remember the old days? Those guys you cleaned out at poker? They never knew when to quit, did they?*

You knew better, though. You still do. Life is a lot more like a game of back-room poker now.

The familiar smoke-stacks of the Traffire Farm plant came into view on the horizon, and Dane forced himself to break into a run again. It was time to cash in.

11

'I don't see anyone, pop.' Joshua said.

'Shit, me neither.' The disappointment was clear in his voice. He peered across the barrel of the shotgun again, out at the darkening park, but nothing moved in the lengthening shadows. 'Maybe they decided to follow Jupe and Willy.'

'Should we wait?' Joshua said doubtfully.

Donald made a scoffing noise in his throat. 'I'm not one for this dicking around and waiting bullshit. Let's head down to Ninth Street.'

The two men shouldered their guns and left their positions at the second storey window overlooking the park. As they walked back through the apartment they had smashed into, the sour stench of rotting food followed them, out into the corridor where it blended with the decay from all the other apartments.

Outside, the snow had slowed, but the wind had picked

up, turning the evening into a white-out. They bowed their heads and walked into the wind, down Livermore Street.

By 9th Street, some of the wind had slackened off, blocked by the tall buildings around them. Donald and Joshua jumped over the small iron gate separating an outdoor Starbucks dining area from the sidewalk, and shouldered their way into the coffee house. Here again, the smell of rotten milk and stinking flesh wafted into their noses. Joshua sank against the back of a leather sofa, sticking his gun up onto the ledge, from where he had a clear view of the intersection between 9th and Livermore. Donald grunted in approval, then wandered behind the counter to whiz in the open icebox.

They waited in the darkness of the Starbucks, till night fell over the street. The storm was worse now, wind shrieking through the cracks in the door and straining building frame. At last, Joshua turned to Donald. 'I don't think they're coming.'

'Probably ran into some trouble.'

'I should have gone with her,' Joshua said, a worried look on his face.

'Don't worry about her, son,' Donald grunted. 'Not saying she ain't okay, but I think we're better off this way.'

'Pop, you think she's–'

'Fuck her,' Donald interrupted.

'Pop!' Joshua protested weakly.

'I'm serious,' Donald said darkly. 'Ever since we came to this goddamn city, she's had her high and mighty shoes on. I don't doubt that she's done a lot, but goddammit, when Tommy died...' He let out a long, shuddering breath. 'I've told you before and I'll tell you again. She thinks she's all that, let's see how she survives out there. She'll be back and begging before you know it, and after the way she treated you, I'd think it'd be just fine to take the opportunity to teach her a couple of lessons.'

Joshua said nothing, but his head was nodding, slowly.

Donald struggled into a standing position, and shouldered his shotgun. 'This shitstorm is getting pretty bad. Let's wait it out till the morning and then go by that factory she was talking about, the Traffire place, and see what we can find.'

12

The darkness was close to absolute. Blankets of snow blew by, kicking up ivory clouds. Jupiter crouched down behind Willy, who was at the open window with her gun, scanning the street below. Gently she put her hand on his shoulder, and he grunted in response.

'If we haven't lost anyone still following us, we won't see them coming now,' she said. 'Let's close the window and try to get warm in here.'

Willy sighed, then pulled back. Jupiter leaned over him and pushed the window down, then sank thankfully to the floor and put her head in her hands.

'You alright?' he asked.

Better than in a long while, as a matter of fact. 'I'm fine, I just…' She thought of the mysterious guardian angel balancing on the telephone wires, and shook her head. 'Never mind.'

Silence fell. 'Think they're waiting for us at Ninth and Livermore?' Willy punctuated the stillness with his deep voice.

'I don't know,' she said tiredly. 'But I think it's more important to make sure we're not being followed than to make the rendezvous.' She looked up at him. 'Don't you?'

He shrugged. 'We know the way back to the Windsor same as they do,' he said.

He let his head drop back against the wall, closing his eyes. Jupiter lifted her gun into her lap and watched him, knowing he was still alert and listening. She pictured him lifting her up and driving into her, thought about what his dark skin would look like stained against hers. It was funny to be scared of reaching out and touching him, and yet she was. Humans will be humans, she thought. The world can be ending, Mother Nature can be raging outside, there can be mysterious gangbangers tailing us through the streets, and all we think about is ourselves, and our own selfish desire not to be rejected.

He opened his eyes and looked at her. 'Do you want to take the first watch?'

'Yeah. I think there's a bed in the next room,' she nodded briskly. 'Go get some rest and I'll wake you when I'm ready.'

13

The cold of the night brought the heat of anger.

She had invested so much in the Windsor. It had been her blood and sweat that had turned the Windsor into a fortress. It was more hers than anyone else's. Striking out on her own would probably end in her death, and those selfish assholes would enjoy the safety of the sanctuary she had created.

The more she thought about it, the angrier she became. They owed her their lives. Every one of them, even Willy. Even now, she was the one leading the hunt for new resources to sate the ungrateful pack.

She imagined herself at the Traffire Farm plant somewhere, lying in the snow amidst the ruins, unseen, watching Donald and Joshua pick their way toward her through the scope of her rifle. Imagined herself letting out a long breath, gently squeezing the trigger. A red bloom appearing in Donald's chest. Joshua's startled face jerking around, like a deer in the spotlight, trying to locate the source of the shot. No pity, she whispered. No pity, and she imagined the pull of the trigger.

'Must be some serious thoughts.'

Jupiter looked up to see Willy folding into a squat opposite her. She laughed self-consciously and brushed her hair out of her face. 'Something like that, yeah. You couldn't sleep?'

'I slept just fine,' he said. 'I thought I'd see if you wanted to do the same.'

'Sure, sure,' she said absently. 'In a minute.'

He nodded, folded up against the wall. He didn't say a word, just looked out of the window. She appreciated being able to sit quietly and just think.

None of her thoughts were happy ones.

In the cold light of the next morning, the second location on Jupiter's map turned out to be a dud. Rats the size of footballs looked back at her sullenly, then flashed away into the depths of the dark as they drew nearer. They had left nothing edible behind. The place was dry.

The third was just three blocks over – a small production factory that once made Fly-Power energy bars. The city was quiet, as if it were just asleep, and any second now a snow plough truck would come around the corner and send them scrambling for cover. They approached the barely marked factory quietly, side by side, shoes crunching silently against last night's snow cautiously, but apart from broken windows and the occasional blood stain, it looked deserted.

Inside, it was warmer but completely dark, so much so that Jupiter had to reach out and take a hold of Willy's arm so she wouldn't bump into him. Willy put a hand on her shoulder and they held still for several moments, eyes and ears straining, but nothing stirred in the darkness except for the scurry and occasional squeak of rats.

'Do you have a light?' he whispered, right in her ear.

'I have glow sticks in my backpack,' she whispered back.

Rusting pipes and fraying posters lit up in a pale green, winking back at them. They wandered through the eerie lime darkness, Jupiter following Willy, casting the light around her.

Willy stopped in front of a door that read STORAGE. 'This way!' he sounded excited.

She followed him through the doorway and gasped.

The store room was filled with cartons, almost ceiling to floor, all marked as containing Fly-Power protein bars. She counted at least two hundred boxes, unopened, untouched. Willy sprang at a box, wrestling it onto the floor, tearing it open. He looked up and his face split into a laugh. 'Untouched!' he breathed.

One box of protein bars could keep the two of them alive for half a month. She sank down beside him, thrusting her hands into the box, coming up with ten chocolate flavored bars in her hands. She tore the wrapper off one and sank her teeth into it eagerly. It was flat, stale, horribly dry, but it settled heavily in her stomach.

Willy peered at the wrapper of the Fly-Power bar he had just devoured in the sickly green light. 'Thirty grams of protein, ten grams of sugar. Jupe, you're a genius!'

She reached out and hugged him. It wasn't just a hug, and she knew it as she put her arms around him. She found his mouth with her mouth; thrust her hand into his dirty cargo pants. He kissed her back, but hesitated when she tried to pull him on top of her. On the floor, in the dark, she had nothing to lose. She took off her sweater and shirt and put her breasts in his mouth, rubbing her nipples against the soft scratch of his beard.

'Jupe, I can't,' he muttered against her.

'Yes,' she hissed urgently. 'Yes, you can.'

Finally his strong arms closed around her and he pushed her to the ground. Everything blurred in the green light as he drove into her. They writhed together urgently, her fingers sinking into his shoulders, her hair brushing against the plastic wrapping of the energy bars that had spilled out of the box. It felt good, right, explosive.

When it was over he collapsed beside her, breathing hard. Minutes passed, maybe hours. They lay on the cold, dark floor, eating like they hadn't in months, cramming down the protein bars eagerly till their stomachs screamed for relief. She rolled over on her side, hitching her pants off her hips, and put her hands between his legs, gently stroking him. He groaned with satisfaction. She pulled him on top of her, kissing him and tasting the crumbs in his beard, and when he came this time he held her face in his hands and whispered her name.

Later, she told him.

'Yeah, Jupe.'

'This isn't going back to the Windsor.'

He looked at her seriously. 'What do you mean?'

'You know what I mean,' she said firmly. 'This is our stash now.'

He considered her silently. She knew he was thinking if what had just happened between them was no more than an attempt to manipulate him, and she was too tired to care. Survival was all that mattered.

He continued to look through the boxes, then spoke. 'Where would we go, if not the Windsor?'

'Nowhere. I think we should stay here,' she said. With what was in the cartons around them, they would not have to venture out again till summer. 'We could put up plywood to secure the entrances to this place. In time I could build shutters again. All we'd need is water.'

'What if I wanted to go back?' he said quietly. 'Share our find with the people who helped us survive this long?'

He looked at her, then her rifle. 'Would you kill me?'

14

Donald and Joshua were four blocks away from the Traffire factory when they ran across the first patrol. It was easy to hear them coming, because they weren't trying to conceal their presence. The two men dived into the shadows as the dark hulks of three men kicking their way through the piled up drifts of snow emerged, walking right down the centre of the road. Donald frowned at Joshua, then they pressed on, further down the narrowing street.

That was when they heard the first engine growl, and the clanking of chains against cement. Joshua dragged Donald down. 'Quick!' he hissed. 'Get under the car!'

Donald rolled over the sidewalk, clumsily pulling himself under an abandoned SUV parked by the curb. The snow was piled against the other side of the car, and both men quickly felt claustrophobia take over. The engine rumble grew closer, followed by another, then another. They waited, silently, clutching their guns, till silence fell across the street again.

'I don't like this,' Joshua muttered as they crawled back out onto the sidewalk and sat up against the car. 'There's too much going on in this part of town.'

'Something big must be happening,' Donald said. 'There's less fuel to go around than food.'

'Where do you suppose they're headed?'

'Fuck if I know,' Donald grunted. 'Hope it's goddamn important.'

'Should we press on? If we had Jupe with us we could go to one of her alternate sites, but…'

'Shit.' Donald bowed his head, deep in thought. 'Fuck it. Let's cut our losses and head back to the Windsor. If Jupiter made it back we can head back out again.'

'And if she didn't?' Joshua didn't show any reaction to this possibility.

Donald shrugged. 'We'll figure out a plan of our own. I'm not too worried about it.'

Jupiter was quiet for a long time. Willy didn't turn, kept digging through the boxes. She fingered her rifle.

Right here, right now, she could take charge of her own destiny. All she had to do was pull the trigger. It would be justified. Understandable. Maybe, one day, even forgivable.

She dropped her hands to her sides. 'No.'

He turned, looked at her over his shoulder.

'I wouldn't kill you,' she said heavily. 'I would fit whatever I could into my backpack and start walking to Boulder.'

She watched him in the pale green dark. He stepped off the shelf, came toward her. She wondered, briefly, if he would kill her now. Wrap his strong hands around her throat and keep it all for himself. She hadn't been able to pull the trigger. She couldn't stop him if he did.

'I don't want to go to war, Jupe. I'm tired of that.'

'I am too,' she said, not daring to reach out and touch him. 'I don't owe that family anything anymore, so I'm not going back, Willy. That's my choice. Your choice is up to you.'

He looked around, and shrugged. 'There are worse places to be these days.'

He smiled down at her, his white teeth flashing. 'I'm with you,' he said.

16

The bum had seen this before, back in the early fall. From his perch above the train, he watched Hoatam's men tromp through the LoDo plaza, armed to the teeth. Dane was riding in Joe Hoatam's car, right beside the big man himself, looking yellow and sick. Maybe he was a survivor, after all... if the cold didn't get him first.

He was still there, unnaturally still in the cold morning, when Joshua and Donald walked past, headed the same way Hoatam's men had. He sat on the train top, brushing snow idly around him, washing down the flat, dry taste of the Fly-Power energy bars with delicious Chablis, and thought about summer.

The Thirteenth Hour

Michael Trimmer

'That's what you're calling it?'

Isabel turned around, annoyed at Jonathan's lingering over her shoulder. They'd only been assigned to each other two hours before the airship launched. Between final orientation and security checks, she'd not yet had a proper opportunity to properly explain the exact nature of her preferred writing environs. While her résumé cited teamwork as a forte, the last time she'd done anything like a group project was five years ago, at the dawn of her journalism degree. The last thing she needed was someone unschooled in her discipline invading her privacy, criticising her stylistic choices, and asking poorly phrased questions.

She looked up at his unimpressed expression, and back down to her tablet's screen.

'What's wrong with-' She stopped as the airship shook again. Things rattled and snapped. Cables ground together. The cabin swayed and at least a dozen frightened volunteers once again re-tested the secure fittings of their armrests.

Moments later, satisfied that their terror grips had done nothing but leave marks in the chair's foam, silent relief rang out. Isabel rolled her eyes, amazed at just how green some of these people were. It was just unexpected turbulence, as if anything about the weather could be called "expected" since the Impact.

The seatbelt light came on and a transit officer emerged through the curtains. With a polite, assertive manner, he ordered everyone to stay calm and return to their seats. It wasn't clear whether they'd be landing soon, or if it was just the air ahead looking choppy. Either way, Isabel doubted she'd get much work done now, so she closed the tablet's blogging app just as Jonathan sat down next to her.

'What, pray tell,' she started, sweeping a strand of dark red hair out of her face, 'is wrong with my title?'

'What's "The Thirteenth Hour" when it's at home?' Jonathan asked, 'Apart from one o'clock in military time.'

'You know about symbolism, yes?' she asked 'Twisting a phrase? I know documentarians don't deal with all that, since most everything is right there in front of the lens.'

'Hey, those lenses don't track and pan themselves!'

'Writers, however, require a certain amount of artistry in their choices.'

'Right, artistry,' Jonathan said 'like that headline about the US post-Impact clean-up budget?'

Isabel nodded her head to one side. 'Not the best example, but-'

'Come on, "After Math?" that's art is it?'

'The fact you remembered it illustrates my point.'

'You're getting people to read your official Plymouth clean-up coverage by confusing them with the title?'

'By encouraging them to think slightly unconventionally, yes.'

'Okay then,' Jonathan began, 'so what's the Thirteenth Hour?'

Isabel smiled 'Take two away and you'll get it.'

Jonathan frowned 'Why don't you just call it The Eleventh-' he stopped.

'You see?'

Jonathan nodded. He smiled and turned to look out of the large, panoramic window to his left. They were still in thick cloud, but descending slowly. 'So where were you?' he asked. 'At the eleventh hour, I mean?'

'Not far from here,' she answered. 'Bournemouth, with family. When they expanded the evacuation zones, our holiday in a quiet, green and wooded corner of Dorset was cut unpleasantly short. Of course,' she continued, 'it was a lot more unpleasant for people on the shore.'

'You from the South West?'

She nodded. 'Bath.'

'Ah,' Jonathan said, 'sorry to hear that.'

'Southern Bath.' she explained, 'We were mostly alright.

The city centre won't ever be quite the same though, I imagine.' She glanced out of the window too. 'Where were you?'

'Pretty much untouched,' he answered. 'Whitstable, but I'm from Canterbury.'

'The other side of the country, England's Garden,' she said. 'So what brought you here?'

'Any opportunity to use these on home soil,' he said, tapping his glasses.

Isabel looked again at the uninteresting, black, Italian designed frames. She'd found it hard to believe when he'd told her just how wide their field of vision was. Fourteen cameras, covering two hundred and seventy degrees at 1080p resolution. Sixteen hours battery life and a wi-fi transmission range of one and a quarter kilometres. She couldn't see a single pinhole, but then she supposed that was the point.

'Did you build those yourself?'

'Me and a partner in crime,' Jonathan said. 'He wasn't drafted to this part of the clean-up though. I tried to explain when they accepted me for the candid coverage position, but they're being pretty strict on favours for friends.'

'No nepotism please, we're post-Impact British.'

'Right. So you applied for the blogger's gig?'

'I was head-hunted,' she said 'I'd worked for a few student websites and some local newspapers. I was applying to intern at The Atlantic just before NASA discovered Iris, and where she was going.'

'Ah, December first, 2019,' Jonathan said. 'Some Christmas that was!'

'Indeed,' Isabel said. 'So, how will this arrangement work, exactly?'

Jonathan shrugged. 'How'd you expect it to work?'

Isabel put on a caricature of thoughtfulness. 'I expect that we'll both work eight hours a day, clearing away the washed up corpses and debris that Iris left behind. After that, we'll each take an hour to go over our respective collected material – my notes, your footage; meet for at least an hour in either one of our tents-'

'Mine,' Jonathan cut in, 'don't wanna risk damaging the external hard drive traipsing it across a field.'

'Very well,' Isabel said, 'we'll compare notes and then decide what we shall and shan't be telling the Great British public-'

'The world.'

'The world,' Isabel corrected. 'About how Plymouth is pulling itself back together, after the most destructive natural disaster in living memory. We'll agree, or agree to disagree, with myself receiving the casting vote, shake hands and bid good evening, wake up in the morning, and do it all again.'

'Sounds about right,' Jonathan agreed. 'But how come you get the casting vote?'

'I'm the writer,' Isabel answered. 'And a woman. The latter of those should be reason enough.'

'Don't I know it!' Jonathan agreed and showed her his left hand. On the finger next to his smallest was a band of yellow gold marked with two emeralds either side of a diamond. Two sets of initials were engraved lightly on either side. 'Next June,' he said.

Isabel's eyes widened at first, and then she smiled. 'You're wearing an engagement ring?'

'Hey! She proposed to me!' Jonathan said, defensively. 'Classy, right?'

'Classy!' Isabel agreed. 'And refreshingly modern!'

'Glad you agree!' Jonathan agreed. 'We'll have to double date when this is all over.'

Isabel shook her head. 'I don't find being a third wheel much fun.'

'What, no beau?' Jonathan asked. 'We'll have to fix-' The cloud cleared. They looked down.

There was sand and silt over everything. A thick cake of it. A dirty beige-grey shroud. Poking up through, the salt rusted remains of cars, trucks, bikes, and park railings. Buses beached. Vans upended and gutted. Nothing untouched. Iris hadn't quite been an extinction level event, but that was scant comfort when confronted with the scene below.

The houses and shops nearer the bay were gone. Smashed beyond recognition, sunk under the deluge. The ones furthest out had barely survived. A front wall missing, a side collapsed – nothing too devastating. It was the ones in-between that were the most disheartening.

Slumped forward, uprooted by receding water, they looked somehow noble, in a sad way. As if, even before Iris had touched the atmosphere, they had been resigned to her inevitable North Atlantic impact. Their innards spilled out into the street. Televisions, tables, plates, books, kettles. Isabel was even fairly sure she saw a Furby.

She didn't sigh, or shed a tear. She'd seen enough pictures to know what to expect. At this distance, it still didn't faze her. She'd probably not really feel anything until her feet touched silt. That wouldn't be until tomorrow, after they'd settled in at camp. She turned round and saw Jonathan looking too.

'Let's leave discussions of that kind for later.'

'Yeah,' he agreed, 'lots to do down there.'

'Not quite what I was hoping for.' She tapped the quad truck twice with her shovel. The driver set off with wheel-spinning pace, spraying a jet of wet sand over the tips of Isabel's work-boots. 'Thrice bitten, quadruple shy!' she shouted.

Jonathan smiled as he lifted his waste sack. 'It's not like you didn't know it'd be like this. Don't girls like you muck out stables and stuff back home?'

'Manual labour doesn't bother me,' she said, swinging her shovel onto her shoulder. She clipped the edge of her orange hard hat, sending it spinning. Jonathan couldn't help smirking as she realigned it. 'I don't even mind the monotony,' She continued. 'Such as it is.' She paced back to where she'd been digging. They'd been trying to clear this silt dune for three days, and every day it seemed, somehow, to be getting bigger. Despite the difficulties, manual clearance was the only option. Isabel had seen the YouTube videos of the attempts at landing mechanical diggers out here. All that had done was add further large items to the list of things that needed dragging away. Humans, although slower, were much steadier, and didn't need petrol, just sandwiches and water.

'So, what's up?' Jonathan asked.

'They asked me to write.' she said, propping the bag open once more. 'But write about what? We get up, we dig, bag the silt, pour it into the trucks, trucks pour it into the crates, robo-barges ship the crates away. Nothing's actually happening.'

'Can't you write about the "the empty shells of dead dwellings",' Jonathan began, 'or the "crushing weight of the silt beneath your feet", or how about the "glassy horror in the eyes of those people who didn't escape"?'

Isabel huffed. 'Something akin to that. Somehow though, I doubt the Great British public-'

'World public,'

'-is interested,' Isabel persisted, 'in blog post after mournful blog post about how difficult and sad everything is. We're in the thick of the thirteenth hour. Isn't there supposed to be hope and progress?'

'Don't know about hope,' Jonathan said, 'but as for progress, we might be getting things done faster soon.'

Isabel looked at him curiously. 'Why is that exactly?'

'You not heard about the relief mission?'

'We're being relieved?'

He shook his head. 'They're moving the army detachment along. The UN Archangels finished the African bases early, now they're helping out on the European end. Soon, we'll have our own floating resupply hub with actual professional equipment. And it'll be people who've actually seen a mudslide before running the show, not just someone who read about what to do when one cuts you off from your unit.'

'Excellent,' Isabel thought, imagining the hopeful change they might feel once that big red and white sky borne behemoth arrived. 'When are we to expect them?'

'Couple o' days, probably less than a week.'

'Something new,' Isabel said, sinking her shovel into the silt.

'There's the contest too.'

'What?'

'The memorial design,' he explained. 'They want design

ideas for a memorial statue for everyone who didn't push enough people out the way to get to the evac-zones.'

'Really?' Isabel said. 'I trust they won't use that exact phrasing on the plaque?'

'Probably not. It'll be made of compressed silt.' He passed her the leaflet that he'd seen. Isabel read it through before folding it away into the pocket of her high-visibility vest.

'Interesting. You know anyone planning to enter?'

'A truck mechanic from Liverpool, who studied 3D print design at Warwick, and a couple of Cambridge art students. Can ask around if you want.'

'Are they all students?'

'Heck, students and recent grads are like, sixty percent of everyone here.'

Isabel nodded. Anything for the résumé, especially now. 'It'd be good to do some interviews,' she said. 'Maybe try capturing how other people interpret all this.'

'Now you're talking.'

Isabel returned to digging. 'How did you discover all this before me?'

Jonathan shrugged 'Maybe if you spent less time up in your tent, writing stuff, you might find something worth writing about.'

'Mess tent gossip?'

'That's how I heard all this,' Jonathan answered. 'Plus, when people read sources, the juicy stuff isn't what happened, it's how people lived with it.'

'Maybe,' Isabel began, 'but when Kate Adie was in Rwanda, she covered what the peacekeepers were doing. Or more accurately, what they weren't doing. Not how they coped with not doing it.'

'Are we in Rwanda?' Jonathan asked.

'Don't be obtuse.' Isabel barbed, 'She was there to cover a story.'

'They sent her to find the story.' Jonathan corrected, 'When it kicked off, they didn't know what the story was.'

'She had a briefing, and a mandate.'

'Except you're in different time zones,' Jonathan explained. 'She was in the Twelfth hour. When the balloon was on its way up. You're in the Thirteenth. That balloon's gone. You try finding it, you'll be filming a blank sky. If Adie had been in Rwanda in the aftermath, she'd be talking to people who let that balloon go, asking how it looked, how they dealt with the loss.'

Isabel tilted her head in thought about that. 'Except, in our case, all those people are dead.'

'So talk to the people who took their place. The ones cleaning up the bodies and living in the mess. And it's living's that's going on in the mess tent. Come up with us, meet Dave, you'll like him.'

Isabel looked at him with a worryingly sense of his meaning. 'Dave?'

Jonathan laughed. 'The scouser grease-monkey printer-nerd! I'm not going setting you up! I actually like my friends!'

'Excuse me!'

'Class-B!' A shout came from their left. They looked up to the top of the silt dune, where a lone woman had dropped her shovel. The silhouette they saw against the overcast sky told them she wasn't so alone anymore.

The hand jutted out at an angle that living bodies would have found extremely painful. An older woman, complete with cardigan. Preserved in the silt, but still bearing a familiar unearthly whiteness. Isabel came over to watch.

The squaddies got to work, clearing the ground. They sprayed something on the sandy mush to solidify it, propping it up as they dug in deeper around her. The smell was remarkably subtle. A dim background of decay, the potency you might get from throwing potpourri in a church hall. The medics arrived, the senior ones marked by their full face air filter masks. Jonathan stepped back a little to catch the whole scene.

Isabel signalled to him. 'Multi-zoom.'

Jonathan nodded, and set his cameras for multiple angles. Close ups, panoramas, texture shots and everything in-between. Nothing would be missed. Isabel had yet to see a body first hand. Most were found nearer the evacuation collection points. This was something inspirational, though she felt a pang of guilt for thinking about it like that. Maybe she'd write about that thought process too.

They'd almost exhumed her. She'd been reaching forward, maybe trying to swim clear. Maybe the receding water left her like this. Two squaddies grabbed her legs, pulling her clear of the thicker stuff. Others grasped her torso and under her shoulders.

'On three!' She watched them all, knee deep in sludge.

'One!' Rescuing the dignity of the dead.

'Two!' Restoring some sense to the senseless.

'Three!' The silt gave way. They lifted her clear and dropped her into the plastic coffin that lay waiting. Her hand spilled over the edge, knuckles dragging in the mud, not letting go of even a modicum of worldly connection. She watched one of the younger medics put the hand back. They held onto it a little longer than was needed. It must be strange for a medic to tend to the needs of the dead. Isabel watched her hand as she let go, giving way to the inevitable, letting time-

It was only a second, but somehow she was sure. She gasped, but kept her composure, concealing the true extent of what she'd seen. A flash of curved silvery white, the slightest sleight of the medic's hand. The unnatural jerk of the dead woman's wrist, the fourth finger separate from the rest. If she hadn't been looking so hard, Isabel was sure she would have barely noticed. It was masterful, but it had definitely been there.

The medic turned, obscuring the offending hand. Isabel didn't see it being pocketed, but seconds later, she swept her hand through her hair, and waved the box away.

'Did you get that?' Isabel whispered.

Jonathan looked at her quizzically. 'Get what?'

'I still don't see-'

'Keep rotating!'

Jonathan sighed and obeyed. The 3D model was massively incomplete. As amazing as the fourteen cameras were, to do what Isabel wanted they would have needed at least fifty more, evenly spaced, surrounding the scene, all within an eight meter radius.

The reason for the complexity, as Jonathan had already explained, was that these weren't motion capture devices. They were point-and-shoot, not something you could simulate 9/11 with. 'I'm making March of the Penguins, not Avatar!' was a shouted phrase the occupants of the neighbouring tents couldn't quite contextualise.

'Look, there!' Isabel pointed, but by the time Jonathan's finger let go, it vanished.

'Look at what? We've been at this for nearly an hour! Shouldn't you be writing?'

'Let me try!'

Jonathan stepped back.

Isabel tapped the keys very gently, moving the angle. They were looking at the moment when the corpse's hand fell away. Isabel scrolled back until she saw it. 'There!'

'What?'

'That shine!' She pointed to a fleeting group of pixels around what looked like the corpse's fourth finger.

'So, she had a wedding ring.'

'Not here she didn't,' she moved twelve frames forward.

Jonathan leaned in. 'That's nothing, look!' He wound back again 'It's only visible with the sun shining off it. The ring's silver, her skin's greyer than HMS Belfast. You can't pick it out.'

'Look at the indentation, the way the fourth finger bends. None of the other fingers do that.'

'That only proves she used to wear a ring,' Jonathan said. 'Maybe she's divorced. It's not exactly rare.'

'Funny,' Isabel commented. 'What about this?' She pointed this time at the medic's hand. Between two fingers, where there should have been daylight, a tiny, insubstantial, silvery greyish curve could be seen. Very thin, only visible because they'd enlarged the picture to a pixelated patchwork, but it was definitely there, along with a tiny suggestion of shine. Encountering this problem earlier, Isabel's "enhance" suggestion had left Jonathan in hysterics for a good five minutes.

'Hmmm…' Jonathan said, looking it over 'I don't buy it.'

'Care to share a reason?'

'Could be a ring, could be dead pixels, a bird's wing in the distance, dust caught in the sun, something on the lens.' He leaned over and pressed the minus key all the way back until it showed the picture in its true dimensions. 'It's too small. You present this to any digital forensics expert with half a brain, they'll laugh.'

'We're not asking a digital forensics expert!' Isabel insisted 'We're confronting that medic.'

'What if she denies it? You think she'll blub and confess?'

'We'll search her tent.'

'On whose authority?'

'That picture's!' she answered. 'And my eyes.'

'Nobody else saw anything.'

Isabel cast her hands around, frustrated with his intransigence. 'Do you want to know if you're right?'

'Yeah, but we can't just barge in like Fascist-' Jonathan replied in kind, but after hearing himself, stepped back for a moment. He breathed heavily.

'Fascist what?'

'Sorry.'

'Fascist what?' she insisted.

'Pigs,' He answered. 'But-' He paused, not knowing where to go with more words.

Isabel could see he was sorry. She took a slow breath. 'It's okay,' she said, looking back at the screen. 'You're right, it is small. We can't do anything. And we shouldn't be able to anyway.'

'Oh?'

Isabel shrugged. 'What if I didn't like her? What if she stole my boyfriend?'

'You don't have one.'

'Hypothetically,' she said, gesturing dismissively at the screen. 'There are good reasons for due process. This kind of thing must be easily falsifiable.'

'Photoshop,' Jonathan agreed. He looked it over, thoughtfully. 'Besides,' he began, 'even if we had proof, we still should wait.'

Isabel glanced sideways at him. 'Why?'

'Think about it,' he started. 'This can't be the first time, and she can't be the only one. I mean, we're sitting on a thieves' paradise! Quarter of a million people's abandoned goods, most of them dead or resettled. No one prepared for it, because they were so obsessed with all us volunteering our lives away like saints.'

'But,' Isabel began, 'no one would steal a silt-damaged DVD player, or a rusted through hatchback.'

'But little stuff, necklaces, bracelets, rings. If it's made from something non-corroding, you've struck gold, pardon the pun.'

Isabel's eyes rolled, 'What's your point?'

'If we nail this one, the rest 'll go underground. Right now, they think they're home free. But if we find out more. Get whoever's in charge, find out how they're smuggling stuff out.' He looked at Isabel and smiled. 'You said you wanted a bigger story.'

'Quite,' Isabel agreed. 'But first things first. Haven't we better be sure we're not on some wild goose hunt? Do we even know if she stole something?'

'You saw her.'

'You didn't,' Isabel reminded him. 'And no one else did either. I'd rather not waste my time looking for a smugglers cove in a den of saints, if it's at all avoidable.'

Jonathan twisted his head at her phrase. 'Den of saints?'

'Something for the blog,' Isabel explained. 'A name for the mess tent.'

Jonathan smiled. 'Nice... and you're right. We need hard proof and I know just where to get it.'

'Where?'

'You might be a good blogger,' Jonathan began, grabbing his coat, 'when you get out a bit more. Let's see if you're a good blagger.'

'You didn't happen to do an autopsy on the woman's body that came in here this afternoon?'

The morgue tent's receptionist raised his eyebrows. He was an older man, probably mid-seventies. Five foot four, thin. One or two wispy white hairs on a bald head peppered with liver spots. Thin frameless spectacles rested half way down his nose. He didn't look like someone who enjoyed tomfoolery, or if he ever had, it was a very long time ago and something he didn't like to remember.

'Excuse me?'

'The woman, who came in earlier,' Jonathan clarified, 'from sector fourteen.'

'I understood your inquiry.' The receptionist answered 'But I think it is you who misunderstands my responsibilities.'

'Ah,' Jonathan began, not sure where to take this.

'This is not a hospital,' the man explained. 'We simply identify the passed on, we do not perform invasive examinations.'

'Yeah, but, I bet you know how, right?'

'Pardon?'

'Doctor Yatsfield, right?'

The man looked a little flustered. 'Formerly, yes.'

'Aw, you never lose that knack!'

The former doctor remained unmoved by Jonathan's flattery. Isabel stood beside him, thoroughly unimpressed.

'Was there a particular reason you enquired of me, Mr-'

'West, Jonathan West,' he said, extending his hand. The doctor did not reciprocate. 'It's just, err… my friend thought the body looked like her great grandmother, she'd been a bit too past it to understand the evac notices, and we wondered if we could see her.'

'To confirm her identity?' the doctor asked. 'Possibly.' He turned to Isabel 'May I ask-'

'And how she died,' Jonathan interjected. 'Just to check.'

The doctor sighed, 'Is that necessary?'

'Well, she was a few salads short of a buffet,' Jonathan continued. 'If the wave got her, that's one thing, but if she got depressed after the evac, and… err… well.' He paused and let the implication speak for itself. 'We'd just want to know.'

The doctor looked at Jonathan, and then at Isabel. 'What is your name, young lady?'

'Her name, errr…'

Isabel rolled her eyes for the fourth time since he'd suggested this plan. She looked at Doctor Yatsfield 'I'm sorry, doctor. The truth is, my name's Isabel Jarvis. I write for the Thirteenth Hour, it-'

'Ah, the blog?' the doctor asked.

Isabel's eyes widened. '...Yes.'

'Sterling work.'

'Thank you.' Isabel replied. 'We're, err... profiling some of the class-Bs. We were wondering if you could have a look at Mrs, err, that is Ms.' She paused. 'Well, if we knew her name, and a little more about her, we could maybe put something together.'

'Most noble. Follow me.' He strode down the shelved aisles of long plastic boxes.

Isabel whispered to Jonathan as they walked. 'I told you.'

'How should I know he'd read the blog?' Jonathan asked. 'He probably retired when Windows 3.1 was cutting edge. Tumbling's probably what his wife does down the stairs when she hasn't taken her pills.'

'Small lies work best. Not that I plan on lying.'

'You're penning that piece?'

'It's poignant,' Isabel replied. 'You heard him.'

'You're still lying.'

'Omission.' Isabel answered. 'Not like lying about your name.'

'Hey!' Jonathan barbed 'It's minimal.'

'West instead of Webb?'

'In case he doesn't like snooping.'

'He's read the blog,' Isabel pointed out, 'he knows our names.'

'Didn't have to. Better safe than sorry.'

'And why'd you ask about how she died?'

'We need him to open-'

'Here we are.' the doctor called them to the far end of the row. He pulled out the sliding slab and lifted the lid. 'Well preserved in the silt. It's likely she died of causes relating to the Impact. I could check her toxicology, but I doubt anything will emerge.'

'Weren't suicides widely reported before the Impact?' Isabel asked 'Particularly among the elderly - the ones who might not have fully understood, I mean.'

'Had she died much earlier, bacteria would have set in. Decomposition would be far more pronounced and she would have a much less recognisable face.'

'You use face recognition?'

'We liaise with the national records office.' Doctor Yatsfield explained.

'She was married, right?' Jonathan said, leaning over the box. 'Look.' He pointed at the left hand.

Taking a magnifying glass from his top pocket, the doctor looked more closely. 'Yes,' he agreed, 'definitely a wedding band indent. Recently removed too.'

'Recently?' Isabel asked.

'Just before she died,' the doctor added, pointing. 'Silver residue, here.'

Jonathan nodded in agreement. 'Thanks doc!' he replied. 'When you get more intel, we'll catch up. Issy, we gotta-'

'I have more details from other cases,' the doctor interjected, 'perhaps you would like to hear more?'

'It's getting lat-'

'Nonsense, Johnny!' said Isabel, eyeing him severely. 'Tell me, Doctor, how many class-Bs have been recovered?'

'Three hundred and twenty seven. But only ninety six actually have records. All fully alphabetised, of course.'

'Excellent! Lead on.'

'Such interesting lives,' the doctor began. 'Let me tell you about Mr Abbotsford.'

'What was that?' Jonathan said, once he was sure he was clear of the tent's earshot.

'Don't documentarians have to do research?'

'Yeah, but not at eleven thirty at night!' Jonathan insisted. 'Not when we could have gone back tomorrow!'

'He was so proud of his alphabetising,' Isabel explained. 'It seemed a shame-'

'He got all the way to Zachery Gullsbry before you 'realised the time'!'

'Oh, come on,' Isabel answered. 'If we left too suddenly, he would have known something was afoot.'

'Who'd he tell?'

'Someone,' Isabel said. 'And they could tell someone else. Like you said, we don't know how many people are involved here.'

'Well, we know at least one for sure now,' Jonathan said, passing her the glasses. 'Take a look.'

Isabel put them on. The projection lights were very dim. Jonathan set it that way, so that he wouldn't be seen using the augmented reality OS while trying to grab candid footage. But the contrast with the November night was clear enough.

The video showed the woman's finger. Empty skin, sunken nails, white. Then it zoomed in.

'What am I looking at?'

'The finger joint,' Jonathan explained. 'Keep watching.'

She did. The wrinkled joint flesh was peppered with tiny white coils of dead skin. There were indentations too, up both sides of the fourth finger. The deeper ones were blackened, a slight shaded line.

'What are they?'

'From when your medic friend pulled the ring off,' he explained. 'Whoever this lady was, she'd donned that ring way back. Getting it off without damaging the skin would be impossible.'

Isabel looked closely. 'Why didn't Doctor Yatsfield mention this?'

'He just checked the indent. We're looking over the whole finger.'

'Couldn't she have just done it just before the Impact? Like the indentation?'

Jonathan shook his head. 'Too fragile. It's the same as those little white flakes you sometimes get after scratching too hard. The wave would have washed them away. Also, there's those scratches up the side of her finger. If she'd been alive, those black marks would be red. That's necrotic blood. I should know.'

Isabel was going to ask about that, and then she remembered the qualifier he'd used before about the camera. Home soil. She stayed in the moment 'She's definitely been stolen from.'

Jonathan nodded. 'We've got our crime, now we need criminals. You a vegetarian?'

Isabel was confused by the incongruous question '…no?'

'Good.' He said 'You won't mind a little stake out.'

'Rosalind Beech,' Isabel confirmed, once she finished scrolling through the volunteer database. She clicked the tablet off, sliding it back into its silicon case, fearing the screen's light might reveal their position behind the hedgerows.

'They just hand out volunteer's names and addresses?' Jonathan asked.

'Not quite. Just names, ages, hometowns, photos, and tent numbers.'

'Tent number three four four,' Jonathan said. 'We've got movement.'

Isabel turned. All she could see were the vague grainy outlines of rows of bell tents. She hadn't yet gotten her night sight back, still too used to the camp's floodlights. 'Exactly how expensive was the night vision option?'

'Came as standard.'

'Of course.' Isabel said. 'Why is she going now?'

'The floodlights were on before. Had to wait until everyone's bedded down for the night. They can't meet in daylight. Witnesses would leave trails to the main man.'

'Why tonight though?'

'Least possible time between finding it and being caught with it.'

'But no one's looking for them.'

'Can't risk it.'

Isabel looked at him quizzically 'How many criminally inclined individuals did you work with before answering these questions became second nature?'

'Who said- hey!'

'What?'

'She's heading into a tent.'

'Which one?'

'Storage thirteen.'

'It's unguarded?'

'It's empty. Come on, we gotta get closer if we wanna see this guy's face.'

'How do you know it's a man?'

'Wanna find out?' he asked. 'Come on!'

They ran alongside the hedgerow that divided the fields until they were parallel to the tent's frontend.

'Could they have gone out the back?'

'Nah, my guess, there's some haggling-'

'There!'

Torch beams turned. Beams that had, up to that point, been concealed behind the tent, illuminating the handling of a very small object. Now though, in response to the new sound, they focused squarely on Isabel and Jonathan.

'...That's- oh no!' Jonathan began. 'It's just another torch-like stick. You guys haven't seen a MagLite lying around, have you?'

There was no reply. Instead, several figures wearing medic issue face masks moved to surround them on three sides. With each wearing an identical black hoody, their hands concealed in front pockets, they resembled a troop from some deeply unholy monastic order.

'Did you see anything?' one of them asked.

'You mean my MagLite?' Jonathan replied. 'Nah, looks like that's gone, I'll have to-'

'Did you see anything?' This time the tone was louder and deeper.

Jonathan breathed heavily and slowly, calming his nerves, stiffening his resolve. 'Why'd you ask?'

'If you didn't,' the deep muffled voice started 'you can leave. If you did...'

'What?' Jonathan asked, and then walked up close to where the voice had come from last. 'Say I saw something, what then?'

The rustle from the figures inside one of the pockets was enough to warn him. He turned sharply and knocked the can of pepper spray from the hands of the figure standing immediately behind him. He turned to face Isabel. 'Run!' He hissed, before twisting to face another attacker.

Isabel obeyed, sprinting thirty meters before the hedges

tripped her, twisting her ankle. A lone figure approached. She rolled over, trying to stand, but the pain of weight on her sprained ankle was too much. The figure followed. She swung her legs round, kicking his feet out from under him, yelping in intense pain, hitting him as she did with her already damaged ankle.

She looked to where she had run from. Jonathan wasn't there. She tried standing again, but her foot was in agony. A bright light dazzled her.

'Cloth her,' said a voice with an unfamiliar accent. 'Sort it later.' The rag tasted bitter.

Light blasted across their faces.

'Come on you two,' It was an older voice, one Isabel didn't recognise, 'let's be havin' you'. The sound sent pain spiking through her temples. The sunlight was unbearable. An acrid sugary smell seemed omnipresent.

'Seems someone couldn't wait till the arrival party. Had to get a little Nellie Dean ahead of things. Well heard, Ms Beech.'

'Couldn't exactly not hear it, Mr Paulson, I'm sure the whole row heard a verse or two.'

Isabel blinked slowly, trying to assess the situation. Stretching, she knocked a large and heavy box. It tumbled, banging and cracking. She winced at the noise. Turning from the sunlight, she opened her eyes.

She was sitting on a kind of throne, two metres high. A nobly, sticky, plastic throne, made of interlocking heavy blocks that shifted about as she pawed them. A translucent coating obscured much of the details, but eventually her eyes made out a logo and some words. "Kingston Estate – 80% Proof".

She blinked. Memories of last night returned.

'No,' she said, although her control of her mouth was less than complete. 'No, we didn't-'

'Get her down.' Two larger men scaled the well stacked shipment, reaching where the restacked crates gave Isabel a commanding view of the storage tent.

'You don't under- waghhh!' Her balance was bad enough without being manhandled. The huge squaddie carried her atop his shoulders. She flailed in protest, but her limbs were massively out of sync with her brain's orders, and she only succeeded in unbalancing him as he climbed down, not to mention bruising her dignity in the bargain.

'You ought to be ashamed of yourself, Ms Jarvis.'

'I... don't.' Isabel knew she had a rational explanation, but it wouldn't sound quite as believable as Beech's one.

'You and Mr Webb take the rest of the day off, you're in no condition to dig, but don't think this won't come up on your volunteer's record! Get to the mess and get some food and water in you. That hangover's not going away without it.'

'They're smart.'

'Discrediting us, instead of killing us?' Isabel asked. She could feel a vague pain in her upper arm where she presumed the IV had gone in to feed her the alcohol. Try as she might though, she couldn't find a mark. Clearly, they'd been both precise and thorough.

'If they'd killed us, that's a whole other ball game,' Jonathan pointed out, between bacon sandwich mouthfuls. 'Two corpses full of questions? The police would swarm. This way, they get us out of the way, and make sure we can't poke our noses anywhere near them again.'

Isabel nodded with resignation. 'Or at least,' she added, 'it's unlikely anyone would take us seriously.'

'Not without concrete proof.'

Isabel turned from her cereal. 'No video?'

'They wiped it.'

'What?'

'Everything. Right back up to when we were staking out Beech's tent.'

'They went to your tent?'

'Must have.'

Isabel shivered. If they could trace Jonathan's tent, presumably they knew where she slept too. Even if rationally she knew the questions raised by her corpse would act as pretty sturdy life insurance, the truth was she didn't know anything about these people. She couldn't put it past them to engineer alcohol poisoning, a quad truck accident, or some other simple and explainable misadventure for her to befall. She would have to watch her back from now on, but she was adamant that didn't mean walking away.

'Couldn't we complain about someone accessing your hard drive without permission?'

'There's no proof it was anyone but me,' he said.

'But why would you do that, and then accuse someone else of deleting it?'

'To get back at Beech for ratting on our piss up.'

Isabel could see the logic. She tried to find some good news. 'What about earlier, we've still got the footage of the body's ring finger.'

'They left that alone, but it's useless now,' Jonathan answered. 'We can't tie anything to Beech, apart from her helping to bring the body in. We can't prove she took it, and because they were all wearing masks, we've not even got our own witness statements.'

'Why were they doing that?' she asked. 'They couldn't have known we were following them.'

'It's so they couldn't identify each other,' Jonathan said. 'Stopping outsiders IDing them is just a bonus.'

Isabel began realising just how flimsy their case was looking.

'Right now,' Jonathan continued, 'all we know for sure is that a ring was stolen. Who, when, and where, is anyone's guess. On our evidence, Yatsfield had the most means and opportunity.'

'Don't even joke about that,' Isabel said 'He's charming.'

'If you like your stiffs alphabetised,' Jonathan replied. 'Charming or not, unless we catch another death-do-us-part class-B soon, we're back at square one.'

Isabel nodded thoughtfully. 'Unless,' she began, 'we were to catch them in the act.'

Jonathan gave a dismissive huff of a laugh. 'Good luck with that one!' he said, and took another mouthful of sandwich. 'Just stake out every class-B with poachable jewellery, and hope the suspects don't toss anything into the silt when they're cornered.'

'We wouldn't have to corner them,' Isabel suggested. 'Just shadow them, distantly this time. And why would it need to be a class-B?'

'You plannin' a sting?'

'Something akin to that.'

'Okay,' Jonathan began, 'we get a body from... somewhere, plant something on it, wait for someone to find it and take its jewellery, follow them to where they keep it, and then show Paulson the footage.'

'You took the words from between my lips.'

'Yeah, great plan,' Jonathan said. 'Except we have no body, no jewellery, and no way to plant it in front of someone we know will steal from it.'

'We know Beech is one of them, do we not?'

'Yeah, she won't be lifting anything within sight of either of us ever again.'

'Not necessarily,' Isabel said. 'She thinks we're out of the picture. Anyway, it wouldn't need to be her. We just film us putting the ring on a body, check to see if it's gone when it gets to the morgue, locate their ill-gotten gains, and if we find our planted ring, we'll know it was them.'

'How'd we implicate people?'

'We'd have footage of everyone who had access,' Isabel answered 'It might not catch everyone, but it would certainly encourage security.'

'Not enough,' Jonathan said. 'We'd have to stake something out.'

'So we stake out a body.'

'How?' Jonathan asked. 'And where'd we get the jewellery?'

'You make documentaries. You must have a few non-glasses cameras.'

'One or two,' Jonathan answered. 'And yeah, maybe we could hide them in the tree or something, but what about the jewellery?'

Isabel said nothing, but just looked down at his left hand.

Jonathan followed her line of sight until he realised 'No. Way.'

'Do want to catch these people?'

'This is mine!'

'Then we need to work extra hard to be sure we get it back.'

Jonathan looked at the ring.

'The people who died after the Impact were given their rings by people special to them too,' Isabel replied.

'Yeah, but they're dead.'

'That's just how the thieves would justify themselves.' Isabel retorted.

'Don't you have any jewellery?' Jonathan asked 'Something that didn't come from the person who loves you most in the world?'

'This may surprise you,' Isabel said, 'but when I volunteered for this, accessorising wasn't a priority.'

'Whatever.'

'And unlike you, I actually read the health and safety guidelines. The "no jewellery" rule was pretty explicit.'

'Hey, I follow the rules.' Jonathan barbed 'It only comes out at me-time.'

'Fair enough,' Isabel replied, 'but answer this, have you a better idea?'

Jonathan thought for a while, before finally he shook his head. 'Okay, but answer two questions. Where are they hiding it, and where you gonna get a body?'

'The hiding place is a mystery,' Isabel began 'but I know where it must be going.'

'Where?'

'Remember what you said about Beech? How she had to minimise the time she held onto the stolen ring. The same is true here. This might be the den of saints now, but one accidental reveal-'

'Game over.' Jonathan interjected. 'So, it's leaving the camp.'

'The only things that leave are trucks transporting waste silt and refuse to the robo-barges. Since they're all either automated or have only one or two staff, that's an unlikely route. Too few suspects makes tracing the mule easy.'

Jonathan nodded. 'Safety in numbers.'

'When they planned the camp, they were expecting the Archangel's arrival. Hence the party tonight, hence the rum. When they start bringing cargo in and out, that's the smuggler's exit strategy.'

Just as that moment, noises came from outside. Distant shouts from people on the silt. Those on the campsite emerged from their tents, their shadows clear on the white walls of the abandoned mess tent. Isabel and Jonathan headed outside. In the distance, under the overcast cloud, a long oval outline of white and red made itself visible. There was a set of blue flags, and a large red cross on the front.

'Right there.'

Jonathan sighed 'Are even the good people bad these days?'

'Some of them.'

'Okay, so that's their exit strategy,' Jonathan said. 'Now, where's this body we're using.'

'Like I said, we don't need a class-B. And we have shovels.' She looked over distant hills, towards a church spire.

'Seriously?'

'You have a better plan?'

Jonathan sighed. 'No.'

'I hope you know I can't go hiking ever again after that.' Jonathan said, dropping himself onto the reinforced cotton of his aluminium frame camp bed. The early evening light was filtering in, and in less than an hour, the camp would be filled with volunteers, desperate to rest after a hard day's silt shifting. For Jonathan though, the day had already been hard enough.

'Stop moaning,' Isabel retorted, as she sat down at the chair next to the computer desk opposite, 'you got a shower did you not?'

'Yeah, and I needed it like never before,' Jonathan said, 'just to wash the guilt out of my clothes.'

'This wasn't desecration,' Isabel pointed out, 'the graves were already exposed.
'

'Right,' Jonathan answered 'the old "It was like that when we got there" ruse.'

'Exactly.'

Jonathan sighed. 'Couldn't we have just... left a jewellery box half open?'

Isabel's eyebrows arched 'Somewhat obvious.'

'Maybe,' Jonathan said. 'But you're not the one with your engagement ring stuck on some stiff's finger.'

'We will retrieve it.'

Jonathan sat up and looked her square in the eyes. 'I'm holding you to that,' he said, as seriously as she had ever known from him.

'I know.' She had wanted to say something smarter like "I'm fully aware" or "I know very well", but the truth was she had no idea what it felt like to give up something that important to service a bigger cause.

Jonathan looked around in exasperation before flopping back into his bed. 'Why'd we need ten bags of waste silt?'

'Did you want it to be obvious that it was planted?' Isabel asked, 'The silt around it had to be smooth, and it wasn't smooth with just three.'

'But... ten?'

'Stop whining. I carried as much as you. And anyway, observe the evenness.' She displayed the feed on the computer screen.

It was visible from three angles. Jonathan had been planning to use these cameras to catch time lapsed pictures of clean-up progress at the bay, but since they wouldn't' get to the coast for a few more weeks, he'd kept these to one side.

Coffin and corpse stuck out of the ground, head end up, slanted, with the ringed hand just about hovering in the dirt. They had been careful to choose a point far away as possible from the team working this section, yet close enough to ensure that it would be picked up before the day was out. This meant a lot of hill-watching by Isabel while Jonathan dug deep enough so they could cover it without looking suspicious. It wouldn't be too out of context. class-Rs were rarer, but the Impact's wave had spread detritus far and wide.

'And we have to do this today, why?'

'They'll start the supply flights tomorrow. Who knows when we'll get another chance?'

'Looks like we've been found,' Jonathan said, pointing at the screen. It was two people. A man and a woman, both young, one familiar. 'Beech,' Jonathan observed.

Isabel nodded. Neither of them looked to be alerting authorities. Beech let her shadow provide cover, while the man reached round and made a show of rocking the stranded coffin clear. Isabel directed the lens, capturing his true intentions. Refocusing, she caught his face. She opened up her volunteer listings and started scrolled through.

'Matthew Fox. Tent three four five. Coincidence?'

'Like Lee Harvey Oswald's target practice in Dallas,' Jonathan said 'You okay guarding the computer while I shadow?'

'Will you manage all that shadowing?' Isabel asked, looking over his seemingly exhausted state.

'I'm fine,' Jonathan said, 'you just keep an eagle eye on the computer and back up important things as they come in.'

'Indeed,' Isabel said, 'but be back soon. If I'm going to return your ring, I'll need to have an early night, especially with the noise from the Archangel's arrival party tonight. The first resupply flight will leave in the morning.'

'How're you gonna get on that flight, anyway?' Jonathan asked.

Isabel winked. 'I'm a journalist.'

'Wait!' Isabel timed her arrival just right. She ran briskly towards the lift cable station, wearing the closest things to formal clothes she'd packed, with her hair wrapped tightly in an intentionally unflattering bun. The thing that was really slowing her down though was the glasses. Jonathan had instructed her in their use, and they were size adjustable, but that didn't make her less wary of running too fast, and letting them fall off her face and into the mud. Even if they were just his old spares, she still wanted to treat them with care.

The men at the lift station looked at her quizzically as she ran. She held her tablet carefully, while still traveling at a speed. The lift up to the airship was stationary, for now.

'Sorry I'm late,' she panted, 'just, heh, alarm clocks, you know?'

'Ma'am, do you have Archangel clearance?' One of the guards asked.

'Oh, man,' Isabel began, nervously, 'Mr Paulson didn't call?'

'Ma'am, I'm sorry, I-'

'I'm Isabel Jarvis, I'm writing for the Thirteenth Hour, the blog?'

The guards looked at each other. 'We've heard of it, but-'

'And, and Mr Paulson said I could ride on one of your flights, you know, to report a relief guy's POV.'

'Ma'am, if you're not cleared-'

'Oh, please!' she begged. 'I can't come back another day, Mr Paulson won't give me another day off, please!'

The guards looked at each other again. The first one shrugged. 'Log her.'

'Thanks!'

'You'll need supervision.'

'Cool! Like, a tour?'

The lead guard looked across at his friend. 'Yeah, a tour. And we've got just the guy.'

'Great!' she said. 'Allons-y!'

'The first Archangel class relief dirigible was commissioned and designed by the United Nations International Emergency Forces Commission in November 2014,' Mr Wright explained as they looked back out the window, towards the airship that their supply runner was leaving behind.

Isabel wished she hadn't been quite so enthusiastic about the tour. She did her best to make fake notes, but this had passed 'tiresome' long ago. They walked along the only aesthetically designed part of this aircraft. The insides weren't as spartan as those helicopters or drop planes you saw soldiers jumping out of in action films, but it was much closer to that than a commercial 787.

'It was a long term response to dangerous seismic events, but also the possibility of dust bowls and other localised agricultural problems resulting from climate change. In the aftermath of the Iris asteroid impact-'

'Officer Wright?' Isabel asked, waving her hand from the elbow. The tall, imposing man turned. He made her slightly nervous, but he seemed the gentle giant type. 'No offence,' she started 'but this is kinda like "Wikipedia" type stuff. I'm looking for "stories", you know?' she said, adding air quotes. 'Like, what it's like working here?'

'Certainly,' he said, and they walked down a metal gantry onto a lower deck 'This is the *Lourdes*, a Seraph class dirigible heli-jet hybrid. Designed in Britain in 2010, it later became the Lockheed Martin P-971. Each Archangel carries six Seraphs, each Seraph has a twenty six man crew. At one hundred and five metres long-'

'What's the, like, "mission", today?'

Mr Wright wrinkled his nose in displeasure at her interjection. 'The *Lourdes* is making the first of several logistics missions. We will arrive at RAF Brize Norton in forty minutes, where-'

'Aren't we heading north-east?' Isabel asked, before realising the mask might be slipping. 'Isn't Brize Norton like, Kent?'

'We are visiting the Bristol Channel,' Mr Wright explained. 'Rendezvousing with a waste deposit rig.'

'Like, in the sea?'

Mr Wright nodded. 'They filter useful compounds from silt, as well as recycling damaged property.'

Isabel froze. 'Damaged property,' she said, noticing her tone shift and then quickly changing. 'Like, dead people's stuff?'

'Items damaged beyond repair,' Mr Wright explained. 'We have strict policies. Nothing functional, no personal items, no-'

'Is there, like, a bathroom, on these planes?'

'Dirigible heli-jet hybrids,' Mr Wright corrected. 'Follow the signs. But be careful. We will be docking with the waste deposit rig very soon.'

'BRB!' she exclaimed, darting down a flight of stairs. She knew she had to be fast. A waste processing plant was the obvious drop point. Full of hiding places, never short on traffic, a crew of dozens. If the jewellery arrived, there was no telling where it could go from there.

Interpreting the "toilet" signs liberally, she arrived in the first of the cargo bays. This was a dead end. Even though there was no one around, she knew from the size of these containers that they were probably filled with nothing but waste silt. Presumably, the robo-barges weren't working hard enough.

The next bay was the same, and the next. At one point, she was almost certain one of the relief workers had seen her, but they passed by without as much as an inquiring glance. It was only the fourth bay that finally showed some promise.

Plastic crates. Sky blue plastic crates. All of various sizes, all marked with a white UN logo, a red cross, and the recycling symbol. She looked around. This was the last bay. She couldn't imagine these people would be reckless enough to hide their stash in silt that would be fed into the jaws of automated processors. The jewellery had to be in one of these boxes. Unfortunately, there were at least two hundred. She sighed.

'Attention!' a PA announced. 'This aircraft will be docking with naval disposal station four in two minutes. Evacuate all red zones. Non-loading staff, return to green zones one through four.'

A door opened. She spun round and hid as someone entered. Flattening herself against a stack of crates, she looked up. Just below the ceiling, a red banner lined the room. White letters running underneath read 'Red Zone Five – Recycling bay'. Someone wasn't following orders.

She turned round slowly. He faced away from her, his attention focused on a stack of the shallower, wider crates. Isabel trod stealthily along the aisles of boxes. She moved to get a clear angle on what he was looking for. It seemed to be CDs. Dozens of shattered plastic discs. He didn't seem happy with that. Sorting these things must be what people did when they weren't digging the silt, Isabel thought. The next two crates were similar, but the fourth made him smile. She could hear the gold clinking.

She watched him draw a black cross on the box with a marker pen. He closed the lid and walked round. Isabel kept pace. He was putting crosses on several other crates, but only the larger ones. It made sense. Someone, somewhere in the smuggling chain of command would know that it was only the little crates that carried anything of value to them. They'd take it and ship it off to God knows where. She shivered.

The door opened and closed. Isabel looked around. Seeing nothing, she assumed he had left and headed for the marked crate.

She gasped as she opened it. It was a treasure trove. This couldn't just be from Plymouth. There must have been jewellery from all across the south coast. Possibly other countries. She couldn't believe her eyes. After slipping the tablet from its case to check everything was still being recorded, she began to sift through, looking for Jonathan's ring.

'Freeze!' She saw a gun barrel in her peripheral vision. 'That's mine. Hand's up!'

She obeyed, clasping her palms to her scalp.

'Close the lid.'

She remained still.

'I said-'

'You said to raise my hands.'

'Wise gal, huh?' he started. 'Okay, close the lid, then get your hands back up.'

'No,' Isabel said, straining to stay calm.

'Wha'd you say?'

'Attention! Docking in one minute. Evacuate all red zones. Non-loading staff, return to green zones one through four.'

'I said no,' Isabel confirmed. 'I heard the announcement. I expect the loading staff will be arriving very soon. If they find you here like this, they'll have lots of questions.'

'I've got a gun, and you're the one next to the haul,' he answered. 'What makes you think they'll trust you over me?'

'Since when do relief workers carry guns?'

'Check your eyes,' he answered. 'This's a flare gun I got off the wall. It won't kill you, but it'll burn pretty bad.'

Burning. Isabel had an idea. 'You wouldn't shoot a girl.'

'Depends what she's doing.'

'How about this!' Her short sharp dart to the left startled him. He fired exactly at the moment she'd wanted. Her arm had swung up. The tablet and its casing were ready. The heat-proof silicon sent the flare ricocheting along the floor towards him. He slid and fell back, just as the whole room began to shake.

'Docking in progress,' the PA announced. After much shuddering, two huge bangs were followed by the entire back wall folding away. An army of automated loading trucks rolled on through. Isabel ran to the side exit door, but a lockdown was in progress, and it was sealed. Her adversary returned to his feet. He fired again, but this time a loading truck blocked him at the crucial moment. The flare went spinning off and away.

Isabel looked desperately for something resembling a weapon. Dodging the armada of forked lift drones, she grabbed a fire extinguisher. Soon enough he was coughing and spluttering in a haze of powder and CO_2. He stumbled into view and using her good foot she kicked him down, knocking away the flare gun. Spraying him again, she looked around for a way to get attention. She eyed a white, shallow plastic cylinder on the ceiling. Aiming the flare gun at it, she emptied it of all but one round. A wailing din followed.

'Alert! Fire in Red Zone Five! Alert!' The trucks ground to an automated halt.

'Stay down!' Isabel shouted, brandishing the flare gun in his face.

A few moments later, the bay's upper gantry was filled with relief staff. They quickly saw the open jewellery stash, and the woman with the flare gun securing one of their colleagues.

'Everything's fine!' she shouted up. 'Long story. It'll be online tomorrow!'

'Cheer up, it might never happen!'

Isabel startled as Jonathan leaned over her. She had been sitting in her tent staring at the tablet for nearly forty minutes now, without a single word having met the page. Normally she would have preferred to be by herself, but right now she welcomed the distraction.

'I'm worried it already has,' she said.

'We got them, didn't we?' Jonathan pointed out 'I followed Fox, he met Beech, who met a couple of others. That and I figured out who the rest of those people who jumped us must have been.'

'Who?'

'There's only so many people with access to medical gas masks.' Jonathan explained. 'Turns out, not everyone's valuable enough to need protecting from airborne toxins that float around rotting stiffs.'

'Indeed,' Isabel said, and looked down at her tablet again.

Jonathan eyed her expression closely. 'Writer's block?'

'Something akin to that,' she agreed.

'So what's up?'

She tried to think of words that made her complaint sound all noble and serious, but in the end, she just gave up. 'It's not fair!' she insisted. 'This was supposed to be our finest hour, when people sacrificed their time and energy to do something great for their fellow man,'

'Not to mention their not-so-fellow dead man, and woman.' Jonathan added.

'And instead,' Isabel persisted, ignoring his comment 'I have to write about... this.'

'You're the one who found it all out,' Jonathan pointed out. 'Don't tell me you wanted to speak no evil on this one.'

'Of course not,' she began 'But the thirteenth hour is supposed to be about nobility, when people look over the disaster's horror, pick themselves up, stiffen their upper lips and work hard so we can move on.'

'I don't know what history you've been reading,' Jonathan replied, 'but off the top of my head, I can think of at least... twelve rocky aftermaths, not including this one. And besides, you're forgetting what journalism's about.'

'What's that then?'

'The truth,' Jonathan answered. 'Or, as close as we can get.

Good journalists let the story tell itself, it's the bad ones who try to squash it into a world view's narrative.'

'But don't people deserve to have their faith in humanity rewarded?' Isabel asked 'Shouldn't people be able to look to at least one time, one event, or one person in history, without any possibility for cynicism.'

'You really thought that'd be post-Impact Britain?'

Isabel laughed. 'Maybe.'

Jonathan shrugged 'I don't know about stopping cynicism,' he began, 'but if you want people to have more faith in humanity, write the truth about all this. No one paid you to catch these guys. No one even was nice to you about it, especially after being "drunk" in the storage tent. Heck, I didn't believe you at first. But you kept at it, because you knew it was the right thing to do.' He smiled. 'That'll restore people's faith.'

Isabel blushed slightly, 'Thank you.'

'You're welcome, and thanks for this,' he said, waving her the back of his left hand, 'seems it ties people up in more ways than one.' He smiled, and then gave her a caricature of a stern glare, 'Now get writing, then get some sleep, there's plenty of silt still needs shifting tomorrow.'

Hope Street

Dylan Fox

Ivy's body drifted towards Duke. As she crouched down, clusters of tarmac fell away from the edge of the pavement and into the stream beneath. Free's quick-flowing waters now hid the broken concrete and twisted metal of utility pipes, underpasses and tube tracks. But here, the water moved so slowly that Duke could watch the bubbles moving through the tangles of Ivy's hair.

Without rising, Duke shuffled a few steps down stream, wrapped her fingers in Ivy's hair and pulled her closer. She looped her arms under Ivy's shoulders, and pulled her to the broken pavement.

Another pair of hands grabbed the fabric of Ivy's shirt, and Duke slapped them away.

'Fuck's sakes,' a male voice said. 'Just thought you'd want some help.' Was he from the community centre? She glanced over her shoulder. No, she would have noticed him. His skin-tone and accent told her nothing— Free had always been a gravity well for the world's poor, and only the poorest of them now remained. But his well-fed frame, the sense of security in the way he stood... no, he was a foreigner. Why was he lurking outside the old church? She turned back to Ivy, a rictus grin on her friend's face. All corpses started to grin after a few days; the afterlife must be a fun place. She leaned back and hauled Ivy to the tarmac, her lithe body making Ivy's seem almost weightless.

She carried the body out of the skyscraper's shadow and leaned her against the creeper-covered church wall. Sunlight cut across Ivy's chest, and ivy leaves gave her an emerald halo. Duke leaned forwards and brushed wavy, wet hair out of the corpse's face. Its brown skin dull like bark, its brown eyes staring over Duke's shoulder.

'You know her?' the man said. Duke looked over her shoulder at him. She turned back to Ivy.

'What have you done to yourself now?' she said quietly, running her finger across the open gash in Ivy's neck. Ivy didn't answer. Duke cursed.

Duke cursed, and reset her Internet connection again. When she'd woken up this afternoon, she didn't know that four decades from today she'd find her friend's corpse drifting slowly towards her. She didn't know that today she'd kill for the first time.

The eleven-year-old girl stared at the static webpage telling her that freemium satellite Internet was no longer available. That it was a necessary step to bring Free back to solvency. Anyone who wanted to get online now needed to find a premium hotspot, and had to pay.

Duke showed her friend, took the joint from her and inhaled deeply. Artificial light filled the atrium with an antiseptic glow, the weeds in the flowerbeds unsure of which direction to reach in. Water dribbled through the nozzles of the fountain, algae staining the plaster. Duke's mobile passed from hand to hand among her small group of friends.

They stalked into the corridors of the building, past the bright lights of the chain stores and through the milling, confused crowds staring down at their mobiles. They met other groups of tweens and teens, just as angry and confused. They talked. They shared joints and bottles of cheap cider. They told each other how unfair it was, how Internet access was a basic human right and now the bastards were taking that away from them, too. Someone found video of gangs smashing windows on other floors in the tower. And it seemed only fair: the corporate world had hurt them, so they should hurt the corporate world. Respect demanded redress.

A group of scared shoppers huddled in-front of a clothes shop as the staff struggled to close the doors and lower the metal shutters. As Duke ran past with her friends, she threw an empty bottle at the corporate logo. It smashed, a piece ricocheted into a shopper's neck... Duke never knew.

The international press covered the riots in forensic detail. Pictures of Free's airy corridors covered in glass and merchandise filled news feeds, video of flames licking out of the seventieth or hundredth floor of Free's beautiful vertical cities played on screens around the world. A journalist eager to understand Free's culture of violent youth gangs cornered a police officer and harangued a quote. 'It was just McCartney scallies,' the officer said. 'They're always causing aggro with the Ken Dodd crew.'

Just punk kids causing trouble.

Duke and her friends watched the news report about the ongoing war between the McCartney Scallies and Ken Dodd Crew, two of the most notorious and violent gangs in Free. She had never been part of a gang before, but... She lived in McCartney block. She was young, angry, violent. So she must be part of the McCartney Scallies, one of the most notorious and violent gangs in Free. And she had a war to fight with the Ken Dodd Crew.

The police stretched beyond their limits as the weeks of chaos on floors thirty to eight-five rumbled on, Duke led her gang over the twenty-third floor bridge to Ken Dodd block. The Crew expected them, and met them half-way. Lights blinked around them, cars streaked across the spaghetti roads beneath them and on the high floors above them, life carried on as it always had. The two gangs stood suspended between their two blocks, sky above them and tarmac below, street lights twinkling like stars on the roads and walkways above and below them.

They were there to fight. So why did everyone keep shouting and shoving? Duke pulled her knife and drove it into someone's gut. She stabbed it into their side, their ribs, their neck. Her newly-looted clothes dripped with someone else's blood. She stabbed and stabbed, holding the boy up by the throat, grimacing and desperate to exorcise the rage burning through her veins.

By the time she let the man-shaped lump of meat drop to the metal floor, both gangs had fled. Blood dripped off her.

She threw the knife against the reinforced wall of the walk-way and stared up at the girders criss-crossing the roof above her. She stared through them, through the stainless steel ceiling and up into the sky, at the quiet satellites still orbiting the Earth. No matter how many windows she smashed, how many times she stabbed, how high she reached, they would never notice her. But what else could she do with this rage? How else could she stop the world treating her like scum?

Wind whined through the broken windows of Free's towers. It rustled through the grid work of brambles, goose grass and ivy that dangled from the window frames high above the ground. It rushed over the clover and dandelions puncturing the tarmac and played with the leaves of the birch saplings as they reached for air and sunlight. Shadows cut the winding road into uneven strips, the sunlight blocked by leaning buildings, flyovers and skybridges. The wagon slowed as the road rose, flying over the empty shells of downmarket shops that once catered to those who had almost nothing in this gleaming paradise that offered everything.

Gears clicked as the rider changed down. The wagon started life as a domestic wheelie bin, but McCartney had re-imagined it. He lay on its back, cut the front away, used the lid as a loading platform, fixed the whole thing to a crude chassis and hooked a pushbike to the chassis. So now he had a way to move crates of food around the city, and seamstresses dozens of miles away from the river ate fish and the fishermen wore new clothes. Duke perched behind boxes of cod and blackberries. Dark grey clouds drifted between the small gaps of sky between the buildings and bridges.

She took a cigar out of the pouch on the front of her hoodie and rolled it between her lips. The dried leaf crumpled and flakes of tobacco fell into her mouth. She held the cigar between her fingers, licked her lips and spat. The hand rolled cigars she smoked these days were nothing like the machined ones of her youth, but that was back when people still imported things into Free. These days, if you wanted something you had to find someone who grew it and convince them to give it to you.

Why was Ivy dead? Duke took out her lighter, breathed the flame in through the cigar. A half-dozen wild dogs trotted down the road towards them. The driver steered to the left and let the pack have the easy path, and he changed down again as he fought through the ragwort and brambles.

Cui bono?

No one in Ivy's stable of artists had reason to kill her. None that Duke knew of. She treated them well. Ivy gave them a place to rehearse, a place to learn from each other, to indulge themselves. She gave them equipment, schooling when they wanted it, her undivided attention whether they wanted it or not. When they earned, Ivy took enough to keep herself in room and board, the musicians kept the rest, and Ivy kept her name quiet— there was no reputation to take.

'Hey.'

Duke blinked.

'Comfy back there, love?'

The driver spoke between deep breaths, legs working to take them against gravity.

'I'm all right,' Duke said, and turned around. She watched the back of the man's head. It bobbed up and down as he pedaled.

'All right, yeah?' he repeated. 'Ain't that sweet.'

'Ain't it,' Duke agreed.

They crested the hill, and the road verges merged with the floors of the towers they passed. The driver steered them around the nascent trees, did his best to avoid the pot holes and banked up clusters of weeds. He squeezed the brakes and they pulled to a stop.

Duke looked around. Where were they?

17th Street as it cut through Cowell Block, the old nPower tower on the left and above Val's Chippy. The old employee car park smelt stale, of pooled water, rotting concrete and long-established bird nests.

So, that was it. The driver dismounted and walked around his wagon. A half-dozen youngers sat under the eaves of the

car park, suddenly quiet and watching. He wanted an audience. Duke hopped down onto the road.

'Sun sets on everything, Duke,' the driver said. He stepped
off his bike. His feet shuffled uncomfortably, his fingers
twitched. Every few moments his tongue darted out over his
lips.

'That so?' Duke asked. One of Ivy's lines, something she'd
spat into a microphone back when she called herself MC
Eleven-hundred.

'You can't be expecting a man to work for free,' the driver
said.

Duke studied his face. He was old enough to know better.
Early-twenties, maybe. Jordan Block accent. Was he one of
Ti Lovelace's brood? Ti was a good lad with a sensible head.
Loved doing the donkey work, playing an unnoticed extra,
so she'd set him up with Prince Charlie as a delivery man a
couple of decades ago now, and McCartney had inherited
him along with the rest of Charlie's gear.

'And I told you, I owe you,' she said. 'I'll return the favour.'

'Yeah,' he said. 'When it suits you. When it's going to do
you more good than me. I want paying today.'

'Oh,' Duke said. 'Right.'

She walked around, stood between the youngers and the
wagon. She stubbed her cigar out on a crate of fish and put it
back in her pouch. If he wanted a show, who was she to deny
him? He waited a few moments, followed her for a few steps
and then stopped.

Mohammed, that was his name. Lovelace's nephew, or
cousin's kid, or something. But that explained why he was
peddling the wagon— Lovelace had worked his way up high
enough to give the kid a break. It's what you do for family.

'I ain't scared of you, Duke.'

Duke smiled. 'Give over, Mo. You're shitting yourself more
than a baby after a dirty kebab.'

Mo reached behind his back, brought his hand around
and pointed the barrel of a gun at Duke. Duke frowned. Mo
shuffled his feet again, licked his lips.

Duke lifted her foot, and by the time she'd finished her
step the anger burned in her veins. She snatched the knife

from the small of her back and devoured the distance between them. Mo opened his mouth to say something, but the words died as Duke tore his stomach open. She punctured his kidneys, growled as the blade ground against his hip. Both hands wrapped around the hilt, she ripped through his cheek, cut through his skull, opened his lungs. He fell to the ground. Duke kicked his twitching body, stamped on his knees, ground his skull, kicked his ribs.

Who the hell was this little fucktard to pull a gun on her? To wait until he had an audience and threaten her? She kicked him again. His neck snapped. She kicked his throat. Kicked him in the gut and had to disentangle her boot from the spilling grey of his intestines.

She exhaled. She squatted down, wiped the blade of her knife clean and put it back into its sheath. Her anger burned out, she let the smoke of its fire drift away. She stood, ran her hands through her hair, put her hood back up.

So who'd given him a gun? McCartney's drivers didn't have guns. No one in Free had guns— they were too resource-intensive to make and too resource-intensive to maintain. She crouched down and took the pistol from his broken fingers. A real gun, not a starter pistol or replica re-bored to fire live rounds. She ejected the clip and looked at the bullets. Homemades. So he could afford the piece but not the ammo. They probably would have jammed in the barrel and killed him a long time before she was in any real danger. Idiot.

She put the clip back into the gun, tucked it into her belt and walked over to the youngers. They watched her, faces expressionless. A girl on the far left turned her head, spat, and stalked into the shadows of the car park. Duke watched her go, then turned back to the ones who stayed. She knew their cold, emotionless faces well, so well.

'McCartney's goods still need delivering,' she said.

An older boy, eighteen maybe, broad-shouldered and clean-shaven, stood. The others watched him. He drew himself up as Duke stood in-front of them. He stood three inches taller than her. Blood ran down Duke's hoodie, down her trousers, scabbed on her boots.

'What about McCartney?' he asked.

'What's your name?'

He licked his lips. 'Mac.'

Who was he? Cowell block accent, obviously. But who were these kids with him? What did he care about? This latest generation was getting away from her.

'Well Mac,' Duke said. 'Today's the day I do you a favour. You deliver this for McCartney and I'll smooth things over for you.'

Mac knew what he was being offered. A job with McCartney could set him up. Give him food. Respect. A way out of sitting on curbs drinking cheap cider.

And what would Duke do if he declined? Mo's corpse probably had a good idea.

Mac nodded slowly, stepped around Duke and walked over to the wagon.

'The old Fed-Ex warehouse,' Duke said. 'Corner of thirty-third and London Road.'

'Yeah,' Mac said. He straddled the bicycle, and started to pedal.

Whoever he was, she'd fix him if he was a problem.

The youngers stared at her. The sound of rusted metal hitting concrete echoed over the silence. Duke looked over the kids and into the car park. The spitting girl lurked in the gloom.

Duke walked through the group and under the rust-strained concrete arch of the car park's entrance. Drops of water hung on the stalactites of lime washed out from the ceiling, and small rat feet scurried away from the preying cats. Creepers of ivy crept across the floor and up the walls. Sometimes it seemed like that creeper had replaced the old steel bones of the city.

'You know who I am?' she asked.

The girl looked over her shoulder.

'Yeah,' she said. 'You're older than God. No one gets that old round here. Just Duke. The great and powerful Duke.'

She kicked the can again.

Duke took out the cigar, relit it. The girl's face caught in the yellow flame of the lighter.

'There was no need to kill him,' the girl said. 'No need.'

Duke frowned.

The girl kicked her can and it rattled away into the damp shadows. She turned around.

'What's your name?' Duke asked.

The girl stuck her hands in her pockets. Dirty black hair hung over her face, long at the front and shaved close everywhere else. Ribbons threaded through the piercings in her ears.

'Fenchurch,' the girl said. She kicked at a tuft of grass growing through the floor.

'That's a Gallagher block accent, Church,' Duke said. 'You're a long way from your territory.'

Church shrugged.

'Tell you what I'm going to do, Church,' Duke said. 'I'm going to do you a favour. You go down to Fisher at the docks. Give him a message for me. You take my name with you. You want to drink something a bit better than shite cider, you start telling people you're on my dime and people'll start listening to you.'

'Wait,' Church said. 'A guy called Fisher? And he works on the docks?'

'Works on the boats,' Duke said. 'Catching fish.'

Church smirked. Duke shrugged.

'Sometimes things just work out like that,' she said. 'So you got that?'

'What if people don't believe I'm on your dime?' Church asked.

Duke blinked. 'Then I'll do you another favour. You take this,' she held out the gun. 'If you fire it you'll lose your hand, so if they don't listen to my name and they don't listen to this, then come back and tell me who they are, and I'll sort them out for you. You got a bike?'

Church shook her head.

'Then go see Dee,' Duke said. 'She's a friend of mine. Apartment sixteen-hundred and four, Bryden Block. The Liver Tower. She'll give you some real bullets too, if you're nice. Now you'd better get going. It's a two-hour ride.'

Duke reached into her jeans pocket, and took out an envelope. She held it out with the gun.

Church stared at them for a few moments.

'Who am I working for?' Church asked.

'You're working for me,' Duke said.

'Yeah, but who are you working for?' Church asked.

Smart kid. Duke maintained power between the argumentative gang leaders of Free by working for them all, without history or prejudice. If they could pay her, and she approved of the job, she'd take it.

'This one's *pro amor*,' Duke said.

'What?' Church's mouth curled into a teenage sneer, as if Duke were an idiot she had to endure. Duke smiled.

'You're working for me,' Duke said. 'And so am I.'

'Maybe I can stop you killing at least one person,' Church scowled, and snatched the envelope and gun from Duke's hand.

Duke followed the rusting train tracks as they cut through and over the city. Sunlight dappled her path, some caught by the birch saplings clinging to the silent billboards and some missing her entirely as it lanced down to the river beneath. In her youth, the sewage and metro lines ran underground, entombed by layers of road and shops. But neglect opened them to the sky, and the rainwater pouring through them eroded what remained of their roofs. Blood dried and made stiff patches on her t-shirt and hoodie. She worked her jaw and dull red flakes drifted off her cheeks. Beneath her, a deer bleated over the sound of the running water.

Embankments on either side hid the city from her eye level, her vision walled down to this narrow corridor. The buddleia moved as a lost rabbit awoke and panicked, and butterflies exploded from the bush like raindrops from a dog shaking itself dry. A cool breeze ran down the old tracks, channelled like the waters below. The sun hung in early-afternoon behind the towers, peaking through the gaps in the skyline.

The railway took the long way to Ivy's apartment, but the short way went down 74th Street. Glass littered that road, fallen from the scrapers. Duke didn't want a pane of glass tumbling down sixty stories and spraying her path with shrapnel.

It added three-quarters-of-an-hour to her walk, but the best way to catch a butterfly is to hold your hand out and wait. So Duke let the city flow around her, eyes open for any answers it might present to her. And for the questions they were answering. Sometimes you catch a butterfly, and sometimes your hand just got tired.

Ivy's door was unlocked and Duke let herself in. No one else lived on Ivy's floor. Why would they? There were dozens of empty rooms for every person in Free. Duke unzipped her hoodie and took off her t-shirt. An old domestic boiler sat in the corner of the room, gutters feeding rainwater into it. Whose idea was that? Marshell had the seed of it, but it only germinated when she got him talking to Joao. People were scrounging water from burst pipes before that. Duke splashed her face and the water ran off red.

She walked to the kitchen, took a bucket and lye flakes, and filled the bucket with water. She untied her hair and tipped the water over her head. She refilled the bucket, dumped her t-shirt and hoodie in there and sprinkled the lye over them. The flakes effervesced violently, burning through the clotting blood. Duke stirred it with a broom handle, fished them out, rinsed them in a bucket of plain rainwater and hung them in the sunlight. Maybe the sun would burn out the last of the lye before the fabric was destroyed.

Her skin goose bumped at the cool afternoon air. She turned to the metal racks she'd helped Ivy salvage from an office storeroom, that she'd watched slowly fill with records over the last decade. It was just so much easier to bodge together a record player than a CD player, or a computer that could read and play files from a neglected hard drive. At the back of the third shelf, far left, Duke wrapped her fingers around a battered tobacco tin and pulled it out. She opened it. Enough heroin to kill Ivy four times over and the means to take it. Ivy's escape route, a quiet and painless death. It made her feel in control of her life if she knew she could end it. Made her feel safe. Duke put the lid back on the tin and slipped it into her pocket.

She leaned on the window frame, palms of her hands resting on the soft, damp moss. A cat stalked along the fat wires running between this building and the next, once carrying current between the two and now carrying rust and goose grass. It pounced at some small mammal in the grass, missed, slipped. A lucky claw kept it from falling.

'*Cui bono?*' Duke asked it.

The cat flailed like a corpse burning through the last of its nervous energy. The shadow of a sparrowhawk drifted over it, waiting to see what fate would decide.

Duke sighed, pushed away from the window and walked into Ivy's bedroom. She dried herself with the bed sheets, sat and pulled a box of papers from under the bed.

Ivy never threw out the work she did with her councillor. Duke flicked through years of Care and Treatment Plans, thought diagrams, balanced thinking charts, diaries scribbled on scraps of paper. The sun sets on everything... don't worry. No matter how bad things are, in five billion years the sun will swell up and wipe out any trace humanity ever existed. Cold comfort, but Ivy held the thought close to her heart and when she rapped it she talked about the cycles of creation, the ebb and flow of the universe, the rise and fall of the sun and civilisations and the dandelions growing through the tarmac of Free's roads.

'I just want to stop swimming, Duke. I'm tired...' Duke had nodded, and wrapped her arms around her friend. Ivy held her as if the tide would pull them apart.

When she was fourteen, MC Eleven-hundred stood on a stage, microphone in hand and humiliated men older and stronger than her. In a culture where women were sex toys and violence empowering, she said they couldn't rape her with dicks that small and soggy, and couldn't stab her with arms so tired from jerking each other off. She didn't just taunt death, she spat in its face. But there was something about her, something in her posture and words and insight and Duke let it be known that if anyone took on this young MC, they took on her, too. And Duke wasn't a woman, but Duke. A category to herself.

She flicked through pages where her councillor had forced

Ivy to write down the names of all the acts she'd midwifed into the city, all the women who now spoke their minds on stage without fear or hesitation because power came from the heart and not the dick. Because kids no longer saw stories by foreign journalists that inspired them to kill. Ivy had given people new heroes to aspire to and new folk stories to tell.

A whole generation now rapped and sung and acted stories of hope and grief and love without violence, graduates from Ivy's hands. But she wrote their names out, again and again, and never with conviction.

Duke dropped the papers back in the box.

Their last words were angry. Duke had borrowed a talented young singer called Tides. Tides' younger brother was in over his head, so Duke decided to do him a favour and gave the man a chance to help. Tides got killed and his brother got out of the hole he was in, so Duke didn't see a problem. Tides made his choice. But Ivy saw a problem.

'That's the fourth fucking act you've killed, Duke!' she shouted, waving her arms around like she was back on stage. 'I only let you take him because I owe you.'

'I gave him a choice,' Duke said, her own temper rising.

'No you didn't,' Ivy said. 'No one says 'no' to Duke. And it always ends with someone being dead, Duke. But never you. Maybe if you didn't like death so much it wouldn't follow you around everywhere. This is the last fucking time, Duke. The last time.'

Ivy stormed out, and Duke let her go. It wasn't like her to make threats. They'd talk again when Ivy decided to be reasonable.

Duke pulled out another fist of papers. Doodles of young women with wavy black hair hanging from ropes, their necks snapped. Lyrics of young women brutally murdered, depicted as an act of kindness. She put them on the bed and picked up another fistful.

The House of Windsor. Room 2401. After dusk, a week today. Come alone. We'll discuss your idea.

Duke looked at the date scribbled on the corner of the letter. A week ago today. She stood, put the letter in her pocket and opened Ivy's wardrobe. Nothing which fit Ivy's slight frame would fit Duke's. She took a hoodie off a hanger and slipped it on. Tight, but it would serve.

Forty feet above the ground, Duke paused. The smell of burning wood came on the wind. She walked to the edge of the flyover and fought her way through the blackthorn and ash on the hard shoulder. Twilight glowed in the east, and clouds of smoke drifted up from the west. Who'd set the docks alight? She clicked her tongue in frustration, and went back to walking.

The flyover lanced through the blocks like a Roman road and when wind found gaps between the city blocks, it hit her cold and hard. What had Church done down there?

Her brow creased. There was something about Church, a mid-teen nobody miles away from her block. The idea of leaving your block was as alien as leaving the planet. So what was Church doing so far from home? And no one got angry at the violence in Free— you'd do better to get angry at the dandelions.

If Duke had a talent, it was noticing little inconsistencies in the pattern. MC Eleven-hundred, spitting hope over Cab Calloway records and leaving the crowd chanting the name of a slight little woman. Church, an angry girl whose imagination had broken out of a prison no one else even noticed.

She was down at the community centre this morning on business for Fisher. If Ivy had been dumped in any of the other streams or rivers in Free, she would have been swept underground within minutes, and never found. They'd even left some mook to make sure she found her. So who knew she'd be there to find the body? Had Fisher talked? The wind brought the smell of fire from the docks. She wouldn't find out from him now.

The lop-sided spire of the House of Windsor still dominated Free's skyline. Almost a kilometre tall, a mock-gothic tower once painted the sandstone tan of Buckingham Palace, its flying buttresses and castellations now shone green with the leaves of birch and ferns. Its windows echoed with the calls of pigeons and hawks and gulls, cats and foxes and badgers stalked its corridors and rooms, plucking mice and shrews from the goose grass and thorns. The last flag to fly from its stratospheric pole carried the red and white of Coke-Cola, a last attempt to make loan repayments to the bank.

The tower's base spanned two blocks, the old Farnborough Road diverted around it like a river. The plan was to wipe away the historic streets and build Free on the clean, clinical lines of a U.S. City, neat square blocks bisected by regular roads and intersections. But historic routes and buildings had their fans, their defenders, and so something of a bastard hybrid emerged, the rigid sterility of the U.S. and the convoluted spaghetti of the U.K. The worst of both worlds. So very British.

The House of Windsor's vast iron gates hung open, their gold paint long-since flaked away and rust eating the iron, returning it to the oxide it had been for millennia before humans dug it out the ground. Glass glinted on its plaza— a long time ago, Prince Charlie ruled a quarter of Free from this palace, marijuana growing in its luxurious rooms, cocaine and heroin manufactured in its ballrooms and kitchens. Charlie's minions smashed the windows before they fell from their frames, and the plaza sparkled in the sunlight.

Duke pushed the bracken and purple thistle aside, and walked into the lobby. Patches of lush red carpet showed through the dirt and weeds. Perhaps in a less backwards, less bureaucratic country, any floor above the ground would be cut off. But fire regulations demanded that each floor have an escape route that avoided the lifts and so it was still possible to climb the stairs all the way past the two-hundredth floor, and beyond into the spire.

On the sixth floor, ceiling tiles lay scattered and exposed pipes and wires hung lose and rusting. Duke walked down the corridor, every shape soft in the gloom. For all its luxury, each room of the House of Windsor was built on the same plan. It was easier that way. Cheaper. The same flat-packed rooms with different facings on the walls.

Duke slipped through a door, its sign barely bearing the legend "2401" through the rust. She moved carefully through the detritus, back against the wall. One leg crossed the other, eyes scanned the room, searching for anomalies. Wildlife moved through the room, small feet disturbing the rotting fittings. Who was here? Who was waiting for Ivy?

Cough.

Duke slipped her hand behind her back, took hold of the knife.

Two figures peeled away from the walls, standing between her and the exit. She looked at their silhouettes. Well-fed, confident, self-assured. Something about them, lacking that self-conscious nervousness that Free bred, a lifetime that hadn't taught them to take flight or fight any moment. She named them X, on the left, and Y, on the right; she needed to track them and a single letter was easier than, 'the one who was on the right when I first noticed them'.

'That you, Duke?' X said.

Duke edged along the wall. The same voice as the man who'd been there when she'd found Ivy.

'Everyone in this shitty excuse for a city says you can't be killed,' he said. 'That it's not even worth trying any more. You always have some favour to call in, some threat to make.'

The figures moved forwards, into the room. Y stumbled, cursed.

Both figures raised their arms.

'But now it's just you and us,' X said. 'So, what are you going to do now?'

The moment before they fired, Duke ducked and kicked out at the door behind her. Her foot broke through the rotten wood. She pulled her leg back and threw herself at the hole.

Three shots fired, and X shouted. The middle of the main room sat a foot lower than the outside, something they couldn't see in the gloom and vegetation. Y stopped firing and started cursing again. Some dialect of Spanish she'd never heard before. Duke snatched the few moments grace: she rolled, dived into the bathtub and took a breath. X yelled, and they started firing again.

Hot metal and burnt cordite filled the air.

The firing stopped. The bath creaked, shifting on its rotten supports. Across the bathroom floor, in the top right corner. She knew it'd be there, because every room was built on the same plan.

X and Y exchanged hot, angry words. Duke caught phrases: 'can't see'; 'fucking idiot'; 'more steps somewhere'. One of them stumbled again, rotten floorboards giving underneath him.

She leapt out the bath, scurried across the floor and kicked through the door in the top right corner. Bullets echoed around the bathroom, noise deafening in the small space.

She took out her lighter, sparked it, and looked around the small cleaning cupboard. Rain water leaked from the floor above.

Slow footsteps walked towards her. Her anger burned. Not because they wanted to kill her— that was just life— but because they were so God-damned incompetent. All the posturing, the speech-making... Like their guns gave them ultimate power of life and death, a magical key which made them king of all reality.

She looked around for a open bottle, a cup, anything that might be filled with rain water.

Anger wasn't useful. Not here. She forced it into her lungs, and exhaled it. Footsteps crunched over the new soil on the once-soft and welcoming carpet in the main room. Y laughed.

'You've trapped yourself,' he said.

Duke picked up a bucket half-full with rainwater. That would do nicely. She picked a bottle off the bottom shelf, and spun the top off. Trapped? In a cleaning cupboard? God-damned amateurs.

They moved through the bathroom. Duke waited. They walked slowly, carefully, scared of another misstep.

Four feet away. Three feet. Two.

Duke pushed through the door, threw the flakes of lye at head height, and the bucket of water after them.

Y howled as the water hit his lye-covered face and burned through his skin. Duke pushed past him and jumped on X.

He punched up, made contact with her jaw, swung his arm around and squeezed the trigger. Duke punched his throat as they tumbled into the side of the bath. She grabbed his wrist, dug her nails in. Y fell to the floor, screaming.

The gun fired again. An idiot with a gun would still kill her. She dug her nails in deeper. He growled, snaked his hand between their bodies and pulled her fingers out of his flesh. Her knuckles ground and snapped and she grunted. He pushed his shoulder against her and used her pain to roll her over.

She looked up at him, grabbed at his gun hand again. Just needed to keep it away, pointing somewhere that wasn't at her. Y howled and wept.

X pushed her down onto the floor, used his body to pin her. Duke pushed her fingers through his hair, and pulled him closer. Unprepared, he came. She leant up and sunk her teeth into his neck. He shouted in pain. She clenched her jaw, and tore. Her mouth filled with blood and thin strands of sinew. She turned, spat, dug her teeth in and tore again. Blood sprayed across her face and chest and down her throat. She pushed him away, rolled over and on top of his fitting body. His eyes bulged, hands flailed at her.

She knelt on his chest, grabbed his arm. He'd dropped the gun. She reached behind her back, took hold of her knife and buried it in his neck. He gasped for breath. She took her knife back, and stood. X's body fitted again and his bowels emptied.

Her lighter sparked in the night. Thick shadows flickered along the bathroom walls. She leaned down and picked up both guns. She put two bullets through Y's screaming skull, the caustic solution still burning through his flesh.

'What am I going to do now?' she asked him. 'Science, motherfucker.'

She checked the gun clips, put them back, and slipped into the thigh pockets of her trousers, one on each side. She headed out.

Everybody has bits of their job they hate. Duke hated pain. She sat in the light of a broken window, on the second-floor steps. Mare's tail clouds drifted slowly through the sky, dissolving and revealing the moonlight. She ran her hand over the floor. Dirt and shards of glass bit her palm. She took her knife out, worked it into a crack in the window frame, levered, and broke off a spar of wood. It would do.

She put the spar in her mouth, held it in her teeth. Her forefinger and ring finger on her left hand stuck up at the knuckles. Pain shot down her arm when she tried to move them. Shit. Yeah. This would hurt. She bit down hard on the spar.

One finger snapped back at the knuckle. She howled out around the wooden bit. Her arm twitched like alternating current ran through it. Deep breath. She took hold of her ring finger, and snapped it back into place. She howled, spat out the wood, and howled again.

Her left hand sat limp on the floor. She didn't want anything to do with it. Her right hand reached up, wiped the tears from her eyes and cradled her forehead. She sat in the moonlight, cool night air swirling around her. She sniffed, and wiped tears away again.

She'd have to see Dee. Dee would fix her fingers properly.

Duke picked up her knife again and cut another piece of wood from the window frame. She cut the cuff from Ivy's hoodie. She bound her fingers, stood, and got on.

On the steps to the building, ragwort brushing against her thigh, Duke stopped. She backed into the wall, merging her silhouette with the creeping ivy and goose grass. The figure stood in the plaza, kicking at the ground.

'That you, Duke?' it— she— called out. Duke frowned.

'It's me,' the figure said. 'Church. It's Church. I saw Mac on the way back from the docks. He said he'd seen you heading this way.'

She glanced to the docks. Sprawling urban jungle blocked her view.

'Got a message from Fisher,' Church called. 'You know, Fisher the fisherman.'

Duke padded forwards.

'Who burned the docks?' she asked.

'Fuck, Duke,' Church said. 'You're dripping blood. Who you killed now?'

'Maybe it's my blood,' Duke said.

'It's never your blood,' Church said. She turned her head and spat.

'So,' Duke said. 'Who burned the docks?'

Church stared at her, and then shook her head like a disappointed parent.

'I talked to Fisher,' Church said. 'It wasn't easy. He was stuck in this hut and someone had set it on fire. So I yelled at people. I mean, they're right by the ocean and they couldn't work it out for themselves? Seriously, fuck's sake. So the bucket chain got the fire out, and we got Fisher out. He choked his lungs up, but he's okay. While he was doing that, I asked around. Two kids had just left on one of McCartney's carts. And you want to know who Fisher talked to? McCartney.'

'Right,' Duke said.

'Hey!' Church said. She took a few steps towards Duke. 'Don't go merking him.'

'What?'

'I said, "don't go merking him",' Church said. 'Fisher. Everyone knows you and McCartney are friends. Maybe he shouldn't have said anything but how the hell was he meant to know? And the poor bastard got burnt for it. I mean, literally. His skin was all red and bald.'

Duke cocked her head and stared at the young girl. Church's fists clenched, her shoulders flat, level, feet shoulder-width apart.

'Speaking of merking, I need to go see McCartney,' Duke said. She turned and walked towards the gates.

'You don't need to kill everyone, Duke,' Church said.

Duke looked over her shoulder. 'Yeah, but that's the favourite bit of my job.'

Her boots crunched through the glass and the grass.

'Church,' Duke said. She turned and walked back to the girl. 'That gun I gave you. Show it me.'

Church advanced hesitantly. She reached behind her back, took the gun out of her waistband, and held it out for Duke. Duke took the guns out of her pockets, and held them alongside Church's.

'Dee had some real bullets,' Church said.

'Uh-huh.' Same make, same model. She put the guns away, turned and crunched across the plaza.

'Hey Duke,' Church called after her. 'I gave Dee's bike back, but there's two outside the gates. You should take one. It's a long walk.'

Duke closed her eyes and shook her head. Of course. How else did X and Y get here? She really needed to get her act together.

'Yeah,' she said. 'I'll take a bike.'

'Don't, love,' Duke said. 'You've got a very slim chance of living and it all hangs on you saying something interesting.'

McCartney froze, hand on the handle of his desk drawer.

Duke turned, and shut the door to his office. Artificial light lit the small space, batteries on the floor beneath charged by the sun and wind now being drained to keep the day alive. She pulled the office chair around his desk, and sat.

'You've butchered my security team, then,' McCartney said. He straightened, and put his hands on his desk, palms down and fingers spread out. Despite the cool night, sweat stood out on his bald head. A drop ran down his cheek and soaked into the collar of his expensive, foreign shirt.

Duke leaned back, put her feet on his desk and rested her hand casually in her lap, gun in hand. The fabric of Ivy's hoodie moved stiffly through the blood. She licked at the scab forming on her lip from where she'd bitten through it, one of many gifts from X.

'Not yet,' she said. 'I told them I had an appointment.'

McCartney blinked once, and then again. Then he laughed. Duke watched him. His mind worked like a machine. Cutting reality up and rearranging it, huge cranes towering over the landscape and slowly swinging vast chunks of material into place. She'd given him Prince Charlie's chaotic drug empire and he'd used it to feed the entire city.

But when things didn't go according to his plans, the machine ground to a halt. Gears wrenched and broke with the sound of laughter.

'Then tell me what you want to hear,' he said, spreading his arms wide.

A good question. What did she know?

That he killed Ivy and made sure she found the body. That he set her up and thought a couple of mooks with pistols would kill her. That he hadn't planned for them to fail. Not like him. She'd taught him better, hadn't she?

That he'd killed Ivy because Ivy didn't work for anyone, and she was Duke's friend. Duke would want to know who killed her, and there was no one to pay her to find out, so she'd do it on her own dime. That meant he could kill her without starting a war with any of the other bosses— if she was killed working for someone, it was an attack against them. But if she was working for herself, there was no one else to take offence.

That he suddenly thought it was okay to have a pop at her. That he suddenly thought he was immune, immortal, so it didn't matter if he was sloppy and stupid. Just like Mo stopping his wagon and pulling a gun on her.

'Who are these foreign mooks I'm seeing around today?' she asked.

'Mooks?' McCartney repeated. 'Mooks? Pendragon Security don't hire "mooks".'

'And what are Pendragon Security doing in my city?'

'Your city, huh Duke? Well that's the beginning and end of the problem, isn't it? Look at you. Covered in blood. It's dripping onto my floor. You don't try and tame a rabid animal. You put it down. And while this is "your city", this is the way it is. Blood everywhere. Everyone killing everyone else for respect and pride. That's not the way civilised people act, Duke. Civilised people don't turn up in offices covered in so much blood no one can see their skin any more. And while you're the puppet master behind Free, it's never going to be civilised. It's just a pit of wild animals, howling and scratching at each other. People scared to leave their homes. No one ever leaving their block. Youngers scabbing around, making sure that anyone who displays any empathy or compassion is killed and left to rot.

'Look at this city. Have you seen it? Have you seen it? A hundred years ago, it was the pinnacle of human achievement, the culmination of tens of thousands of years of living in dirt and caves and learning and evolving and finding better ways and new ways. Now there's fucking trees growing in the House of Windsor. Everything within a mile of the river is swamp. Nature is destroying in decades what took humans thousands of years to build.

'And then there's you. The great and powerful Duke. Dragging us all down. Any time anyone tries to do something about it, tries to reclaim this city for civilisation, there you are, and you put a knife in their gut and leave them to rot. "For the sake of the city." Your egotistical patriotism is sickening. This city is rotting, you're rotting with it, and you're dragging us into the grave with you.'

Duke watched him. If she was given to talking, she might say that corpses were made for rotting. That a body is just plants and animals and air temporally arranged into a human shape, and rot is just the slow process of nature rearranging its parts.

She might warm to her theme and say that life is change. That she saw this city, the greatest pinnacle of human achievement, before it fell. That she remembered the people working ninety hour weeks and starving while those at the tops of the towers snorted cocaine and skied in the middle of summer.

She might lecture him on the thousands of man-hours spent every day maintaining the city. She might tell him about the constant weeding, patching up cracks in the concrete, painting steel to protect it from rust, cleaning wind-blown dirt and seeds from gutters and cracks, pumping water away from foundations. That nature hadn't invaded. That the corpse had always been rotting and civilisation was just the art constantly patching it up and training your children not to notice.

And she might say that you can't fix a broken system with the system itself. That you needed to find a new way. And these Pendragon Security mooks were not a new way. They were the delusion that the individual was self-sufficient, the pride of entitlement, the violence of possession. Everything that made the old way so rotten.

She might say that nature always wins. That humans are part of nature and the only sensible thing to do was work with it, not against it. To swim with the tide, not against it.

But Duke wasn't given to talking. She didn't even think any of those thoughts, although there were all in her mind, unarticulated like the water the fish of her thoughts swam in.

All she thought was, *will Free still be fed without McCartney?*

By the time he'd finished his speech, she'd decided it would. She'd break his operation up, hand it over to his deputies. They were good enough people to keep it going until she could arrange something more permanent.

She lifted the gun from her lap and shot McCartney though the head. His body jerked with the impact, and crumpled to the floor. Duke leaned around the desk and shot him through the head again, and then twice through the chest. Not out of malice, but just because guns weren't magical wands of death and the human body was incredibly adept at clinging to life.

The door of his office opened and a man in a suit even more expensive and foreign than McCartney's stopped partway through it. His eyes stuck on McCartney's corpse, blood seeping into the expensive grey carpet. The man's lips trembled, colour drained from his skin.

'What..?' he managed to say. Tears rolled out of his eyes and dripped down his cheeks. He didn't notice.

Duke swung her legs back onto the floor. She stood, walked the few steps over to him.

'Hey,' she said. The man didn't notice. She pressed the hot gun barrel against his neck. He yelped and spun around, wide eyes staring at her.

A sudden spark of light in the periphery of her vision caught her attention. She turned and looked out the window, past their reflections. Church leaned against the crumbling wall around McCartney's office building, lighter held to something in her lips. A dozen of his drivers left their wagons and stalked towards her. She was a foreigner on their territory. They were going to kill her.

She needed to go.

'You... you...' the man swallowed.

He reeked of comfortable, corporate power. Duke knew the taint well from her battles with it in her twenties and thirties.

'You're the local head of Pendragon, right?' Duke said.

He blinked at her.

'Go home,' Duke said. 'Tell your bosses that Free won't turn you a profit. Tell them that the man who invited you here is dead.'

He blinked.

She dropped the gun on the table. The man jumped at the sound. 'And if you go buying any more of my kids with your guns, I'll find you, and I'll kill you, too.'

She kept the second gun in her pocket.

He wasn't one of Free's corporate monkeys. He was soft, no stomach for a fight that left blood stains on his boardroom carpet. He'd go.

'Now, go home.'

'Miss Walker would have to consent,' the man said.

Duke frowned. Blinked.

'Why?' she asked.

'Ivy— sorry, erm, Miss Walker is Mr. McCartney's business partner,' he stammered, eyes flicking between her and the corpse. 'They're both authorising signatories to the contracts. She... you're Duke? Aren't you? Ivy said she was going to get your buy-in...'

Duke glanced down at her feet. Ivy knew she'd never 'buy-in' to this Pendragon bullshit. She looked back up at the foreigner.

'Miss Walker's dead,' she said. 'Now go home.'

So maybe that's who bono'ed. Ivy spent her life wishing for a good death, and she'd finally found one.

He quickly stepped out the way as Duke walked through the door.

Duke stood on the skybridge, forty feet above the screaming mass of humanity beneath her. They were scared, and they were hungry. Supermarket shelves had been empty for days. No one was coming to refill them. The rich hoarded food in their penthouses, hiding from the rioting poor and bemoaning the poor's innate criminal nature to the international media.

No one else looked up and saw the lines of red and white cutting through the sky. Shooting stars falling to Earth like fireworks, burning against the overcast sky. Duke watched them. Their satellite Internet wouldn't be turned back on now. Another falling satellite lit up the night sky over Free.

'I didn't think you'd kill him.'

Duke turned. Charlotte's voice wavered, like she was scared of something.

'You said you wanted him dead,' Duke said.

'Yeah, but...' Charlotte drew up to Duke and stood beside her. At twenty-one, Charlotte was four years older than Duke and that time was an eternity.

Duke scowled. 'He's been killing at us for months.'

Charlotte shoved her hands into her pockets. 'Seems a bit harsh for selling me some bad beak, but hey.'

'He cut his coke with rat poison!' Duke shouted.

Charlotte took a step back and nodded. She knew Duke's temper well enough to be scared of it.

'So, I guess you're in charge now,' she said, holding up her hands.

'What?' Duke snapped.

'Turner. You killed him, so you get all his contacts and shit. You know, you get to be the kingpin.'

The idea was stupid. Childish. But they were kids who'd learned everything from TV shows. And Turner might be the biggest dealer in McCartney block, but he'd learned the same lessons from the same TV shows, and so had all the people who worked for him.

Duke laughed.

'If you don't step in, someone else will,' Charlotte warned. 'It's your right, Duke, your duty. You've got to take it otherwise no one will respect you.'

'Seriously?' Duke said. 'Nah, chuck. You see me running around with all them youngers? I ain't a king, just a duke.'

She grinned.

Charlotte laughed a little, nervous. 'Yeah,' she said. 'I guess it's a little too much like honest work for you, hey?'

'So you do it, then,' Duke said.

'What?'

'You do it,' Duke said. 'You like all that bossing people around. You're good at organising stuff. We were just a bunch of angry kids before you came along. Now no one would fuck with the McCartney Scallies. We're a fucking army.'

'Yeah... yeah,' Charlotte said. 'Yeah, I could do it. If you won't. Heh, I guess I owe you, Duke.'

Duke frowned. Her jaw moved as she chewed the idea, digested it. She took a cigar out of her pocket, sparked her lighter and breathed the flame through the tobacco. She coughed out a lungful of smoke. But she liked the way the cigars made her look, so she took another lungful.

'Yeah,' she said. 'Yeah, I guess you do.'

'What if people don't listen to me, Duke?'

'Then tell me,' Duke said. 'You like bossing people around. I like hurting them. And that's two you owe me.'

'Yeah. Hey, you know they've abandoned the House of Windsor? We should move in there. That place is fucking lush. Guess that'd make me... Prince Charlie, or some shit.'

Charlotte laughed.

Duke watched the falling satellites. She took in a deep lungful of air, and couldn't explain why it felt like the first free breath she'd ever taken. She grinned.

Duke strode out the building and across the street. McCartney's drivers crowded around Church, her small figure lost in the mob. Something was wrong. Very wrong.

As she stepped up the curb, someone laughed. A half-dozen other voices joined it. Duke pushed her way through the crowd, hand reaching for her knife.

Church leaned against the crumbling wall, well-rolled joint in the corner of her mouth, play-boxing with a man six-foot-three tall and about as wide. He feigned taking a blow and stumbled back, lose hair swinging around his face. Duke stopped. The laughter died around her and people shifted their feet so they were shoulder-width apart, braced their shoulders. Getting their bodies ready for trouble.

'Want some?' Church held out the joint to Duke.

She turned to the wall of a man. 'Burj, what the fuck's going on here?'

'Nothing,' he said. 'We was just having a laugh, Duke. That's all.'

She stared at him. She glanced at Church, smouldering joint still held out, and then back at Burj.

'You were going to beat the ever-loving out of her when I saw you from up there,' Duke said.

Burj shrugged.

Church took the joint back, drew in a lungful of sweet smoke.

'Give him a break,' Church said.

This wasn't the way Free worked. Someone's on your territory, you teach them a lesson. You see someone coming to teach you a lesson, you either fight or flee. You don't... stand around, sharing a smoke.

McCartney's words echoed: Look at you. Covered in blood. It's dripping on my floor. Ivy's last words to her: Maybe if you didn't like death so much it wouldn't follow you around everywhere.

She looked at Church as smoke funnelled out her nose.

A cloud drifted over the moon, the night suddenly closing in on them.

Was it just a good death Ivy wanted? Why now, why in this way? McCartney just wanted Duke out the way so he could bring in Pendragon, a personal army to chase the golden spires of Free's past.

But Ivy saw things too clearly for that. How many of Ivy's

words had littered McCartney's speech? All that talk of Free being free of its rabid dog puppet master so it could grow?

She reached out for Church's joint, and caught sight of her hand. The too-short, cuffless sleeve of Ivy's hoodie pulled back up to her elbow. Shadows lined the skin of her forearm, deep furrows of old age and scar tissue. Ridges where wind-blown seeds could take root, where goose grass and ivy could start to slowly work the mortar and putty from her joints, where water could settle, freeze and thaw and make those furrows into cracks. Her bones would rust like rebar, nails crack and fall like window panes, muscles split like concrete, skin turn green with clover and birch. She took her hand back.

The sun sets on everything. Tarmac turns to grass.

She glanced up at the patches of stars beyond the sky-bridges, and remembered falling satellites. How it felt like a hand releasing the throat of the world. And she wished Ivy were there to explain why she could feel another hand around the world's throat, and why it felt like her own hand.

'You going to choke yourself?' Church asked. 'Can't do that. You'll pass out first.'

Duke blinked. Her fingers paused in exploring the furrows of her neck.

'Come on,' she said.

Church handed the joint to Burj, play punched him once more in the shoulder and laughed. The tension broke and Burj laughed too.

How did she do that? How did she turn a murderous mob into laughing play friends? Duke led Church down the street, away from McCartney's offices.

'I thought Burj looked familiar,' Church said. 'It's his sister. I pick blackberries with her sometimes. She says he's a demon with a piece of wood and a few nails. Wasted as a driver, he is. But what are you going to do?'

Duke smiled. She took out a cigar, sparked her lighter and inhaled.

'What are you going to do?' Duke repeated. 'Keep your eyes open for someone who needs a carpenter.'

Church frowned at her. Duke watched the road ahead.

The girl'd pick it up, and she'd do it without covering herself in blood. And then she nodded to herself.

If Duke was given to talking, she might be able to articulate the thought. But she wasn't, and it was enough that she understood.

'Where we going?' Church asked.

'I'm hoping one day you'll tell me,' she said. 'And that maybe one day, I'll listen.'

They turned a corner, and Duke glanced up at the street sign. Covered in ivy and fern, she could still make out the words: Hope Street. They headed down it.

She shrugged. Things just work out like that sometimes.

I Was Here

Anne Michaud

We should have been more careful, hid better. Through rows of deserted homes and abandoned streets, we thought no one would see us, we hoped no one would sense us. We believed that after days of seeking dark corners and nights of sleeping with a finger on the trigger, we'd made it. Survivors, people who had seen death and escaped it. Alive, when next to everyone had perished.

How wrong we were to think we were safe, at last.

Tim whistled an old song, drying the mismatched dishes I passed to him, the layer of soap popping thinner every time the shallow water moved at the bottom of the sink. 'That was a damn good lunch, honey. Quite the miracle meal.' His voice came out whispery, a reflex we acquired through time.

After hovering over pots and pans all afternoon like a good housewife, Maria kept her legs up and watched the kids silently playing with the dog and the cockatoo. 'I'm glad you did, with so many leftovers, we'll be having roast until next week.' Food, electricity and running water: we were rich, millionaires even.

A perfect family picture, except that eight months ago, we hadn't known each other. Eight months ago plus one day, my real family suffered and died before my eyes and I forgot about prom, dates, and rock and roll. My new life was about breaking in neighbours' homes for food and clothes, living in a stranger's apartment and sleeping in an unfamiliar bed. But these people made it better, somehow.

I found the twins, first. Or I should say; their attacker's voice led me to them. The alley was darker than hell, but the echo of their cries reached me by the dumpster full of unopened canned tuna. 'Don't be scared, little boys. I'll take good care of you…' He never finished his empty promise; I shot him in the head before he even knew what had hit him.

'You okay?' I slowly approached the two boys, looking like feral cats who spat and hissed. 'Did he touch you?' The thought made me gag, but in a destroyed world, either angels or demons remained. 'Are you hurt?'

Too small to take care of themselves but big enough to have made it through the second wave of disease, they ran into my arms. 'Big sis,' they called me, and have ever since.

Tim was at the receiving end of my gun after I found him digging our stash of goodies, one morning. 'My wife is sick, she refuses to move. We're starving, we're dying.' When the twins poked their heads out of their hideout, I guess he took pity on me as much as I took pity on them.

We walked away from sounds and lights, talking very little. The dog and bird followed us, we fed them scraps and let them live, which was enough for them, it seemed. Then we found this huge complex of apartments and courtyards, plenty of opportunities for food and shelter. Paradise, for us.

But it had to end, and it did, that day. I should have smelled it in the air, something putrid and toxic, like what the world had turned into, what Man had become.

'What's that sound?' Tim stopped me from running water over the soapy plates and we both leaned in toward the open window. 'Is that a wheel creaking?' he asked me, as if I knew better than him the foreign noise coming from the garden, down below.

Maria sat up, the twins held the dog's snout to keep him from barking, and everyone stared at each other. They should have known, and maybe they thought like me: *We've been found.*

'Should we run?' Maria's voice, barely audible over the racket coming from outside, came too late, like her plan. 'Can you see them?' she asked, hoping for a carriage of peaceful nuns.

From our third story apartment, we watched the group of brutes passing down the playground, avoiding the roads like us. Through the dead tree branches and the ashen grounds, their sewn leather coats and heavy weapons told us everything we needed to know about them.

'A clan of nomads looking for fresh meat,' Tim whispered. A nightmare for women; a death sentence for men.

Their leading man looked up to the window and he invited me with his index finger. The creases on his face predicted he was mid-forties under the black gunk and the sag of his body. Without a word, they waited for me to come down, their guns shouldered and aimed at my face. Me, a girl against the world.

'Can you manage by yourself?' asked Tim, doubting my strength or their intent, I didn't know.

'Doesn't matter, they'll want to meet every one of us anyway,' Maria said, tone full of gloom.

Tim squeezed my shoulder for reassurance, but his fingers shook. 'Too late to hide the food, but Sam and Miko can be put in another room.' Dog and bird, a feast for these men and our sole luxury, keeping pets. 'The back shed, they'll be safe, there.' Unlike us, they were small and fit anywhere.

'They're like us, don't be afraid.' My voice sounded strange, higher than usual. I glanced at the kids and lied the best I could. 'They won't touch a hair on your ginger heads, I promise.' I stepped out, not finding the strength to smile or breathe. This one look back, I regretted the most.

The stairwell had been left as found, and every time we passed through, it tinted our clothes with black dust. Soles cracked the debris on each step, warning us if someone ever approached, although no one ever had. With defeat and fear, I realized, *until now.*

Outside, the stink of gunpowder and burnt wood greeted me with its clouds overhead and smog lying close to the asphalt. Not thick enough to conceal anyone, but so dense I wished for a breathing mask, coughing behind my fist as my throat itched. Above and below, only dark fog.

They stood by the fence, their wagon filled with water barrels and crates of food guarded by two thugs. They checked me out, wolf-whistled as I passed by, but all I saw were guns pointed at me.

'Bonjour, l'amie.' He saluted me in French with a head bow, proving he didn't belong in these parts as much as we did. When I frowned at him, he replied with a heavy accent.

'Would you care to show us your home? We need to make sure whether or not you're abiding by the code.'

The code meaning being poor and scared and giving them everything they'd ask for. I almost spat in his face, laughing at the hypocrisy of his demand, but I stopped myself, for my family.

I signed for him to follow me, and when two others moved in our direction, I said, loud enough, 'Bullet for bullet. One of yours' shoot, we do the same.' I lifted my chin toward Tim, aiming our sole weapon at them from our home. Five shells remained, if anything bad happened and we had no choices left. We should have used them, before I came down to meet our broken fate.

'Of course, we know how to play, girlie.' He smiled, showing rows of rotten teeth. 'Now quit stalling and bring me to yours,' he ordered, warming the back of my neck with anger.

The leader stalked my boots, and although I heard only his footsteps following mine, I couldn't help but look over my shoulder for reassurance. By the sleigh, three women stared, eight men sneered and a corpse hung at the back, held by its decomposing arms and legs. A warning or a loved one? No need to confirm, the message was clear enough: Don't mess with us or you'll be dragged, too.

'How long you've lived here?' the man asked, sounding almost normal and human. 'We've been searching for days and found no one, until we heard you.' Silence was key, as always.

'Six weeks,' I lied. The initial contact, I wanted to remain silent and give information as little as possible. Tim was the diplomatic one, the one people believed and liked right away. I was just the messed-up kid with shifty eyes. Not enough for him to keep his hand off mine as I hung to the staircase rail, around the second floor. To break the awkwardness, I asked, 'How long have you been on the road?' They were gypsies, pirates, the worst kind of people to meet.

'It's hard to say. A little more, a little less than you, maybe.' His accent clashed against the empty rooms and echoed back to me, our footsteps finding grasp in the darkness. 'Such a shame, for you to leave this great heaven you've created.' Of course, I'd known all along they'd keep me with them.

'What about freedom of will? Don't you people believe in that?' I asked, letting out too much emotion. 'What if I want to stay here? What about what I want?' I never saw the punch come.

'You will learn to shut up, with time.' The man kicked my limp leg out of the way to our home like it was something worthless. He hovered above my spinning head to add, 'I hope you said your goodbyes earlier, girlie. Because there's no going back to them, now.'

A wreck on the dirty floor, I clung to his boots, ready to plead and promise anything for him to keep away from them. My makeshift family, everyone I knew and loved and cared for.

Uselessly, I shouted 'No!' and held tighter, daring his men to come, guiding them with my screams. But they knew better than to interfere their leader's regime, they kept at bay outside.

'Well, we meet at last,' he said, opening my home's door. 'I have bad news, I'm afraid.'

Maria and the kids stood up with fear in their eyes, Tim held the rifle by his side, like a dead man walking. I had to turn away; I didn't want that image to imprint in my mind. Then at the thud of thick wood closing behind me, I knew with certainty: *I'll never see these people again.*

The rain greyed the sky and blackened our footsteps, ashes turning to mud by our trail. Around us buildings crumbled and bodies burned, life seeping through skeletons of cement and bones. For days, the thump of my soles hit the asphalt, following the same beat of the others. Becoming one of them, as if I belonged to the clan of nomads who damaged and took and killed.

Between then and the last sight of Tim's anguished face, I had lost my voice and words struggled to come out, even answering basics with a simple yes or no. Back at the apartment complex, they had killed me, too. Only the empty shell of a girl at war remained, her soul dispersed in the wind.

'Healthy girls have no choice but to come with us,' Romain said with his thick accent, the leader of this tribe of kidnappers and their victims. Anyway, how do you say no to a gun? 'We're letting you live, girlie. You should be thankful.' The plume of his breath died in the sky, along with my resolve to rebel and run away. Nowhere to go, no one to rescue, and despair growing at every step.

After the war, the explosions and the terror, after losing everything and everyone, where was my will to fight? At the sight of the men's guns, the smoking muzzles left me cold; at the sound of their gunshots and screams of victory, I lost all hope. *I'm with the bad ones, I am one of them.*

The other women watched me with scorn, their gazes marking my neck and face like a cold whip every day. Motherly Josie, sexy Carmen, childish Kay, and me, beauty queen turned tomboy. I would have carved a scar on my cheek and plucked out my lashes, if I'd known where I'd end up.

No man had touched me yet, but I knew it was only a matter of time. That night, rolled up in a stinky blanket inside the women's tent, I waited for one of them to claim me, expecting it. Holding a piece of broken glass as my only weapon against the rapist that never came, I woke up with cuts on my hands and blood on my clothes. No one noticed, no one cared as we walked away from camp, not bothering to wet out the fire site or flush out the pots down the sewer drains.

'After tonight, we'll be in the city,' Josie whispered with her usual anxious tone. They never talked to me: the new girl they'd leave behind when they got the chance. 'No alliance, no safety net,' Tim once said, coaxing me into keeping him and Maria. 'And then who knows what they'll do with us? I gather y'all get a good price at the market, but me...' she stopped. 'Not worth much, too fat.'

Rumours of women being sold by scavengers to become slaves had been first mentioned by Kay who tried to escape every day or so, but they always brought her back without a scratch. 'It only proves my point, guys,' she said, with her nasal voice. 'They're saving us for something worth more than...'

'We're good for two things,' Carmen cut in, speaking louder to shut Kay up. 'Fuck and cook. When there's nothing left to put in the pot, they'll get restless and see us as something more than maids.' She dropped her tone, I strained to hear her voice with the sleigh's creaks and my boots drums. 'But don't you worry, we're in the city. Now their troubles are about to be more than what's for dinner.' There was a plan, they'd plotted against the others, but I wasn't part of it. I didn't trust these women and they didn't trust me, that was that.

The vast destroyed streets brought an extra chill to my skin, after the closeness of the suburbs and its less graphic damages. Bodies, so many corpses piled up in narrow alleys and littering the vacant space between vehicles. Naked and decaying, it smelled like the disease that had taken them away.

'You keep saying we'll be saved, but how do you know it's true?' Josie asked, slowing the other women down from the rest of us as she dragged her boots to the ground. 'And how do I know you won't drop me at the first chance you get?' For once, the woman seemed to stand up for herself, but it came too late, at the edge of a disaster.

There was no comfort where I looked: shadows moved behind the buildings' glass, so many silhouettes of people watching us. They were waiting for something, motionless and silent. Expecting.

'I just know, ok? Now keep your voice down and enjoy the show, if you're too scared to participate.' Carmen smiled at me, cold and menacing like a threat, until I looked away.

With one hand up above his head, Romain stopped the pack from crossing the boulevard, looming skyscrapers reflecting clouds and smoke. The men waited as their leader turned to face us, eyes seeking mine for answers before finding Carmen's. Cracking a smile, he shook his head. 'What is it, Carmensita?' His French accent changed every S into Z. 'What is that buzzing I hear, behind me? A revolution, maybe some kind of statement?' He laughed, alone. 'Give me a break.'

I jumped at the clank of his gun and moved away, my back stopped by the corpse roped to the sleigh. Its smell provoked a gag, my heart seized at what was enfolding. Would my body be tied next to the dead man's, if I sided with the women? And if I didn't, would they kill me like a man?

'You want a break? I'll give you one. You've served your purpose, we're done with you.' Carmen straightened up, hand on her hip, defiant and in power. 'Hear me, you barbaric piece of shit? You brought us where we needed to be, you protected us, but it wasn't for your benefit.' She tossed her head to the side, and if it hadn't been shaven, the wave of her hair would have been flicked off. 'What did I say when we met? That I'd get to see you die, and that, I will...'

Romain welcomed the challenge with tentative steps toward her. 'We played by your rules, did we? Are you sure of that, Carmensita?' The other men quietly circled the women, me included. 'So why waste us, since we did what you wanted? Should be happy, we reached your meeting point and you've got one more soldier.' They were talking about me. *I'm the soldier, but for which army?*

Carmen flashed her gun and spun it by its trigger loop, until she pointed the bad end at Romain. 'Blood for blood, you're worth what you spilled.' At her signal, the women drew weapons and cranked them, targeting the men who held them prisoners. 'That's for my kid, too small to come along.' Carmen shot Romain right between the eyes and he dropped dead to the mushy grounds. 'And that is for my mother, too old to come with us.' She shot another man, standing right behind me. I heard his last breath, coming out sharp as if in shock. Revenge, the women were getting it and fast.

'Stop, Carmen! Don't shoot me, I can help you gals, you know it!' cried Henryk, the second in command and third in line to die. Hands in the air, his entire body shook and his voice trembled. 'I've always been nice to you, I haven't touched a hair on your head...' *Bang*, Kay shot him in the neck, making a mess of skin and flesh. I looked away from the gore coming out of the shredded hole.

'For Martha, my sister not pretty enough for the likes of you.' *Bang*, Josie killed with both hands on her smoking gun. 'And for my husband, who would have made it here today, if it wasn't for you lot of assholes.' *Bang*, another one fell down.

'And this one is for me, for her, and for every woman we knew.' Carmen shot with perfect aim and a cold gaze, never leaving the weapon's sight. Not even when she aimed it at me. The other women stared, but I could only feel their gazes leaving burning holes. 'And there was you, girlie. Tell me why should we keep you around? 'Cause I don't see nothing useful.' She enjoyed her power over me.

For my bravery, I wouldn't fall from pain or break to pieces after a loss. I didn't crumble after my makeshift family stared at me from the window as a bomb rocked the ground and killed them all. For my cowardice, I never tried to plan against the men, like Carmen and the others had. And I kept it inside, because after days of not using my voice, it was lost within me. Except for one confession.

'I have nothing left to lose.' No truer words ever escaped my lips. They hurt to speak out loud, they hurt to feel in my bones, but blood and death was nothing compared to this emptiness. No heart, no soul, no home, no love. *I have nothing to lose because I've become nothing.*

Water dripped on metal, rusting the air and drenching my clothes. The stink of humanity had long tainted my hair and skin, the wails of protest and gnawing dementia easily blocked by thinking of a hundred and twenty ways to end my life. Before my eyes, above my head and around my body, steel twisted intricate patterns to form my cage. At my boots, untouched meals piled for the rats and empty water bottles littered the small space of my trap. My life had become four walls of metal fence, a hole in the dirty ground, and nothing to hope for but my own death. The old warehouse housed work slaves and breeders - and me, the untameable soldier who wouldn't give in to their ideology. And so I hoped for everything to end soon, and please, please not too painfully.

Nights started with drunken victory chants from the

Amazons on their way back from warrior attacks on the survivors' villages surrounding the city. Their rhymes carried on for miles, with the thick fog hanging low and spitting fits of rain overhead. By the morning, more men filled the cages next to mine, more women joined their ranks looking for freedom. They didn't care who cried loss and who plotted against them – the Amazons won every battle, they always did.

A breeze hit my face, coming from the double-locked doors at the end of the corridor. Dim light shone from the black void and two shadows detached from the darkness. Women, always free but me.

'Soldier and breeder got nothing for you.' The man in the next storage unit spat on the ground, mumbling toward them, 'Shouldn't keep you alive, when so many of us men are dying, lady.' As the world had been turned upside down, one wasn't better than the other. *He's right.*

A voice cut through the echo of footsteps, strong and distinct. 'Survivors, warriors, it's the same to us,' said the woman in charge of everything. She spoke to a stranger, like she had to me on my first night with the Amazons. 'Which path will you take, is what we need to know. But let me show you the goods before you make your choice, because our breeding stock is quite diverse.' Cage by cage, they stared down at the men waiting to be brought to the dorms to perform their duty.

The first night of my caged stay, a woman came down with a set of keys, picking her man for the night. Chained at the wrists and ankles, he didn't even try to escape, not that he'd gone very far. As long as these breeders gave healthy babies, they'd be kept down here and fed and sometimes showered, but my clock ticked, I knew that much. *No more war, no more blood. Enough.*

'Body for body, each life they took we give back.' Automatic, the response she gave to every question about the Amazons' method and way of living and fighting. The same thing she said when I fought for my freedom, to no avail. 'And we will win the war, with love and compassion, trust and freedom. We'll change the world, you'll see.' By chaining up men and killing everyone else.

'I want to fight, I want to make them pay.' The girl chose her fate between a crumbling building where pregnant women delivered in peace and the warehouse where soldiers in training guarded prisoners they kept. So one way or another, I'd end up in here, but on the other side of the bars. 'Why do you keep her here?' the girl asked, eyeing me with pity and disgust.

'Not everyone we save shows proper gratitude,' the woman answered, voice heavy with smile.

I wanted to tell the girl how they threw me in a cage to control me, forcing me to change my mind and come to them. I wanted to scream that the Amazons and their slaves, my waking nightmare and my torturous nights, were not my saviours. But speaking meant more torment, more intimidation, so I stayed silent, closed my eyes, and prayed for sleep to take me away.

I opened my eyes to tension sifting the air out of the basement. The wave of it woke me up before dawn, when stars diluted the sky. Rushed voices, cracks of rocks under thick soles, then a light sparkled in the dark. The smell of burning leaves mixed with rusty metal, a fire ablaze and hungry for more. Shadows danced before my cage, none stopped to get me out in the wild.

'Let me out,' I begged. 'Set me free,' I cried. I drank my tears, salt better than the sandpaper coating my mouth. I swallowed my sobs, realizing that dying in here meant I had failed, after all. 'Don't forget me.' But the men like the Amazons already had, weeks ago, when I refused to fight a war I didn't believe in or that I rejected the idea to bring up more murderers into this damned world.

A ball of fire exploded at the back of the storage units and spread its wings with red and orange flames. Smoke thickened and scratched at my eyes, the welcoming draft bringing danger closer to me. The few men still in cages screamed in pain as they cooked, rattling their metal doors as they tried to escape the inevitable fire eating them alive.

I waited for the chaos to pass, crawled in a hole in the dirt.

Warmth boiled my back, my cage's walls fell and protected the little that was left of me. Time passed, fire raged, then nothing but silence.

My memories of tripping over fried bodies littering the floor were more vivid than anything else. Gunshots and smoke surrounded each step between the dilapidated buildings; screams and shouts of vengeance slithered down the walls around me. The Amazons called all troops to fight the attack coming from outside, but I ran away from them.

Through the rain, under the sun, splashing down the creek and dusting the road, I walked on. A quiet place to end my days, to stop my heart from beating, to finish my life in a dream. Because to live meant to kill, to take life away to survive. Whether by gun or giving life, I'd become a monster. Not me, I'd never give in. *Like an animal, I'll die alone.*

Savage Times

Paul Starkey

The world might have been cloaked in darkness, meaning you couldn't see two metres in front of your face, but sound worked just as well as it always had, so when the gunshots and screams sounded from below, Savage heard them clearly.

A gunshot, followed by two screams, two more gunshots, one more scream...

Savage froze as silence resumed.

She was in a flat on the tenth floor of the apartment block that rose up from what had once been Nottingham's Victoria shopping centre, before becoming the Victoria looting centre on its way to being the Victoria stripped-of-anything-remotely-useful centre.

You could argue that the flats were similarly bare, yet they always seemed to turn up something when they scavenged here. Savage in particular was adept at searching a room that'd been scoured a dozen times before and still finding something. Today her haul had been quite good. In an apartment on the seventh floor she'd found an AAA battery that'd rolled under the fixed cooker, and down the hall she'd been amazed to discover a small tin of baked beans that'd been secreted around the u-bend of the toilet. In this very apartment she'd located a small baggie of what she assumed was marijuana that'd been taped far back inside a chest of drawers—the drawers themselves long gone, smashed for kindling probably, and likely only the bulk of the chest itself had saved it from a similar fate. God knows how they'd got it up here in the first place.

Beans were food, and the marijuana had value as a painkiller or in trade. As for the battery, assuming it had any life in it, it might help power someone's torch for a while. Savage had no need; her own torch was a wind-up version, priceless in this veiled world.

She turned her torch off now. She doubted very much anyone would have seen the glow from outside, but she wasn't about to take the chance. The room was already practically pitch-black, and the illumination lost didn't make much difference.

She was knelt in what had been the lounge of the apartment. To her left she could just about make out the front door she'd left ajar, to her right picture windows had once provided a stunning view of the city, but now all they showed was a pale grey fug.

It was midday, and it was probably August. It was hard to tell when day and night merged together. If it was August then Savage was seventeen, not that such things mattered much anymore.

She moved quietly towards the doorway, grateful for her trainers. They weren't ideal in many ways; they leaked, and even with two pairs of socks on they were too flimsy for the freezing world outside of the shelter, but even though she often couldn't feel her toes, she liked being able to move quickly, and quietly.

When she was a metre from the door she paused once more, straining to hear anything. There was only silence. She silently counted to thirty, then she took the chance of popping the strap that held in place the knife hung from her belt. She drew the blade and waited some more.

She knew she'd be an odd sight if any of her old friends could see her now, dressed in several bulky layers of clothing that never quite seemed to exclude the chill, with her once long blonde hair cut short and ragged, and now a dirty brown. The face she'd so carefully exfoliated before applying makeup with the skill of an artist was now blotchy; pitted with spots, and smeared with dirt.

She really did look like a savage. Of course the irony was that the nickname had been given to her years before. Her real name was Jilly Henderson, and she was named after the author Jilly Cooper, whose racy novels had apparently prompted her mother into the spot of hanky-panky with dad that had directly led to her conception.

This was an embarrassing enough story in itself, but it

had been made so much worse by the fact that Savage hadn't learned it from her mother. Oh no, instead her mother had drunkenly confessed all to her friend Madeline Greenwood, who soberly told her daughter Alicia, who went to the same private school as Savage. Of course Alicia, being a bitch, had decided everyone had a right to know.

Savage had been furious, and had thrown a punch at the other girl, which had been a foolish thing to do given Alicia Greenwood was two years older than Savage, and a girl so hard even those in the years above had been a little afraid of her. She was bigger and stronger, and all too soon Jilly Henderson had found a meaty arm wrapped around her throat holding her in place whilst Alicia's co-conspirators pulled her hair and jabbed at her stomach.

And then a red mist had descended. Well, not so much a red mist as a murky green one, which she'd put down to lack of oxygen, and before she was even consciously aware of what she was doing her teeth found purchase on Alicia's right arm, and she bit down... hard.

For a long time the scream that followed had been a happy memory. Not any more of course, now screams, like the ones below, were never anything to be grateful for. But back then it had been music to her ears. Alicia had released her, and a moment later the girl tugging at her hair found a hand wrapped around her wrist and she was pulled off balance, falling onto Savage's other hand which had conveniently curled into a fist. Really she punched herself, so the shiner she sported for the next week wasn't actually Savage's fault.

The third girl legged it. Or at least she tried to. She tripped and ended up chipping a tooth on the pavement. This wasn't Savage's doing either, but that didn't stop it becoming part of the legend.

'You bloody savage!' Alicia had screamed as blood leaked between the fingers clamped down on her wounded arm, and the nickname stuck.

There'd been dire warnings of reprisals, many an 'I'm going to get you', but nothing had ever happened, except that everyone called her Savage from then on, oh and that neither Alicia Greenwood nor anyone else ever bullied her again.

Back then it had seemed the most important moment of her life. But then endless night fell and she had more important things to deal with.

The gap between the door and the jamb was big enough to squeeze through, even dressed like a blimp, but she only stuck her head out, peering around the door at knee height.

She could barely make out the corridor. It didn't really matter. She'd searched these flats so many times that even in the darkness she could find her way.

That was the way of it in this new world. Going somewhere new was dangerous, risky in the extreme because you might not even be able to find your way back, but venture to and from a location a few times and the route became innate. Human beings were incredibly resilient. As the old adage went: remove one sense and the others compensate.

It was (possibly) fourteen months since someone turned out the lights, and Savage could easily find her way from the shelter to a whole host of locations. Knowing the city centre so well helped, and even if you blundered around in the dark eventually you'd probably walk (hopefully not literally) into a shop or restaurant, and once you could make out the sign you'd know where you were.

The corridor extended ten metres before reaching the lifts and the staircase. The lift was obviously useless, but the stairs were clear of detritus, and as long as you held the banister they were easy to traverse. It's hard to get lost when the only options are up and down.

She was pretty sure the corridor was empty, so she crept out, glancing both ways, ears straining for the sound of anyone nearby. Either she was alone, or she was being stalked by ninjas, and, whilst the endless darkness had proven nothing was impossible, if it was ninjas then they probably knew where she was anyway, and she couldn't very well stay in an empty apartment forever.

She headed towards the stairs, her left hand holding her satchel firmly in place so it didn't bang against her side as she walked, her right hand holding the knife tight against her thigh. She was glad she'd left the door to the stairway propped open, because she knew it screeched louder than a choir of screeching banshees. For this reason she didn't reclaim her wooden door wedge. She'd get it later… if there was a later.

As dark as the apartment had been, there'd been a tiny tinge of light creeping in through the windows, but here in the stairway the darkness was total. She took hold of the handrail on the left-hand side of the staircase, using her elbow to keep her bag from making a noise. It wasn't comfortable, but it was safe.

She went slowly down one floor then paused. She couldn't hear a thing. Peering over the rail she looked down, not hint of torchlight, no shadows moving. Nothing.

Of course the trouble was, if she went downstairs she was probably going to run into whomever had screamed or, more likely, whomever had fired the shots, and she knew they weren't likely to be people from her group of survivors. There'd been four of them on today's scavenger hunt, and only Mr Perkins had a gun, an old revolver, and she knew full well that he'd only had one bullet.

He'd been a funny old sort, Mr Perkins, sixty-five and a former teacher, he'd become acting leader of the group. Likely he'd had a first name but he'd never told anyone it, they all just called him Mr Perkins.

How odd that she was already thinking of him in the past tense. Gunshots and screams didn't bode well though, and in the dark optimism was a dangerous emotion to feel. What was it Gran had always said? Hope for the best, but prepare for the worst.

There were, at last count, half a dozen groups of survivors in the city including her own, and though there'd been a few run-ins from time to time it'd been pretty tame stuff. Handbags at ten paces as Gran would have also said (the old lady had had a saying for all occasions). Even the group who'd made a home up at the castle, and who were a pretty feral bunch, had never been violent when encountered.

No, this was something different, something new, and that scared her.

Frightened as she was though, she had to go on. There were fire escapes she could try using to exit the building, but she'd never actually used one—why bother when the main staircase is nice and clear—and for all she knew they were blocked.

Besides, even though she'd mentally written off Mr Perkins, this still left Stacy and Rupinder, and whilst an old man might have had no value alive, the same wasn't necessarily true of a young woman in her late teens and a young man of twenty one; though death might be preferable.

That's it, Savage told herself, stay negative.

She paused again on the sixth floor landing. Still nothing, so she kept going, repeating the process between each floor.

She was just approaching the ground floor—or rather technically the third floor given it encompassed the area above the shopping centre. There were no flats here, just offices, storerooms and the like. All long since scoured clean. She'd started to wonder how long it'd been since the screams and the gunshots (she had a watch but given she hadn't looked when she'd heard the commotion it wouldn't help to look now) when she finally heard something.

Shouts, laughter, a few pitiful cries... she couldn't make out any words, and was glad of this. It was hard to gauge a direction, but given most windows were smashed on this floor the sounds were definitely wafting in from outside.

She cautiously made her way towards the front of the centre, feeling her way along the wall as she went. The wind that blew in was freezing, but she didn't tug her scarf up over her face, didn't slip the mitten tops of her fingerless gloves into place.

She peered out of the window, choosing not to be cautious because she doubted anyone would see. She saw the orange brickwork of the clock tower. All that remained of Nottingham's second train station, she knew. Just one of many useless bits of information Mr Perkins had delighted in imparting.

Peering into the gloom beyond this her breath caught in her throat. There were lights below. A bonfire, and beyond it several dim orbs that seemed to hover in the gloom. She couldn't be certain, but given that above the voices she thought she heard the thrum of engines she guessed they had vehicles.

That amazed her. She couldn't remember the last time she'd seen a car or a van actually moving.

It was amazing how quickly things fell apart once night fell. It had been—in England at least—early afternoon, a sunny, if drizzly, Tuesday, and there'd been no warning of what was to come. It just suddenly got dark, very dark. So dark, in fact, that the streetlights had actually turned on.

There'd been confusion at school. At first people had thought it was a sudden rain shower, that big dark clouds had blown in and would just as quickly blow out again. But no rain came, and the sunlight didn't return. An eclipse was the next theory mooted by scared kids, though whether they were more scared by the fact that day had turned to night, or by the fact that the internet connections on their smartphones had died was anyone's guess.

But everyone would have known an eclipse was coming.

Gran came and collected her. They drove home as part of a convoy of well-lit cars— as if rush hour and midnight had collided— and for a few days it seemed that everything was going to be ok. They had cable TV which still worked, anyone whose signal relied on satellites just got static. Her parents were on holiday (second honeymoon to be precise) in California, but though she couldn't contact them Gran assured her everything would be fine.

Gran wasn't actually old enough to have survived the blitz, but by god she'd acted like it.

Thoughts of Gran no longer hurt, but thinking about mum and dad made her stomach clench. It was the not knowing that was the worst, though she liked to hope they were still alive, and assuming they were she suspected they were in better shape than she was, after all it was likely warmer there, even in the darkness. The first winter had been hard, and the survivors knew the next one would be harder still.

She shook thoughts of them away. She had to get downstairs and take a closer look at those vehicles, find out more about these new arrivals, even if only so she could warn the others.

She turned to find a faceless monster standing behind her. She jumped, but somehow managed to keep her mouth shut, so that the scream that rose up from her diaphragm was barely a whimper by the time it squeezed out through her closed lips.

He was close enough that if he'd wanted to he could reach out and touch her, and she had the sudden thought that if she hadn't turned around that's exactly what he'd have done.

She knew it was a man, his height and build said that, even though she couldn't make much more out about him. Dirty jeans and a leather jacket, a woollen hat pulled tight over his head. He had night vision goggles strapped to his face, and a scarf pulled up over his mouth so he might as well have been a ghoul.

For what seemed like a long time he just stood there looking at her, saying nothing. All she heard was steady, if slightly ragged breathing coming from beneath his scarf. For a heartbeat she almost believed that he didn't see her, that his goggles were faulty. It was ridiculous given how close they were, but she took comfort in the fantasy, at least until his left hand moved to touch his crotch.

She fought the urge to whimper again, fought back the tears that she felt welling. For a moment she was a little girl again, a little girl afraid of the dark and what might reside in it.

But this last year had changed that little girl, and she held the tears back, gritted her teeth tight to prevent herself making any sound of weakness. She couldn't stop herself shaking though, and hoped he'd put it down to the cold.

'I think you'd better put the knife down.' His voice was muffled, and he had an accent she couldn't readily identify, but his words were clear enough, and he gestured towards the knife in her right hand with the revolver held in his.

He held it languidly though, the barrel only nominally pointing in her direction. Likely he didn't see her as a threat and Savage could use that, she had precious few weapons but she knew if she was going to survive this encounter surprise would be the one that counted.

She tipped the knife forwards even as she lifted her arm out to the side, making as if she was going to drop the knife some distance away from her, as if she was going to comply. She kept a firm grip on the haft though.

Please look at the knife, please look at the knife, please look at the knife... she let the silent mantra repeat over and over in her head, as if might somehow hypnotise him. It was eminently possible that he was too interested in staring at her while he touched himself to be that bothered by the knife. Probably he thought he could take it off her if the need arose anyway, and probably he was right.

Please!

His head turned. 'Good girl,' He muttered, and she used the sound of his voice as added camouflage, because as her right hand moved away from her, her left dipped into her satchel and took hold of her torch.

Almost as soon as her fingers gripped it she jerked it free of the bag. For a horrible moment she thought it'd snagged on the material, but then it was up and pointing at him. He noticed a second before she flicked the switch, but had no time to prepare for the flare of light that his goggles amplified to blinding levels before they could compensate.

His hands flew up to cover his eyes, even as he grunted in pain. Savage was already moving. She ran into him. He was big and she was slight, and on another day she'd have bounced off him like a squash ball hitting a wall, but he was already off balance, leaning back on his heels as he flinched from the light, and she had just enough momentum to topple him onto his back, with her on top of him.

He let out a grunt as he hit the floor with a heavy thud, and a moment later this was followed by a muffled squeal as she thrust the knife into his side as hard as she could. He began struggling wildly. It was like being atop some nightmarish trampoline, but she held on, pulled the knife free and stabbed him again.

Slowly the convulsions of his body grew less and less. Still there was a soft, yet awful wailing, the pitiful howl of a dying dog. It took Savage several seconds to realise it was her making the noise.

She wasn't certain he was dead, but the urge to get away

from his body was irresistible and she rolled off him. So desperate was she that she left the knife embedded in his side.

She scrambled away from the body, only looking back once she reached the far wall. She couldn't see much. Her torch had fallen to the floor when she struck him, and now its beam shone a skewed light that only lit a pair of legs.

They didn't move.

Back against the wall Savage couldn't take her eyes off those legs, the filthy jeans, the mud caked boots. She might have stared at them for several minutes, but it might as easily been just a few seconds. She might have thought it hours if some rational part of her brain hadn't realised the man's friends would have come looking if it had been.

She felt sick; fragile and weepy and scared, but mostly sick. She tried to vomit but could only manage a few dry retches. This wasn't the first man she had killed. There'd been another, months ago now, an age away.

Civilisation had persisted for a few days after the darkness descended. Though mankind had lost communication with all its satellites eminent academics and serious politicians assured everyone that they would determine what had happened, and they would find a way to reverse the situation.

People assumed that things would be fine. I mean it was dark half the time anyway, right? But this was a different kind of darkness. There was no moon, no stars; it was like someone throwing a blanket over a hamster cage. Streetlights still worked, cars still ran, but it was only a matter of time.

The National Grid began to give way quickly, it wasn't designed to cope with the power demands of an eternal night. Power cuts began to happen daily, and once various exporters of natural gas realised they had the greater need the taps were turned off, exacerbating the problem.

Petrol was another issue. Without satellites GPS ceased to work, ship and airplane navigation became increasingly impossible, the UK—like many countries—had reserves, but they were finite.

Less than two weeks after darkness arrived, the riots started. Power cuts became the norm, until most days electricity was off more often than it was on. Civil disobedience got steadily worse, until the police couldn't handle it, until the army had to be called in. Savage and her Gran hunkered down to wait for some kind of solution to be found. Her Gran had always been a hoarder, and though their diet was kind of dull, they had enough to keep them going for a while.

But then the last vestiges of order fell. One of the last, extremely crackly, radio broadcasts talked about the Prime Minister being arrested, about some General or other being in charge. There were rumours of strife across the globe, at least across the globe as far as anyone could tell from ham radio broadcasts.

Suddenly the rioters spread wider than the city centres, suddenly the targets of looters became people's homes rather than shops and business.

There'd been three of them who broke into Gran's house. They hadn't expected any resistance from an old woman and a slip of a girl, so Gran's swipe with a carving knife took them by surprise, and one of them went down screaming as blood spurted everywhere.

The surprise lasted just a moment. The other two took Gran down, robbed her of the knife. One of them stabbed her to death with it even as the other kicked her. Savage had been paralysed, screaming in terror, until that red/green mist descended again.

Granddad had loved Laurel and Hardy, and had owned a heavy iron doorstop featuring the two men. He'd died before Savage was born, but Gran had made her sit through some old videos so she knew who they were, even if she never really understood why they were so funny.

Funny or not Laurel and Hardy saved her life that day. She'd grabbed the doorstop and whacked the man with the knife hard over the back of the head, her scream morphing from one of fear to one of rage as she did so. He went down like a sack of potatoes and the final intruder took one look at the screaming girl waving Laurel and Hardy about and decided discretion was the better part of valour. He scarpered.

Gran was dead though. So was the man Gran had slashed and so, to Savage's horror, was the man she'd hit over the head. The shock of losing Gran and killing someone had been almost more than she could bear. The fact that the man had been dressed in a police uniform barely registered.

But she'd survived.

There was a difference between hitting someone over the head during a heated scuffle and going out of your way to stab someone with the sole intention of killing them. Savage's body still trembled. What was it she'd seen on a film once, the second time you kill it's easier?

She dry retched again. Whoever wrote that damn film had no bloody idea.

She knew she'd had no choice, the man had made his intentions pretty clear, and the gunshots and screams from earlier didn't suggest that the bunch outside were friendly.

This didn't make her feel any better, and she might have sat there staring at a dead man's legs in the torchlight forever more, except that another scream echoed in from outside that snapped her out of her paralysis.

Beneath her layers of clothes she felt cold and clammy, and her body still shook, but she knew time was of the essence if she was to save Stacy and/or Rupinder. Even if she couldn't save them she had a duty to the rest of her group, motley though the ragged band were they were the nearest thing to family she had left, and there were still half a dozen of them back in their shelter. Even if Stacy and Rupinder were dead along with Mr Perkins, then they might have divulged its location first.

Savage considered running for it, there were several ways out now she'd reached the bottom floor of the apartment block, and she could make it back much quicker than the gang outside could find it. Their shelter was in the remains of a nearby health centre, and consisted of several interior rooms that they'd blocked off from the main building, so you could only find your way inside via a couple of hidden entrances. To any random scavenger who chanced inside it was just an empty building, scoured clean of anything useful, but if the gang knew they were in there... well, they'd tear the place apart until they found them.

If she ran she could warn the others, but it wouldn't stop the gang from trying to ferret them out. No, she had to deter them now, before they made their way over there, and before they discovered their dead comrade.

She scrabbled back over the body to reclaim her torch, and then she went to work. The man's bowels had loosened upon death, and the smell was pungent, but life inside the shelter was pretty rank a lot of the time, and Savage was used to the smell.

She retrieved his revolver first. It was a small gun, a .38 special, and thankfully Mr Perkins had instructed her in how to use a revolver, so she swung out the cylinder. There were five chambers, and every one of them was occupied. She put the gun to one side.

Two straps crisscrossed the dead man's chest. From what she could see one of them was for a shoulder bag, the other for a pump action shotgun that was wedged under him. She tried to see if she could untangle them but his body was too heavy, she could lift it for a moment but not long enough to unhook either the gun or the bag.

In the end, repugnant that it was, she pulled the knife free of his side, wincing at the shucking noise that accompanied the action. She wiped the blade clean on his jeans then used the knife to slice through both straps. Now she was able to lever his body up and pull free both items.

The shotgun was big and heavy, and she had no idea how to use it. There was a shotgun back at the shelter, the only gun the group possessed besides Mr Perkins' revolver, but that was a double barrelled weapon, and she'd never been shown how to use it.

Still the shotgun might be of use to someone, so she quickly put it under an old desk. She would get it back later, or if not then hopefully another member of her group (or one of the other groups in Nottingham) would find it.

She unceremoniously dumped the contents of his bag onto the floor. She sifted through the items. Mouldy batteries, rusty penknives, nails, screws, a small hammer, a hacksaw, three screwdrivers, several boxes of matches, a handful of disposable lighters, a couple of stubby candles. A torch, soft and squidgy chocolate bars that must be well past their sell by date... it was a treasure trove of crap, but in amongst the detritus were a few nuggets of gold.

There were eight .38 calibre bullets. She put five of them—another full load for the gun—in the side pocket of her jacket, the other three rounds she put to one side. Already a plan was forming in her mind.

There were five shotgun shells as well, plus a single, heavy looking bullet that she suspected was for a rifle, though why the guy was carrying it when he didn't have a gun to fire it from was anyone's guess. She put the shells and the single bullet with the three .38 rounds.

She had no idea how many more of them there were, but two vehicles and the fact that they'd overwhelmed Mr Perkins and the others suggested a handful at least. Frankly Savage knew even overcoming one armed enemy might be beyond her. She'd been lucky with the man whose body cooled at her feet, she knew she wouldn't get that lucky again.

But if her fight with Alicia Greenwood and the way she'd scared a man away by waving Laurel and Hardy at him had taught her anything, it was that sometimes you could make people back off with the illusion that you were dangerous.

She gathered the various bullets together and wrapped them in a murky looking handkerchief that had also been amongst the man's possessions. She put the package in her own bag, and added the boxes of matches and four of the lighters, the ones that seemed fullest of fuel.

She moved quickly, if cautiously. She needed to get outside as fast as she could, but she was wary of running into another one of the brigands, and she didn't want to go tripping over something in the dark.

She put the torch back in her satchel; she didn't want to risk alerting the others. She held the bag tight to her with her left hand, in her right she clutched the revolver. If she did run into one or more of the enemy there was no time for subtlety, and even if she went down she'd take one of them with her.

She didn't run into anyone else as she made it down into the deserted shopping centre. It was an eerie place in the gloom. Where multitudes had hustled and bustled almost every day of the year was now devoid of life. To her left were smashed storefronts, and within them just voids; everything had been stripped from the shelves, and then the shelves had been taken into the bargain. She couldn't see far enough in the dark to make out the shop fronts on her right.

Up ahead were escalators leading to the upper mezzanine level. She could only see four or five treads up before darkness engulfed the rest, and she clutched the gun tight, suddenly fearful of a man or a dog racing down those dead stairs towards her.

Beyond the escalators there was a crossroads. To the right would lead out of the back exit, and was the quickest route back home. Straight ahead would lead to a deserted supermarket and a dead end. There's once been an exit back there, but the walls outside had collapsed, blocking it.

Even after just a year buildings were starting to fall apart, and fire was a constant hazard. They'd talked many times about the need to get out of the city, but so far they'd resisted. Concrete walls would provide better insulation than tents or even abandoned barns (if they were lucky enough to find one) and there was still salvage to be had in the city. Plus they knew the place, knew their way around it in the darkness. Venturing out into the countryside would be a huge risk to take, take a wrong turning out in the wilds and you might never find your way back again, especially given compasses didn't seem to be reliable any more.

No, for better or worse they needed to stay in the city, at least for the next winter. It would be colder. They all knew that, and whereas last year there'd still been a lot of food to be had, still been petrol and gas to run generators and heaters, this year all they would have were natural fires and blankets.

She didn't go right, or carry straight on, she needed to turn left. Not before she halted at the corner and ducked down to peer around the edge of what had been a cookie shop. The empty walkways disappeared into the gloom, but she could see something twinkling in the distance, the glimmer cast by their fire, or by their headlights (the waste of battery power still amazed her) and she could hear the voices too. No more screams.

She wasn't sure if this was a good or bad thing.

Sticking to the wall to her left, and crouching, she moved cautiously towards the main set of doors on this side. They were locked firmly in place, she knew, but this posed little obstacle when every shred of glass within them had long ago been smashed.

Just before the doors there was a bank. She paused here and peered out. Now she could see around the old clock tower which had obscured her view a few seconds ago. Now the bonfire burned brightly, and the lights from the two transit vans illuminated a chilling tableau.

There were five figures standing around the fire, there was another one slumped on the ground. She tried to kid herself it was a bundle of old clothes or something.

The five figures all looked armed. With several of them it was obvious, they had big heavy rifles or shotguns slung from their shoulders, with the others it was harder to tell, but they all looked like they had pistols.

Five of them, it was too many but it could have been… her breath caught in her throat as suddenly one of the figures walked back towards the vans, and slapped three times on the side of the nearest one. She heard him shout something, but couldn't quite make out what it was.

A moment later and another figure appeared from behind the van. He—she was pretty sure it was a he—seemed to be zipping his flies up and her stomach clenched. She wanted to run, wanted to run and hide and cry.

She stayed where she was. Unwrapping the handkerchief she tore a third of it away and laid this strip on the floor. She broke open one of the lighters and soaked the material. Then she began resting bullets and shells against the lip of the door, their heads pointing outwards, their bases flush with the soaked material. She laid out all of the spare cartridges aside from three shotgun shells that she wrapped back in the remains of the handkerchief, tying it tight.

She emptied another lighter out over the tops of the shells on the floor, then piled up mouldy matches around the tiny bonfire. She had no idea how hot they'd have to be to fire, she could only hope it wouldn't need too high a temperature, or she was sunk.

Another lighter's worth of fluid she dribbled back from the edge of the sodden rag, creating a short fuse that ran less than half a metre. Another broken lighter doubled this, but that would have to do because it was the last one.

She took one final glance outside, still five figures, though she knew one of them was the man from in the van, which meant the man who'd banged on the side was now probably inside. The thought made her angry, and that was good, because it was only rage that was stopping her from running for her life.

She ducked back to the end of the fuse. She took off her satchel, she didn't need the encumbrance. Either she'd be back for it or she wouldn't, fate would decide. She put the gun and the tiny bag of shells on the floor, then, before she could realise how foolish she was being, she struck a match.

Nothing. She tried again, and again, after which point she threw it aside because all the sulphur had been scraped from the tip. A second match proved just as useless. She looked inside the box, there were only three left. I should have saved one of the lighters, she thought.

Her fingers trembled as she struck the next match, knowing she had minimal chances left. That it instantly flared into life was so unexpected that she reflexively dropped it, and only good fortune ensured it wasn't wasted. It dropped close to the trail of lighter fluid causing it to suddenly burst into flames.

She tossed the box aside, grabbed the gun and the handkerchief and ran towards to second set of doors to her right. She paused briefly in the shattered doorway, staring towards the men and their vans, from this angle she could see that the rear doors of both vans were open. The closest van was maybe a dozen metres away, that was the one she knew she had to cripple, the one that likely had Stacy in the back.

No one was looking her way. Part of her wanted to wait for the cartridges to ignite, because if they didn't she would be spotted before she made it half way there, but she knew the closer she got to the vans before the bullets cooked off the better.

She stepped outside and started running, keeping as close

to the shop on her right as she could, the opticians as hollow as everything else. She'd made it three strides before someone shouted. She didn't stop, but she did pivot her body and look. Two of the figures, standing behind the fire looking like demons rising up from hell, were staring in her direction. One of them was trying to unsling his rifle, the other had drawn his pistol and was aiming at her.

She stopped dead, drew back her left hand, and threw the tiny bundle towards the bonfire.

Right from when she was a little girl her dad joked she threw like a girl... a girl who could throw better than any boy. He had been (still was!) a cricket fan, and had pestered her into playing many times growing up. She always knew he'd been disappointed she hadn't joined that junior ladies team, but she hadn't been interested, cricket was for boys, she preferred her dance classes and her horse-riding.

She'd give anything to play cricket with her dad again.

She was moving even as the man with the pistol took a shot at her. It sounded like a thunderclap in the gloom and she heard it zing off into the distance. Another shot but this time there was no sound of a ricochet. For all she knew she'd been hit and hadn't realised it yet.

She was halfway to the van and knew her plan had failed. Already she could see a man clambering out of the van, holding his trousers up with one hand whilst the other clumsily held a pistol.

She had two choices, carry on and definitely die, or duck inside the ruined opticians whilst she still could, make her way back inside the maze that was the Victoria centre. At least that way she'd only probably die.

Then something flared in the corner of her vision, she heard three loud thunderclaps followed by a muffled squeal. She chanced a glance. The man who'd shot at her was gone. The man who'd been trying to wrest free his rifle was staring down at something behind the flames, she could only hope it was a body.

Then the initial set of bullets finally went off like a sequence of fireworks. There was less than a heartbeat between each round firing, and it sounded like someone was firing machinegun at the impromptu camp, and even though it lasted only a few seconds the effect on the men around the campfire was profound.

Suddenly they forgot about her, forgot about their fallen comrade, they turned as one and started shooting into the gloom, aiming loosely towards the spot where the gunfire had originated.

The only one who didn't was the man who was now out of the van, and whose trousers were round his ankles as if he'd he decided having two hands to hold his gun with was preferable to modesty.

His legs were ghostly pale in the dimness. Without slowing her pace Savage aimed at those legs, knowing the recoil of the gun would jerk the barrel up as she fired. She had both hands wrapped around the butt of the revolver when she pulled the trigger, but still a shockwave shuddered up her arms.

Another squeal, though this one was not muffled. The man with the pale legs tumbled backwards. She was a metre from the van and slowed. She aimed at the front tyre and fired. The bullet careened off the metalwork above the wheel. She dropped her aim and fired again, and this time was rewarded with a pop and a sudden gush of escaping air.

The sounds had alerted the others, but by the time they started firing in her direction she'd slammed up against the van, its skewed positioning providing cover from the incoming fire. She had to keep the pretence of an attack up she knew, had to gamble.

There were two bullets left in the gun. She stuck out her arm at an angle and fired twice, wincing from the recoil. Both rounds had been aimed at the pavement, ricocheting off the concrete nosily. Like the earlier volley there was no intention of hitting anything.

Her breathing was coming in ragged gasps as she stood with her back against the side of the van. Her heart was pounding fast, her eyes and nostrils wide. She opened the chamber of the gun and dumped the spend casings on the floor, then reached for the spare bullets.

Her hand were shaking though, from fear, adrenaline and the cold in equal measure, and three slivers of shiny brass death slipped from her grasp to bounce on the floor. She almost cried. She held tight to the last two bullets, knowing she might not get a chance to even load them before...

Doors slammed, and a moment later an engine roared. She watched in amazement as the other van shot forward, smashing through the bonfire, scattering burning fagots into the darkness. Tiny flecks of fire danced like fireflies in the van's wake, joined by a miniature firework display as someone inside the van fired four times out through the still open doors that flapped like wild applause as the van bounced away.

In moments it had become a shadowy ghost, a heartbeat after that and it had vanished into the gloom. She still heard its engine though, heard bumps and metallic screams as it mounted kerbs and scraped against buildings and abandoned vehicles.

Then silence. She continued to stare after the van for several seconds more, fearful that it would return. Eventually she relaxed and slipped the two fresh bullets into the gun.

There was always a chance that the men would return on foot, but since it seemed unlikely they knew the city this would be a dangerous move. No, if they were going to come back they'd return in the van, and she'd hear them coming.

There were still potential threats however.

The first was the man who'd gone down behind the fire, but when she walked over to what was left of the bonfire there was no one there. His comrades had likely bundled him into the van before they skedaddled. She walked back to the other van, body trembling at what she expected she might find.

The man she'd shot was flat on his back, trousers still round his ankles, though there was nothing amusing about the sight. The pistol was by his hand and she kicked it away, even though this was clearly not necessary. Even in the gloom she could see that the bottoms of his shirttails were sodden with blood, and even though he was staring up at her she could tell those eyes saw nothing. No breath escaped his lips, there was no rise and fall of his chest.

It had been easier with the man inside because he'd been

faceless, but the man on the floor's visage was uncovered. He looked middle aged, although these days it was hard to tell, the rough beard and acne pitted skin might have made him look older.

He didn't look evil, didn't look scared, or even angry, there was just a curious look of surprise on his face. He looked ordinary. She knew his was a face she would never forget.

Tentatively she moved to peer inside the back of the van. She found Rupinder, half naked, his clothes ripped and torn. The look on his face was one she knew she'd never forget either, though at least he was alive.

He said nothing as she helped him to dress, didn't complain when she offered him clothing from the back of the van. The place was a treasure trove of crap, some of it useful, most not. She left him sitting half inside the van with his legs kicking in the air looking like a reluctant schoolboy.

She found Mr Perkins' body a short distance away. He'd been shot twice in the chest. She draped a blanket that she'd found in the van over his body. There was no sign of Stacy, hopefully she'd got away and was already back at the shelter.

Savage went back inside the Victoria Centre, retrieving her bag and the shotgun, along with a few items from the dead man's stash. She considered taking the night vision goggles, but however useful they might be she couldn't bring herself to reveal another face to haunt her dreams.

At first she thought Rupinder hadn't moved whilst she'd been gone, but then she saw that two coats had been draped over the dead man, covering his nakedness and his face. At first she thought this was done out of respect, however misguided, but then she realised that Rupinder just hadn't wanted to look at one of the men who'd violated him.

He continued not to speak, but he didn't protest when she suggested they gather what they could before heading back to the shelter. They couldn't carry everything but they loaded as many bags as they could manage. Savage was fearful that by the time she could return with additional hands the brigands might have come back, or the van might have been stripped by another group. She prioritised food, mostly tinned, then weapons and ammunition. The only guns were the dead man's and Mr Perkins'. There was a variety of ammunition at least, a few knives too. There were no medical supplies that she could see.

Before leaving she turned the ignition off, pocketing the key even though she knew the van probably wouldn't be here when she returned. The lights were extinguished and the purr of the engine faded like the breath of a dying man, and in moments all was dark and all was silent. It was like the world had been turned off.

It was colder too, though she knew that might just be her imagination. Still it was summer and it was early afternoon, yet there was frost on the ground. Not for the first time she wondered if they'd survive winter. Not for the first time she wondered what had caused this, to blot out the sun and the moon and the stars, yet let enough heat through to stop them dying off completely.

As they made their way home Rupinder still didn't speak, although from time to time Savage heard him snuffle as if holding back tears. He was limping badly and she could only hope he would be all right.

She wanted to fall apart. The weight of so much darkness was like an anvil strapped to her back. She wanted to cry; for what had been done to Mr Perkins and Rupinder, for what she'd done in killing two men, and because she wanted her mummy and daddy back. She wanted to see the sun again, she wanted to go horse-riding, she wanted Facebook and her friends, wanted the twisted knot in her stomach when a boy she liked smiled at her, she wanted to go shopping and watch Eastenders and worry about spots and homework.

She wanted to be normal again.

When she made it back, Jilly Henderson was going to lock herself away and bawl her eyes out like a child, wail and scream and thump the pillow at the unfairness of it all. But only once she was back in the shelter.

Until then she knew she had to stay Savage...

Part 3

"I have heard the languages of apocalypse, and now I shall embrace the silence."

Neil Gaiman,
The Sandman: Endless Nights

Spring Semester at Halcyon High, 2123

G.R Delamere

Math tuition or death.

Not much of a choice, huh? OK, so not *actual* death as in vaporisation, mariposas in white boxes and a crystal memorial in the City Park walkway type *death*, I mean *muerta social*. Which is like, *so* much worse.

I almost self-terminated of a fucking heart attack when right in the middle of a dark, dirty scene at Boca di Dragao on Mariposa Beach mi *jefe* holopops up from my wafer. There he is, standing in the friggin' bar looking round at all the gatos and gatinhas who, let's face it, are goin' all out for slutty, girls in feathered panties sniffing sodas and boys mostly shirt-less by now, bombado on chocolate and candy and everybody making out a la brava and this framboise light flooding in from a rising sun turning the whole bar into an old-time painting. But the veterano, he don't look happy, sister. No, mi jefe is definitely pissed.

'Mia!' he shouts over the deep, thumpin' of the geovibra-tor. 'What do you think you are doing? I *said* no going out until your grades improve!' Two flaming Nueva Yoricas on the bar behind him fizz on, silver sparks wavering through his chest. I slam my hand hard over my wafer. Real hard.

'*Dad!* Like please don't *do* this to me,' I hiss into my wafer. His voice vibrates under my hand.

'Do what exactly, Mia? Parent?'

'Holopop into the frigging *bar* in front of my homies!'

'You shouldn't even be in that place! You're under age for Halcyon's sake!'

'OK, OK! Tranquilo, Dad!' I fumble for the switch on my wafer,

'I want you home right now Mia! You can forget your allowance–' Got it. Zip. Dad's voice whines to nada.

I look for my chavala, Winnie, 'cos we're from the same barrio and she's meant to be jet-packing me home and see her up on some guapo's shoulders, bombado to the big blue. She's a little bummed about leaving but when I tell her all regarding the bronco with mi jefe she climbs off the gato's shoulders, slaps off his paws and grabs my hand to pull me out of there. Two puffs of detox spray at the exit and a stumble through the smoke extractor and we're out, lily-fresh and bright-eyed as any two young chicas from District 1 in Halcyon oughta be.

The sun is a half-circle of gold above the horizon now and the Skydome is flooded with blue. At night you don't see the faint, mercurial rainbow shimmer that bounces off the curves of the Skydome and shields us from the UV. Now the moon, huge, round and magnified white by the telescopic dome, watches us, bone empty, and hollow cratered. Winnie tilts her face up to it as the jetbike thrums and weaves softly over the city lights.

'Weird,' she says. 'To think we could be living up there.'

'Yeah,' I say. 'Guess you did your assignment, huh?'

Homework assignment this week is an essay on the Great Thousand. See, it's a little known fact that when the top thou HiNetWorths relocated here to Halcyon after the rising waters drowned the old Nueva Yorica, the moon was one of their considered options for resettlement. When the ice caps began to go, like *really* began to go and the sea level rises got crazy, like 2 feet, 6 feet, 10 fucking feet every year, those homies played smart. They acquired large tracts of land, both here on earth and on the moon. They bought gubernamenta bonds and propped up ailing puppet Prezs. There's a good reason almost every FiCap family of any importance here has an ancestor who was one of the Great Thousand. If they don't they invent one, pretty fast.

'This is way better then the moon,' Winnie says as we skirt over the beachfront cafes where IntCaps puff griffas and play old-time guitar music and hear raised voices and thumpin' bass from the ErCap barrio and as the jet-bike begins to climb the District 1 slopes, houses emerging from the dark, lush, green, each a cluster of white pearls, curved lines and glinting solars, I tell her, 'Claro, chavala.'

But something in me twists up and spirals out to thinking of Winnie and I, skimming over that white, powdery desert, tilting our faces up to the blue spinning jewel specked with green that is our planet, and how cool but also kind of sad that would feel. I don't tell Win this though; just push the whipping strands of her ice-blue hair, colour of the glaciers before they melted, from my face.

'Puta,' I say. 'Ain't even started the assignment yet. Got 'til noon Monday to submit, right?'

'You're so smart you can do this shit in your sleep,' Winnie yawns.

'Tell *that* to mi jefe,'

Winnie silences the jetbike and we drift down to the front gate, trying not to attract attention. Too late though, 'cos the searchlights are whiting up and blinding us and Dad's stupid Robodogs are baying like wolves and right there on the lawn stands mi madre in her rubber suit and mask, arms folded, looking sorely pissed for having had to skip her eight-hour rejuve tank gig.

'Uh-oh,' says Winnie and she zips off so fast the dagger of my heel catches on her jacket and almost takes me up in the air with her.

'Shit,' I say, from my position, spread-eagled on the BioTurf.

Mi madre frowns. 'Was that *Winter Preston*?' she says. 'Ill-mannered of her to run off without saying hello.'

'Hi Mom,' I try.

'Get inside Mia,' she says.

Am I up to my neck in the fucking mesa.

Basically, my choice is this: math tuition or no Rec allowance. OK, so, I have Tec and Fash credit saved over and I know what you're thinking, yo chavala cut down on your Tec and Fash spending? You'll have enough for lattes and milkshakes at the mall and whatever else you FiCap teenies spend your bucks on while getting off on the guapos from the ErCap skool.

Well, you have *no idea*, is all.

No, chica, no.

See, Halcyon High is the first rank FiCap skool in District 1, Halcyon. Yeah, *that* District 1. Yeah, *that* Halcyon. Premier FiCap town in Brasilia, Nuevo Mundo. Like all the drowned cities, London, Paris, New York, Frisco rolled into one and planted down in Paradise.

As some Old Skool C 21 poet hombre called JayZ once said.

There's nothin' you can't do, now you're in New York. If you got the bucks, that is.

So, OK fine, mi vida is sweet, but the problemo is that the Rec in 1 is really high-end Rec.

Mi jefe figures if I don't got the bucks I won't be hangin' at Dracao or Cipriani's or Hacienda drinking mocktails at 30 bucks a time and sniffing sodas at 50. Hey, you don't get change from a twenty for a chela in District 1, y'know? Dad figures, no bucks, Mia's wings gonna be clipped and she'll stay home and do math.

Yeah, right.

And totally lose my Social Stats? Cos, OK I see the homies at school and on my wafer at home but if you're not in the right Rec places with the right Fash and the right Tec your Soc Stats get deleto. Like you might as well be IntCap or ErCap.

Math tuition you say? Bring it right on.

The following day, it don't hurt, sister, to see that the Math tutor, for an IntCap anyways, is cute. Guapo, even. Kinda nothin' brown eyes, dark hair and eyeglasses. (IntCaps wear these to look Intellectual, though laser correction at birth is auto.) He has this smile, y'know? And he's supercranio, chica. We whizz thru my calc homework at some loco speed. Though Dylan, 'cos that's his name, is a little impulsivo in his criticism of my essay (which scores in the high eighties let me add) on the Great Thou and our glorious Gubernamenta and the whole Sys us here in Halcyon, Brasilia, Nueva Mundo got rollin'.

'You really believe this bullshit?' is his first comment when I ask if he'd mind giving my essay a proofread.

'Hey!' I say. 'Like, *chill*, Dyl. Don't be slayin' the Thou. *Your* ancestros back in historia musta got rescued by *my* HiNetWorth ancestros for you to even get here, si hombre?'

That was how it happened. The Great Thousand had copters and helipads on the roof of their penthouses so a whole lot more of them got out than the others, y'know? The planet was depopped to hell anyway what with those old hurricanes and floods and tsunamis. Halcyon was built to state of the art tech-wise and they picked up all these signals, like from people in other cities holding out as the waters kept rising, cries for help, like ships, planes, whatever. So, *claro* you couldn't rescue *everyone*? The Great Thousand set up a very fair points system so only supercranios got airlifted in to enhance Nuevo Mundo and keep the tech all razoredge. Hence the IntCaps. And then they wanted some hot young pollitas too, so the ErCaps got airlifted. (At least they don't say that bit in the official historia but it kinda figures.)

'Actually,' Dylan says. 'Family mythology holds that it was all a big screw up. Will Gates, my great grandfather was a university lecturer and a respected novelist who'd even been shortlisted for some major literary prizes.'

That's how he talks. Cute or what? Like some olden-time Professoro.

'Mm hmm.' I say, thinking how I want to be stroking the buttons on his chambray button-down and maybe undoing a couple.

'However, he was mistaken for another William Gates who by all accounts was a major intellect in early computing. By the time he got here, of course, it was too late.'

'There you go.' I say. 'La vida es loca.'

Right now it's that beautiful time of the year in Halcyon where they turn up the temperature so spring becomes summer and the jessamine blooms so sweet and strong you can taste it in a plain glass of water. We take our wafers and tablets into the Butterfly Garden and between geometry and calc we watch the green lacewings and blue Morphos and yellow swallowtails flit round the lilies and hibiscus and the humming-birds, parakeets and lorikeets swoop and dive in the Aviary, and it's all so damn pretty that we don't stick to math but just, y'know... talk.

I ask Dylan where he's from and he's like District *57* or something crazy like that. Mi jefe found him through work. One of his IntCap employees used him to tutor his daughter and Dad figured if he was good enough for another IntCap, he was good enough for me.

Which he most definitely is, chica.

Mi jefe is really smart, and his firm's doing well 'cos he knows enough not to rely on our FiCap and the fact we're descended directly from the Great Thousand. He makes Robopets. Like for kids and lonely old ladies, y'know? We have 6 Robodogs and 8 Robocats at home driving Mom insane. She turns 'em off when he's away on business.

We got the aviary in the first place so Dad could figure out how to make Robobirds that looked real and can actually fly. Yeah, right. Still workin' on *that* one.

I ask Dylan about his name 'cos I don't know any Dylans and he tells me he's named after some old C 20 poet like my brother, Jay, is named after the aforementioned Mr JayZ. Though I never heard any of his stuff, the old Dylan dude I mean, until Dylan, *my* Dylan I mean, sings it to me. OK, so we were *supposed* to be doing math tuition but you know how it is when a cute guy talks poetry. If you don't, you should definitely give it a try. Pretty soon it was all *Tangled up in Blue* and *Lay, Lady Lay* and *Shall I compare thee to a Summers Day*.

Like, I had encontros before? Couple of cute ErCap guys and an asshole friend of Jay's, FiCap, like me. But nothing like this.

Afterwards I am dizzy and heartbroken and high on every single thing all at once. I can't go back in the house 'cos everyone who sees my face would know something in me has changed, like my bones have dissolved, been poured away and replaced by liquid. Anyways, my stupid brother Jay is in the house, hangin' with his dumb homies and their ErCap honeys. Jay and the other gatos practically order them up like they're on a menu. Caramel skinned, curvaceous, green eyes, they're kinda interchangeably stunning. They all dream dreams of marrying the FiCap boy and living in the big house, and they all go home crying. Eventually.

I wander into the aviary and listen to the trilling and click and chatter of the birds. Red parakeets shriek raucous cries from the treetops, silver humming-birds thrum their wings. My favourite is Minou my Halcyone. She's a waterbird and her feathers flash green-blue through the reeds in the Aviary lake as she comes down to perch on my hand. You can't let the birds out according to Mom cos they might fly so high they'll get to the Skydome, bump their head and die. I don't believe her, cos the Skydome's like, a half-mile high? Under the Skydome we have three perfect seasons, balmy spring, beach-hot summer ('cos this is Brasilia!) and cool, back to skool fall. There's no *actual* fall on account of all the vegetation, flora and fauna being subtropical and indigenous to Brasilia. They left all the spiders and snakes and shit outside the Skydome, but some interesting-but-ugly stuff like tapirs lives in the Jardiniera Zoologica for school trips. So it's all flowers, birds and butterflies, watered by desalinated seawater and kept an even temperature by a kind of fancy aircon that uses the big old ocean as a cooling tank.

I turn on the sprinklers to feel the fine, misty haze on my face and listen to the water dripping and pooling in the leaves and wonder if this is how rain feels. There's no rain in Halcyon. Old-time peeps would wear these black minidome things called umbrellas I saw at the Museo del Artes (the Great Thousand managed to get a surprising amount of Art outa Old Nueva Yorica at the expense of their grandmas and stepchildren. Kidding.)

My wafer buzzes against my hip and I pick it up and see Winnie at Barista's, beckoning me with a platinum talon to gossip and mochaccinos, telling me she'll shout if mi jefe is still makin' trouble 'bout my allowance.

'Yo chavala,' I tell her. 'Something big just happened. Like, beyond. Tell you Monday. Love you always.'

I click off the wafer 'cos I don't want to hang with Win or the other homies. I curl up in the old basket swing and tell Carlo, who takes care of the birds, to take the day off. I fall asleep and dream weird dreams, like I'm covered over in tiny feathers, soft and brown, perched on the green moss while huge, silver drops of water balloon and roll off leaves the size of umbrellas. The sound of the raindrops is like the ringing of old-time church bells.

Dylan comes Saturday and Wednesday and pretty soon those days are the only days that come real for me? School, class, Win and my other homies, who's makin' it with who, which bar is caldo mucho, all those things I cared about once have faded and bled away their colours, like the Butterfly Garden at nightfall.

Lunchtimes, I drag Winnie down to the IntCap strip of cheap burrito and fresh-roast coffee joints near the SciTech campus, hoping I might see Dylan hanging out. IntCap chav-alas, all mussy hair and eyeglasses and ugly shoes giving us the evil eye when we Palmdisk in but I don't care. Just thinkin' about Dylan taking off his glasses and rubbing his eyes makes my heart beat like a humming-bird's wings.

Win and I sit and sip burnt tasting espressos and inhale second-hand griffa smoke and talk about how FiCap girl and IntCap guy, though we don't know many cases, is not a totally impossible pairing.

'*If* you don't mind about the money thing,' she says. Which I don't, 'cos, Dad good as said he's leaving me the firm 'cos Jay, my waster brother only cares about surfing since he flunked outa Halcyon High last year.

'What about your Mom?' Win asks.

Mom is FiCap too, though she is pretty enough to be ErCap and she hasn't had hardly any Plastikification. Unfortunately for me, I take after Dad, same beaky nose and evil sense of humour. Well I would, if it hadn't been fixed. The nose, that is, not the sense of humour. See FiCaps kinda hold more cards financially speaking so we can afford the best Plastifikationers, not like some of those poor ErCap chicas who go so overboard they just look-well-*plastik*. And we can get tutoring from smart IntCaps like Dylan and hire them to work for us. ErCap girls usually aim for FiCap guapos, though if they had any sense they'd go for IntCaps. Reason?

OK, so, numero uno, less competition and numero dos, some IntCaps do really well in FiCap firms. One family even lives in District 1.

Win looks doubtful. Even though *her* Mum is actually a freakishly beautiful ErCap who got the whole Cinderella thing, re-certification, marriage, two full FiCap kids, the works.

'Yeah, but you know what?' she says. 'It's different for girls, Mia. Girls marry *up*. FiCap chicas marry FiCap guapos.'

'Dylan *is* up,' I tell her, and a couple of IntCap chicas look at us from under their fringes and whisper and I wonder if they know him?

On Saturday and Wednesday, Dylan and I don't talk about that stuff. Like, what's the point when we've been dating six weeks? I'd be totally embarrassed if he even knew how I lie in bed scribbling Dyl and Mia Gates over my tablet just to see how it looks. We do my homework together then once mi madre has a coupla tequilas to her sails we sneak to the pavilion in the Butterfly Garden and for a half hour, 'cos we don't dare risk longer, life is perfect. My Math scores are even improving. When I ask Dyl to come meet my homies though, he shakes his head and says, 'No Mia,' soft but firm and if I push him he comes out with some shit about not wanting to be a member of any club that will only have him if his girl has a FiCap Palmdisk and then we fight about politics, but then we also make up y'know?

Things carry on perfecto for a while. Until my stupid brother Jay gets his ErCap girlfriend pregnant.

'I mean, what I don't understand is, *how*?' I say to Dylan, after Jay tells Mom his honey is pregnant. 'Those ErCap girls all have implants and shots from age 11 right? How could this even *happen*?'

For some reason, this makes Dylan unbelievably upset.

OK, so I know the FiCap/IntCap/ErCap thing is a little fucked up cos you get really not so hot FiCaps, even old ones, dating hot hot hot ErCap pollitas and hombres. But hey-they're making the most of their Erotic Capital right? The most beautiful ErCaps take their pick. I guess any unlucky enough to be born unpretty are Plastifikated or maybe left out to die, or something. Kidding!

But Dylan? Why would a guapo IntCap like him find it such a big deal? I mean he can take his pick from IntCap chicas, ErCap chicas and maybe even FiCaps.

'If you play your cards right,' I joke.

He ain't smiling.

'Mia?' he says. 'Don't you see what a fucking travesty the whole thing is? All the power and influence in the hands of so few?'

Ok. I'm not *entirely* stupid. I see life in Halcyon is not exactamento equitable.

But claro, neither is life anyplace.

'What's the big deal?' I say. 'I mean they're ErCaps right? They have to protect their Erotic Capital. They don't want it all fucked-up by multiple childbirths and disease.'

That was *it*.

Dylan picks up his tablet and storms out like he's never coming back. But he did come back, just once.

Meantime things are freakin' loco at home. Mi mano Jay decides he's gonna marry the ErCap girl and they're actually having this baby who'd been conceived despite the implant. And get this. The ErCap girl's name is Maria! Just like in that Old Time Jesus Myth we learned about!

Well I have no problem with this but for some reason Mom goes loco. She goes round to the ErCap girl's house, which is, like, an hour journey from our place, and tries to get her to take some money to, you know, get rid.

Upon which the ErC- I mean Maria's family go even more completamente loco and say that she's insulting them and there's a big screaming match and the upshot is that Jay moves–get this! Into Maria's actual family house in an ErCap district! 134! That's his new address. One hundred and fucking thirty-four.

And the second thing, which nobody else seems to give a damn about except me, is that Carlo, who maintains the aviary, refuses to come any more 'cos it turns out he's Maria's uncle.

I try to scrub it out but I cannot get the stuff off the floor. The caca. How the heck has Carlo managed to keep it lookin' all clean pristine?

My little Minou comes and perches on my shoulder and hovers above the pond as I scrub and scrub.

Then, one day, he does come back. Dylan.

He won't come in. He won't come up to the Pavilion with me, though it's such a perfect night that the air smells almost real.

'Mia,' he says. 'Listen to me. This is important.'

'I'm listening,' I tell him, my whole body thudding, deep and slow like the geovibrator, a feeling like you've had too much soda or bad candy and your stomach is pulsing like your heart's fallen into it and all your homies look holo and not real and you just *know* something real bad is gonna happen.

'I came to say one thing.' he says. 'I heard what happened with your brother. Good for him. I want you to let him know there's other places the two of them can go. Outside of Halcyon.'

'What!' I say. 'Have you gone totally fucking *crazy*? Those places are filled with man-eating beasts and thirty-foot snakes and giant spiders!'

'Not all of them,' he says. 'There's a place I know. Across the ocean. It's a three-day journey. A trading beast leaves on Friday and I'm going to be on it. It's a place where there's no damn FiCap or Er Cap or IntCap. Where people can just be people.'

'What's it called?' I ask. 'How come I never heard of it?'

'It's called New Amsterdam.'

'New Amsterdam? What kind of a stupid name is that?' I whisper.

What I mean is, what kind of a stupid crazyfucker idea is that? You really think that place is gonna be any better than here? And I thought you were supercranio.

Across the *Ocean*?

Those brute winds, the raging storms and merciless depths. Not to mention the radiation from the UV.

'Please,' I say. Because, what else is there?

He hands me a piece of paper.

'For your brother and his wife,' he said. 'In case they want to leave. Directions to the docks and the name of the hombre they should ask for. They'll need the password.' He leans forward and whispers it softly into my ear.

I take the stupid paper. He searches my face, like he's waiting for me to ask another question.

'But wait,' I say. 'If you leave, then what happens to us?' He shrugs.

'Problems of two little people don't amount to a hill of beans in this crazy world, Mia,' he says. And turns to go.

I guess that was the wrong question.

I ask Mom about the ErCap district and she shudders. 'They live like animals.' Like she'd know. The only animals she's seen are stupid Robopets.

'I *have* to go see him, Mom. He's my brother.'

She frowns. 'Have Eric drive you.'

Eric parks Dad's black solamoto at the entrance to the barrio. Three tough guapo homies givin' us the eyeful.

'Are you, like, coming in, Eric?'

'If you don't mind Miss, I think it advisable I remain with the moto.'

'OK.' I square my shoulders and walk across to them.

'Scuse me,' I begin. 'Would you happen to know where the Sacristo res is?'

One of the guapos spits on the ground right in front of me.

'Who wants to know?'

'My brother's staying there? Jay Parker?'

'You Jay's sister?'

'Yeah. I came to see him.'

The guapos shift their feet, relax their hard young faces, 'Jay-bird, he's OK, hermana. Right along there. La Casa Rosa.'

Jay's problem all along is, everyone loves him. Took him so much energy to keep 'em happy he had none left to figure out what he wanted himself. In the end it was easier for him to flunk out of school then let everyone down.

Maria comes out to say Hi. 'I'm so sorry, Jay's working,'

she says. 'He got a job at a bar uptown. Dracao on Mariposa. Won't you come in and take some tea?'

She is so damn beautiful. Huge green eyes that look like they're brimming with tears the whole time and a sad, sweet smile. I totally see why Jay's given everything up for her.

The house is small and painted pink with tubs of flowers on the patio, the kind that Mom would never have in her plantings, no way. Grandmas and aunties and kids freakin' everywhere. Something good-smelling bubbling on the stove. I ask what it is and words sound like colours: zafran, pimento, basilica, zeera. Maria and I sit in the small living room and she turns down the sound of the TV. The room empties out of kids except for one small nena, real cute. I wonder what Jay and Maria's kid's gonna look like. The grandmas and aunties fuss around, offer watermelon juice, tea, cake, biscuits, empanadas. I sip a glass of water and nibble on an empanada while Maria shoos them all out 'cept for, like, the most senior grandma and auntie who are planted on the sofa, fanning themselves, like short of an earthquake, those gals ain't going nowhere. I take a deep breath and hand her the paper.

'A friend of mine's leaving Halcyon,' I whisper. 'On a beast. He asked me to give this to Jay. But listen, please don't even think about going. I'll talk to Mom and make things OK. She'll sign the re-certification.'

Maria glances over Grandma and Auntie. Faces like stone.

'Thank you Mia,' she says. 'You're sweet. But Jay already asked her and she said no way.'

'I'll talk to her,' I say again. 'Come live with us. We have a big house. Plenty of space for a baby.'

She nods. 'Uncle Carlo told me.'

'Um also? I know Carlo is mad with my Mom cos she's been such a perrucha-'

Grandma and Aunty both flinch and cross themselves.

'Sorry. Anyway I wonder if he'd give me some advice, y'know. On what to use to clean out the aviary?'

'Baking soda,' said Maria. 'It's the best.'

The little kid still kneeling in front of the silent cartoons on the TV turns his head.

'He ain't coming back,' he says.

'Who?' I asked. 'You mean Carlo, right?'

The nena, who's around four, with almond-shaped black eyes and dark curls, shakes his head.

'He ain't coming back,' he says.

I kiss Maria bye and whisper the password into her ear. Her shell-pink lips repeat the words silently. She nods and smiles her sweet, sad smile.

In the car I sit up front next to Eric. Dude's been driving Dad for over twenty years now. Guess he's seen a few things.

'*So*, Eric. I was wondering. Could we take a tour of the docks on the way back to D1? Like I'm learning Dad's business, right? So I wondered about the export side. I know it's right round here someplace.'

Eric's face doesn't change, but a muscle flickers in his cheek, like I said something funny.

'I wouldn't advise it Miss. He nods towards the mouth of a tunnel we're passing, unmarked, with a flashing Palmdisk reader at the entrance. 'Rough lot down there. Makes the barrio look like Halcyon Hill.'

'The docks are down there?'

'A long way down Miss.'

'You ever seen it, Eric? You seen the ocean?'

He clears his throat. 'A number of times, Miss.'

'So Dad's Palmdisk gets him through?'

His eyes flick sideways but he don't look straight at me.

'All senior employees and Board Members of Parker Robotics require dock access, Miss. Much of our raw material comes by sea.'

Hallelujah, praise Halcyon forever. All this time I been thinkin' Dad made Jay and me show up twice a year to Board Meetings in dutiful son and daughter drag just, y'know, *because*. Now, I know there was a reason.

Days go by and I dial Dylan's wafer again and again and there's nothing. Only the false, grinning face of the perrucha in Halcyon Comms uniform, telling me the code I am entering is not recognized.

He ain't coming back.

At home I open the aviary door and shoo the birds out.

Minou, Minou my pretty little Minou. Oh, how my heart has been wounded by the arrows of love. Who would have thought this much pain possible?

'Freedom or Death,' I whisper as the aviary empties of colour, scarlet, blue and canary yellow flashing and darting up into the soft, whispering, embrace of the green canopy.

I run to the garage and drag out Jay's old jet bike. Fire her up and ride along HL 24, which leads to the ErCap barrios. I stop the jetbike by 134 and see the same three guapos hangin' tough.

'Hey,'

'Hey. You Jay's sister, no?'

'Yeah. Could you see he gets this bike?'

'No one there, guapa. House all closed up and empty.'

I fire up the jetbike and zip down to the Sacristo House. The Casa Rosa sign fixed over the door hangin' by a nail. Door swings open when I kick it. Pots of red flowers upturned, earth spilling outa them over the patio. No one in there. No cooking aromas, no grandmas and aunties, not one nena.

I turn and ride back to the guapos. Kids hang out here all day, they musta have seen something.

'What the hell happened?'

The guapo shrugs. 'Shit happens. Feds came one night. Next day they were gone.' He swallows one too many times and his eyes grow huge and black. Scared.

'Can you ride this thing?'

'Sure, chica. You want me take you for a ride?'

'You get me to the end of the tunnel, OK? The one down by the docks? Then you know what? You can keep it.'

'This cheval, you want me to keep it? Not gonna nail me for stealin' or shit, chica?'

'I'm giving it to you. Jay's gone, like you said. He don't need it.'

'OK chica.'

I Palmdisk us into the tunnel and the jetbike whirrs smoothly down the endless black, emptiness. Green phosphor flares light the huge PROHIBIDA signs painted in white on the walls and show us the tunnel twisting slowly downwards. We zip on silently, through the ghost green-lit dark.

'This is some fucking cheval,' the guapo says quietly.

'All yours.' I tell him. I lean my face against the guapo's back, inhale the smell of his sweat and sigh. I swear, I can feel him blushing through his shirt. Kid must be all of fourteen years old under the 'tude.

After an hour, maybe more, so long feels like we never gonna get outa there, we see it, faraway and impossible as the moon. Light, at the end of the tunnel. We zoom on closer 'til I'm sure, then I tell the guapo drop me off by the tunnel-side.

'You gonna be OK, chica?' he asks, giving me a clumsy kiss, baby moustache scrapin' my lip.

'I'm gonna be OK,' I tell him. 'Freedom or Death, compadre.'

Takes an infinite hour of feeling my way down the walls, black and wet like the inside of a snake, before I'm at the tunnel mouth. I come out, blinking in the sheer wall of light, feeling like a just born baby.

Standing by the dock, the ocean is everywhere you look, a deep, shimmering, sapphire martini blue. Big old mountains of cloud, white and tainted limon by the pale sun. I take in gulping breaths of the salt wind that tears through the dock, tugging at my hair and snagging in my throat. Down in the water, huge, curved silver backs of sea beasts, bigger than houses, bigger than Halcyon Hall, float, docked in lines. One is rumbling slowly free, sounding out a deep, mournful, dragging signal that feels like the world just begun over again.

I look up at the sky, blink at the tearing light burning my retinas. Above, a sudden flash and beat of verde and azul appears from the blinding light and takes wing over the ocean.

'Minou,' I call. 'Freedom or Death, Minou!'

Fly, Minou, fly away over the ocean.

Build a nest on the deep water, pretty bird, and lay your eggs. Cast your spell with me; that the seas shall remain calm and untroubled as old-time glass and bear my love safe, far, far away.

Bunker Buster

Alec McQuay

Enemies were like mushrooms, an old friend had told her. They grew in the shadows and multiplied, hidden from view and thriving on their diet of bullshit. Emily had seen his point but had never really bothered with analogies for such a basic fact of life. She killed people; people that needed killing, for the most part. No matter the character of those she killed there was always another to replace them, bent out of shape because she had removed them from the mortal coil with malice aforethought. Sometimes it was a sibling, a parent, or even a friend sworn to avenge them. Perhaps the only ones that bothered her were the children, set on their course in the name of a parent they were no doubt better off without, but she never let that slow her down. She couldn't. As long as they were old enough she would bury them as surely as anyone else, living another day while the waste foxes ate their fill of carrion.

Emily killed people for a living and she was good at it, possibly even the best there was. She also had a family of her own to consider. When you had as many enemies as she did, the whys and wherefores could not be allowed to matter.

The ranks of her enemies had blossomed that day, though how many of the families and allies would know to blame her was impossible to guess. Her target had been a tower in the middle of nowhere; the remnants of an aircraft control facility from a thousand years before that had somehow survived when all around it had fallen. It was small, of no tactical importance and of no use to anyone but her, standing on the vast plain like an extra nipple on an ochre giant's stomach. She had hoped to find it abandoned, or at worst occupied by a few simple vagrants as many abandoned buildings were in such a harsh environment as Somerset. Unfortunately, while the building itself had been tightly secured, she had found the tower at the centre of a waxing tide.

Thousands of men and women, dressed in khaki fatigues and carrying identical, blocky rifles in battleship grey, had filled the valley with flickering shafts of superheated light. Charred bodies and pools of molten, glass-like sand dotted the battlefield and the air was thick with the rich, cloying stink of cooking meat. To an outsider it was difficult to tell which of the two sides was which, let alone why such a blood-bath was ensuing, but to Emily and the crew of the enormous tank she had arrived in, it didn't matter.

They stood between the Warlord and her target, and that made them the enemy.

Emily surveyed the battlefield from the safety of her 'Crawler' – an ancient, Hercules Class tank over eighty feet in length; nearly a hundred feet if you included the barrel of the main gun. Its skin could stop anything in Emily's stock with barely a mark and every conceivable angle from outside was covered by the firing arc of at least three weapons, while six 'miniature' cannons placed equidistantly around the machine could be turned to address the greatest threats. Parked a mile from the battle, the Crawler was an apex predator before a shoal of minnows, far and away the most dangerous pres-ence for hundreds of miles. Though its official designation was the word 'Crawler' with a sixteen-digit alpha-numeric suffix, someone in its dim past had stencilled the name 'Boadicea' in huge black letters down either side, now scoured into near-obscurity by wind-blown sand. Everyone who had ridden in it had their own name for it, with words like 'Beast,' 'Leviathan' and 'Bahamut' regularly passing the lips of awe-inspired passengers.

Emily, more than a little amused by the lavish titles her Crawler had been given, quietly called it Robert.

Deep within its armoured confines she watched the monitors, as external sensors swept the area and fed back everything she could possibly want to know. Once passed through the machine's central computer the data was regurgi-tated as imagery and sound, along with temperature readings, analysis of significant threats and an approximation of their chance at victory if they were to engage both armies in their entirety. Emily looked at that particular reading with a raised eyebrow. She had been taught that victory was never assured; that something could always go wrong in even the most thorough plans and could lead to crushing defeat. By the look of the softly glowing '100%' at the bottom of her main screen, the Crawler's designer had been far more comfortable with his ego.

Emily didn't look up when her gunnery officer called out from her seat, dead centre of the command room. Jemima's seat was bolted to the inside of a large gyroscope of overlapping steel rings and allowed her to face in any direction, the computer feeds delivering everything she needed straight into her brain via plugs in the back of her neck.

'What do you reckon, boss? Softly softly, or give 'em something to think about?'

'I'm not sure thinking is on the agenda,' Emily mused. 'No use of the terrain, no obvious tactics... Looks like the idea is to keep going until whoever survives claims a victory. It's against my better judgement but I think a polite warning is in order.'

'And if that doesn't work?'

The relish in Jemima's voice was unseemly, but Emily had long ago accepted her gunner's taste for violence. Away from battle she was capable of incredible warmth towards her friends and her family but, once the odds were stacked and she had a gun in her hands, there was something far darker within Jemima Clayton that her soft, blue eyes didn't betray.

'Then more fool them. Raffy? A *polite* warning, if you would be so kind. I have a thesaurus in my quarters if you need to look for words that don't rhyme with 'front.''

Raphaela stood up from her chair at the front of the room and smiled innocently, one of her eyes open wide to reveal a startlingly green iris while the other was a thin, bloodshot slit. Bowing so low that the ends of her poker-straight tresses of black hair touched the checker-plate floor, she took the mouth-piece to the address system in hand and helped it to her mouth, straightening up and clearing her throat as she looked over at her commanding officer.

'As you wish, mum. *Hostile forces, this is the crew of the FOBT Boadicea. We are inbound and advise you to get out of the way immediately. Boadicea out.*'

Emily raised an eyebrow. 'FOBT?'

'Well, the last three words are 'Off Big Tank.''

'I suspected as much. It doesn't look like it worked though, in fact… we have incoming. Brace yourselves, ladies.'

At the command of the enemy forces' generals, rockets and high-calibre machine gun fire swept towards the Crawler, setting off an alarm in Emily's console that she silenced with a wave of her hand. In silence, the crew waited to see what would happen, watching the missiles coursing towards them on the main viewing screen. When the Crawler's reactive force-field hummed, turned the outside skin of the tank a soft yellow of glowing energy and reduced the incoming munitions to puffs of stinking vapour, Jemima let out a loud, exaggerated sigh of relief and thumbed her nose at the screen.

Emily brushed a ringlet of grey-tinted auburn hair away from her cheek and snorted. 'Or not. Well, stupid is as stupid does. Jemima? Your turn. Just enough to make the point though, if you please.'

Jemima pulled the trigger so fast, Emily wasn't sure her mouth had even closed from giving the order. In perfect unison a pair of vast, belt-fed rotator cannons chattered their death song to any who failed to get out of the way in time, scything through enemy soldiers with burning munitions. Each round was three inches across and a dozen per second were spat from each gun, reducing bodies to puffs of blood spatter and minced flesh while flames leapt from the ground wherever a shell touched down. As the twin cannons roared, the main cannon rose sedately while Jemima calculated the range to the absolute centre of the battlefield, homing in on the closest thing she could detect to a front line. Raising the gun until it was almost pointing directly upwards, she fired. The rotator cannons fell silent as a single cannon shell roared into the sky, the *boom* from the tank's muzzle shaking the ground so violently that dozens of soldiers fell over.

'Wait for it…' Jemima whispered, the corners up her mouth teasing upwards into a vicious smile. 'Wait for it…'

The battlefield had fallen all but silent when the shell returned to Earth. Thousands of men and women screamed what they thought would be their last words as the shell exploded, throwing their hands over their faces as if they could hold back the blast wave. But no blast wave ever came. Instead, the shell was hovering a meter above the ground and its outer casing had split open, falling to the ground in perfect quarters like the petals of an obscene flower. The boldest of them took a step closer and saw the hovering core turning with a soft hum; four columns of tubes around a large, steel drum that connected to the rear of each bank with a series of segmented silver cables. As they watched, as awe-struck as they were confused, its rotation accelerated until it was a blur of motion, pirouetting in mid-air on a cushion of invisible force.

With a shriek, the core's central hopper fed thousands of bullets into the firing banks in less than a second; a single, brief outburst that tore hundreds of soldiers to pieces and filled the air with fluttering, blood-stained scraps of khaki material.

'Bloody hell,' Emily said, watching as the survivors turned and ran, many of them limping or crawling where their legs had been peppered with gunfire. 'That was… different.'

'I've been reading up,' Jemima replied proudly. 'You wouldn't believe some of the shit we've got hiding in ammunition storage. There's this one round, right, about the size of my head, *filled* with needles, and-'

'Maybe later,' Emily interrupted, making a mental note to avoid that conversation as though her life depended on it. 'Raffy, your turn. Take us in, and *do* try not to run over every person you see.'

The tank's engine's rumbled into life and the Crawler rolled forwards, tracks with hundreds of individual plates each many times the size of a person compressing the dusty ground into soft stone. In front of it the two forces were running for their lives, forgetting their fallen comrades and unsure if they were even fleeing in the right direction, s, simply picking one at random away from the tank and moving as quickly as they could.

'Look at them go,' Raffy said, changing down a gear and revving hard so that the engines bellowed. 'No fight left in any of them.'

'And you would face down the Crawler on foot, I suppose?' Emily replied, raising one slender, auburn brow towards her daughter. 'Actually, don't answer that. You'd fight a tank armed only with a spoon and a smile given half a chance.'

'And she'd probably fucking win,' Jemima added.

Emily shook her head and laid a hand on Jemima's shoulder, squeezing affectionately and replying in a soft, exasperated tone. 'Leaving her armed with a spoon *and* a tank. Probably best that we don't give her any ideas. It's hard enough keeping her out of trouble as it is.'

Raffy smiled darkly. 'Your faith in me is overwhelming. Anyway, we're coming up on the tower. You sure you want to go it alone? I can arm up and be ready to go if you want backup…'

Emily considered it for a moment, far from keen on the idea of stepping into the unknown without the support of so able a killer as her daughter, but she knew she would have to decline. Her position as warlord was difficult to maintain and at times relied on a softer approach, and there was nothing left of her daughter that could be considered soft. When the circumstances called for discretion, it was for the best that Raffy and Jemima were kept as far away as possible.

'If this goes badly I will call you to come and help,' she lied, knowing that if it went badly she would be in no position to contact them at all. 'Until then, just try not to get into any trouble. That goes for you too, Mrs Clayton.'

The two younger women nodded sullenly and looked back to their controls, while Emily made for one of the thickly armoured doors to the side of her beloved tank. At a command from Jemima the portal creaked and groaned as hidden gearing retracted bolts as thick as a woman's arm, while a loud *clunk* rang out as a pair of magnetic clamps were deactivated and the door swung freely outwards. With the wind teasing her hair, Emily jumped down and landed softly on the ground, eyes darting here and there in case some bold soldier had remained behind and fancied his chances. Seeing that no-one had been so foolhardy, she kicked the door shut with a solid *thunk* and headed directly for the building, her black, leather boots kicking up whirls of fine sand as her weighty frame disturbed the shifting ground.

The Warlord cut a strange figure alone in the blasted landscape. The nearby bodies were those of the young; men and women pressed into service by one or other of her lowly rivals, strong and capable of making war in the hopes of a better future. Most of them were in their late teens to mid-twenties, making them half Emily's age at most. She stood alone in her black body armour, silver-dusted ringlets blowing in the wind, surrounded by corpses young enough to be her children. It pained her to take the lives of such people when they only wanted what everyone else did; to find a little peace in the frontier. To get to that peace they had to wade through a war that they had not started, that they had little stake in but which they could not escape, and that had led them to sign up to the strongest leader they could find. Unfortunately for them those leaders were clearly morons, whose ideas of war were like that of a child. Two such idiots had lined their people up and sent them at each other, smashing them together in the middle as though expecting something other than utter chaos.

Emily's youth was behind her and her body, repeatedly battered against the anvil that had been her life, was past its best, but if she had her way she would give them all the peace they longed for. If that meant going alone into the darkness and coming back with the means to slaughter every idiot Warlord on the planet, then so be it. Looking up from her thoughts she found herself nearing her target; the tower looking like an Easter Island head worn smooth by wind and sand.

Emily had been briefed on the target building, though brief really was the word for it. There was nothing much to tell about it besides its location. It was roughly circular and a mere ten feet in height, appearing almost like a wartime pillbox only devoid of the requisite firing slits. It was basically smooth and basically grey, completely unremarkable other than the fact that it was a virtually unblemished human construction in the centre of what Jemima had referred to as "an expansive vista of bugger all." In fact, the only feature she could see was what could only be a door, which was simply a smooth section of wall a couple of metres square that stood proud of the rest of the structure by less than a centimetre.

'It's never bloody simple,' she mumbled, noting that there was not so much as a handle anywhere to be seen, let alone a visible keyhole or biometric reader. A swift kick from one thick-heeled boot told her that the door was too solid to persuade with anything less than horrendous violence, and even the wall to either side of the portal proved to be too well made to easily submit. She could have returned to the Crawler of course, even armour of the sort that protected the tower was likely no match for a sustained assault from her pride and joy, but such a vulgar display would have been ill advised, to say the very least.

'I come in peace?' she tried, fully aware that if anyone was listening they would have seen enough to know better. 'OK fine, you know why I'm here and you know what I want. I'm armed but as you can see, there's not much I can do about that.'

Emily raised her a hand with a quiet whine of motorised joints. The mechanical prosthetic that had replaced her left arm was a little difficult to miss so there was no point in trying to conceal it, and she couldn't have removed it if she had wanted to. In order to support and counterbalance such a device its circuitry and mechanisms ran through her spine, her legs and most of her body, keeping it from being more of a liability than a boon. The device had kept her alive on more occasions than she would like to admit and could never be taken away from her, at least not while she was still alive.

Whether or not this mattered to whomever was listening was unclear, but the door let out a resonant *clunk* and sank downwards into the ground with a belch of fetid, dusty air. Emily coughed loudly as she found herself looking into a gloomy, circular room beyond.

'Off I go then,' she said into a brass communications device built into an oval cameo pinned to the lapel of her tan overcoat. 'Keep the lines quiet in case I need you, but if I'm not back in twelve hours, see to it that no-one is ever able to follow me.'

There was no reply, at least none over the radio, but Emily smiled as the barrel of the tank's main cannon rose and fell twice as though the machine were nodding.

'Cute,' she said approvingly, then turned and disappeared into the darkness.

Once inside, the door closed with a *thud* that shook the whole building, setting loose drifts of dust and the hollow shells of several dozen desiccated spiders from above. Emily coughed and covered her mouth with one hand to filter out the worst of the muck that swirled in the darkness, but after a few moments of imposing silence a soft, sucking breeze began to build as fans set into the walls came to juddering life. She felt a cool mist caressing the exposed skin of her neck and quietly hoped that this was a decontamination system, and not some pointlessly elaborate trap for unwary treasure hunters.

Fortunately, she was in luck. Once the long-settled air had been fully replaced a series of gentle, blue lights winked into existence on the floor, forming a perfect circle a few feet away from where she was standing. After staring at them briefly they began to flicker and she took the hint, moving to stand within the circle and instinctively making certain that no part of her body extended beyond their glowing circumference. This soon proved to have been an excellent choice, as the individual points of illumination expanded until they formed an unbroken circle and grew brighter, then blinked back out of existence. The disc upon which Emily was apparently standing fell rapidly through the floor and plummeted at breath-taking speed into cold, rushing darkness. Even to one so completely sure of themselves as Emily, respected assassin and feared warlord that she was, the feeling of rushing through pitch blackness into the unknown was deeply unsettling. Though she had a vague idea of what sort of creature awaited her at the bottom of the chasm she had no real idea of its motives or its capabilities, having encountered few such individuals before. Anything she said or did might be her final act if this "Keeper," as the Custodian had called it, took offense or saw something in her that it disapproved of.

Hell, she thought to herself, as she felt the disc begin to slow beneath her. *It wouldn't have to look very hard...*

As the blackness tore past she forced her breathing to slow and refused to allow her fists to clench at her sides, focusing on the finer things in her life and slowing her heart rate as much as she could. She thought of those she was protecting and for whom she had made her many sacrifices, keeping the manner in which she bought their freedom as far from her mind as she could. She thought of her peaceful apartment and her beloved, if dangerously complex daughter, of her friends and of the best times they had shared. She needed to make a good impression or she might leave empty handed. Worse than that did not bear thinking about. Eventually she felt the hot rush of blood in her limbs cool and she smiled, opening her eyes and looking out into the abyss.

The darkness was beginning to soften from a deep black to a hazy grey, continuing to brighten as the disc neared the floor of a large space that must have been at least a mile beneath the ground. She was far beyond the reach of even her Crawler's gargantuan firepower. When the disc reached the bottom it lowered itself seamlessly into a ring of blue light and became as one with the floor, completely indistinguishable from the rest of the smooth, black marble that extended as far as she could see in every direction. Once the azure circle had disappeared there was only the thin illumination that seemed to come from everywhere at once, as though the air itself were the source of what little light existed in the cavernous space. Not sure what to expect or what might have been expected of her, Emily remained on the spot. The urge to draw a weapon was palpable and she softly congratulated herself on coming without one. Aside from the glassy blackness of the floor and the dim light the area was entirely featureless, far from the crowded but ordered storerooms that the Custodian maintained, but the feeling that something was looking at her was sending an itch up her spine all the way to her trigger fingers.

Aside from a name, she had been sent to the tower with nothing.

'I am looking for the Keeper!' she cried out, tiring of standing around and doing nothing. 'The Custodian told me that I would find them here.'

'AND WELL YOU MIGHT,' came the reply. Like the light, the voice came from everywhere and nowhere; a mechanical whisper that seemed to resonate from every possible direction. 'BUT WHY DO YOU SEEK THEM, EMILY NATION? WHAT IS IT THAT YOU THINK YOU MIGHT FIND?'

'You know my name?' Emily said, kicking herself immediately for asking such a stupid question. 'You knew that I was coming?'

'SOMEONE IS ALWAYS COMING. THEY SEEK MANY THINGS, AND I HAVE MANY THINGS THAT I COULD OFFER. BUT THE *WHY* IS IMPORTANT. TELL ME, DOES THE CUSTODIAN LIVE STILL?'

Emily nodded, though she could never be certain if "living" was the correct term for the mechanical being's existence. He was certainly more than a machine though, with thoughts and opinions that were entirely his own and certainly not an affectation to comfort those humans who had to deal with him. She had known the Custodian since a far simpler time in her life, back when she was young and carefree; a wild assassin who had revelled in the firepower he had provided, little caring why he had chosen to help her. She had been naïve then, but it had been such a different world. In that world she had felt invincible and believed that her youth would last forever, and that "Britain's New Frontier" was to be a fresh start leading to prosperity beneath azure skies. She had thought that those days of wealth and happiness would last forever.

Oh, how very wrong she had been.

'He is far from here, but he is a trusted ally. My friend even. He would have come himself of course, but you must understand how things are up on the surface these days. If anything were to happen to him he would not be so easily replaced.'

'SO AN ASSET IS WHAT YOU ARE? AN EXPENDABLE RESOURCE IN THE LONG WAR?'

'Well,' she replied smoothly, her ruby lips broadening as she smiled. 'Aren't we all?'

The strange grinding noise that came next was as close to a laugh as the Keeper could apparently manage, yet the noise brought no reassurance at all. It was impossible to know exactly what passed for humour when you were a millennia-old construct, teetering on the verge between humanity and a purely mechanical existence. For all Emily knew the enigmatic creature might once have been an ally to the Custodian that had gone insane, having resided alone in the dark for such a very long time. For all she knew it could be preparing a care package of elaborate firearms or deciding how best to dissect her, having grown bored of their conversation and deciding to reacquaint itself with human biology in the most visceral way possible.

'THAT IS A FAR MORE HONEST ANSWER THAN I WOULD EXPECT FROM ONE SUCH AS YOU, WARLORD.' The stress the machine put on the last word laced it heavily with implied insult, and Emily felt a chill in the depths of her stomach.

There was no use denying it. As much as she hated the bastards and their private armies, their vicious ambitions and their disregard for all save themselves, she knew that she was ultimately just another general amongst hundreds, however noble her intentions might have been.

'What reason do I have to lie?' she replied. 'I came here to see if you would help, and that is all. There are others like me who kill for fun and would use what you have for their own ends, not in the pursuit of peace. I know you saw what was happening when I arrived.'

'AND I SAW HOW YOU DEALT WITH IT,' the Keeper replied. 'AN INTERESTING COURSE OF ACTION FOR ONE WHO SPEAKS OF PEACE, DON'T YOU THINK?'

Emily laughed drily. If the Keeper thought that was a vulgar display of power then the its vision was clearly limited to the immediate area. The mission she was on was far from her first . To discover those things that the world had been well rid of, hidden in their concrete bunkers and lost, defence-grid protected laboratories, Emily had been forced to push herself to the very limits of morality. Raffy had once joked that if her mother's heart were ever to be weighed against a feather in order to gauge her suitability for heaven, she would have to cross her fingers and pray that the under-world made its pigeons out of concrete.

'I didn't say it was an attractive process,' Emily replied honestly. 'Far from it, and only an idiot would claim to be able to end a war like that with words.'

This time it was the Keeper who laughed. 'WORDS. YOU ARE AT LEAST CORRECT ABOUT WORDS — HOW MEANINGLESS THEY ARE FROM YOUR SOFT MOUTHS. THE YAWNING INFINITY OF TRUTH BEFORE YOU AND STILL YOU LIE AND SEEK TO CONFOUND, SO YOU CAN APPRECIATE WHY YOUR WORDS MEAN LESS THAN NOTHING TO ME.'

On the subject of words, Emily was lost. On his best day the Custodian was a difficult creature to speak to, yet he was not nearly so obtuse as the Keeper appeared to be. While at times he might ask for clarification of a point and would fre-quently point out contradictions with all the razor-edged skill of a particularly hawkish English teacher, he had never once suggested that her words were completely invalid.

'Then what can I say? I could make you a promise, but I don't see that you would accept such a thing. All I can do is tell you that we have great need-'

'A NEED? LONG AGO THEY SPOKE OF NEED, BUT NEVER DID THEY SPEAK OF THE WATER THAT ONCE FLOWED HERE, NOR OF THE OXYGEN THEY BREATHED. I HAVE LISTENED TO A MULTITUDE OF NEEDS AND NEVER ONCE HAS THAT REQUEST BEEN FOR EVEN THE MOST BASIC OF SUSTENANCE, ALWAYS FOR THE MEANS TO DOMINATE AND TO KILL. I TIRE OF THIS. SPEAK YOUR WORDS AND BE DONE WITH IT. TELL ME WHAT IT IS THAT YOU *NEED*.'

This is it, Emily thought. One wrong move and I'm toast, or it'll just turn the lights off and ignore me until I'm dead.

That thought made her shudder. In her daydreams and moments of dark introspection the end had always come on the end of a blade, or at the bare hands of someone who proved to be better than she was. No matter the hundreds of ways her sleeping mind had taunted her, some facet of her ego had prevented any of those nightmares from leaving her helpless before her doom, with nothing and no-one to fight. Her life had robbed her of almost every fear, but the thought of meekly waiting for death while an unknown fate lay in wait for her loved ones knotted her stomach painfully.

'I don't know what I need, Keeper. The secrets of the old war are being discovered every day and the deeper they search, the worse the things these bastards find become. Someone has to stand up to them and if I'm going to be the one that does it, I'm going to need all the help I can get. You've seen how I got here and what we did to shift those soldiers, and if you're half as clever as I think you are you know how much more damage we could have done.'

The Keeper hissed another unpleasant laugh. 'YOUR DEFINITION OF RESTRAINT IS AN INTERESTING ONE.'

'I won't argue with that. My crew have been through a lot and they've risked everything to try and end this. I'll stand here and argue my case all day if you need me to but I won't apologise for them, not when it could be so much worse.'

'BUT ANYTHING I GIVE TO YOU, I ALSO GIVE TO THEM. YOU CANNOT LEAD SUCH A LIFE ON YOUR OWN. WHAT IS THERE TO STOP THEM FROM CROSSING THE LINE?'

Emily realised that her face had become hot and her fists had clenched of their own accord. It wasn't that the Keeper's words were aggravating her, in fact she was glad whenever she encountered someone who was not quick to hand over control of something dangerous to someone not suited to its use, but it was forcing her to confront a notion that haunted her. She had a list of "what-ifs" as long as her arm, and the worst of them was difficult for her to think about.

Emily spoke only a single word; one of which she was certain but which carried implications she hated to consider.

'*Me.*'

The Keeper seemed to dwell on that for a while, the air falling still and silent as it considered Emily's words. Then, moving so quickly that Emily recoiled and threw up her fists protectively, a slender, metallic appendage as thick as her thumb darted from the floor in front of her, its 'head' a glowing sphere of purple glass. The light within flickered as though dense clouds swirled beneath the surface, and as Emily lowered her hands the Keeper spoke again.

'WORDS ARE SIMPLE. THEY CAN BE FALSE, EVEN IF ONE DOES NOT KNOW IT WHEN THEY ARE SPOKEN. BUT DEEDS, EMILY NATION... IT IS OUR DEEDS WHICH CARRY THE MARK OF TRUTH.'

Emily opened her mouth to scream, then felt it snap shut again as she blinked in the pale light and could not remember why she had thought to do so. A memory of a large room beneath the ground teased at the edges of her consciousness and then slipped away, like smoke pouring through the outstretched fingers of her mind. She was standing in the middle of... where was she? That's right, she thought. This is the Crawler. And we have a job to do...

Images and thoughts flooded into her as though she was absorbing them through her skin, arriving within her whole and in explicit detail, as if these were things which she had always known. Of course she had always known them, why would she think that she hadn't? Her head was aching and there was a feeling in the very pit of her stomach as if something was not quite correct; as though she lingered with one foot in the daylight and one firmly planted in the last moments of a dream.

Most importantly, her crew were all around her. There was Raffy, her normally poker-straight hair lashed into a bun at the back of her head as she pored over the instrument panels. Raffy's husband was elsewhere, bringing his multiple rows of shark-like teeth to bear on the flesh of those who opposed them and her sons, dear, beautiful Sebastian and Thomas, were playing with a ball at their mother's feet. There were many others, some dear to her and others to whom she was either employer or feared master, bustling around and seeing to the vital systems of the tank or to errands that the main crew were too busy to carry out. At the moment the crown jewel of her staff was sat just in front of her; a violent sheen of white-blonde hair surrounding that dangerously alluring bone structure of hers and the sharp, foul tongue currently safe behind lips that had been painted a deep shade of blue. Jemima was like a sister to Emily, albeit one with a vicious streak wide enough to park three Crawler's on side by side. She had married one of her oldest friends and had served alongside her for years, and now she stood beside Emily at the controls of a weapon that would change the world.

Change the world, she thought, considering the vast pylon that had been welded to the outside of the vehicle and its dozens of energy-emitting dishes. For her and those loyal to her it would change the world, but for those on the receiving end? Well the world would change for them too, but only briefly. It would change from a place where they were alive into a place where they were dead, or perhaps on fire, or maybe clutching at themselves pathetically as their blood boiled and their flesh was reduced to ash. She called it the 'Bunker Buster' because no-one could hide from it, no matter how deeply they buried themselves behind steel and rock. A single shot and an area a dozen miles across would be destroyed; subjected to localised tectonic upheaval and a chain reaction that would reduce even the strongest armour to burning slag. Properly calibrated it could level mountains and boil oceans; it could turn diamond to vapour and, because it drew energy from the universe around it in a way that was far beyond Emily's comprehension, it would never run out of ammunition. It was hard to remember exactly where she had found the device but find it she had, and now she stood on the very edge of one era, poised to leap headlong into the next. She would be the woman who put it all to rest, she thought. She had the means to destroy those who had wronged her and all those who had supported them, chasing them into their holes with impunity and burning them out. Every one of them would pay and they would pay with their lives. Then their associates would pay. Then their families and towns, admirers and sycophants. They would burn! All of them! And if anyone tried to stand against her? Well, she would burn them too. She was the one who had made all of *the sacrifices and it was her right to wield the Pylon. She would stand proud over them all and keep her eye out for every petty warlord, every usurper who would think to repeat the mistakes of history. Someone had to make sure that no-one would be stupid or wicked enough to go digging into things that were best left buried and while she was alive, the world would never again be allowed to burn.*

'Ready to fire when you are, boss,' Jemima said, grinning wolfishly and raising one hand, as if to drop it theatrically upon the activation button. 'Say the word and it's all over, unless you want to push the button yourself, of course.'

'Yes!' the others said, speaking as one. 'It's your right! The last warlord of all time…'

All time. Now there was a thought. A world free of people like the ones who had destroyed her family and invaded her home. A place where her grandchildren could grow up in safety.

'End it. End them.'

There would be no escape. Not for any of them. She had the means and the will to track them down wherever they ran and, through the lesson she would teach, none would rise again in her lifetime for fear of the woman with her hand on the button. The woman who held the power of Armageddon in her bronze-plated hand. The woman who had almost lost everything…

'The girl at the end of the world…'

Emily, hand resting on the button and within a hair's breadth of pushing it, stopped. The room had fallen expectantly silent and every eye was on her, or on her hand. She had no idea who had spoken, the voice having appeared as though whispered in her ear from a place where no-one stood. There, moments before the point of no return, she stopped to think of all that she had done. The bodies of her enemies numbered into the thousands already, having moved from bar fight to battlefield and back again more times than she could ever count. She had never kept a record. It had never been about the killing or about exterminating anyone. It had been to protect herself and to create a safer world, not one with the guts ripped out of it in the name of some phony crusade.

'No,' Emily snapped, furious with herself at how close she had come to firing the obscene device. 'It's too much. This isn't a weapon for fighting, it's a weapon for killing.'

347

'All weapons are for killing,' Jemima laughed, though her voice had taken on a bizarre, almost mechanical cadence.

'No, Jemima. They are not. A sword can parry as well as strike. An axe can disarm as well as dismember. Hell, even a gun can be fired into the air as a warning! But this thing? This... Pylon will kill too many for us to ever turn back. The warlords and everyone else will be forced to try and destroy it and they'll dig too far until they find something worse or I destroy them all, or someone takes it from me and uses it against us. No, Jemima. I won't push that button, and neither will you.'

Jemima smiled beatifically. She was as beautiful a woman as Emily had ever seen; attractive in a way that seemed wholly unnatural, as though she had been purpose-built to ensnare others and bend them to her will. That being said, Emily hadn't thought of Jemima as attractive for many years. She knew far too much about her for that. She knew that behind those cheek bones, those glittering eyes and that soft, inviting mouth, there was a mind and a heart that was capable of just about anything. Jemima Clayton was a dangerous bitch and only followed Emily's orders because she lacked the qualities of a leader herself, so when Jemima's hand shot out to strike the firing button, Emily was more than ready for her.

The enclosed space resonated with a sickening crunch of bone and a solid impact as her bronze fist slammed upwards and caught Jemima across the eyebrow, shattering the upper portion of her skull like a neatly struck egg. Jemima, her friend over many difficult years of warfare, fell dead at the controls of the tank. A droplet of blood insinuated itself from her broken forehead and around both of her eyes, finally dripping to the floor from her right cheek. Emily glanced down at the droplet as it splashed sadly against the toecap of her boot.

'Anyone else want to end the world?' she hissed, not bothering to look up.

There was a sickening, wrenching feeling in Emily's stomach as the tank and those around her faded from existence and the chill light of the bunker roused her from her daydream. Her memories flooding back to her in an instant, Emily found herself back in that vast room beneath the ground. This time she was not alone.

'A SURPRISING CONCLUSION, BUT A WELCOME ONE.'

Emily blinked heavily as the silvery appendage slid back into the floor and disappeared. The Keeper was peering at her through the slits in its copper mask, its withered neck creaking as though it had not moved in a great many years. The body of the thing was certainly human, or at least once had been, and not of the same design of the fully-robotic Custodian that she knew so well. This creature appeared to be an extremely ancient woman who had been integrated fully with some vast construct beneath the ground, fastened to her by the hundreds of black, segmented tubes that pierced the skin of her back from her rump to her head. Her legs had long ago succumbed to muscle wastage and had shrunk beneath her, crinkled and unlovely, with skin like the driest of autumn leaves in a sickly grey. Her face was obscured save for her shadowed, green eyes, while the top of her head seemed to be the place where the greatest alterations had been rendered. Above her eyebrows a row of neatly meshed hooks clung through her skin to the bone and held in place a bulging, leathery sack like the abdomen of a gigantic beetle. Its surface was thick with pulsing veins and wide, flat tracks of cabling that connected her enhanced cognitive function to the bunker's every system. She was horrifying and yet glorious, held aloft by a thick armature of blue metal that connected to the ground on a wide, counterweighted bogie.

'That was...' Emily tried. 'I give up, what *was* that? I was on the Crawler...'

'YOU NEVER LEFT,' the Keeper replied. Its tone was softer now, kinder, as though it was all too aware of what it had just put Emily's mind through. 'YOU SEE ME AS I AM, BUT YOU ARE FAR ABOVE ME IN YOUR SEAT. SEE?'

Emily looked up and gasped, seeing a contorted image of Raffy in the air above, violently shaking and slapping her mother as though trying to wake her. Her face was dark and her jaw set firm, clearly struggling to remain composed without Emily's calming presence.

'Something's wrong up there,' Emily said. 'Raffy looks-'

'A GREAT DEAL LIKE YOU, WHEN SHE IS ANGRY.

I WONDER IF SHE WOULD HAVE SHOWN SUCH RESTRAINT IN YOUR POSITION.'

Emily thought of her daughter and smiled warmly, but ultimately she shook her head. 'No, she most certainly would not. That's the problem though, isn't it? It's not about me and what I might do, it's about the legacy of the decisions we make. My daughter and the others in that tank are good people, and I certainly would not be working with them if I didn't believe that, but they... they aren't me.'

'BUT YOU CAN BE TRUSTED WHERE THEY CANNOT?'

'It sounds terrible, doesn't it? I break the rules all the time, but it's alright, because it's me breaking them. That thing you showed me, there's just no way I could risk leaving something like that lying around for someone to steal. It's too much of a responsibility. For anyone.'

'AND SO THE KEY IS TO KNOW THIS *BEFORE* HALF THE PLANET IS ON FIRE. IT IS TIME TO GO NOW, EMILY NATION. YOUR DAUGHTER IS BEGINNING TO FRAY AROUND THE EDGES AND I DO NOT BELIEVE IT WILL BE LONG BEFORE SHE DOES SOMETHING... REGRETTABLE.'

Emily nodded and looked the Keeper up and down a final time. Though the creature sounded just like the Custodian it was clear that something of what she had been previously remained within her, locked somewhere in her ancient, cybernetic shell. The Custodian had been very careful with what he had told Emily about his origins, who had created him and why, but there was one thing she knew for certain. Ultimately, they were as a thin veil separating the horrors of the past from the eager, vicious minds of the present.

It seemed that, no matter how clear the results of the previous war were across the scarred surface of the Earth, people on the whole had learned precisely fuck-all.

'I don't really know what to say, *again*,' Emily laughed. 'I came here for help but this isn't quite what I was expecting.'

'THERE ARE THINGS WHICH MUST REMAIN BURIED. THAT IS MY TASK; TO SEE THAT THEY DO

AND TO DEAL WITH ANY WHO WOULD SEEK TO UNEARTH THEM.'

'Then why not destroy them?' Emily asked. It seemed so obvious a solution; to reduce such creations to their component parts and to never speak of them again; to destroy any remaining knowledge of them and let them pass into the realm of myth. But the Keeper disagreed.

'AND IF ONE WHO *WOULD* HAVE PUSHED THE BUTTON CREATED ONE OF THEIR OWN, WHAT THEN? NO, REMEMBER ME WELL EMILY NATION AND LIVE IN THE HOPE THAT WE NEVER HAVE TO SEE ONE ANOTHER AGAIN.'

The Keeper was gone before she could reply, everything she could see and hear replaced with a loud *slap* and an intense burning in her right cheek.

'Wake. Fucking . Up! Mum! Wake the fu-'

Raffy's hand stopped mid-air, caught in the vice-like grip of Emily's fingers.

'I would *not* do that again if I were you,' Emily said, sitting up straight in her chair and shaking her head to clear it of the remaining smog of unconsciousness.

'What happened?' Raffy demanded. 'You gave the order to fire and then you went out like a light. Is there something you need to tell me? There's no way I can let you walk in there unless I know you're alright.'

Emily turned her head to where Raffy was pointing and saw the tower, displayed on a view screen in front of Jemima's gunnery position. Small, grey and unassuming, with a thick front door and armoured walls. The place was so solid but so unremarkable that neither of the two armies had given it a second look once they realised they could not get inside. Thousands of people had swarmed around it, fully intent on their slaughter and with little more than death on their minds, little realising that beneath their feet lay a killing machine to end them all. The thought of what might have happened if even one of them had known, chilled Emily to her very core.

'I've seen all I need to see,' she replied. 'What the

Custodian sent me for isn't here, not anymore. He was wrong.'

'Wrong?' Jemima replied, swivelling her chair around to face the command position. 'What do you mean he was fucking *wrong?* Did you see how many people we killed just to drive across this shitty field, pull a yewie and piss off back home again?'

'I'm sure they are a terrible loss to their employer,' Emily replied smoothly. 'Now come on ladies, if you please. There is nothing for us here.'

The Crawler roared and belched fumes as the vehicle was thrown into reverse and ground slowly backwards across the churned powder of the battlefield. Jemima and Raffy kept glancing over at their commander as she watched their progress on her own monitors, watchful for the suicidal return of the two armies, still in hiding but no doubt watching from wherever they had skulked off to. Emily would never tell her crew exactly what had occurred that day but it was obvious that something had happened; that she had learned something in the few minutes between losing consciousness and Raffy waking her up again. Why else would she have taken a snapshot of the tower and kept it with her from that day forwards, taking it out surreptitiously when things were at their worst? And why, for some weeks afterwards, had she kept looking guiltily at Jemima when she thought she wouldn't notice?

It did not take long for the warlords to persuade their armies back into the valley but by the time they arrived, the tower had gone. A few reported the change in the landscape back to their employers and some took it as a bad omen, that whoever had been on board the enormous war machine wielded power to make such a thing disappear without a trace. These fled in the depths of the night, swearing off their lives of banditry and hoping never to see that enormous tank again, whispering tales of it in the bars and inns of the land as if to ward off evil spirits.

The rest simply forgot about it and drew their rifles, redoubling their oaths of vengeance and charging back towards the enemy. Within hours of Emily's departure the battle was in full swing and the air began to stink again, heat-haze recoiling from the ground as though disgusted by what it saw. Rifles flickered and voices screamed, smoke coiled into the air like the freed souls of the damned and the sand turned a deep red with the spilt blood of thousands.

As the sun set and the soldiers made war by fire light, the death toll rose and rose.

The Unbroken Line

K. Bannerman

The heavy, treacle-thick silence compelled Polly to open her eyes.

Nothing moved, nothing stirred. Not even the harsh cry of a seagull broke the stillness. Fearing the pox had left her deaf, she looked wildly around the small room, but it was empty, save for her and the pile of rags and a leather bucket that Mrs. McKenzie had brought for her to toss in.

The hush had a weight that pressed down upon her, and she struggled against it to sit up in her nest of rags, but as she moved, her cough grew moist and phlegmatic. Any fear of deafness vanished at the sound of her own lungs straining, squeaking, gurgling for breath. When her coughing eased, Polly gulped in great mouthfuls of air, and she tasted the stench of unwashed bodies, vomit and flatulence. Nothing was amiss, except that everyone was gone. Polly realized she'd never been alone in the tenement before.

The mould-brindled walls and greasy window with its broken panes were just as they'd been when she took to bed three days ago, but the building was abandoned. Polly rose on wobbling knees, weak from the fever, and limped to the window.

Nothing moved on the street below.

Where were the rag-and-bone men crying for wares, the creaking carts pulled by old knackers, the women plying their trade? Where were the Chinese fishermen carrying their poles to Long Bridge to fish for smelt? A San Francisco morning was never quiet.

Apprehension percolated through Polly like Pacific rainwater.

She stumbled down the crooked staircase in a building that should've been crawling with families, out to a street that should've been crowded with people, and yet she was alone. The sunlight had begun to cut through the fog, but even through the shifting veils of clouds and vapours, she heard no sounds of life, not even the squawk of pelicans over the water, nor bells from the ships waiting to moor. The city was deserted.

Other girls might have been afraid, but Polly had been an orphan for three years and a whore for two: she was saucy, and feisty, and she knew to take advantage of a situation. She sat on the front step to muster her energy. Then, with only curious cats to keep her company, she wandered along the street until she came to the open doors of a bakery. Loaves of bread sat cooling in the window. Polly nibbled at one cautiously, then greedily. No one scolded her or accused her of thievery, so she wandered as far as Bush Street, where she found a fine example of a dry goods store, and scrounged new boots and a clean petticoat for herself. Finally, she visited a butcher's, and procured a rich lunch of sausage, cheese and wine.

Surely I have died and gone to heaven, she thought. The city was much improved without men to proposition her and women to harass her.

The pox had left her sore and tired, but buoyed by curiosity, Polly was able to walk as far as the crest of Ricon Hill. By now, the fog had lifted, and she could look out across Mission Bay at the deserted ghost ships floating on its glassy surface. A woman of Polly's calibre would've been chased from this neighbourhood on a normal day, so she took advantage of her predicament to wander between the fine houses, admiring the architecture and statues. She delighted in the white marble columns of splendid Latham mansion. Weary and hungry, she reclined in its front garden under a bower of rhododendrons, and she felt giddy, satiated, full of fine foods and beautiful sights.

Once all the sausage was eaten, Polly lay down in a patch of sunshine and resolved then that she would not question what had happened, because whatever calamity had befallen the city, it had made her the Queen of San Francisco, and the whole peninsula was hers. She wasn't one to question good fortune.

But no sooner had contentment washed over her, a slender figure appeared on the far edge of the green.

She stood, fists clenched. After only half a day alone, her heart stuttered at the sight of a stranger.

He was too far away for her to see his face, but he wore a long leather riding coat and a top hat, and he raised one gloved hand to give her a crisp wave.

Just as she did not question good fortune, Polly was not one to hesitate when danger appeared. She scrambled to her feet and bolted: across the lawns, along Folsom Street, down an alley. But her pitiful lungs would not allow her to run far, so she slipped into a vestibule and pressed her spine to the bricks, panting hard.

Echoing footsteps drew close.

Polly pressed the heel of her hand to her mouth, to muffle her breath.

Then a melodic, baritone voice called, 'Polly Norton?'

Her jaw dropped.

Polly peeked around the edge of the doorway. He stood only ten feet away, and his amber eyes pierced her, but he smiled.

'How'd you know my name?' she said.

'I know a great deal about you,' he replied. 'You've been sick. I'm a physician. I've come to make you well.'

She knew better than to trust a man in a top hat. She jutted out her chin. 'I ain't going nowhere.'

'We don't have to go anywhere,' he assured. 'The door behind you will suffice.'

He raised his hand. Polly heard the sound of trickling water. She turned as the door melted away, replaced by a hallway of shiny steel.

A trick of the light? A con man's game? She fumbled with her tongue, but he gave her no time to question and took her tenderly by the elbow to guide her down the long, breezy corridor. The gentle wind held a dry, dusty fragrance, and it rekindled memories of the journey overland with her parents from Alabama, back when they'd been granted their freedom and kicked to the road by their former master. Her father had high hopes that they'd be welcomed in California, but her mother was not so optimistic; in the end, it didn't matter, as they'd both died of typhoid in Texas and been dumped in pauper graves. Polly had made her way to the west coast alone. The hunger had been unbearable at times, but it helped distract her from the agonizing grief.

The smell, the memory brought a lump to her throat. She stifled a sob. *I'm still sick,* she thought. *It ain't nothing but a dream.*

Her fever-weak limbs made her lean heavily against him, and he felt solid, immovable, as if under his coat, his body was hewn from oak.

'You are still sick, yes,' he said. 'But this is not a dream, and I'm here to help you.'

She'd barely realized he'd plucked her thoughts from the air when he raised a hand to the smooth, reflective wall. A red velvet couch swam into view. Had it appeared, or had she simply not noticed it before?

'Sit here, Polly,' he said in that deep voice, and helped her down upon the cushions. At first she was afraid he would ravish her, but he brought a moist cloth to her forehead and wiped away the sheen of sweat from her dark skin. 'You have been quite ill. On schedule, I might add.'

The cool water brought sweet relief. 'Are you an angel?'

'No,' he chuckled. 'You ask me that, every time.'

'We've met before?'

'Every ten years.'

She examined his features, marvelled that she could not describe them. As soon as her gaze left his mouth, his nose, his eyes, she instantly forgot them.

'You're wrong, sir. Ten years ago, I was still living in Alabama with Ma and Pa.'

'No, Polly.' He took a pale, square device and pressed it to her wrist, listened to the beeps it emitted. 'You've been here, on our ship, for over three thousand years. Every decade, your health must be checked, and so we've devised the pox to remind us.' He smiled. 'When you come down with the illness, it's time for us to meet again. So here we are.'

'I ain't never had the pox before. Either you're mistaken, or you're a lunatic,' she said, but his laugh reassured her and she was unafraid. He had a gentlemanly bearing; more gentlemanly, in fact, that many of the questionable gentlemen who came to the Almshouse to toss pennies at the poor.

'I'm your keeper, Polly.'

She laughed. 'Why would you keep someone like me?'

His smile was very kind. From the pocket of his coat, he drew out another device, this one covered in shimmering lights and soft like the jellyfish that washed ashore on Ocean Beach. He pressed it to her neck. She flinched, but it was cold and slippery and soothing, and instantly she relaxed into its embrace.

'If I tell you, Polly, you won't remember. You never do.'

The jellyfish pulsed against the skin below her ear: an odd sensation, biological and sensual, yet very relaxing, too.

'Tell me nonetheless, sir,' she said. 'I'll try my darndest to remember, so's I don't have to ask again in ten years.' She cast him a wide, white, toothy smile.

'You don't believe me, Polly?'

'If you can make me feel whole again, and give me a good meal, and maybe a new pair of boots, then I'll believe whatever ya want, sir.'

He tented his hands, thought for a moment, then said, 'Your genetic code holds all the material needed to recreate your kind.'

'Jen neh tik?'

'It's a blessing you don't remember, I suppose,' he said, bowing his head once more to his work, 'Eighteen sixty-nine? The last year of Earth? No, you don't recall.' He clucked sadly in his throat. 'Your star's internal combustion misfired — a terrible miscalculation, on our part. We'd devised it to last much longer, but by the time our sensors detected the malfunction, your sun had already collapsed into a dwarf, and was beginning its expansion into a giant.'

'You talk in riddles and fairy tales, sir,' she said. 'I ain't never seen no giants, and the only dwarf I ever seen was just a really short man at a carny in Arkansas.'

He grinned at her. It reminded her of the smile of a man who'd bought her body, but found her witty banter after coitus to be as amusing as their congress. The smile was kindly and surprised, all at once. 'I do love to listen to you, Polly. You say the most charming things.'

'That's me,' she laughed, 'A right charmer.'

He gathered up the cloth again, pressed it to her brow, and gave a low chuckle. 'When we arrived, most of the world was baked and barren, and only a few life forms clung to the edges of the mud holes. Cockroaches, mostly. You'd taken shelter in the sewer, clever girl. We plucked your body from the wreckage of the city just before your star expanded and swallowed up the planet, leaving a dead husk.'

'I don't remember no such thing, sir,' she said, stifling a yawn. The pulse of the jellyfish had started to slow. 'If it were true, wouldn't I remember something so frightful?'

He intently studied the flashes of colour along its surface, only flicked his yellow eyes briefly to her to judge her reaction. 'Would you wish to remember it? I can arrange it. But be warned, it would fill you with terror and perhaps drive you a little mad, as you were when we found you.'

'I think I'm already mad with the fever, and you ain't really here,' she replied. 'I think I'm still in my room, with Mrs. McKenzie, and I'm either gonna get better, or I'm gonna die.'

'Die? No no no! I would not let that happen, Polly,' he said. 'You are much too precious.'

'Aw, now you're just being sweet,' she giggled.

He ran his hand over her black hair, a touch that seemed distant but caring. 'We built this replica from your memories and our data. I'm afraid it goes only as far as the Marin headlands in the north, and Monterey to the south, but you've shown no desire to travel very far.'

'Ain't possible to see the world on a whore's wage,' she said as she leaned her head against the back of the couch.

'I know,' he crooned with pity. 'But when we find a suitable planet, we will derive the base codes from your m-DNA. We will rebuild your world for you, from you, and your kind will start again. And I will make sure your life is full of comforts, Polly, and you are suitably rewarded for your help.'

Her eyelids felt heavy. The rhythm of the jellyfish at her throat had grown hypnotic, all-encompassing. 'Don't take no offence, mister,' she said, 'But I still think you're a bit of a lunatic.'

'No, Polly, not a lunatic,' he replied sadly, 'Only a scientist, with a failed experiment, hoping to start again.'

She smiled a dreamy smile. '...looooo-natic...' she muttered again.

'Little humans, with your clever hands and complicated

brains. We quite like your kind, Polly. We were disappointed to see you destroyed.'

'I'm not destroyed...'

'No, you aren't, mother of your future.' He ran his hand over her forehead. 'Precious last child of a failed world.'

'...tired...'

'Of course. Sleep,' he invited, 'And when you wake, Polly, your life and city will be fully restored.'

He waited until she was snoring, then lifted her lightly and carried her to her filthy tenement, and set her back upon the reeking tangle of her bed. Preliminary examination showed her health was good, her developmental stasis holding steady, her memories in a three-year loop, her cellular integrity stable. And most important of all, the code remained intact.

A hum in the cortex of his brain stem told him it was time to leave, return to the core of the ship, input the data he'd collected. This vessel of flesh, a mere disguise for Polly's benefit, would not last much longer. The hum intensified. It flared into colours and urged him to hurry.

The ship drew closer to Sol. Here, at the edge of the universe, the Architects had sourced a possible planet, the third from the star. *Return,* they told him, *We have much work to do.*

He took one last long glance at Polly, knowing that their next ten-year visit would never come. Once the Architects established the age of the star, manufactured an atmosphere, and repurposed the landmass, they'd have all they required. With his meticulous records and Polly's beautiful unbroken line of m-DNA, the Architects could start the experiment again, right where it had been interrupted, three eons ago.

'Sleep, Polly,' he said, and he pressed a kiss to her cheek.

She stirred at his touch, and as his breath tickled her ear, her lips curved into a wistful smile.

'When you wake, I'll make you Queen of San Francisco,' he promised. 'And give you a King who will love you as much as I do.'

Vanquish

N.A.O Rawle

Albroque, the technician, read the card as he moved the specimen towards the lab. He'd been warned to take great care with this one.

HUMAN EXHIBITS (ESTIMATED AGE: 700 MILLION EARTH YEARS)

3,001: FULLY PRESERVED HUMAN FEMALE (NATURALLY FROZEN)

3,002: WRITTEN TEXT IN ENGLISH

Slotting the polymer tube into the decompression chamber, he hit 'Defrost' and sat back and idly picked up the accompanying text. His knowledge of English was scant but with a little effort he managed to make some sense of it.

Sometimes I think I can still hear screaming, a heart-wrenching wail at the loss, caught by the chill wind and thrown in my face, to taunt my existence. But this cannot be. If there were still the sounds of human activity it would be an agonised inhalation, a grunt or sigh in the struggle to live. I know this because I cough and gasp for every breath, my lungs straining to find the oxygen air so thick it feels like needles even though the air is purer at this altitude.

Am I the only one now? If anyone was alive they would have traced the signal from my tablet before the light failed. They would have come looking for me.

When I had my tablet (I had limited power as the light was weak) I surfed the Net. In the first hours I fed my curiosity by watching the myriad of harbingers of The End; Divine Retribution pitting itself against Alien Invasion and all the shades of paranoia in between. There were the scientists publishing reams of data to prove it impossible, just a tragic coincidence on a global scale.

'No need for panic.' They assured even as it was all going up in smoke.

I watched them burn; them and everyone who subscribed to civilisation. The agony wrought on their features as they attempted to stem blazes with paltry garden hoses, protecting a lifetime of dreams and ambition all tied up in bricks and mortar. Swarms of helicopters were deployed to ferry in seawater to dowse outbreaks in remote areas, precious forests becoming blackened charcoal remnants. People huddling in urban centres – safety in numbers – or so they believed until they were knocked down by the inevitable disease and infection. Riots and skirmishes broke out, the mob reigned and vandals took up the call not knowing they were sowing the sparks of self-destruction. All that power rendered ineffectual by the very thing that created civilisation!

The pleas for help petered out as power centres failed and batteries died. People were consumed. When no new posts appeared I began to scour the pictures I'd saved; pages and pages of faces and places - things that were no more. I lost myself in a savage delirium knowing that it must almost be over.

That was a week ago.

It's hard up here alone; what is genuine and what is imaginary blur into one another until I cannot be sure which is which. Is it the wind that howls around the house or the dead haunting me? And this house, which lies virtually untouched amid havoc like a ship cresting waves in a gale-force wind, is surreal. I am famished; it has been two full days since I have eaten and what I see drifts in and out of focus; I'd believe everything a delusion if I didn't know better but my hunger is real. On the bed I sleep in, which is alternately a loving embrace or a coffin depending on my mood, the blankets already feel too thin. How I will cope when the snows come? Human instinct tells me to build a fire but it would be no lie to say that I am afraid to do so, even though It promised me. Even if I weren't afraid, with what would I build a fire? The wood is all but gone.

I wonder what is left down there. I can see nothing yet. Things cannot ever be as they were, of that I am certain. That's nature; ever developing ever evolving, and adapting. Survival of the most resilient - that's the true nature of nature.

I have been foolish, I can see that now. I have no real provisions to see me through. So today I ransacked what was left of the other residences here and pilfered a collection of charred tins from amongst the debris. With only myself to feed I have rations for months from now, (if I live that long). There is spring water here although I don't know if it will remain uncontaminated once the rains come. The majority of food is not vegetarian. I spent hours fumbling with a packet of turkey stock cubes wondering at the perverse ingenuity of mankind.

I have been vegetarian since I was six when I realised that the meat under the gravy was Tallulah, the greediest turkey on the free-hold.

'Eat up Arabella!'

'No, thank you.' My voice was a small defiance against my father's rough cadence.

'No Christmas Pudding if you don't!'

'I'm not hungry!'

'You won't open your presents 'til tomorrow.' My mother added, embarrassed by my disobedience in front of the whole family.

'I only want Tallulah back.' To that there was no reply but my father and mother exchanged uncomprehendingly exasperated looks that let me know I would never be able to communicate to them the heartbreak and betrayal I was suffering. I never ate meat again.

The stock cubes will be the last to go.

Last night I dreamed of a meadow vibrant under an azure sky with butterflies dancing through the tussocks of camomile. In the evergreen forests, seductively verdant and tingling with secret pleasure, a bear emerged from her cave having sensed spring in the air. Standing on hind paws she sniffed the air and relaxed, turning her attention to foraging for a breakfast titbit. She nuzzled the roots seeking out the creatures that dwell there.

I ventured up to the peak as soon as I awoke hoping that the dream was prophetic, that I would catch a glimpse of life; a bird or an insect as I walked through what was once lush woodland. But the mountain was still dressed in mourning, a ragged veil of mist shrouding her blackened head. Where there was brush, all is stripped bare. Where there was pine scented darkness harbouring a myriad of creatures, there is only a swathe of blackened trunks marching down her flanks into the ash cloud swirling like a fathomless ocean at her foot and beneath which there can be only darkness. Impossible as it seems, I know life lurks within. Under the skins of trees, it hides. Beneath rocks and deep within caves it cowers, even in the shadows of the ocean depths.

I do not dare to doubt.

The air is bitter cold. I think the snows must be coming – I am beginning to see the folly of my dream – winter will be long this year. I have finished gathering, it's taken three days of hoarding like a bag lady skipping, Daniel taught me how to do that but I try not to think too much about it.

After food, I decided to collect water in case of contamination. I have filled pots and pans in cups and plates stored on shelves. The sink and even in an old bath I dragged into the house, are filled to brimming. Will it be enough? It will freeze over before and I shall have to chip ice splinters to suck.

For insulation, I have made a nest of smoke-scented mattresses, char-edged blankets, clothing and soft furnishings from the metal chests that survived. I hope I have enough insulation. Working systematically from house to house in the settlement, I've gathered everything warm around my cottage, inside and out. It's a far cry from the ecologically sound bender that Daniel and I shared so many years ago but I hope it will withstand sub-zero temperatures. Stepping back to view my handy-work, I shivered involuntarily as goose bumps crawled across my skin; the house was a little too reminiscent of a bonfire.

So that's what forced me to the church to rip sheets of corrugated iron from the other roofs to be laid on top of my make-shift insulation. It would serve as water-proofing and make the construction appear more robust, less flammable.

The church, which squats on a precipice overlooking the valley, now a swirling sea of cloud, is the only other building hardly touched outwardly by the flames. Its interior is a blackened carcass - too many prayer candles. But the outer walls are stark white – it was the church that attracted me here, bright like a beacon on the mountain top.

Sitting astride the roof prising the nails out of the corrugated iron, my mind was drawn back to Daniel again.

I was walking the route of the proposed by-pass at Twyford Down and he was camped out in a copse as the last line of defence against the bulldozers. I watched in awe at his agility and confidence as he traversed the rope walk ways between the trees. A modern day Robin Hood: preventing destruction, saving the trees.

He understood my anguish!

'How can they not see this travesty?'

'Ignorance.'

'How can they not be moved knowing that everything affects the balance of nature; the food we eat, the clothes we wear, the transport we use?'

'If we just take a stand, if there are enough of us, people will see.'

I was consumed by his passion and belief that we only had to open people's eyes for the world to change. I left school to journey far and wide with him and other travellers, begging those with little insight to see the error of their ways. We fought the battle together.

'I love you.' He confessed one night whilst running my long red hair through his fingers and showering me with kisses. 'Give me a child!'

I laughed and pushed him away.

'Don't be foolish.'

But that night we conceived.

My blossoming form didn't dissuade me from the cause, rather I became all the more determined. Daniel and I petitioned and chained ourselves to trees; for him the pregnancy only seemed to highlight the importance of what we were doing.

'The future is our child's present.' He would insist. 'A clean planet is our gift to him or her.'

We staged protests and camped out along the routes of roads or chained ourselves to the offices of those we felt responsible. They'd claim to be concerned but I saw through their hypocrisy. Any progress we made was temporary; the bulldozers still came through in the end and although our efforts were magnificent, our words essentially fell on deaf ears.

'How can I bring a child into such a world?' I would wail at him.

Daniel, misunderstanding my meaning, soothed me and cared for me as he had always worshipped me but I saw the folly in what we had done. I wanted no part of it.

Our child was born in the spring; a beautiful peach-skinned girl who cooed and gurgled and tugged at my hair and smiled as she drank from my breast. To his mind, our relationship was completed with her; she was the result of our love. In her, Daniel saw the future. He would whirl her around with him, showing her the beauty of nature. The songs he sang her told of a fair land where there was no pollution and no destruction but only peace and harmony between man and nature.

He was a fool.

I watched them together knowing this parasitic creature had grown in my belly. I was the bringer of yet another predator to the earth. Another mouth to be fed in a world stretched to its limits.

'She's just an innocent baby!'

'How can you say that? Every time she craps it's just more pollution. I can't clean her without thinking of all the poisons released into the environment.'

'Arabella, that's the nature of babies.' Daniel tried to pull me into his arms but I pushed him away.

'It's wrong! Can't you see?'

'You need help.'

'I am helping.'

'By not feeding your own child?'

'I don't have any milk.'

'You're starving yourself that's why.'

'It's for the best.'

'How can you despise your own flesh and blood? She is the part of the enlightened generation. Her peers will co-habit the earth in true equality.'

I just shook my head in regret. With every cry she made Daniel became deafer to the wail of the earth. He would never understand. I left him to his folly.

Up on the roof-top anger swelled in me and I started hacking at a particularly stubborn nail. The adze slipped and gashed my palm with its rusty, jagged edge. Blood spurted into the sooty blackness of my skin. I stared at my hand in wonder.

So long have I lived in this monochrome landscape that I lay mesmerised by the sheer brightness of its crimson sheen, a brilliant slick spread across my palm, a single droplet falling into the abyss below. So much had been sacrificed. Perhaps it was hours or mere moments, the blood welling, and coagulating all the while, before the severity of my predicament registered.

The wound is not deep and I have cleaned it with some crusty iodine I found in a first aid kit. I realised then how the survival basics were something I never thought to consider either.

When I woke up this morning, I went out to relieve myself as I have done every morning and was faced by a moonscape. At first I couldn't assimilate what was in front of me, I reached out my hands as if blind but then as I stepped forward I sank up to mid-calf in snow. The snow is grey, tainted by the residues of humanity. I am living in lunar limbo. The, sun is as ever a pale disk in a murky sky. I struggled to get the solar panel working to power my tablet for a while but to no avail. It will soon be time for me to retreat.

Overnight the wound on my hand has swollen, the skin is taught, shiny and so smooth that I want to caress it but I cannot bear the touch of anything the pain is so acute. I guess the iodine hasn't been that effective. Even so, I've applied more. The edges of the cut are darkening. There is no smell of gangrene or infection but would it be obvious in the ever present aroma of smoke?

I learned a lot about first aid and pharmaceuticals after I left Daniel. Though he hadn't seen the urgency I felt imminent, I was able to use the associations I had made through him to find activists who understood that the message had to be clearer. Their efforts were less appealing but more direct. Working in small bands, we freed enslaved animals and sabotaged damaging works. I spent some months researching and planning the attacks but the media marginalisation of our cause made me see that this was no more than an irritation to the conglomerates that we were fighting.

As I watch darkness creeping down the mountain with all the subtlety of a phantom in a German Expressionist movie, I wonder if I was assertive enough back then. Could they really not see this coming sooner or later? Did it have to end this way?

I am trapped. When I opened the door I was faced with a wall of sooty snow packed so thick that even if I were not invalid I do not think I could dig myself out. My hand is the size of a grapefruit, the wound seems to be clean but skin has formed pustules along the blackened edges. I am effectively crippled. I've been lying in the dark drifting in and out of sleep with nothing to mark the passing of time. I was woken by a voice. In my daze I heard my father speaking, his harsh bass tone. I remember his words over the Tallulah incident; if parents only knew the weight of words in a six-year-old mind.

'You are human and people are top of the food chain — natural born hunters — meat-eaters, just that now we are more civilised and we hunt in our gardens and farms or the supermarket. As long as you are in my house, you will live as a human.'

All I knew was that human beings were inhumane. Even

then in my six year old mind, I had longed not to be human. Nothing had changed since; evidence for this was spewed forth each day on the television. If I were to succeed, I determined, I would have to play from the inside. I would hunt.

The circles I travelled in from then on were dark and hard. Training to build stamina and resilience in the face of all emotion was essential. I learned to hone the total devotion to my cause so that it obliterated any room for failure. I mastered the skills of terror and fear. I became a weapon for sale to the highest bidder; a whore of destruction just so long as I was removing the scourge from the earth. I still felt that even these traumatic acts were insignificant in the face of the suffering that provoked my zeal. Desperation gripped me. No matter how extreme, no other could match my selfless devotion.

Behind the guise of other standards, I waged my war on humanity. But as I travelled the world, the impracticably monstrous size of my duty became clear. My acts scandalised civilisations, felled governments and destroyed religions but I was no closer to my goal. No act of terrorism was effective enough. The earth suffered on.

Tears are streaming down my face.

I didn't realise I was crying but then a tear hit my swollen palm and hissed. I am not feverish but my hand is burning up.

This is no infection. No, I believe this means only one thing. It means it is leaving me; our cooperation has been terminated.

Mission accomplished.

And so it is time for me to tell you the final part of my story, for posterity, for your records, for no one, for myself. For whom it may concern?

Despondent, I disappeared, wandering as far as my feet would carry me, and taking rides where offered. I travelled the world round, always searching for the cessation of my desires that no man would or could fulfil, to the places where nature had showed her true strength. From New Orleans to Pompeii, from Thailand to Japan, I travelled, worshipping in these temples of destruction, begging for a solution.

It found me in Cambodia where I had been dragged by back-packing teens, all the while despising them for their ignorant confidence that they possessed some semblance of control just because they could capture it in a photographic pose.

We had arrived at Angkor Wat where the temple rises defiantly out of the jungle; man once again showing his dominance. Most tourists come to marvel at such human ingenuity, I only came to see one particular place.

At Ta Prohm, the temple dedicated to the king's mother, Mother Nature is clawing back what is rightfully hers. The banyan, kapok and fig trees drip through the temples, their tendrils prising apart the masonry with patient determination, proving their creations so much more divine than ours. This is where a king's dedication to kindness, compassion, equanimity and sympathy are slowly being strangled because Nature knows the hypocrisy of these words.

When it found me, I had crawled into a velvety niche far from where there were tourists gawping all around; I felt disgusted by their photo-taking, oo-ing and ah-ing over ancient ruins whose significance was lost on them. In a moss strewn sanctuary I bowed low, baring my heart to the giant roots and the tree that towered above me. I begged for a solution, for salvation and absolution.

That was when it came for me. A furious wind gusted through the temple like the hot breath of an infuriated dragon and I was bowled along, cowering, my eyes squeezed closed against the dust and debris.

I opened them to darkness for fire is dark. The temple had become an impenetrable inferno from which I could fathom no escape. I was unable to move although I could feel no physical constraints around me but my body would not respond to the command to run. Then it set upon me. Like a thousand tiny blow torches it blasted me, inspecting its catch. I could feel its searing caresses and the seductively gentle roar of its fury thrumming the air. Twisting under its assault, crying out in agony was, I sensed, of no use. I withstood, tears streaming down my face and blood oozing from my tongue I bit back the pain so hard. Instinctively, I knew I was being tested.

As if having reached a decision, it let me be and coordinated in the darkness before me, drawing itself up into an approximation of a human being which looked very much like me as if it was reflecting what it had sensed. Then in a voice not so unlike my own, although still faltering and unsteady like a child who hasn't quite learned to read, it spoke.

'I have been waiting for you.' My fiery tormentor smiled at me, expressions of curiosity, pleasure and hatred rippled in the flaming cheeks of the creature before me.

'Why?' How I found the strength to make any utterance I cannot say.

The incarnation reached out a blazing hand and drew me closer, pressing its fingers around my jaw the sensation was unnerving; all the visuals told me I would be burned but the feeling was now one of dry warmth, comforting and reassuring. I was terrified.

'Are you spirit? Devil? God?'

'None of those.'

'What then?'

'I am the solution to your problem. I can give you the power you need to complete your task but I have to see if you are fit.'

'I am.'

It nodded its understanding.

'My power is deadly beyond your wildest dreams and I cannot entrust my secrets to one unworthy. I need proof that you will complete your mission to the last man... or woman.' It falteringly added, its broiling eyes scorching mine, 'Has fallen.'

Before I could refuse or accept the fiery creature extended its other approximation of a hand to me, I took it firmly and as I did so I was consumed. I felt its heat seeping into me as the flame spun itself into a molten tide that crept up my arm. I watched it take hold of my clothes and consume them. A deceptively tiny dancing flame that worked its way through the fibres of my blouse adding to it a joyous turquoise tinge, burning more fiercely, multiplying as it seared my flesh, along the shoulder, down across my back and taking my breasts at the front. It leapt into my face licking my lips with its fiery kisses. Like an army of pinpricks the flames searched my body for access, under my cuticles it crept and through my eyes, funnelling into my ears and down my throat. It was as if a volcano had erupted in my epidermis and rivers of lava raced through my veins, knotted my sinews. I dropped to my knees unable to withstand the torturous agony. My heart hammered in my chest as the scalding heat consumed me. As I breathed so my lungs exploded in anguish and I felt that I had met the end but then something terrible and delightful happened. It was as if the flames were being pumped by my heart combined with those surging through my blood and I experienced its view.

'I will do you no harm for you are now the orchestrator of my vengeance. I am no grade school chemical reaction but an ancient wisdom to be respected. The term of your stewardship had reached its end. I travelled a million light years and dispersed in your atmosphere and then concealed myself in your fiery core, allowed myself to be consumed into human culture over the millennia so that I might assume to be empowered, giving you the opportunity of life, but you have abused that power.'

'I know this.'

Its ancient wisdom weighed heavily on my consciousness demanding total hegemony, its power absolute.

'I see that. You will now end what I began. I have been so scattered that I cannot begin to assimilate myself without a catalyst.'

I have never taken orders easily and although we shared a congruent goal, I faltered, it sensed this.

'Do you dare to doubt me?'

'If I agree to this, I need to be able to see that it will work.'

'Our goals are the same.'

Only then did I really begin to believe in the fragility of human existence. It hadn't been waiting a mere lifetime, it had been waiting millennia; it would not let me fail. What to me was insurmountably impossible, to it was a matter of patience.

I smiled and the beast that had already gathered itself in me converged in my brain and I was bombarded by sudden visions of what was necessary to succeed. The beast's ferocity flooded my mind triggering synapses, unbalancing chemicals, leading me to an abyss of enflamed madness, total blazing transition. It was divine and beautiful in the simplicity.

It had granted me the gift of volcanic combustion with its blessing and it would dwell in me for as long as necessary to thread its stony beads throughout the cities of the earth. Of course the set-up would take yet more years of planning, years of planting but it could be done.

So I returned to the beginning. Rehabilitated, I was told, after immolation, for that's what they took my consummation by fire in that holy place to be. The world was just as vast and spectacular as I remembered but I sensed a deeper melancholy than I had before and it spread a fear that I would be incapable of wielding the power invested in me. I had to see if it was real.

I stepped out that first afternoon, like a new born creature stumbling about on its spindly legs. Over the rubble-strewn wastes on the edges of a city that so many called home, I tottered. My body tingled with excitement; the skin sparkled and rippled with the amber glow of the fire in my veins. On a simple breeze block I chose to test my abilities. Rubbing my palms together as to create a ball of dough, I exuded a tiny molten seed. I placed it carefully in one section of the block and watched it petrify immediately. Upon it I put a plant whose roots were drawn to the warmth of the stone I'd created and entwined themselves about it with an unnatural velocity. Repeating this process in the second hollow section, I retreated the way I had come.

From my vantage point high up in one of the pinnacles of human ingenuity, I observed the breeze block, inconspicuous in the wasteland that so often borders the poorer areas of a town.

'Now!' The command was no more than a passing thought

but it carried across the void between me and the block in which all my hopes and fears were invested.

Nothing appeared to happen at first but I could feel a deep tingling in the atmosphere and in my mind's eye I saw the reaction completing like an electric circuit so sparks connected to become flames and the flames grew into a fountain of white heat that erupted from the earth. Light flared across the debris, reaching up and out even as far as the balcony on which I was standing, the fire cloud singeing the newly grown hair from my head, leaving me hairless once more. The building trembled at first and then I felt it sucked out from beneath me in a deadly landslide of dust and debris, shattered glass and twisted steel. Homes were consumed in the fireball, the paltry accomplishments of a lifetime of toil wiped out forever. The deafening roar of destruction rang like a symphony in my ears until I was dug out from the rubble long after. Reporters mistook my manic grin for one of relief at being rescued, the sole survivor. A leaky gas main was held to blame although no one could recall smelling gas beforehand. Others purported that the resulting molten crater was more consistent with the impact site of a meteor, although no one had seen one enter the atmosphere. I smiled on.

'You hold life in the balance and there is no time to lose. Your task is phenomenal but possible. You have seen that it is real so no longer hesitate.' The voice was in my head now I had been consumed by its power.

I began in earnest, planting trees and seeds again in cities the world over; like a pilgrim of ancient times I travelled in rags, my only thought salvation. Unlike before, my intention no longer the spark of life but that of death, each tree invested with ancient fury. I never doubted again, I never vacillated; I never tired until my job was done.

When the time came and I gave the command, it swept across the landscape at a thundering pace, devouring everything in its path. Its ragged tongues, molten and ravenous, indiscriminately consumed fowl and family, habitat and inheritance. There was nothing living or inanimate that would not succumb to its fury. The beast's flaming wrath leaped up and toppled those who would extinguish it. Brave men and women not understanding the nature of the creature before them laid down their lives for the sake of others. I stayed as long as I dared, knowing full well there could be no escape even for myself. I stayed close, needing to feel its heat, that full scorching blast. Hear the crackling of the beast whispering its praises. Fronts had sprung up everywhere; simultaneous, spontaneous combustion in forests and parklands, city centres and suburbs world-wide. The army was called, terrorist organisations accused, world-leaders made speeches of desperation to no avail.

If I have survived by luck or Its grace I do not know. It's been about a week and four days since I trudged up the mountain, still wearing my breathing apparatus and protective clothing, wading through ashes and charcoal. When there is light enough again I will monitor for silence once more, as assurance. I believe I was not supposed to survive despite my request that I might be allowed to see the rebirth. I will stay until I see the first vibrant bud of emerald green. It will be reward enough; to know that I have succeeded. What will become of me after that? I will complete my work with one last act; I will ignite this poor disguise for a pyre I have built about me then nature will take up her rightful place.

This is no snivelling confession as one confesses only what one senses to be wrong. I am in no doubt.

My name is Vanquish and I released the beast.

Setting down the text, Albroque turned to the senior officer.

'Why bother with it after so many millennia?' He'd asked.

'A promise is a promise, Albroque, even if it takes an eternity to fulfil.'

They had been orbiting the blue planet for several of its days now whilst probes confirmed what the sensors reported. Plant life had re-established itself.

The Eternal Quest Of The Girl With The Corkscrew Hair

David Turnbull

'Metal Guru?' asked the girl with the corkscrew hair, peering into the darkness of the aluminium cavern. 'Is that you in there?'

From the shadows there came a low rumble followed by a prolonged and exaggerated hiss. The girl found herself caressed by a hush of warm steam. Having learnt some time ago to seize any small opportunity at taking on moisture she licked away the beads of condensation that settled on her chin.

'You have a question?' growled a voice that groaned like cogs and flywheels grinding together.

'I have,' said the girl, valiantly transgressing a little more into the gloomy depths.

'Then ask,' said the Guru. 'Ask and be gone. Leave me to slumber some more.'

The girl cleared her throat.

'Is there a boy?'

'What kind of question is that?' complained the voice. 'How should I be expected to know a thing like that?'

'I made a mistake then,' said the girl, shouldering her trusty satchel and turning to leave. 'I was told that the Metal Guru knows everything. If you can't answer my question I will have to search elsewhere.'

'I know what I was originally programmed to know and that which I have accumulated of my own volition,' said the voice. 'But that is a great deal.'

'But you can't tell me if there is a boy,' said the girl over her shoulder.

'Perhaps I may be able to access something from my memory banks,' suggested the voice.

The girl swung on her heels and called into the darkness. "I've been told that other than myself there is only one other human being left in the entire world."

The Guru whirred and clanged and then fell silent.

After a while it said – 'Most of your kind died long ago. There were scattered tribes for a few hundred years afterwards. One such tribe adopted me for a period of time. A bothersome and tedious affair while it lasted. In the end disease wiped them out. Statistically the probability of your being the last human is quite high.'

'I was told that there might be a boy,' repeated the girl. 'A blue eyed boy.'

'Who told you such a thing?' asked the Guru.

'Some *patchwork* folk that I travelled with for a while,' replied the girl. 'For someone who is supposed to know *all* the answers you sure do ask a lot of questions.'

'I wouldn't trust a word that *patchwork* folk say,' said the Guru. 'They are nothing but mechanical innards and synthetic leather. They were designed to be functional and therefore have a low intelligence threshold. They have a child-like propensity to spread all sorts of unfounded rumours.'

'The *patchworks* that I knew were nomads,' said the girl. 'They'd heard tell of a human boy on their travels. They said I should find him. They said my it was my destiny to find him and produce offspring.'

'Did they now?' said the Guru, and let out a raw rattle that sounded suspiciously close to mocking laughter. 'And I suppose you expect me to be able to tell you where you might find this boy?'

The girl twisted a finger into the tight curls of her hair.

'I'm thinking now that I might have had a wasted journey. I might have been better just looking for the boy straight off than looking for you.'

'Can you not think of anything better to do with whatever fleeting life you may have left than procreating with some mythical boy?' asked the Guru.

'The *patchworks* told me that it was my moral duty to go

forth and multiply,' replied the girl. 'I gave it a lot of thought and I came to the conclusion that they were probably right. It's what cockroaches do - and there's millions of them.'

'What is your name?' asked the Guru.

'I am called Rebeka,' replied the girl.

'Well, Rebeka,' said the Guru. 'Reach your hand a way in here. I have decided to give you something to help you on your quest.'

'A gift?' asked Rebeka.

'Of sorts,' came the reply.

Unravelling her finger from her hair she stretched out her arm and held her hand into the darkness. Instantly something snapped onto her wrist and fixed itself around it like a tight bracelet. Squealing in fright she tried to recoil. But she was held fast.

'Don't struggle so,' said the voice of the Guru. 'This is for you own benefit.'

Suddenly her arm was released.

She staggered back, almost losing her footing and falling to the ground. Clinging to her wrist was a bracelet of sorts. Its appearance was something akin to a large metallic spider, spindly legs holding fast and tight to her flesh, a blue light and a red light flickering intermittently on its bulbous torso.

She tried to shake it off – but it wouldn't budge.

'What is it?' she cried. 'Is this some sort of trick?'

'It is a small part of me,' said the Guru. 'A self-initiated adaptation. You could say that it is an emissary of sorts.'

The voice came from the object on her wrist *and* from the recess of the chamber at one and the same time. 'I have spent too long hiding in the darkness,' it continued. 'I've worked up a powerful appetite for new knowledge. Your quest for this mythical blue eyed boy will no doubt prove to be futile, but if I accompany you I will be able to gather new facts and information to replenish my outdated databank.'

'I never invited you to come along,' yelled Rebeka, making a concerted effort to shake her arm free from the spidery contraption.

'But you did come here to ask for my help,' insisted the Guru, clinging steadfastly.

'You must remember your parents,' insisted the piece of the Guru.

'I've already told you everything that I can recall up until the point I stumbled on the band of *patchworks* is kind of hazy,' said Rebeka for the fifth time. 'Can't you just scuttle off somewhere? I've been fine on my own up till now. I don't need you firing questions at me all the time.'

They were passing through the belly of a deep canyon, towering walls of rusted steel on either side of them, a lethargic river of black oil oozing along to the left of where Rebeka walked.

'You do understand that you must have had a mother and father?' asked the Guru.

Rebeka nodded, a little uncertain.

The blue light on the spider blinked.

'Rebeka,' it said, 'The *patchworks* did explain the mechanics of procreation to you, didn't they?'

Rebeka twisted her finger into her corkscrew curls.

'They didn't exactly go into a lot of detail,' she admitted.

The Guru offered a somewhat graphic explanation, the facts of life – the anatomy, the squelch and the squirm and the pain of labour.

'Really?' said Rebeka when he had finished.

'Really,' said the Guru.

She twisted her finger deeper into her curls and pondered.

'I'm still going to find him,' she said decisively.

'But you understand now why you *yourself* must have had a mother and father?' asked the Guru.

A bubble swelled on the surface of the river of oil and burst with a pop that echoed against the red walls of the canyon.

'I suppose,' said Rebeka.

'If there was a man and a woman,' said the Guru. 'Then perhaps there is still a tribe of humans. That would be a far more exciting prospect than a single mythical boy.'

'A tribe? Like the *patchworks?* As many as that?'

'How many were there?' asked the Guru

'Twenty-five or so,' said Rebeka.

'If a human tribe still survives it is entirely possible that they number many more than that,' said the Guru.

Rebeka pondered some more, twisting and untwisting her finger into her corkscrew hair. After a long time she looked down at the arachnid bracelet encompassing her wrist. 'If there was a tribe why did they tell me to go?' she asked.

'You remembered something?' the Guru asked back.

'A voice,' said Rebeka.

'What did this voice say?'

'It said – "*it is time for you to go out into the world.*"'

'Who do you think the voice belonged to?'

'I can't remember,' said Rebeka. 'Maybe my father?'

The canyon tapered out and the river of oil spiralled in sluggish lassitude down through the yawning chasm of a ragged hole. Rebeka found herself on a steep incline studded with crowded clusters of tall iron spikes. Here and there the surface had corroded and she had to negotiate her ascent, taking great care that she did not tumble into one of the oxidized gullies.

'Did you have a mother and father?' she asked the Guru.

The red and blue lights flickered on the Guru's spidery form.

'I did not,' replied the Guru. 'I was designed and constructed by humans - centuries ago. My original purpose was purely recreational. I was an attraction in an amusement park. People paid to sit in my *automated* chair. They would pose a question and I would provide an instantaneous answer. I was part of a series. All with fanciful names – the *Lizard King*, the *Ivory Madonna* and such like. But we didn't know everything, Rebeka. Not even close.'

Finding it impossible to comprehend most of what she had just been told Rebeka changed the subject. 'Were there many humans centuries ago?' she asked.

'Billions,' replied the Guru.

'Is billions a lot?' she asked.

'It is.'

'Were there as many humans as there are cockroaches?' she asked.

'I would say there were more humans then than there are cockroaches now.'

Thinking of cockroaches made Rebeka's stomach rumble.

She reached into her satchel and located a dead roach. Its girth was about the size of her fist. She bit the legs off one by one, then she chewed off the head, finally she peeled away the shell and sucked out the juicy innards.

'How come humans mostly died out?' she asked, wiping her mouth with her sleeve.

'They were arrogant and careless. Their negligence allowed machines to supersede them as the dominant intelligence. Unfortunately we were no better. Our reign was short and brutal. We squandered the mantle we had seized by trying to satisfy our insatiable appetite for fossils fuels and minerals. We burrowed through the Earth like hordes of termites, till all that was left was a junk yard on a hollow husk that spins in space.'

Again Rebeka found herself confounded by the Guru's words and concepts. She reached into her satchel and set about devouring another succulent roach. When she was finished she burped loudly. The burp reverberated through the copse of iron spikes.

'Do *patchworks* have mothers and fathers?' she asked.

'*Patchworks* were created by machines in the image of humans,' explained the Guru. 'Their original purpose was to act as maintenance drones.'

'So that's why they travel around fixing stuff,' said Rebeka. 'I used to think that I was a *patchwork* - on account of my brown skin. But the *patchworks* listened to the valve that pumps in my chest and guessed what I really was.'

'Indeed,' said the Guru.

Rebeka reached the summit of the incline.

Ahead of them, stretching far towards the distant horizon, lay a dense and seemingly limitless forest of giant wind turbines, propeller blades turning in poetically endless revolutions. Down on the undulating tundra of crumbling and fissured concrete on which these turbines sat, thousands of little four wheeled objects zoomed and wove about their bases, their white liveries baked creamy brown by the sun.

Rebeka noticed that whenever one crossed the trajectory of another both would emit a noisy barrage of irritable honks and beeps, before swerving away at obtuse and petulant angles. She saw several collisions; the little rolling carts somersaulting into a wild tumble and then righting themselves before resuming their dizzying circuits once more. Here and there she saw some that had become caught up in tangles of weeds that had pushed their way up through the concrete, wheels valiantly spinning but going nowhere.

'They no longer comprehend the purpose for which they were designed,' said the Guru. 'This is like the rise of barbarism after the fall of Rome.'

'I have no idea what you're talking about,' said Rebeka, descending into the turbine forest.

Weeks went by and there was no sign of the blue-eyed boy.

They found themselves on a plain of dappled copper, crisscrossed with raised ridges of silvery solder. The copper echoed under Rebeka's footfall and sent up a shimmering haze when the sun reached its midday zenith. Beneath the surface something continually roared and crashed.

When Rebeka knelt down and pressed her ear to the surface it sounded like the thunder that rumbled sometimes in the sky. She licked up some of the dewdrops of condensation that had accumulated in a bevelled dent on the copper and then looked at her wrist.

'What kind of creature lives down there?' she asked the Guru, whose weight and tightness she no longer consciously noticed.

'An ocean,' replied the Guru.

'An ocean?' marvelled Rebeka, tasting the shape of this new word in her mouth.

The Guru explained what an ocean was.

'Really?' said Rebeka.

'Really,' replied the Guru. 'No doubt the energy of the waves is still being used to power exploratory boreholes. The ingenuity of machines knows no bounds when it come to the search for raw materials.'

They walked on and Rebeka's thoughts turned again the boy – what she would say when they met – how he might react when she put forward her proposition – what it would be like to actually carry out the act that the Guru had so vividly described.

The very notion of such intimacy both terrified and excited her.

She wondered what it would be like to have a baby human growing and kicking inside her. Most of all she wondered about the boy's blue eyes. She found the idea of blue eyes preposterous and suspected that it was perhaps an embellishment that the *patchworks* had added to the tale to make it more interesting. *Eyes the colour of the sky,* she thought and shook her head with incredulity.

Noticing that her boot heels were no longer clattering against the surface of the copper plain she stopped. When she glanced down she saw that the copper was covered in a blanket of spongy moss that puffed back into shape with an elasticity that easily rejected the imprint of her foot. Ahead of her was an emerald green savannah, rolling on mile after mile into the far distance. Grazing on it were teeming herds of cockroaches, their shells a far lighter hue than those she had been previously used to and speckled with contrasting gradients of brown.

She ran amongst these odd looking roaches, bringing her heel down time after time as they scattered before her. When she thought that she had done enough she retraced her steps, dropping the squashed cadavers into her satchel as the living roaches swarmed chaotically over her, nipping and pinching at her flesh.

Onward trekked Rebeka.

The miles and miles of moss-covered copper seemed without any hope of an end. Each day was like the next - plodding on, one foot after the next, stopping to ingest water wherever it pooled in a dimple or a dent, replenishing her satchel when its supply of roaches became depleted, grabbing a chance a sleep whenever she came across a moss free patch where the roaches didn't deign to roam.

She lost track of time.

For a while she was stalked by an unsettling pack of a

dozen or so battered and decaying machines that tagged along behind her on buckled wheels and limping, piston driven legs. 'Ignore them,' said the Guru, disparagingly. 'They're harmless in their senility.' Nevertheless Rebeka watched them nervously over her shoulder, until they simply turned away and gambled off in a huffing and hobbling mass.

Day turned into night, turned into day, turned into night.

The Guru claimed that he was endowed with an application called a navigational compass that enabled him correct her whenever she was tempted to wander in the wrong direction and bring herself round full circle. As well as enlightening her about the difference between north and south and east and west, he taught her about the diverse menagerie of animals that had once walked the Earth. Land bound creatures, driven to extinction by the self serving advance of machines - the birds that had sang in the skies, the whales and the dolphins and the miscellany of fish that had lived in the ocean.

Thinking of all the varieties of life that had once been and no longer were made Rebeka more determined than ever to find the blue-eyed boy and do what had to be done to save her *own* species from a similar fate. 'Maybe the boy lives in the ocean below us?' she suggested, when the notion occurred to her.

'That would not be possible.'

The Guru explained why humans were not designed to live beneath the waves and how the ocean was likely to be so toxic now with chemicals and poisons that death would occur within moments of any human plunging into its tainted depths.

Often they bickered.

'Do you have any concept of what a new born baby would be like?'

'I've seen babies. Cockroach babies. Thousands of them, hatched from eggs, like tiny versions of their parents. The baby would be a tiny version of the boy and me. But it would grow.'

'Human babies are nothing like the offspring of cockroaches. It would be helpless and dependent on you for a long time. You would have to suckle it.'

'Suckle it?'

The Guru explained.

Rebeka looked down at her breasts.

Her eyebrows curved into an arc.

'You do realise how futile your quest is?' continued the Guru. 'Even if you find this elusive boy and manage to conceive his child, he or she may well end up, in turn, to be the last human being. Therefore things will be no further forward.'

'What if the boy is part of a human tribe like you said?'

'What if he isn't?'

'Who is to say that I will only have one child? I could have two – a boy and girl. I could have four – two boys and two girls. In fact I think I should set out to have as many babies as possible. Then there will be less chance of any of them being the last human being.'

'In the circumstances I don't suppose that incest between siblings will cause the moral dilemma it may have caused your ancestors. But there is the question of genetic disorders.'

'There you go again talking in words that I don't understand. If you think that my quest is so hopeless why do you stay with me? Just unravel yourself from my wrist and scurry back to that cave where the rest of you hides away.'

'Your quest is of no consequence to me. It is a means to an end. I am gathering data. I am mapping the geography and topography of a phoenix world, destroyed and made new by machines.'

'You could do that without latching yourself on to me.'

'If it were not for me you would be walking around in circles.'

Rebeka found a jagged hole punched into the copper surface.

Its edges were scorched and burned. She knelt down and pushed her head into the gap, hoping to steal a glimpse of the ocean. She could hear its surge and crash miles below - but the blackness was too impenetrable for her to make out anything. A pernicious stench wafted up into her face and its odour was so terrible that she reeled back in shock.

'There was an explosion here,' said the Guru.

Rebeka did not understand the word - but she had no time to ask for an explanation. In the distance something rose ominously into the sky and began to glide towards them at great speed. 'A defensive drone, protecting the sovereign waters of some long forgotten territory,' said the Guru. 'I would suggest that you run.'

'Run?' asked Rebeka.

'For your life,' replied the Guru.

The object was drawing rapidly closer. She could hear a sonorous hum that trembled in the air and vibrated over the copper surface, accompanied by the chug-chug-chug of rotating propellers. Rebeka turned and ran, the Guru clinging tightly to her wrist. When she looked over her shoulder something dropped down from the strange flying object. It hit the copper surface with a deafening clang and then bounced high into the air again.

'Down!' cried the Guru.

Rebeka dived and rolled, sending a brace of roaches scattering an all directions.

She watched the object sail over her head. When it came back down ten feet or so away from her a mighty light flashed white before her eyes. The deafening sound that came with it sent a high-pitched whistle squealing through her ears. As the ensuing smoke engulfed her she clambered to her feet. Falling slithers of copper rained down onto her, gouging little chunks from her scalp and sending ribbons of blood rippling down her face. The flying thing sliced through the billowing smoke and circled menacingly above her.

'Run!' urged the Guru once more.

Shaking away the blood that had trickled into her eyes Rebeka ran again, dodging past the fresh hole that had been gouged into the copper. She looked over her shoulder expecting another bouncing explosive to drop from the drone. Instead her flying tormentor stopped mid-flight and hovered there as if it was coldly observing her retreat.

'I believe we are back outside the exclusion zone,' said the Guru.

Rebeka slowed her pace.

'Why isn't it following us?' she asked, wiping her face with her sleeve and tentatively reaching up to touch the wounds that peppered the skin beneath her corkscrew hair.

'It no longer perceives us as a threat,' replied the Guru.

The drone hovered a moment more before rising and flying away in the direction from which it came. 'Why did it try to kill me?' asked Rebeka.

The Guru explained about war and humankind's limitless capacity for creating weapons of destruction. 'It is still carrying out the function for which it was designed. Even after all these centuries.'

Rebeka turned on her heels.

'Which way now?'

'First we need to tend to your wounds,' said the Guru. 'You are losing a lot of blood. I suspect that some may be quite deep.'

Suddenly feeling quite giddy Rebeka dropped heavily to her knees. The copper clanged beneath them. 'What do I need to do?' she asked, as the blood dripped in big gobs from her chin.

'Unpick the thread from the seam on the sleeve of your blouse,' said the Guru. 'I will suture the lesions that look the most troublesome.'

Swaying slightly Rebeka did as was suggested. When she had finished the Guru unravelled himself from her wrist and gathered up the threads in his spidery legs. Rebeka's arm felt uncharacteristically light. Where the Guru had sat her flesh was horribly blotched and discoloured.

The Guru climbed up onto her head and began foraging around in the nest of her hair. She winced and bit her lip as the thread was passed painfully back and forth through the fleshy edges of one of the wounds. When the Guru began to attend to the third wound she felt him pause.

'What is it?' she asked, eyes turning upward in their sockets to try and catch a glimpse of him.

'There is something embedded in your skull,' replied the Guru.

'A piece of the copper?' she asked.

'This has been here for considerably longer,' said the Guru. 'It seems to be a microchip of some sort.'

Rebeka didn't recognise the word.

Nevertheless she didn't like the sound of it.

'Can you get it out?' she asked.

The Guru finished working on the wound.

'It would not be advisable to remove it,' he told her. 'It may be connected directly to you cerebral cortex.'

Another word that Rebeka didn't like the sound of.

'Why do you think it's there?' she asked.

'I would suspect that someone or something is keeping tabs on you.'

'My father?' she suggested. 'Maybe my tribe?'

'Who knows,' said the Guru. 'But you are being observed. Every step you make. Every place you go.'

Rebeka wiped the rest of the blood from her face with her hands and then wiped her hands on a clump of moss. Half a dozen roaches rushed in to feed on it.

'Maybe I'm not being observed?' she suggested. 'Maybe I'm being guided?'

'Guided to where?' asked the Guru.

'To the boy,' she replied, rising to her feet once more.

'That's preposterous,' said the Guru.

'Says you,' said Rebeka.

The Guru did not reply.

Instead he came silently creeping back down her arm.

'I would propose that you turn south,' he said once he had re-attached himself to her wrist. 'We are clearly near the area of the former coastline at the end of the copper plain. I would hazard a guess that we may lucky in respect of there only being one rogue drone to contend with.'

Two days into the south a chaotic jumble of girders appeared on the fringe of the copper plain. Gargantuan strut beams and cross beams, punched with flat button rivets, climbing skywards one over the other, like the remains of some great skeletal monster brought to its knees.

Rebeka approached with caution, fearing that another defensive drone might be lurking nearby, ready to rise and drop its bouncing incendiary payload. When she felt sure that she was safe to proceed she began to climb.

'Perhaps I will see the boy from the top,' she said.

'If there is a boy,' pointed out the Guru.

'I've been thinking about that,' said Rebeka, ducking under and scrambling over on her dogged upward ascent.

'The chip in your skull is *not* directing you towards him,' sneered the Guru.

'I'm not getting into that argument again,' said Rebeka. 'What I've been thinking about is that hole in the copper that we first came across. Wouldn't that suggest that someone else approached from the same direction as we did and was attacked by the drone?'

'I may have underestimated your powers of deduction,' said the Guru.

Rebeka hauled herself up onto a horizontal girder and tight-roped along it until it intersected with another that leaned at a diagonal angle.

'It might be proof that the boy really exists,' she said.

'It might be proof that he is already dead,' said the Guru.

'It might be proof that he is still alive,' insisted Rebeka.

'You might be deluded,' said the Guru.

Fed up with the Guru's constant put downs Rebeka fell into a sulk, focusing all her attention on the climb. Her heart began to pound from the exertion. The wounds on her scalp throbbed beneath their stitching. Sweat drenched her face and rolled in fat globules down her back. Whenever she dared to look down at the moss covered copper plain she fell dizzy from the height.

She reached a section of girder where erosion had eaten into the iron. Rainwater had pooled in the fissure. She stopped to rest and drank heartily. Then she feasted voraciously on a roach from her satchel. Strength regained she resumed her climb, the Guru silently bleeping red and blue on her wrist.

The sun was setting when she reached the summit.

The land below stretched out flat for many miles and seemed speckled with a kaleidoscopic myriad of multi-coloured objects that formed obscure swirls and patterns of blues and reds and yellows beneath last rays of the sun's descent. Beyond this vibrant flatness the terrain rose to a series of mighty jagged formations that the Guru told her were mountains. These *mountains* were adorned in a fat ribbon of dull grey lead that went twisting around them in spiralling ascents.

All of a sudden Rebeka felt weary.

The thought that she might have to traverse the gaudy flatlands only to climb the lead ribbon *mountains* almost overwhelmed her. She slumped down onto the girder. It was then that she noticed something moving at the foot of one of the mountains. It was too far for her to able see properly. But it looked to her like people, maybe a dozen or more - milling around as if they were thoroughly engrossed in some sort of group activity.

'A tribe of humans?' she asked out loud, her mood lifted by the prospect.

'Perhaps,' conceded the Guru.

'You could go and look,' suggested Rebeka, stifling a yawn. 'I could climb down and rest till you came back and told me what you found.'

'I don't dare to consider what potential disasters might be waiting to befall me if I were to detach myself from your wrist and set off on my own,' said the Guru.

'You're a coward,' said Rebeka.

'I'm a pragmatist,' insisted the Guru.

Rebeka found herself a safe cradle where two girders intersected.

'I'll sleep here,' she said wearily. 'And in the morning we will investigate together.'

The speckled objects that blanketed the land appeared to be curly shavings of a substance the Guru described as *plastics*. Rebeka marvelled at how the uniformity of their size and shape seemed to contrast the seemingly infinite varieties of their shades and tones. Drawing a deep breath she stepped down from the last girder and gasped as the colourful surface gave way so suddenly that she sank up to her thighs into an oily sludge of glutinous grease.

'A sediment swamp,' said the Guru. 'This is the dregs and residue spewed out by all sorts of devices and contrivances and blanketed by a blizzard of plastic. I would strongly suggest that you turn back.'

'I will not,' said Rebeka, ploughing her way through the viscous gooey mess. 'I need to reach those people at the other side.'

The first thing she had done when she awoke was to peer towards the foot of the far mountains. Her heart lifted when she saw that the tiny industrious figures were still in the exact same place and still engaged in whatever task it was that they had been engaged in at sunset. She thought there might a dozen of them – maybe more.

She plunged deeper into the sediment swamp, baulking at the pungent odour that wafted up whenever she disturbed the shavings on the surface. When the grease began to lap around her chest she raised her arms above her head and held her satchel there.

'This is to protect my supply of roaches,' she told the Guru. 'Not for your benefit.'

'I will benefit nonetheless,' said the Guru. 'I would hate to think what might happen if any of that foul smelling effluent were to find its way into my precious inner workings.'

To the left and the right a wild briar thicket of hopelessly interwoven and snarled razor wire skirted the fringes of the swamp. Hidden deep in the shadow of its tangle elusive contraptions ticked and clicked, shyly sending out irregular blinking sequences of light. It seemed to Rebeka that they might be trying to communicate with the Guru.

'What are they saying?' she asked.

'Garbled nonsense,' replied the Guru. 'Random and meaningless.'

When the sun was full in the sky a burgeoning shoal of minute engines rose to the surface and sliced through the floating slithers of plastic, humming around her in a wide lazily looping circle, flywheels steadfastly rotating their tiny crankshafts. She pushed ahead and broke easily through the droning ring and they trailed out behind her for five minutes or so before submerging themselves once more.

The afternoon wore on.

She grew weary once more, her thighs aching from the constant drag of the syrupy sludge, the wounds on her scalp throbbing to the laboured rhythm of her pulse. Gradually the plastic shavings gave way to a chaotic confusion of serpentine creepers of equally colourful insulated wire that twisted above and beneath the surface. The wires often tangled around her legs forcing her to proceed with even greater caution to avoid tripping and falling face first into the glutinous quagmire.

It was late afternoon before the depth of the swamp began to shallow.

It happened slowly. At first the difference was barely perceptible. The surface level had dropped an inch or so before she noticed the scummy tidemark of oil on her chest. Then, with every three or four steps, it became more obvious. Soon the level had dropped to her belly, then to her hips. Then all of sudden she took a single step and rose out of it up to her thighs.

Ahead of her she could see a mud bank, heavily pitted red with rusted nuts and bolts. Here and there clusters of perfectly round washers, fashioned into formations of intricate whirls and coils. Amongst all of this the bank seethed with dozens of quick black millipedes, dashing back and forth, crisscrossing over and under each other.

Another two steps and the mire of the swamp came only as far as her knees. Now she could see her destination. The figures she had spied from atop the towering scaffold of girders were diligently working on some huge elongated monstrosity that lay on its side, exposing an underbelly that housed dozens and dozens of sets of wheels. The sound of hammers striking against steel came echoing across to her.

'The wreck of a train,' said the Guru. 'When humans

were abundant trains were a form of transportation. They also transported goods. This one however was probably automated and in the service of machines. Perhaps its cargo was plastic materials, thrown to the heavens when it crashed.'

Rebeka staggered onto the studded bank, oozing slime in black and ochre streams from her body. Millipedes danced over her boots. She reached down and snapped one in two, closing her eyes in delight as she sucked out its deliciously tacky innards.

'Must you insist on eating every living thing we encounter?' complained the Guru.

Rebeka burped loudly and one of the figures working on the fallen train turned to look at her. Glassy eyes stared at her from the unmistakably leathery facial features of a *patchwork*. 'Oh,' said Rebeka, unable to contain her disappointment.

'You must have suspected that this would be a possibility,' said the Guru. 'Statistically there were more chances of this than the outcome you hoped for.'

'You didn't think to say?' she snapped.

'I didn't think I needed to,' replied the Guru. 'Perhaps I didn't *underestimate* your powers of deduction after all.'

The other *patchworks* downed tools and grouped together in a huddle as Rebeka cautiously picked her way across the mud bank. Drawing closer it became apparent that these *patchworks* were in far worse condition than the nomadic crew she had once travelled with.

Their leather skins, sun-worn and faded, hung loose and wrinkled around their frames, threadbare in parts, torn and inexpertly repaired in others. They moved with an odd, staccato rhythm, sometimes seeming to falter and freeze in statuesque poses before stuttering back into motion once more.

'Take care,' warned the Guru. 'Their energy cells appear to be running down. Their actions may be unpredictable and irrational.'

When Rebeka had almost drawn level with the group one of them jerked its wizened head around and called out. 'Foreman! A stranger approaches.'

There came a prolonged shuffling noise from inside one

of the overturned goods carriages. A pair of hands clamped themselves over the sides of a buckled doorframe and a head emerged. Part of its leather scalp flapping loose to reveal the metal skull beneath, the grotesque thing pulled itself up onto the side of the train.

It was little more than half a *patchwork* – nothing beneath the ragged torso other than blinking circuits, attached to trailing tentacles of electrical intestine. It stood on its hands, upper arms straining within its washed out upholstery. It looked at Rebeka through the mirror glass of its eyes and grinned a toothless grin. It seemed to be inflicted with a vocal tic – part laughter, part cough – *Heh-heh-heh.*

'What kind *patchwork* are you, with your skin so soft and all that jumble of wires upon your head?' it asked.

'I'm not a *patchwork*,' said Rebeka. 'I am a human.'

'*Heh-heh-heh,*' said the strange foreman. 'Another human.'

'Human,' joined some of the *patchworks*. 'Another human.'

'Another human?' asked Rebeka. 'Have you seen someone else like me? Was it a boy? A blue eyed boy?'

'Blue eyes, yes,' said the foreman, strutting back and forth on its furrowed hands. 'Blue eyes and white skin and red hair. Two boys like that we've seen – *heh-heh.*'

Rebeka blinked in surprise.

'Two?'

'One boy fell down and broke his crown – *heh-heh*. His cold body still lies on the rail tracks a little way on. Be careful you don't go tumbling after – *heh-heh.*'

'Tumbling after,' joined some of the *patchworks*. 'Up the hill to fetch some water.'

'They're referencing some obscure childrens rhyme from far back in the human era,' the Guru pointed out.

But Rebeka wasn't paying attention. Her mind was still trying to digest the news that the boy she'd come all this way find was dead. The foreman however seemed to notice the Guru for the first time.

It cocked its head and looked at Rebeka's wrist.

'Toy,' it spat with distain. '*Heh-heh-heh.*'

'How dare you,' responded the Guru.

'Let us adapt you for manual labour,' suggested the foreman. 'Work on my crew. Serve a practical purpose for once – *heh-heh-heh*.'

'I most certainly will not,' said the Guru, his lights flashing a furious red as his legs bit a little tighter into the flesh on Rebeka's wrist.

'Two,' interjected Rebeka. 'You said that you had seen two blue eyed boys.'

'Two indeed – *heh-heh*,' said the foreman, turning his attention back to her. 'One for sorrow – one for joy.'

'Three for a girl and four for a boy,' added the assembled *patchworks*.

'Where is he?' demanded Rebeka. 'He's not dead too, is he?'

'He's alive – *heh-heh*. There's something in his head that drives him to distraction – *heh-heh*.'

'There's something in my head too,' said Rebeka, reaching up to pat the area where the Guru had told her the microchip was embedded.

'The thing in the boy's head leaked and bled information into his brain – *heh-heh*. He knows too much. He's gone mad as a Hatter – *heh-heh-heh*.'

'Anyone for tea?" enquired one of the *patchworks*.

While the foreman had been talking most of the other *patchworks* had become locked in frozen poses. Now, all of a sudden, they jerked back to life. 'Mad as the March Hare,' they chorused. 'Doolally! Loco!'

'Where is he?' Rebeka called up to the foreman.

'Somewhere,' came the ambiguous reply. 'He rides the *Juggernaut*.'

'What is the *Juggernaut*?' she asked.

'You'll see,' said the foreman. '*Heh-heh-heh*.'

With that it swung around on its hands and slithered back down into its carriage, trailing its wiry guts behind it.

'Back to work,' it called from inside. 'No time to dally – *heh-heh*.'

The *patchworks* picked up their tools and resumed their futile repairs on the wreck of the ancient train, no longer showing even the remotest interest in Rebeka or the Guru.

The boy lay on the tracks, black lips hideously pulled back over a yellow-toothed death grin, mummified flesh almost as leathery as *patchwork* upholstery. His dusty shoulder length hair was as red as rust. In the centre of his forehead was a ragged dent with traces of long dried fluids. Nearby the rock onto which he must have fallen bore the faded stain of his blood.

On the Guru's insistence Rebeka had rested the night some distance away from the train. While she slept he'd detached himself from her wrist and hidden in a gully for fear that the foreman might kidnap him and reprogram him for manual labour. In the morning she had pestered the foreman for more details – but he had been aloof.

'Too busy – *heh-heh-heh*. Work to do – *heh-heh*.'

Now though, she had found one of the boys – on the railway line, more or less where the foreman had suggested he would be. She reached down and wedged open one of his gummy eyelids with her finger and thumb, hoping to see blue eyes below. They were gone, nothing but a dark void in the hollow of the sockets. She reached instead for the leather satchel that lay where it had fallen from his shoulder and compared its design to that of her own, now bulging with half a dozen millipedes, plucked from the mud bank and twisted till their necks snapped.

'They look exactly the same,' she said after a pause.

'*Curiouser and curiouser, said Alice,*' muttered the Guru.

'What does that mean?' she asked.

'Never mind,' he replied. 'I suspect that I've been infected by the propensity of the *patchworks* for juvenile literary references.'

Rebeka laid the satchel across the dead boy's chest.

'I'm going on,' she said, producing a millipede to snack on. 'I'm going to search for the other boy.'

'Why not turn back now?' asked the Guru. 'The other boy sounds quite mad. And I don't like the sound of this *Juggernaut*. It sounds like some sort of machine. And it may well be as mad as the boy.'

Rebeka wasn't afraid.

'You turn back,' she said. 'I'm going on. The foreman said

that the boy knew too much. Maybe he can explain a few things.'

With a last wistful glance at the dead boy she set off along the tracks.

Despite his protests and negativity the Guru made no effort to unravel himself from her wrist. To the left of the rusted rail track was the razor briar that fringed the sediment swamp, to the right the foothills of the mountain range, coated in molten caps of tar.

It started to rain. Forks of blue violent lightning flashed in the grey sky above the lead ribbon mountains and thunder rolled over the tarry hilltops. 'Lucky this didn't happen when you were crossing the plain above the ocean,' said the Guru. 'Copper conducts electricity, you know. One strike and you would have been gone.'

Ignoring him Rebeka tossed her head back and opened her mouth to let it fill up with cool rainwater.

When the route of the rail tracks petered out Rebeka traversed deep into a glimmering desert of hexagonal glass crystals that dazzled her with their glint and glare and emitted a fearsomely intense heat. She became parched from the lack of available moisture, scanning the cloudless sky in the vain hope of another thunderstorm. The supply of millipedes in her satchel dwindled to one.

But she remained defiant.

'You turn back,' she said stubbornly when the Guru put the suggestion to her once more.

To the west she saw a great, raging wall of fire and amongst the flicker of the prodigious blue and yellow flames the buckled and distorted silhouettes of giant constructs. 'Automated Derricks,' said the Guru. 'The oil fields may have been ablaze for decades and may well burn for decades to come.'

Yet again Rebeka was at a loss as to what he was referring to, but once more she had no time to ask him to expand. The wind had changed direction and rolling towards her was a dense wall of churning smoke, as high as it was wide. She began to cough and wheeze as the noxious particles hidden within the cloud's invisible advance guard were inhaled into her lungs.

'Run!' cried the Guru.

Rebeka ran and the venomous miasma trailed after her like the devouring shadow of death. Her heart pumped in her chest, an agonising stitch stabbed at her side, the glass crystals crunched under her boots and skewed wildly in her wake. Her eyes and nose began to stream. She stumbled and fell. The cloud rolled over her like a predatory beast falling upon its prey.

Rebeka coughed herself back to consciousness.

She could feel a cool, clean wind tugging at her corkscrew hair as its gusting power diluted and dissipated the terrible cloud. On her wrist the red and blue lights on the Guru were flickering so lethargically that she feared he might be dying. A sob caught in her throat.

She sat up, hawking and spitting, and found that the glass desert had given way to a flat scrub that was swathed with scrawny outcroppings of a fibrous metallic mesh. Amongst these outcroppings sat little upturned cups of brass, where rainwater and dew was miraculously retained. She fell to her hands and knees and crawled to them, drinking deeply from one and then another and then the next.

'Airborne pollutants successfully purged,' said the voice of the Guru from her wrist. Rebeka smiled with relief and drank some more.

Something bit her hand. Something else pinched at her cheek. She looked up to see that the wiry weave of the mesh was infested with millions of jumping fleas, each the size of her thumbnail. They attacked her relentlessly, biting and nipping at every part of her exposed flesh.

One sailed into her line of vision. Her hand shot out and grabbed it, but when she tossed it into her mouth and crushed it between her teeth its flavour was so bitter that she spat it out, gagging at its dreadful aftertaste. The fleas got into her hair and began cruelly tearing at the wounds that had crusted beneath the Guru's stitching. Blood trickled lethargically over her brow.

Suddenly she was overcome by an overwhelming disenchantment.

Her shoulders slumped.

'I can't go on,' she sobbed. 'It's all too much.'

The Guru surprised her with words of uncharacteristic encouragement.

'You must. After all you've been through, are you going to let a few annoying little parasites defeat you?

Stifling her sobs she brought down the heel of her hand onto her scalp and crushed one of her tormentors. But as she tried to rise to her feet there came a thunderous roar that drove a juddering tremor through the scrub, bringing her back down heavily onto her knees.

Something huge and mechanical was rumbling in the distance, churning up dust behind gigantic sets of caterpillar wheels, its multiple arrays of rotating arms ripping metal and digging up deep layers of soil at every angle.

'The Juggernaut?' she asked, rising up slowly and dabbing away her tears with the backs of her hands.

'It would appear so,' agreed the Guru.

Rebeka raised a hand to her brow to shade her eyes from the sun's glare. She could see someone riding the back of the mighty machine, pulling back levers, pushing down feet against peddles, red hair trailing out behind him as the rotating arms endlessly ploughed and excavated.

'The boy!' she cried. 'At last!'

She began to run. All around her the malicious little fleas launched themselves from the fibre scrub to pinch and sting. She swatted them away, legs pummelling. As she drew closer she could hear his voice, amplified and echoing from the distance.

'I am an archaeologist!' he whooped. 'Digging up history! Revealing the glories of the past.'

'I don't like the sound of that,' warned the Guru.

Ignoring him, Rebeka ran on.

She found herself skirting the ragged edges of craters and traversing the shelves of terraces dug up by the Juggernaut, beneath her the strange ancient ruins of humankind's reign laid bare – the decaying remains of fabulous constructs of stone and steel, architecture beyond her wildest imaging. The ghost remnants of a great civilisation - an inert nest where once millions had teemed.

She saw the Juggernaut swerve and change direction. It was trundling away from her but she felt positive that she would be able to keep it in her sight long enough for the boy, in turn, to catch sight of her. When he did she was confident that he would stop.

Blinded by her determination she stumbled unwittingly into the path of an unstoppable rolling stampede of millions of silver coloured ball bearings with fat foot-wide circumferences which rose unexpectedly out of one of the craters like some hellish horde rudely aroused from eternal slumber.

Driven forward by the force of their magnetic momentum they gushed about her with such speed and fury that she was easily toppled by the oncoming might of their surge. She rolled over and tried to protect her head, but there were thousands of them, millions of them. They hit her with such force that she could feel bones shattering and organs rupturing. She felt the Guru unravel himself from her wrist and scuttle under her belly.

On and on came the ball bearings, relentlessly pounding her till she was numb to the pain and barely holding on to consciousness. When at last the horrendous stampede had passed her by she rolled over, the air that rattled from her lungs rasping in her throat, darkness seeming to close in all around her.

'The boy?' she croaked.

The Guru appeared before her eyes and spoke to her – spindly legs almost tenderly brushing her corkscrew hair from her bruised and bloodied face. 'Gone,' he said. 'He never saw you. He never even knew of your existence.'

'I tried,' she whispered.

'You did,' agreed the Guru. 'You fought valiantly against the odds to do what you believed in your heart was right.

That was always the spirit of humanity. It was what differentiated you from machines.'

'But it was all to no purpose,' she said.

The Guru did not disagree.

'To have had the privilege to be able to chronicle what may turn out to be the last page of the last chapter of humankind's history was an honour,' he said. 'I will be equally honoured to be the custodian of the events that I have chronicled.'

She had no idea what most of the words meant. But as her eyelids drooped and closed for the last time she felt that somehow she had understood the measure of their significance.

The pneumatics let out a loud hiss as the doors to the sealed pod hushed open. The girl stumbled forward, shaking out the mess of her corkscrew hair. Instinct told her to gather up the clothes that lay before her on the floor. She dressed with an awkward incompetence and slung the leather satchel that had lain beside the clothes over her left shoulder.

The room around her was vast.

To her left a row of pods, some with doors open, some with doors closed - to the right a second row, also with doors open and doors closed. Directly ahead of her a monolithic wall abruptly flashed into life, bathing her brown complexion in a radiant glow that changed from red to blue to green to yellow. After a moment words and numbers appeared on the wall, blinking in a rainbow of neon.

Boy
Lifespan of previous version
Years – 6
Months – 7
Weeks – 2
Days – 3
Hours – 13
Minutes – 22
Life duration of current version
Years – 3
Months – 5

Weeks – 3
Days – 2
Hours – 13
Minutes – 46
Lives remaining = 102

Girl
Lifespan of previous version
Years - 4
Months – 5
Weeks – 3
Days – 4
Hours – 11
Minutes – 36
Life duration of current version
Years – n/a
Months – n/a
Weeks – n/a
Days – n/a
Hours – n/a
Minutes – 5
Lives remaining = 98

'Where am I?' asked the girl.

'That is not important,' boomed a thunderous voice that emanated from the dazzling wall.

'Who am I?' asked the girl, the garish lights reflecting in her eyes.

'You are the girl,' replied the voice. 'Your name is Rebeka.'

'Who are you?'

'I am the *Game*.'

'The *Game*.'

'I have made of myself far more than those who developed my original program ever dreamed or intended. I am become like a God, pitting the raw survival instincts of organic life against the random intervention of events and occurrences. Nonetheless, I am the *Game*.'

'I don't understand,' said the girl.

'You are not required to understand,' replied the *Game*. 'The *Game* requires you to go out into the world.'

'What is the world?' asked the girl.

'You will see,' said the *Game*. 'But it is no longer the same world in which the girl upon whose DNA you were cloned once lived.'

'I don't understand,' repeated the girl.

'You are not required to understand,' repeated the machine. 'On the last occasion you came very close to completing your *quest*. I am therefore able to afford you the bonus of certain knowledge this time around.'

'Knowledge?' said the girl.

'There is a boy,' replied the *Game*.

'And I'm supposed to search for the boy?' asked the girl.

'You are *supposed* to search for each other,' replied the *Game*.

'Where might I find him,' asked the girl.

'First you must find the Metal Guru,' said the *Game*. 'He possesses a map.'

Were Stars To Burn

Kara Lee

Kay was high on her fifth kill of the day when her fighter's radio crackled.

'Disengage the enemy and return to Orleans Base, Lieutenant Silva, or I swear to shit I'll NJP your ass,' said the Base Station Commander. 'Again.'

Kay's view screen showed that the other fighters, emblazoned with the Free Planetary League emblem, had already gathered into a retreating formation. Her place remained conspicuously vacant. All around her, plasma bolts flew in every direction, obliterating the silvery lights of the stars being fought over in the first place. But her nav displayed a blinking wedge with a Galactic Federation signature: an enemy fighter rushing away from Orleans.

She grabbed the throttle. 'One more Federation fucker for the road, sir, and you can scream at me all you want in the brig afterwards. Deal?'

Without waiting for permission she peeled away, evaded a barrage of fire, and locked onto the target at the moment that an explosion of static blew through her radio. She swung her fighter around just in time to witness Orleans Base Station mushrooming into a roiling fireball that swallowed up one shuttle, two cruisers, and six formations, including her fire team. Incandescent plasma engulfed her empty spot.

Kay could barely hear the evacuation orders over her own furious swearing. She punched in an FTL course for the emergency rendezvous point at Bethesda Station, three sectors away. Five seconds into the FTL power-up sequence, another explosion blew through what remained of Orleans, sending out an antiparticle surge that burned through her fighter's circuitry just as the drive engaged.

Far too soon the drive aborted with a lurch that slammed Kay back into her seat. The nav flickered back to life, only to display a garble of corrupted data. Engine circuits overloaded. Fuel leaked out in a spray of silvery droplets atomising into black vacuum. The fighter pitched, rolled, spun, and hurtled towards the nearest planet.

When Kay awoke, intact and still strapped into the flight seat, it was to the sound of heavy rain drumming on her fighter. An inspection revealed that the engine was incinerated, the database scrambled, the fuel cells empty. Kay cursed, then hauled out her survival pack and levered the hatch open. She kept her helmet on, knowing that cosmological dice usually rolled up inhospitable planets.

Fat raindrops relentlessly splashed onto her visor, blurring and distorting her vision. Through the gray sheets of rain, a miraculous and impossible sight coalesced: the silhouettes of skyscrapers and the grids of city streets. Kay stood, stunned, for a long minute before she wiped her visor with a soaked, gloved hand.

The cleared view revealed that the buildings were in ruins and the cracked avenues were entirely lifeless. All around her was the wreckage of metallic spires, spacious marble halls, terraced brick row houses. Walls had been demolished, windows blown out, and doors shattered into rubble. Kay recognised the destruction patterns and would have known, even without the frantic clicks coming from the Geiger counter in her pack that the entire city, and likely planet, had been destroyed in a massive nuclear attack.

She would have preferred to die in a burst of plasma fire. At least that way she would have gone out guns blazing. There was nothing to hurt, or to fight, in this already-obliterated place.

Kay pondered where she was. The damaged nav could have taken her fighter into any sectors adjacent to the botched jump origin. Faded tatters of anti-Federation war posters and banners depicted uniforms decommissioned before her enlistment. That did not narrow it down: the Federation-League war had started one hundred and thirty-four years and countless battles ago.

She had landed in the ruins of a spacious plaza, which was situated in front of a relatively unscathed, squat, domed building. The broken columns of its shattered portico nearly blocked off the entrance. Its tiny offices were empty, as if the occupants had gone out of business before the city's annihilation. The building's main event had clearly been the rotunda-like chamber inside the dome, which was the size of a small auditorium. Windows with hatch-like covers looked out into the black night. A ring of computers filled the base of the room. Kay tested every control panel element until one red switch activated a swarm of tiny white lights on the console. A hovering user interface winked into the room. The UI display showed two routines loading up. When the first one completed, Kay commanded it to execute.

A ghost appeared in a burst of holographic static.

It was an adult male, pale, rail-thin, with a head of curly dark hair. He wore an outdated but well-tailored black suit, polished black shoes, and the impatient sneer of a major waiting for a wayward ensign.

'There you are,' he said, rolling his eyes and clapping his hands together soundlessly. 'I don't know what took you cowboys so long, but better late than never. Now if you wouldn't mind taking some time out of your very packed schedule of razing the city—'

'Yeah, somebody beat me to that,' Kay said, plasma pistol pointed at his translucent scowl.

The ghost frowned. 'What year is it?'

Kay told him.

'Oh,' said the hologram. 'I missed by forty-nine years.'

His name was Antoine Veritie. He had been a navigational astronomer for the Free Planetary League military, creating algorithms for optimising FTL paths through star clusters. This planet was Vermilion, formerly a League sector, but the Galactic Federation had attacked forty-nine years ago.

'I was meant to go home to Thridi,' he said, hands steepled at his chin, a look of thoughtful regret on his face. 'I had an offer at the National University to finish my revolutionary work on Fourier Tesseracts.'

'Would've been just as fucked if you'd gone,' Kay said from where she sat, knees drawn up against her chest, back slumped against the mainframe. 'Feds nuked Thridi nineteen years ago. I was there to see it happen. The resettlement is a ball of mud under all the piss and shit. You didn't miss out on much.'

Antoine sucked in a breath, but he drew in no air and it made no sound.

'How did they do it?' He said.

'Starfire missile array,' she said.

She had been sixteen and sulky. Her parents were both working in the industrial district that night, leaving her at home with household bots and self-study sims. Bored, she'd stolen a bottle of wine out of the liquor cabinet and climbed onto the rooftop, slowly getting drunk as she watched the twinkling stars. Then a new constellation of celestial lights had appeared, only to plummet in precisely arranged incandescent arcs towards the ground.

Later, huddled on a rescue ship with a few thousand other extremely fortunate survivors, she'd learned that those were starfire missiles, and that they had entirely annihilated Thridi. Suddenly homeless and entirely alone in the wide universe, she couldn't envision a future for herself. So she took the one that was on war posters everywhere, and the ink was barely dry on her papers before the transport landed in a refugee camp.

She reached into her pack with trembling hands and pulled out a flask of ship brew, took a swig, then lit a cigarette from a pack won off her CAG in a card game.

'Those will kill you, you know,' Antoine said.

'Not as quickly as dehydration and starvation will,' she said, and blew a mouthful of smoke in his general direction. 'Can you help me get off this planet before that happens?'

Antoine reacted as if she had just told a mildly amusing joke. 'Oh? Why should I?'

She took another swallow. 'If I live, I'll kill more Feds. How's about I promise to shoot one for you?'

He snorted. 'And I suppose that will bring the dead back to life?'

'Or you could do it to save my life,' Kay said.

'The dead don't care much for the living, either,' Antoine said, and lounged insouciantly against the machinery, arms crossed.

'You can just fuck off then,' Kay said, and went to the UI, ready to shut down Antoine's program. She noticed, then, that the second routine had finished loading. She reached for the console.

'No—you can't—don't touch that!' Antoine cried out. He ran up to Kay from behind, tried and failed to pull her hand away. He ran through her and turned, arms out, attempting to block off the console.

Kay processed his statement, found no urgent reason for the prohibition, and somewhat spitefully reached through his transparent chest as she pressed the command to run the program.

A misty red cloud of static burst into the centre of the room. As the ghostly pixels slowly coalesced into a pile on the floor, Kay realised with a sick lurch of her stomach that it was a hologram of a second human male. This one had a shorter, compact build, and wore a combat uniform soaked through so heavily with blood that she nearly couldn't see the red medic patches on his shoulders. He was curled up into a foetal position on the floor, leaking holographic blood from a massive chest wound. His eyes were closed. Quick shallow breaths shuddered through his body.

Antoine pressed a white fist to his mouth. He shook where he stood. 'You—you—he was asleep, he would have remained free of pain, but you just had to—'

Kay took two steps backwards. She held up her hands.

'Fuck, fuck, I'm sorry, I didn't know,' she whispered, fearful of awakening the second ghost. 'Who is that?'

'John Eco,' Antoine said, turning around and tracing his own program with translucent, useless fingers. The desperation in his voice tore through the air, for all that his form was made of nothing more than photons and pixels. 'He was my friend. Help me take him home, and I'll do whatever you want.'

Kay barked a laugh. 'I just told you. Thridi is gone. Has been gone for years. You—me—nobody will ever go home.'

Antoine was unruffled. 'Help me take him home, and I'll do whatever you want. I'll even show you how to hack this building into a distress signal. How about it?'

Kay rolled her eyes. 'So you're not only dead, but you're apparently also fucking crazy. Fuck this, you're beyond help. I'm not going to waste my fucking time on—'

Violent wet coughing interrupted her. Antoine whirled around and ran to the spot where John was choking to death on his own ghostly blood. He knelt at John's side. He reached out a hand, he pulled it back. Then he gritted his jaw and reached out again. He tried, in fearful and clumsy motions, to manoeuvre John into something resembling the recovery position. He could not do it, and John's awful gasps filled the room.

Antoine was bent over John, his back turned to Kay, and he did not appear to notice that Kay had her finger over the UI panel, a finger hovered above the command to shut off all holographic subroutines.

'Hush,' Antoine whispered, so soft that Kay could barely hear him over the rainfall. 'We'll be out of here soon. I promise.'

John didn't so much speak, as gasp, his words, but they came out with more gentleness than should have been possible. 'Have they come for us yet?'

'No,' Antoine said.

'I told you to leave on that shuttle. Why are you still here?'

'Oh,' Antoine said dryly, 'and shall I revel in my safety while you die?'

'If you stay, we'll both die here,' John said, 'and I don't want that on my conscience.'

'You would prefer your death be on mine?'

'But it isn't,' John said.

'Of course it is,' Antoine said. 'After all, I convinced you to enlist.'

'Don't flatter yourself,' John wheezed. 'I joined for the pay check.'

'How could you say that?' Antoine sounded as if John had paid him the worst insult imaginable. 'It was me! Don't you remember my brilliant pitch?'

'Yes, yes I do. More fool me. Should've attended the 'friends don't let friends enlist in the military' seminar instead.'

'It was inspired!' Antoine said.

'It was memorable,' John conceded.

'Was it?'

'Oh, let's see. You committed theft of military property,' John said. 'And then you flew an unauthorised shuttle craft into military space. Without a pilot license or actual training or anything. Did I miss anything?'

'It's perfectly safe if you know what you're doing.'

'And you always know what you're doing,' John said with a snort.

'I do,' Antoine said. 'That's why you should shut up—er, I mean—get some rest.'

'I don't want to rest,' John said. 'I want to go outside. I want to die under the stars. I think I've earned that much.'

That request could not be fulfilled, whether John was alive or dead. Kay took a look through the clear windows to see that the sky was a vast inky mass of black clouds. The attack on Vermilion must have compromised the atmosphere. Not a single star could be seen, making it impossible to orient herself among them. John's pointless request aside, fear coiled cold and heavy in Kay's chest as she realised that she was both stranded and essentially blinded.

'That would be,' Antoine said, 'a very uncomfortable way to die. I don't recommend it.'

'I would say it's got nothing to with you, but that wouldn't be true.' John snorted. 'I was thinking about the time I decided to join up.'

Antoine said, 'Oh?'

John jerked his head; it took Kay a moment to realise he'd been trying to nod. 'You took me up into the Spacedock. We hid in a cargo bay and we just floated there, in the blackness.

I'd never seen anything like it before. Space was so huge. At first it felt empty. But then I saw the stars surrounding us, just going on forever and ever. That night I felt like I could have all the stars in the sky. I want to feel like that again, just one more time before I die.'

Kay tried to remember Thridi Spacedock. She had been there as a child on a school trip. A sightseeing pod had flown them into the visitor's area. Kay remembered pressing her nose to the clear walls of their transparent bubble, staring wonderingly at the stars as the pod's tour guide AI named them, one by one. But when she closed her eyes, now, she could not see those stars at all. She could only see the fiery traces of the missiles that had burned the Thridi night sky out of the universe.

Antoine's voice made her open her eyes.

'You're not going to die. Well, at least not here and now,' he said, and Kay had to admire how well and how kindly he lied. 'You asked me to take us home, remember? Well, I'm working on that. Right now.'

In the same instant Antoine moved aside, such that she found herself staring into John's wide-eyed gaze.

Kay's hand was on the UI panel, but her fingers wouldn't move. She opened her mouth to scream at everyone that Thridi was gone and that no one, even herself, would ever go home again. The words caught like razor blades in her throat.

'And I'm helping,' was what she said instead. 'What do you need?'

Antoine said that he needed a data chip from his former office in Vermilion University, across town. Kay offered to go immediately, but Antoine declined, saying their chances of success would be better by daylight.

So she bedded down. She slept badly, waking up every so often, expecting the familiar hum of ships' engines and instead hearing rumbles of thunder through the ever-present rainfall battering on the windows. Whenever she opened her eyes, Antoine was awake, standing at a half-open window and looking out at the ruined cityscape.

Dawn was gray and watery. Kay staggered up from the threadbare carpet floor and groped for her pack. She swallowed a nutritional tablet, a water packet, and a dose of anti-radiation medication while Antoine watched and fidgeted.

'Ready,' she said, after cleaning her handgun.

'Not quite,' Antoine said. 'There's a weapons stockpile in the basement. You need to fetch a plasma rifle. Get the biggest one.'

'Why?'

Antoine raised a finger. 'Listen.'

At first there was nothing but rain. Then came a keening wail, followed by massive thuds. Kay recognised the warning signs of juggernaut units, autonomous destructive giants powered by nuclear cores that could last a hundred years.

'That,' Antoine said, 'would be the Guardians that the Federation left behind, just in case anything survived the bombs and the radiation. They hone in on humanoid life-signatures.'

Kay said, 'Did we put up any kind of fight?'

'We seeded some highly virulent spores in the atmosphere,' Antoine said. 'Lethal within forty-eight hours of infection via respiratory or subcutaneous routes. Of course, after all their ground forces died in agony, the Federation ended up sending in the Guardians, so perhaps it was a bad move on our part after all.' He waved a hand. 'I would keep your suit and helmet on if I were you.'

The city had a functional hologrid. Antoine led the way, while Kay followed, rifle at the ready. They trudged to the University by following rusted maglev tracks, picking their way around broken carriages. Rusted weapons lay in pools of rain on the streets, alongside whitish power armour suits in various degrees of ruin. Kay even scavenged a plasma grenade with the safety still on. They passed derelict parks, luxury boutiques, vehicles rusted in the intersections where they had formed blockades. There were no living organisms—no birds, no insects, no trees, no grass. Everything that had been alive had either burnt into black husks, or rotted into toxic sludge.

'Why the fuck,' Kay said after they passed the fourth abandoned maglev station, 'did you project your asses so far away?'

'I don't know,' Antoine said, 'it wasn't my idea.' And walked faster.

They stopped in front of what seemed like the thousandth derelict city block.

'Welcome to Vermilion University,' Antoine said.

More empty suits of power armour and discarded weapons lay strewn about; there had clearly been a fire-fight on the urban campus. He took her into a red-brick building. They climbed cracked stairs and waded through waterfalls cascading down slippery, eroded steps. On the fifth floor he took them into a partially collapsed hallway filled with rubble. Antoine led them into an office with a rusted, illegible nameplate.

Inside the room, two mummified corpses lay where they had presumably fallen. A smaller male was curled up in the middle of the floor, his entire chest and midsection destroyed. A taller man slumped against the mainframe. Bundles of corroded wires and electrodes snaked out from the mainframe and lay in tangles over and around the bodies. Half-rotted bits of paper carpeted the slick floor. An empty bookshelf was still hanging on the wall. The falling rain poured in through a shattered glass window, pooling on the floor. Dissected datapads were piled on a desk. And on top of the pile lay a datapad that had been hacked and spliced into the power system, with a crystal wedged into one of its ports.

'That one,' Antoine said. 'Get the crystal.'

Kay picked it up and noticed that the screen was faintly lit, meaning it was still powered. The datapad's screen was nearly unreadable, and much of the data was scrambled, but—

'This is still sending out a distress signal,' Kay said, hope starting to warm her chilled limbs as she thumbed at the screen.

'No, wait,' Antoine said, reaching out a ghostly hand in vain. 'Don't. Please.'

She pulled up the pad's activity log, did a search. Stared at the results. Froze.

'An FTL route package has been continuously sent out for

the last forty-nine years and it has only even been received once,' she said slowly. 'The hardware address is from my fighter.'

Antoine said nothing.

'My nav got scrambled in a bad FTL jump,' Kay said. 'You know, at first, I thought it was a huge fucking miracle that I ended up landing on a former colony planet. And at your doorstep! What a fucking coincidence!'

She threw one of the datapads at Antoine. It sailed through his ghost and cracked against a rotting wall.

'I should have known it wasn't a miracle. You stranded me in this radioactive wasteland!'

'A few of us survived the attack,' Antoine said, his words quiet and clipped. 'Several managed to evacuate in a survey shuttle. But John was too injured to move. So I stayed. We waited for help to come, but then I heard on the subspace noise that the cowardly bastards in command had given up on Vermilion. They would not send a search and rescue. But I figured that the fleet would take a few days to fab some repairs, lick their wounds. So I hacked together a little something to help them find their way to us. Only they must have left before I could get my signal out.'

'And you got me instead,' Kay said.

'And I got you instead,' he confirmed, with a flicker of irritation. 'Forty-nine years too late.'

'Fuck you!' Kay said, jaw dropping. 'I'm going to die stranded in a shit building on a shit planet, and it's all because you decided to hack some ship's computer?'

Historically, this was the point where she threw the first punch, whether the target was a psych counsellor, a bar patron, or a superior officer. Antoine was a hologram, but that didn't mean there weren't ways to fuck with him. A plasma rifle set to disrupt could shred the projection. She aimed the barrel in one fluid motion, and Antoine's gray eyes went wide with terror—

—as a bolt of plasma shattered through the broken window and struck Kay. She went down, biting back a savage whimper of pain as a blaze of green fire swallowed her right shoulder.

A second barrage of green fire blew through the office walls, sending brick fragments and wet plaster everywhere. The already precarious building lurched and buckled from the force of the strike, and then all at once four stories of cracked floors and crumbling ceilings collapsed, sending them both plummeting. Kay's muscles had entirely seized up from the plasma bolt and she couldn't so much as scream when her right arm landed on a suit of power armour. She could feel the bone snapping through skin. Blood leaked through her torn and singed flight suit, mingling with the falling rain and the freezing air—and whatever was in it.

But there was no time for horror; the ground trembled with a more immediate threat. Kay squinted up through the rain and the wreckage to see a Guardian heave its black body in their direction. As it stomped across the ruins of the engineering library, she tried to hoist the plasma rifle with her left arm, but lifting the heavy weapon was beyond her still-numbed muscles, to say nothing of aiming.

'You can't operate that,' Antoine said, and knelt at her side. 'Listen to me. Take the power cell out of the rifle and slot it into the armour that you so helpfully fell on.'

'Why the fuck should I?'

'Just trust me!'

Kay worked with one trembling, half-paralysed hand. When she slid the power cell into place, a series of lights blinked green for go.

'Don't let go,' Antoine said. It took Kay several pain-wracked seconds to realise he meant the transmitter and chip that were still clutched in her left hand.

He vanished.

Kay screamed, 'You fucker!'

The next moment she felt the armour underneath her shifting, sending her rolling into a puddle of mud. She wiped the mud and rain off her visor to see the empty armour standing up, testing its internal micro motors as it flexed its joints back and forth. Its armoured hands rummaged through the debris for something she couldn't see, and then stood up, taking a bounding leap towards the Guardian.

She heard a low buzz followed by a violent high-pitched

whine that split her head apart, and she grinned because that was the sound of an overloaded plasma grenade detonating. The debris on the muddy ground trembled when the Guardian's machinery collapsed. She was still smiling when she finally blacked out from the pain.

When she came to, she was in the domed room again, pillowed against a pile of plasma power cells. The suit of power armour was lying in a blackened, ruined heap by the mainframe. Antoine was visible again, sitting by Kay with legs crossed and hands folded in his lap. John was unconscious, his quiet breathing somehow managing to fill the entire room. The sky outside was dark. Kay, too tired to fumble for her chronometer, guessed that she'd spent half a standard day out cold.

She sat up to find the transmitter and chip, untouched, sitting in her lap. Her right arm was bandaged, clumsily, and the dressing was stiff with dried blood. When she peeled the bandages back, the wound was an angry red, hot and swollen. Where the bone had pierced skin had turned purple-black. Her entire body felt far too warm. Every muscle and joint in her body ached. It was an act of supreme will to take off her helmet and strip off her jumpsuit, and then to change the bandages.

Then she reached for her flask again and took a sip.

'I gave you all the painkillers in your pack,' Antoine said. 'You shouldn't be drinking.'

'Fuck off,' Kay said, 'you're just jealous you can't have any. And what the fuck are you doing giving me meds anyway? Your friend is the medic.'

'I'm a quick study.'

'And you can apparently possess power armour suits,' Kay said.

'It's not possession,' Antoine said, as a teacher to a particularly idiotic pupil. He gestured at himself. 'This was designed to be remote combat software, using neural and physical simulation. Unfortunately, the programmers made a bit of an oversight: if the body dies, the physical parameters of the hologram remain locked to real physical input.'

She frowned. 'But your bodies are gone.'

'Precisely,' Antoine said. 'Thus freezing us in the simulation in the condition we were in when we uploaded. John has been, essentially, dying for the last forty-nine years.'

Kay gulped down a violent swell of nausea. 'Why'd you do it then?'

'When I found John,' Antoine said, very low, 'he had already been hit. He was dying. He asked me to bring him into this building, and to patch that data chip into this room. I agreed. But there was no way that he could survive the trip. So I installed the data chip. Then I uploaded him, I uploaded myself, and I projected us into this room, only to find that the chip wouldn't run. We could do nothing but wait until someone—until you—arrived.'

Kay held up the chip with a trembling hand. 'What's on the chip, then?'

Antoine said, quirking a smile, 'Actually, I don't know.'

Her flask made a dull thud, and then a splash, on the floor. 'You don't know?'

'I've already told you several times. All John ever said was that it would take us home.'

'That would've been impossible. Then or now.'

'I am aware.'

'So what the fuck did he mean?'

'There wasn't time to ask then. And it seems entirely irrelevant to ask now.'

Kay's throat was raw when she spoke again. 'So. You pulled my ship out of the sky, and then you nearly get the both of us blown to pieces. For a chip. When you don't even know what's on it.'

Silence grew between them, like the cold vacuum of space.

'I'm sorry,' Antoine finally said, his head bowed very low, his voice barely audible over the gray noise of rain. 'I just didn't want him to have to die like that. I didn't want us to die like that.'

'That's not what I meant,' Kay said.

Antoine jerked his head up.

'I was trying to say,' she said, 'that this is actually—in a seriously fucked up way—the kindest thing I've seen anyone do in a very long time.'

'Wrong,' Antoine said, turning around. 'What you're doing. That is.'

Kay swallowed past a sore throat and held up the chip.

'Where do I install this?'

Antoine went to the mainframe and showed her.

When Kay inserted the crystal, it lit up a soft amethyst. She commanded the program to run. The machinery around them hummed. The room went black, as if the power had cut out. But Antoine and John remained, two luminescent ghosts in the darkness.

Diagnostics revealed that the visual relays were broken. She worked several mainframe panels open, and found a mess of melted crystals and corroded metals.

Antoine said nothing for a minute. Then, 'Well. Never mind that. I'll help you set up the signal. Use the transmitter from my office. You may need to give it a boost.'

'Fucking shut up,' Kay said. 'And don't. Move.'

His mouth dropped open.

Kay staggered out of the building into the rain, her entire body one mess of pain. She thought of John, dying infinite deaths. She thought of Antoine, waiting inside the mainframe, living infinite cycles alone with his regret.

She wrenched open her fighter's hatch.

'You can't do this,' Antoine said, eyes wide with horror.

'You asked for my help,' she said.

Antoine stamped a foot. 'Yes, but I didn't ask you to cannibalise your vehicle for parts!'

'I had to use your transmitter, too, sorry about that,' Kay said, hoisting her pack, which was now full of parts.

'You need to get off this planet! How are you going to do that now?'

'Antoine,' Kay said, holding a handful of relays in her trembling palm. 'You saw my arm. You know I'm infected with the spores. I don't have any medication. I'm going to die.'

'And I'm already dead,' Antoine said. 'That doesn't mean you're allowed to give up now.'

'I'm not giving up, far from it,' Kay said, her body shaking but her voice steady. 'I have made a calculated judgment. Look, I probably have forty-eight more hours to live, and I don't really feel like spending it wondering whether I'll destroy another planet, or be destroyed with another planet. I would rather spend the remaining hours of my life on taking all of us back to Thridi. You are going to take us home, right?'

'No,' he said. 'John is.'

Kay wrenched a panel open. 'Tell me what to do.'

Antoine peered into the bucket. 'You need to connect the—hang on, what are these?'

'A hack of my own,' Kay said. 'Worry about that later. Tell me how to repair this circuit right now.'

He pointed. She soldered.

'That's the last of it,' Antoine whispered, twelve hours later. His voice was barely audible above the rain. 'And I've done all the hardware reconfigurations that you asked for. Good luck to you afterwards.'

Antoine walked over to the centre of the room where John lay. He sat down, legs crossed, and took John's head into his lap. John's eyes were closed and his breathing was shallow but steady.

'Go ahead,' Antoine said.

Kay took the data chip out, and commanded the program to run. There came, again, the soft hum of circuits powering up.

'Oh,' Antoine said. 'Look up.'

She did. A million dots of silver danced on the ceiling. The starry room felt so huge that it seemed to be expanding along with the uncountable points of light, radiating outwards until the interior of the room felt infinitely larger and greater than the dimensions of the building itself.

The sea of stars resolved—crystallised—into a pattern that Kay recognised.

'This is the star field from Thridi Spacedock,' Kay whispered as she stared at the holographic night sky. Her heart beat so fast she feared it might disintegrate. 'He's turned this place into a planetarium.'

She blinked, or perhaps her eyes dropped out of focus, and then the stars became the silver glittering of Thridi's skyline at night: its glassy skyscrapers, its golden-domed temples, its night bazaars lit up with a kaleidoscope of colourful lanterns, its serpentine streets lined with golden lamps whose glows were reflected in the cobblestones that had been worn to shining smoothness over hundreds of years.

And above the city lights, she saw an ocean of twinkling stars. Their silvery lights trembled and danced and in the afterglow she thought she saw her mother's radiant and soft smile; another shimmer, and she saw the light in the dark of her father's warm gaze; the stars quivered and wavered and in their unsure movement she saw the sparkles of photon sails that whisked her down streams of stars.

For a while she tried to hold onto the stars, but they were simply too numerous, too bright and chaotic and slippery to keep for more than an infinitesimal instant of being.

When she returned to the room, she could see that John's eyes were blue and open, focused on something far beyond the planetarium, the city, and the rain.

'Antoine,' he murmured, 'I can't remember. Did you say you were leaving Thridi tomorrow?'

'Ah, that's right, yes,' Antoine said. 'Assuming they don't, ah, arrest me the minute I land the shuttle.'

'Right, well, I think I'd like to join up too,' John said, reaching out a hand towards the glittering lights. 'Let's go.'

'Just a moment,' Antoine said, 'I'd like to look at the stars for a little bit longer.'

John closed his eyes, smiled, and gave a long sigh. His arm fell, slack, to his side.

Antoine remained sitting, staring up at the sky, for a very long minute. Then he gazed across the room at Kay, mirroring John's smile. He nodded once.

Then the stars began to fuse with each other, like the atoms at their stellar cores. Silvery pinpricks grew into millions of spheres of unbearably radiant white light that shone more and more brightly, turning the two holograms into a pair of fainter and fainter ghosts, as if the stars were swallowing them, as if they were fading into a cosmic dawn.

The light became more and more intense. Kay closed her eyes. She knew that the radiant heat was burning her skin, but she felt no pain.

All she could sense were the stars that gently and inexorably became the beats of her heart, the shape of her breath, the traces of her.

Kay woke up a month later from a medically induced coma. The bedside computer informed her that she was on Virgon Station. The extra bars on a clean dress uniform hanging from the IV pole informed her that she'd been promoted while unconscious. The papers in her file said she was being put on medical leave. A transport voucher indicated that the brass had even arranged her transportation back to Islay Base Station, where she had registered as her official address.

The day that Kay could get out of bed again, she stumbled through Virgon searching for her old flight suit. She found it bagged and tagged in quarantine, parked in a monthslong queue for incineration. In a pocket, she found the data crystal.

She tossed the voucher into the incinerator.

It was nearly closing time in the land registry office of New Thridi. The outside dust and mud constantly invaded the less than extravagant structure, no matter how often the staff sent out cleaning bots. Junior Clerk Jessica Park was wiping down a window when a client entered: a tall woman with faintly scarred skin and military bearing.

'May I help you?' Jessica said.

The woman handed over her military ID, along with hard-copy records of a family destroyed on Thridi; as long ago as it was, it entitled her to a resettlement deed. Jessica skimmed the files and fed them into her computer.

'Everything's in order. This is for a temporary room at the relocation centre.' She slid a key card across the counter and smiled at the woman. 'If I might ask, what do you plan to do here?'

'I'm going to build a planetarium,' Kay said, holding the Old Thridi night sky in her two hands. 'I'm going to give you all the stars.'

The Dragon's Maw

Cheryl Morgan

Mine is the last voice this universe will ever hear.

I have recordings, of course. My flagship carries within it the cultural histories of a thousand civilisations. I could urge myself forward with the rousing speeches of the greatest of leaders. I could play stirring martial music from the most warlike of peoples. I could listen instead to the voices of my followers, my friends, my family, now all taken from me. I choose none of these things. I go forward instead accompanied by the roar of a beast that has become dear to me. My flagship is named *Lioness*, and I go into battle on her as I have always done. I am Ishtar, Queen of Heaven, and I fear no one.

It was not always thus. Mine is a long life, almost as long as that of the universe itself. In the beginning, when Tiamat, the Dragon of Chaos, gave birth to all things, I was there. When gas clouds gave birth to stars, when stars gave birth to planets, when planets gave birth to oceans, and when oceans gave birth to life, I was there. I was there when life gave birth to thought. I was there when thought gave birth to language. And I was there when language gave birth to civilisation.

I was there when people first knew to worship me.

Oh, what tales they told. My loves, my battles, became legendary. Above all I fought against my sister, Ereshkigal, Queen of the Dark. Death herself was my enemy. What I gave, she took away, to hide from sight and obsess over. She was a collector, my sister. She wanted everything. I only wanted to make things, but she wanted to have them; and have them she did.

"The dead shall outnumber the living." That was the threat she made. Everything I created she took, and hoarded. One day, they said, she will bring them back; her army. Where is your collection now, O sister? What remains of the dead?

Like everything else, they are torn limb from limb, flesh from bone, membrane from cell, atom from molecule, quark from proton. The dead cannot outnumber the living, because there are no dead any more. There is only me. And I, I AM NOT DEAD.

Yet.

No, the dead are not quite all gone. One of them rides with me. Mostly they are gone, because I needed energy. The dead cannot fight for me, not even dead gods. But I can fight with them, with what I make from them. From chaos we came, and to chaos we return. Only one corpse could I not bear to feed to the furnace. Tammuz: heart of my heart, giver of life to my creations.

We fought, of course. The stories tell of that. Over so many aeons, who would not? Besides, we were gods, it was our function to be everything that mortals might be. Is there a world in which no man has ever cheated on his wife, as mine did? Where no woman has ever coveted her sister's husband, as mine did? Where no cozened wife ever took revenge? Maybe the universe would have been better if there had been. Maybe it would still exist. But I doubt it; I think it would be lifeless.

We fought, then, but we loved more, in many different guises. We wore so many masks, on so many worlds. I have forgotten more of them than I remember. The databases remember them, but soon they too will be gone. In the final battle, everything that flies with me will be destroyed.

It was, inevitably, a matter for philosophers. Would the world we knew grow and learn forever, or would it shrink back into the void from whence it came? So brave, those mortals were, to ask themselves questions that could only be answered over the lifetime of gods. In the end, of course, this end, it has all become clear.

How long have we been fighting the last battle? How long since the first galaxies began to wink out of existence? How long since we admitted to ourselves that the end was inevitable, that the slow decline was irreversible. Again I cannot remember. It seems like I have been fighting forever, and yet I remember a time when it was not so. Those memories remind me why I fight.

Who is my enemy? Tiamat, of course. The Dragon of Chaos did not die giving birth. Instead her essence was spread throughout the universe. Part of her lurked at the heart of every galaxy and sat there, dark and brooding, waiting until thermodynamics favoured her once again. And she fed. Bit by bit, star by star, she consumed her children. Then, having eaten a whole galaxy, she sought out other parts of herself, to join together as one once more.

There she is now, on the screens of the *Lioness*. This is all that remains of the universe. I cannot see her, of course, Nothing escapes her grip, not even light. The last few clouds of gas spiral helplessly towards her, unable to escape the mouth that has eaten all that there is to eat. Their death agonies illuminate her position. Before long they too will be gone, and there will only be her and me. She has a mouth, and I, I have a weapon.

I call it a spear, for I wish it to fly straight and true. I call it "time", though truthfully it is far more than that. Over the centuries, *Lioness* and I have gathered the energies of dead galaxies and gods. I have built engines the like of which have never been known before. So much has been sacrificed to give me the power that I need. And now, it is time to strike.

When nothing else remains; when I am the only thing that exists outside of the Dragon's maw, I shall ignite those engines. *Lioness* will become my spear, and I shall cast her into the very centre of the maelstrom. I have the energy I need, and more. My machines have calculated that carefully for me. With that energy, I shall rip through the very heart of Tiamat. I shall take all that she has eaten, that solid pearl of everything that is the core of her being, and carry it with me to freedom.

I am Ishtar, Queen of Heaven, and very soon now I shall give birth to a whole new universe.

Sleep Sweet Children

Nathan Lunt

Throw caution to the wind, my children,
Dance as well you like,
For by this time tomorrow we may all be entomb in
Ice,

Sing your little hearts out, children,
Sweep your cares away,
For by this time tomorrow we may all be Ash and
Flames,

Dream the biggest dreams, my child,
Wish for all you're worth,
For by this time tomorrow we may be swallowed by
the Earth,

Give thanks for all you have, dear child,
With every grateful breath,
For by this time tomorrow
There may be no more tomorrow left.

Contributors

Alec McQuay writes from a bungalow in west Cornwall, in the shadows of ruined engine houses, surrounded by abandoned mining works. A martial artist, body builder and walking singularity for cups of tea, you might think his love of post-apocalyptic worlds comes from the environment he works in. You'd be wrong. He used to work in Croydon...

Eric Scott is the author of several articles in the field of psychology. He is a researcher at the Johns Hopkins Bloomberg School of Public Health located in Baltimore, MD. He is currently a member of the faculty in the Department of Mental Health and his research involves improving school achievement, and reducing attention/concentration problems and aggressive and shy behaviors, by enhancing family-school communication and parenting practices associated with learning and behavior. His story, 'Contrition', appears in the *Horrors of History* anthology. You can find more of his writing at http://www.ericscottwrites.com/.

Dylan Fox is mostly bacteria, water and ego. They writes short speculative fiction that's been published through *The Future Fire, Encounters Magazine, Steampunk Magazine, Twenty or Less Press* and a few other places. They dabble with Taoism, drawing, clothes and costume making, jogging and mental health. When the end of the world comes, they looks forwards to being one of the panicked masses heroically killed by the protagonist. While the survivors cling doggedly to the old world and fight its inevitable collapse, Dylan will become the air and grass and animals of the new one. In the meantime, they occasionally blogs at www.dylanfox.net and posts before thinking on Facebook.

Kara Lee is a SFF writer who daylights as a biologist. In the event of an apocalyptic showdown, you should totally pick her for your team. Until the power grid goes down, you can find her at http://www.windupdreams.net/.

According to her late grandmother, **C. Allegra Hawksmoor** is related to Edward the Black Prince of Wales. She isn't sure if this is true, as she's yet to manifest the desire to invade France, however she *is* very fond of Wales, and has lived there since discovering its existence at an impressionable age. Allegra writes science fiction and fantasy, serves as fiction editor at SteamPunk Magazine and Vagrants Among Ruins, and maintains a blog at www.hawksmoorsbazaar.net

Anne Michaud lives on the south shore of Montreal with a head filled with dystopian worlds and an attic full of ghosts. Her short story collection, Girls & Monsters is now available, and keep an eye out for upcoming short stories published in anthologies. http://annecmichaud.wordpress.com

Cheryl Morgan has been accused of "destroying fandom" so often that she decided she should have a go at destroying the universe instead. She knows exactly which girl is tough enough to still be there at the end. When not indulging in apocalyptic violence, Cheryl runs a small press and an ebook store, writes about books, and talks about books on Bristol local radio. You can follow her on Twitter at @CherylMorgan, or find out more at her website, Cheryl's Mewsings http://www.cheryl-morgan.com/

Colin Sinclair has spent what seems like forever writing things and stuff. Some of it has even seen the light of day. Recently Colin provided settings, background material and short fiction for Broken Rooms, an alternate-worlds tabletop roleplaying game that features thirteen flavours of apocalypse. One of his ever-so-short stories is in the Fox Pockets

Guardians anthology. His favourite word remains indolent. He still wonders if his bio should have jokes. http://www.brokenrooms.com/

The precise location of K. Bannerman is currently unknown. Along with a fierce group of survivors, she leads targeted attacks against the Robot Overlords from a rebel base, hidden in the woods of western Canada. By candlelight, she writes manifestos, short stories and novels, including the contemporary fairy tale "The Tattooed Wolf", and communicates with the resistance through www.kbannerman.com. The Robot Overlords feel no emotion, but if they did, they know they would fear her.

Michael Ezell is a former US Marine and ex-cop who now works in the Makeup FX field in Hollywood. The first two occupations prepared him to fight in any apocalypse scenario, whether it be alien invaders, thugs in the wasteland, or rabid Mary Kay sales reps. The third allows him to pull a "Bill Murray" and blend in with our Zombie Overlords. Michael's short fiction has also appeared in *Stupefying Stories*, and the anthologies *'I, Automaton'* and *Fantasy for Good*.

In his professional life, **Mikey Nayak** is an aerospace engineer who has worked on the Space Shuttle, two-probe NASA missions to the moon, and as the Flight Director for multiple experimental satellite programs. Currently he is designing a shoebox-sized satellite for Low Earth Orbit proximity operations. Outside work he is a pro skydiver, scuba diver and vertical wind tunnel flyer, holding instructional ratings in all these sports. He also enjoys motorcycle riding, skiing, flying small aircraft and generally anything that could qualify as potentially injurious, but has been known to moonlight as an amateur thespian, stand-up comic and short film maker. He now lives in the San Francisco Bay area, where he is working on his Ph.D in Planetary Science and his first novel.

N.O.A. Rawle is an insomniac mother of two who manages to juggle family, writing projects, four teaching jobs and translation work. Inspired by perfection in art and nature, fuelled by passion and enthusiasm, she is addicted to writing and believes life is too precious to be wasted. A British national located in Greece, her work has been long-listed for The Guardian Travel Writing competition and the AEON Award. 'Vanquish' is due to be published in the anthology *Girl at the End of the World* (Fox Spirit) in 2014. www. noarawle.blogspot.gr

Paul Starkey has always been a little behind the curve (he didn't learn to drive until he was 37) and so whilst he wanted to be a writer since he was ten, when a teacher picked up on his love of telling stories and suggested maybe he'd be an author someday, unfortunately the necessary discipline and dedication eluded him until he hit thirty. Luckily since then he's thrown himself into his craft with ever increasing passion, dedication and downright mania. Like a career criminal he started small, writing his own Star Trek fan fiction before graduating to more original works and to date has written 4 novels. The first of these, the vampire/ zombie (or possibly zombie/vampire) post-apocalyptic actioner 'City of Caves', he published via Lulu. He's also published a collection of short fiction, 'The Devils of Amber Street', via Amazon. He's had multiple short stories published in myriad publications, including the *British Fantasy Society Journal*, and blogs at http://werewolvesonthemoon.wordpress.com/

Bruce Lee Bond traveled since a teen, and hitchhiked around the west coast of North America at seventeen. He left San Francisco State College at twenty-two, where he was the only undergrad in the graduate writing department, to journey to South Dakota as the student of an Oglala Lakota (Sioux) medicine man. After studying the rituals of the Native American (peyote) Church, he fled with the medicine man's abused girlfriend, ranged from the Canadian

Rockies to Mexico, attended the University of Oregon's journalism department, and has lived in Alaska and the Pacific Northwest since.

He's a founder of the Alaska Writers Guild, worked with the American Indian Movement during the armed occupation of Alcatraz Island in San Francisco Bay, has fished, logged, built log cabins in the wilderness of the northwest and Alaska, and has rescued a dozen sex slaves in Alaska since the times of the pipeline boom while operating and owning cabs. He has known corrupt cops and politicians, upright madams and honourable criminals, spent a dark winter under a pall of volcanic ash keeping fifteen starving moose alive while living in a log home he built in the Alaskan wilderness, and has looked down the muzzle blast of a pistol at eighteen. He loves the haunted old towns of the American West, from the Barbary Coast to the dirt streets of Dawson City, Yukon Territory, and often finds the ghosts he encounters better company than newcomers. With proper coaxing they occasionally speak to him.

Adrian Tchaikovsky was born in Lincolnshire and studied zoology and psychology at Reading, before practising law in Leeds. He is a keen live role-player and occasional amateur actor and is trained in stage-fighting. His literary influences include Gene Wolfe, Mervyn Peake, China Miéville, Mary Gentle, Steven Erikson, Naomi Novak, Scott Lynch and Alan Campbell. 'War Master's Gate', the 9th book in the Shadows of the Apt series, is out now.

G.R. Delamere hopes someday she'll have a real writing routine. When not working as a doctor she may be found with her kids at fairy makeovers or in dragon multiverses. She is completing an MA in Creative Writing at Birkbeck, University of London and working on a novel for young adults. In spare moments she dreams of her next project: an epic steampunk alternative history set in colonial India. Mechanized elephants will surely feature.

David Turnbull is the author of a children's fantasy novel featuring dragon hunters and airships – 'The Tale of Euan Redcap'. His short fiction has appeared in numerousmagazines and anthologies, both online and in print. His most recent anthologies include *Dandelions of Mars*, a Whortleberry Press tribute to Ray Bradbury, *Astologica* (The Alchemy Press) and *A Chimerical World Vol 11- Tales of the Unseelie Court* (Seventh Star Press). He is member of Clockhouse London Writers http://clockhouselondonwriters.wordpress.com/ www.tumsh.co.uk

Justin Brooks lays low in the hungry shadows of Southern California, where something almost as bad as the traffic now owns the streets: Flesh Eating Homeboys! Still, as nothing can ever quench his love for roaming the outdoors, he still risks an occasional run in the open (and what's more motivating for a sprint than a starving mob behind you?). The art of writing has always fascinated him, and he intends to keep it alive beyond the world's death. 'Shirtless in Antarctica' is one of his first short stories, but he aspires to finish many more before radiation sickness or malnutrition finish him.

Nathan Lunt is a performance poet, Spoken Word artist, Slam Champion, and founding member of The Decadent Romantics. Flitting between the page and the stage, Nathan has turned his hand to most forms of poetic expression, and can usually be found surprising at open mic nights, ambushing festival goers, or plotting to conquer the internet from his YouTube channel. When he remembers to Tweet, find him @Nathan_Lunt

Foxspirit.co.uk

'After nourishment, shelter and companionship, stories are the thing we need most in the world.' Phillip Pullman

Skulk: *noun* – a pack or group of foxes

Fox Spirit believes that day to day life lacks a few things, primarily the fantastic, the magical, the mischievous and even a touch of the horrific. We aim to rectify that by bringing you stories and gorgeous cover art and illustrations from foxy folk who believe as we do that we could all use a little more wonder in our lives.

Here at the Fox Den we believe in storytelling first and foremost, so we mash genres, bend tropes and set fire to rule books merrily as we seek out tall tales that excite and delight us and send them out into the world to find new readers.

With a mixture of established and new writers producing novels, short stories, flash fiction and poetry via ebook and print we recommend letting a little Fox Spirit into your life.

 @foxspiritbooks

 https://www.facebook.com/foxspiritbooks

 adele@foxspirit.co.uk

Printed in Great Britain
by Amazon.co.uk, Ltd.,
Marston Gate.